AXEL

KELLY FINLEY

AXEL

KELLY FINLEY

Axel: Belles & Bratva Beasts, Book Two

Kelly Finley

© 2025 Kelly Finley Publishing, LLC

Visit the author's website at kellyfinley.com

ISBN: 979-8-9916399-0-3 (eBook)

ISBN: 979-8-9916399-4-1 (paperback)

Interior Formatting by Kelly Finley

Cover design by Lori Jackson

Cover photo by Wander Aguiar :: Photography

Cover model: Mario Perozzi

ALSO BY KELLY FINLEY

Belles & Bratva Beasts

Nash

Axel

Sire

Loch

Jace

Interconnected Books

Shameless Play

Shameless Game

Make Him

Tempt Her

The Six

Holiday For Six

Halloween For Six

After Him

With Him

CONTENT ADVISORY
WARNING: THERE ARE SPOILERS, TOO

This book, like all in this series, contains a very spicy plot with swoony angst and witty snark set in an ex-mafia secret society. Congrats if this is your kind of romance.

It also contains topics that readers may be sensitive to. If you have any questions about this list, please message me on my social media platforms @kellyfinleybooks (Instagram, TikTok, and Facebook).

- A stalker romance (in fiction, it's hot; in reality, it's not. Please know the difference)
- Touch her, and I'll kill you vibes (he does)
- An obsessed MMC with a primal kink
- A strong FMC with a disability (epilepsy)
- Age-gap love (He's 40. She's 27. They're adults)
- A taboo moment (Virginity lost. Not hers. Just read)
- A love triangle that's not a thing (the MMC is a one-woman mafia man. Trust and you'll swoon)
- Detailed sex scenes that feature chasing, stalking, exhibitionism, public sex, dirty talk, primal kink,

BDSM, anal, cunnilingus at that time of the month (he's a true man), fellatio, a collar, an audience ... you get the idea
- He doesn't want to share, but he knows he has to, so...
- Is it a why-choose? Meh. Not really but...
- There's a taboo initiation into a secret society involving other men
- Kings who prove their love for their Queens (in front of each other)
- They're brothers, too. But hell no. Never brother-on-brother
- A dominatrix who uses adult toys to *sort of* torture (but her captive loves it)
- There are a lot of knives and salt
- And a FMC who gets real stabby
- A plot surrounding sextortion of LGBTQ people
- A badass woman who survived abuse and being a child bride, and built an empire of revenge
- References to physical and psychological parental abuse
- It's a book in a series about men who escaped the mafia, so they're not big Bratva fans. Instead, they're like the ex-mafia avengers
- And a guaranteed HEA

If this only got you excited, this book is for you.

*For readers who deserve to be chased
and claimed like a goddamn queen*

THE KINGS & QUEENS

ORDER OF THRONES

Ruslan Kholodov	Nadine Faye "The Queen"
Axel King	Ruby Jones
Nash Allen	Vale Monroe
Sire Rutledge	Wren Chapel
Grant Moultrie	Delphine Laurent
Jace Ryan	
Nick Barinov	Zar Rollins
Loch Waring	Alena Allen

PLAYLIST

PROLOGUE
AXEL (A PEEK INTO MY OFFICE)

"Ms. Jones, do you know the difference between a colon and a semicolon?"

I toss my trial binder on Ruby's desk, and she lifts her glare.

"I know what comes out of a colon, and you're about to say it."

I loom over her desk. "A colon introduces a list while a semicolon connects two independent thoughts. Correct your trial notes. I won't accept errors."

"Will you accept this?" She flips her middle finger.

And I fall in love.

Every goddamn time.

"Will you be fired for insubordination?"

But I hide it like everything else.

She shrugs, smiling and flipping her other middle finger, kissing them tip-to-tip. "Let me introduce you to a FUCK and connect it with a YOU. See? No punctuation required."

Helen, my practice manager, snorts at her desk.

Samuel, Ruby's fellow paralegal, feverishly types away on

his keyboard, trying to pretend he's not relishing this daily occurrence.

Our daily war.

When I hired Ruby Jones, I hired the human version of a migraine.

But she's the best goddamn paralegal I've ever had.

I'd never fire her.

Because she's way more than that.

And me?

Who am I?

Well...

CHAPTER ONE
AXEL

You know the saying, "The Devil takes care of his own."

Oh, I take care of her.

I own her.

I *stalk* her.

I have two hours until Ruby goes on her morning run ... and I follow. Every morning, I wake with my heart pounding to see her as she races by. Then, I pace myself two blocks behind her, far enough so she has no idea I'm chasing her, but close enough that I get wafts of her lilac perfume.

Chasing Ruby calms me. It's what I need.

She's what I need.

Not this.

This annoys me.

If I want to chase Ruby this morning, I'll have to forgo sleep. It's four a.m., and murdering this asshole is really fucking with my stalking routine.

Donald Ashcroft squirms in the chair I've tied him to, fighting the rope I've used to restrain him. It'll eventually break with his force, but not before I burn him alive.

"So tell me, is it just helpless old women you abuse?" I lift the metal spout to a paper can of salt, and his eyes widen with fear. "Or when we empty your loaded bank accounts, will we find more than four victims?"

His protest is muffled by the saline-soaked bandana I've stuffed over his busted lips. I punched him in the mouth so many times I lost count. I just wanted him to taste the saying about salt in a wound.

Getting creative with our punishment is part of the thrill. If not, justice gets quite boring.

"What was that, you say?" I hold a finger to my ear. "You have a little dick, so you compensate with violence? You're one of *those* men?"

"Frrrrgh ohhh." His curse is hysterically muffled.

Yes, I hear the irony. But there's nothing little about me, and this isn't violence. This is vengeance.

"I get it. It's hard to talk when your tongue is two inches thick."

I teeter the can of salt over his bleeding bare feet that I bound to the front legs of the chair. I twisted them, exposing the damage I inflicted. It's a trick of the trade I learned in the most excruciating way.

If you want to trap someone? Mutilate their feet. It makes escape virtually impossible.

"But at least you'll die with something of a decent size on you." I wink, pouring a stream of white granules over his bloodstained soles.

His howls are swallowed by the cotton in his mouth, and for a moment, empathy whips through me. Memories, too.

But fuck that.

This man has stolen thousands from four elderly women, the tenants in this dilapidated double duplex north of town. He's trapped them in leases they can't afford to break. He's stolen their checkbooks and committed elder fraud and abuse. Then, he beat Ms. Patel, my client, when she threatened to call the police.

I wanted to murder him that day, but I'm not an impulsive man.

It took a week for my brothers and me to plan our justice. Not like we don't have enough shit going on with catching a ruthless sex trafficker, too, but I insisted on this side gig.

While Ashcroft writhes in pain, I turn and set cans of cooking spray into a rusty microwave in the crumbling kitchen. Then, I turn on a gas burner to the old stove. Conditions like these are illegal to rent. But since when does justice find the poor? The most vulnerable?

Since us.

Since me and my brothers.

We found the elderly tenants new homes. Safe and affordable ones, while this one will look like it perished in a kitchen fire, along with its slumlord.

Do I worry that Ashcroft's pain is oddly satisfying? That his blood is my balm?

Maybe it's in *my* blood. Maybe I'm just like my father, who kidnapped, raped, imprisoned, and forced my mother to marry him at fourteen? Did I learn his brutal Bratva tactics and torture by watching? Or does it lurk in my DNA?

Men like Ashcroft aren't worth my time considering it.

I just press the buttons on the microwave and have three minutes to escape before this shithole explodes.

"This is for Ms. Greene, Ms. Craig, Ms. Eagle, and Ms. Patel." I turn back, smirking at his frantic eyes. "Now you know better than to fuck with women. Karma *is* a bitch," I open the side door, calling over my shoulder, "and I'm her son."

The door closes behind me as I tug my baseball hat down

for any watching eyes, but still, I smile. Concern. Guilt. Remorse. Nope. I don't feel them.

No one is awake at this hour. We made sure there were no cameras on houses or nearby doors. There's nothing to worry about or regret.

With quick strides, I'm sliding into the dark sedan waiting for me at the curb. "Drive," I tell Sire, my oldest brother.

"Wait for it." He looks through the passenger windshield. "We don't leave until we see the hellfire."

He's right, so I turn and admire the spectacle, too. A sudden flash of light accompanies the explosion so percussive I feel it in my chest. The lethal fireworks fill me with relief—like it's July 4th, the day we were freed from our evil father.

"Go," I command.

I need to get home and change before I chase Ruby through the streets of Charleston. And then? I get to torture her all day at work.

I swear that woman lives in my mind. She owns my dreams, and lately, she's invaded my heart.

She's so feisty; I think I'm fucked.

I think I'm in love.

But before Sire can pull away, a light furry flash under the decrepit front porch catches my eye as flames shoot from the structure's roof.

"Stop!" I shout.

Sire slams on the brakes before I swing the door open.

"You've got to be fucking kidding me," I mutter, stomping back to the scene of my crime. Crouching down, I find her crouched like me, hiding under the porch, her fur golden like a little lion. When I reach for her, surprisingly, she doesn't fight. She lets me pick her up. *Great.* "You're going to be a fucking pain in my ass, aren't you?"

Carefully, I lift the cat with my leather-gloved hands,

feeling her swollen nipples and bloated belly. "Of course, you're going to be a mom," I growl, cradling her. "Let me guess: six baby boys."

But she just stares up at me with big green eyes.

"Shut up," I softly hiss. "Yeah, I get it. Karma found me, too."

Why am I talking to this cat like she understands? Don't ask. I'm too annoyed. This wasn't part of my plan.

"Now go," I huff at Sire as I slide into the passenger seat, bracing myself for nervous claws to puncture my jeans the minute we start driving.

"Got a new pussy?" He's amused. It crinkles the tattoos on his face.

"No," I slam the door, "you do."

"Why not." He shrugs. "Wren would love a pet."

"She's pregnant."

"Not yet." He smirks, driving toward the interstate. "But once she's initiated, I'll breed her in no time."

I roll my eyes at Sire's kink. Then again, I have mine, too. "I mean the cat, not your queen."

"Even better," Sire replies. "Wren would love kittens until we have kids."

"Are you sure she's ready for us?" I worry. Wren is our youngest queen. She's only twenty.

"You were there." He checks the speedometer. We don't speed. We don't get caught. "She passed her test with so many orgasms, I thought we broke my little angel. But she gets what she wants, and she *always* wants more."

The memory stirs my cock.

Wren took most of my brothers for her test to be our queen. She wanted us. She moaned, begging for us. She'll do the same when she's initiated as Sire's queen, and I know it arouses my brothers, too.

Yes, it's a taboo tradition, but our queens love it, and we love them. We'll die protecting them.

I won't stop until we, the seven kings, my brothers, find our seven queens. Until each queen has a first king—her husband—and a second king, should the first king die while protecting her.

It's how we escaped my father, Ruslan Kholodov, the head of the Russian Bratva. He forced my mother to take him and then a second king. For years, she endured my father's abuse and bore him six sons while she fell in love with her second king.

It was her second king, Maksim, who got us out. In my heart, Maksim was my father, and he died protecting us. So, in his honor, and in my mother's honor, too, we continue the tradition.

We may have escaped the Bratva. We may be hiding in plain sight in the last place my father would think to look for us—in America. In a genteel, Southern tourist town by the sea. We may take risks using the skills we learned from him to seek vengeance for others.

But still.

We live looking over our shoulders.

We live like a clock is ticking down.

Any day, we can be found.

So, it's my mandate: I want all kings, all of my brothers, to claim their queens. That includes Nash. He's my best friend. He's the seventh king. He's not blood, but he's like our brother, so I insist he claim his queen, too. No matter how forbidden she may be to him.

I want nieces, nephews, and children of my own. I want my mother surrounded by her grandchildren. I want her pain not to have been in vain. She survived for us, so now we fight for her.

We're loyal to her and each other.

Only once did I betray my brothers. In the worst way, and it haunts me. But I did it for a queen. I'll do anything for our queens, and I paid the price for my betrayal. I lost *my* first queen.

So now?

I hunt my next one. I hunt Ruby.

One day, I'll make her my queen.

And if she fights me on it?

Even better.

SIRE TURNS DOWN A NARROW STREET IN THE FRENCH Quarter as dawn crawls up the sky. It's still dark. Gas lamps flicker, illuminating the dewy cobblestones. Expensive cars choke the curbs cracked by hundred-year-old oak roots, feeding the verdant canopy above.

This is an old town of shadows, secrets, sinners, and saints; I should know.

"Tomorrow night..." Sire stops in front of my gold-spiked iron gate. "Wren wants the kings again. We can't treat her like a doll. She wants us for her initiation."

Mindlessly, I take off my glove and pet the cat. "Oh, I'm aware of her demands. Wren called me."

"But is Nash ready?" Sire asks. "He's Wren's second king, and he'd better make it official. I want us bonded. I want her protected and—"

"Don't give him shit." The cat purrs at my touch. "You know why he holds back."

"For his daughter's best friend?" Sire smirks. For a pastor, he's quite the devil. "Yeah, we all know who Nash really wants, but he owes me and Wren. He needs to put his heart aside and put his dick—"

"Yeah, yeah, don't paint me a picture."

Some of my brothers, like Sire and Grant, get off on sharing queens. Some of us, like Nash, Nick, and I, do not. Loch's not allowed, and Jace puzzles me. He used to love sharing women with Grant, but lately, he's abstinent unless it's a ritual. Regardless, we meet our obligations to our queens, and Nash will meet his.

"We'll initiate Wren, and then she's all yours." I insist, "I want a niece or a nephew in a year. Mom deserves her first grandchild."

Sire winces. "Yeah, her *first* grandchild."

"Alena is ours, but she's not blood," I remind him. I remind myself—*she's Nash's daughter and certainly not mine*. "And I fucked up my chance to be first, so now it's yours."

More ire twists my brother's face.

Solemnly, he nods, and it's odd; whenever the subject of my first queen comes up, Sire seethes like he feels my pain for me.

"In the meantime," I tell him, "take this to Wren. She can mother some kittens."

I lift the cat with my hands wedged under her forelegs, and Sire reaches to take her, but she hisses, her back claws swiping and scratching his inked hands.

"Alright. Alright." Gently, he shoves the animal back to me. "She's your pussy, not mine."

"What the fuck am I going to do with a pregnant cat?"

"You still remember your way around pussies. Right?" The fucker smirks. "Figure it out."

"Fuck you."

I leave Sire laughing as he drives away, and I struggle with my arms full with an expectant animal I have no clue what to do with.

Once inside my home, with its dark wooden beams braced under historic, white plaster ceilings and creaking wide pine floors below, I aim upstairs to my bedroom.

"Here." I set the cat on the foot of my bed, snarling, "Don't have those fucking kittens on my white Frette linens." She purrs, staring up at me. "I'll get you a goddamn litter box by the end of the day." Lazily, she circles a spot. "And I swear to God ... if you sink your little claws into *my* duvet, I'll put you under the neighbor's porch."

Yes, I like fine linens and fashion. I was raised in an opulent Russian prison of a home until I was eleven. Then, we used my mother's jewels and tenacity to rebuild our life here, and now, I spare no expense.

We give the money back to the victims we help and donate most of the rest, but we skim a little off the top for our services. You know, for operating expenses.

Suspiciously, I eye the cat as she curls into a golden fur ball at the foot of my bed, and I strip down, warning, "Don't piss on my stuff. Deal?"

She closes her eyes.

"Hey!" She opens them. "Sparky, did you hear me?"

Yep, that's her name, and she doesn't listen. She wedges her nose under her foreleg like *Shut up, asshole, and turn off the lights* while I wait for the sun to rise.

It's a little warm to zip on a grey hoodie with my black running shorts, but I like to sweat. Watching the time pass on my phone, I do my research on pregnant cats, then a nearby vet.

I'm not keeping this damn thing. She'll have a new home by Monday.

At six twenty-three, my daily alarm goes off.

It's stalking time.

With a final warning to Sparky not to fuck up my shit, I lock my door then gate, and aim toward my waiting place blocks away. It's behind a large oak in the park by the battery wall, braced against the wide river to the Atlantic beyond. Shadows cloak my presence while runners and folks walking their dogs emerge, dotting the sidewalks.

Then, exactly where my stare is aimed at the fountain in Waterfront Park, Ruby appears.

Every time, she rips my breath away.

Every time, my heart pounds.

Every time, my cock awakens.

Was it lust at first sight with Ruby? Guilty. Was it love, too? I plead the fifth.

She thought I was interviewing her for a job as my paralegal, while I knew I was talking to my future wife.

A person knows when they meet their equal.

And a real man knows when she's his soulmate, too.

God, she was beautiful.

From under the collar of her lilac dress, I could see the price tag. Making me suspect she couldn't afford it and would return it?

But it was the way she proudly asserted her qualifications for the job. How she crossed her bare legs as I clocked a rivulet of blood drying on her scraped kneecap. Did she trip and fall in her high heels on the way to our interview? If so, it didn't stop her.

No, she saw me note it, but she lifted her chin, looked me dead in the eye ... and kept proclaiming her worth.

Damn, my heart started pounding as I licked my lips in recognition.

Ruby spoke like a queen.

Like *my* queen.

I couldn't believe my luck that she had stumbled into my life.

That was months ago, and I can't go a day without chasing her.

Why?

Maybe it's love, but it's one-sided. The woman loves to hate me. Honestly, I give her a shit-ton of reasons to.

It's my plan. One day, her mad-at-me will ignite into madly in love with me. It's the only way to catch a fiery woman like her.

So, yeah, it's a chase. I lift my hood in case, for the first time, she spots me...

But as usual, she's oblivious.

Ruby runs with earbuds in, her long auburn hair swishing behind her. Her curves tempt in those mint, high-waisted leggings and matching sports bra, making my cock swell as she darts past me.

Like a gazelle, she's fast, navigating treacherous broken pavement, her luscious ass my target to follow.

I give her thirty seconds, and I do.

One day, I'll let myself catch her, licking the sweat off her flesh, pinning her against a brick wall and...

Stop, you horny fuck. Running with a hard-on is hell.

We follow our routine—the same pace and route as locals walk their dogs, waving good morning, and she waves back. But I don't.

I can't draw attention. I always hide and never work alone, but for her?

Imagine my horror when I met Ruby and realized ... *I'm just like my father*, a predator obsessed with a woman. I had to have her. I started stalking her. It wasn't my proudest moment, but ... fuck it.

She's not my first woman, but she's the only one who's ever made me feel so base, so beastial. When I'm near her, instincts overwhelm me. To chase. To capture. To claim.

To love.

And the best part?

As I lurk down the block, hiding in a narrow alley,

watching her. As she finishes her three-mile route. As she slows into a cool-down, nearing The Mercier Hotel. As the bellhop waves to her, admiring her ass—*I'll murder him for looking at my queen.*

The best part is...

Ruby has no idea I'm stalking her.

CHAPTER TWO
RUBY

"Hey, Bruce!" I wave to the hot bellhop. "It's a beautiful morning."

"Yes, ma'am," Bruce tips his hat, "it *sure* is."

I know, as I race up the steps into my brother-in-law's hotel, Bruce is eye-humping my ass.

Good.

Let Axel watch him do it.

Yes, I know he stalks me. Yes, I know *Axel* is his real name, not "Michael Cummings, Esquire," as most know him. Yes, I know he's into some shady shit. And yes, he's my boss, and I hate him with a white-hot intensity.

Lording his law degree over me like he's God. Lecturing me on boring statutes. Finding every mistake in my work and then just making shit up when there aren't any.

Oh, and he's a rich, smug, arrogant asshole, too.

And all the while, he's stalking me? *He's* breaking the law?

He makes me nuclear. I'm one hairline crack in my concrete from blowing and wiping out this entire city.

Axel must think he's so clever. He must get off on it. I bet he listens to Duran Duran's "Hungry Like The Wolf" while he chases me.

I wear earbuds, so he'll think I'm oblivious, but I'm not. I'm listening to his footfalls crunching behind me.

I know he'll be there every morning, waiting behind that oak tree in the park, and then he'll follow me here. Hell, he even follows me home some nights, too.

This shit began a month after I started working for him, and that was a year ago.

Yes ... a *year*.

I was on my run and stopped to tie my sneakers; then, I got that tingling feeling. Maybe only women can sense it, I'm not sure, but it's when you know you're being followed. So, I snuck a glance over my shoulder and caught Axel lurking in a dark alley, barely peeking around the corner of a brick building.

At first, I thought it was funny. Then, I was flattered.

And a little aroused.

Alright, alright ... *a lot* aroused.

I can't help it. The man is a tower of hard, hot, inked, and fuckable flesh.

But after all these months, what's his game? He's never come on to me. He keeps his distance. And with the dickish ways he tortures me at work, too? It's getting old. Real old. I'm so tempted to whip around one day and bust him, but it's my only advantage.

It's the ultimate power play—when the stalked stalks back.

I've been spying on my dickhead boss for nine months, and I've learned quite a lot.

My favorite nugget?

Axel is some kind of mafia king.

Yes, he's a lawyer: one of the best, I hate to admit. But as much as he practices the law, he breaks it, and I'm just waiting to prove it so I can shove it in his sexy, smug face, all while I push his buttons, too. Like a panel of circular lights in an elevator with fifty floors, I punch every one.

But my brother-in-law's hotel has only eight floors, and I punch the button for the second.

With a *ding*, the gold doors slide open. In a furious haze, habit takes me into the high-end hotel gym, where I turn into the women's locker room. Here, I keep one locked and full of my products, with fresh dresses and heels for work.

I can't afford a fancy gym membership, but I won't take a red cent from my sister, Scarlett, or her billionaire husband, Luca. I'm broke on bills and pride. But Luca insisted that I at least make myself at home in his hotel, and it is convenient.

The Mercier Hotel is four blocks from Axel's law office on Meeting Street. So I get free parking, a free shower after my run, and sometimes, a hug from my big sister when I need it most.

Speaking of...

"Oh, god, Luca." I recognize Scarlett's raspy voice. "Oh fuck, don't stop."

"Yes, my whore. Take it."

I roll my eyes, recognizing my brother-in-law's distinct Greek accent, too.

"Oh. My. God!" I call out to the row of pristine showers. Lucky for these horn dogs, we're the only ones in here. "Y'all can literally get a room. You own them all."

I hear a giggle, then a man's voice, not Luca's, reply, "Yes, but darlin', where's the fun in that?"

Zar is the first to emerge from their shower for three as he wraps a white towel around his waist, winking. "Mornin', hotness."

"Morning, you fluid flirt."

I adore Zar. He adores my sister and subs for my brother-in-law. He's also in love with Nick Barinov, the hottest NFL player I've ever seen, and Zar hosts the best parties at his "beach shack." I'm one of the few women he invites to join them, but not in *that* way. I support my sister's poly love and life, but we don't cross that line.

But I do love blurring lines with the other closeted, bisexual football players at Zar's place. I feel honored, protecting their secret. They're safe with me.

"Hey." Scarlett emerges, naked as a jaybird, before Luca steps out, too. She immediately reads my simmering rage. "What's wrong?"

"Nothing."

"Don't lie." Luca is naked, hung, and *still* hard. "You Jones sisters are horrible at it."

I cover my eyes. "Can you put that thing away?"

Luca laughs. "Nudity is natural."

"So is toe fungus, but I don't want to see that shit either."

"Dayum, something's got her worked up." I hear Zar's drawl, thinking Matthew McConaughey is in the room whenever he talks. "And it ain't our dicks or her mornin' run."

"I'm fine, y'all," I huff, shielding my sight. "I just need to shower and get to work."

"On a *Saturday*?" Scarlett asks, disbelieving.

"Yes," I snap. "We're busy."

"So it's work?" Concern laces her voice. "Is that what's wrong because Zar's right, you look one minute from murder?"

I drop my hand and thankfully find all wrapped in towels while I let my sister read my eyes. She's right. I'm furious about Axel, but I don't want to talk about it. She can read that, too.

I'm close to my sisters, all three of them. We've been through hell and back with our father, then our step-father, and for the longest time, it was us and our mom against the world. We put our walls up and protected each other, particularly Scarlett. She's the fighter. Literally, she has MMA titles.

But love changed my sister, and I'm happy for her. Scarlett deserves Luca. He worships her because she fought for him, and he tore down the walls guarding her heart, too.

But not me. I still don't trust love. I don't trust that there's a man like Luca out there for me, too, so I stay safe. I fuck, then leave; it's what I do. And I *certainly* never love.

No one can make me stay. No one can make me trust.

The perfect Exhibit A, your honor? Men like my boss, Axel.

He's so typical; men just want the chase. Because once they catch you and have their fun, they leave, so I leave even faster.

"I'm fine, y'all," I echo myself. "Just going to be late for work, and my yeast infection for a boss will make me itch all day about it."

"Oh," Zar chuckles, "so it's *love*. That's the burr under your saddle."

I arch a brow. "Careful, cowboy, or you'll choke on the shit you're talking. I don't do *love*."

I swear the biggest smiles lift their faces—Scarlett, Luca, then Zar—but Luca warns, "You can't run from love, little sister. Trust me; I tried, but thankfully, she caught me." He reaches for Scarlett and gives her the most disgustingly passionate kiss.

"Yeah, well, please try and let me shower." I tug at my sweaty sports bra.

That's their cue. Zar and Luca leave with waves while Scarlett worries, "You sure you're okay?"

"Righter than rain."

"Whatever you say." She yanks me into a hug and knows I'm full of shit, but I love her for not giving me any. "Are you coming for brunch tomorrow?"

"Maybe. I might be working."

"On a *Sunday,* too?"

"We get paid time and a half on weekends."

"Ruby," she sighs, "just let me pay off your school loans."

"Nope."

"Your medical bills?"

"I got it."

Epilepsy, that is, and I'm not letting my sister help me with that, either. Besides, I have it under control with medication, exercise, and managing stress, which means stressing my smug boss out instead. That usually gives me tremendous relaxation.

"I could just call the hospital and pay your bills," Scarlett threatens.

"Don't." I stand firm and topless. "I'm just like you—a trailer-park girl who doesn't belong in this fancy world, so don't make me swallow any more pride than I do every day. I haven't had an episode in two years, and I've almost paid off the last one. I'm fine."

"I love you" is her perfect answer.

"Love you, too." I give her one more hug before I race through my morning routine. Shower. Hair. Make-up. Smart watch. A dress and dumb-ass heels.

My smart watch comforts me. It's to call for help after I have a seizure, or if I can sense one coming. But the rest? I'd rather wear jean shorts, a T-shirt, and flip-flops, but that doesn't fit in with the Charleston elite. Trust me; they'll let you know. They can afford everything but kindness.

"You have a good day, Ms. Jones." Bruce tips his hat again when I exit the hotel an hour later.

"You, too." I wave, smiling as I find the sun shining, pink azaleas blooming, and a busker playing her guitar outside an art gallery, so I tip her. She has a beautiful voice, and my day is getting better...

Until I get an annoying text.

SPITTING COBRA

Three espressos. NOW

I smirk at my nickname for my boss. One, Axel's a stalking snake, so it's fitting. Two, he's a giant dick, so it's still fitting. And three, he's venomous because no matter how much I hate him, he's in my veins. I think about how much I hate Axel all the time.

If I search ASSHOLE on Google will your face come up

Because fetching your coffee isn't my job

SPITTING COBRA

You suffer fetching delusions of job security

You suffer the assumption being a dick will make yours bigger

...

Why am I smiling and chewing my lip? Why am I turning into my favorite coffee shop and waving to Roberto behind the counter while I wait with bated breath for Axel's reply?

SPITTING COBRA

Listen closely

That's the sound of the sexual harassment lawsuit I'm filing against you

:‑) You're the boss

You're my paralegal who brings up my dick

A lot

Like an obsessive litigant

You're hyper-focused on it

Focus on this

The only thing coming on your dick is

I leave him hanging and order three espressos from Roberto, two lattes, and a chamomile tea.

The coffee shop is packed as usual, with Saturday tourists crowding in.

"Can you hurry it up?" One of them rudely shouts at Roberto, "I thought they had good service in the South!"

I whip around. "Bless your heart; we do. We have that *and* manners. Go buy yourself some at a gift shop." Someone gets my wrath today, and if it's not my hot, dickhead boss, it's this turd.

The man seethes, gesturing to the long line. "This is some shit."

I snap, "Clearly, because shit happened to your face, but you're the only one being a dick about it."

Snorts and snickers fill the small shop. The guy's face turns red, and *whoops,* my temper did it again.

"Look," I reply calmly. "The sweet guy is a college student and working as hard as he can. Have some patience."

I swipe my card, knowing I'll expense it for work. But the tip? I reach into my wallet and leave my last ten for Roberto.

"Thanks, Ruby," he nods, and I shrug, grinning.

Loaded with two coffee trays, I feel better. I practically skip two blocks before using my butt to nudge open the glass doors to our building. Sitting at the front desk, Natalie rushes to help me.

But I chirp, "I got this. You're a thousand months pregnant; sit down. And here's some tea."

"Thank you."

Natalie takes the tea instead. She's about to pop but says

work is the distraction she needs until then. Besides, it's important work. She's one of Axel's lawyers who takes pro bono cases.

It makes my boiling hatred for my boss simmer because he has two signs posted in the window of his law office. One, offering pro-bono services to those in need, and another, educating on the signs of sex trafficking.

I haven't figured out why it's an issue Axel is so passionate about, but I can't wish explosive diarrhea on a man like that.

Just a little shart.

Speaking of the shitty devil…

I take the elevator to the third floor and find him standing by my desk, talking with his practice manager, Helen, who sits beside me when I know … *really* … I left Axel waiting.

For his espressos.

For my inappropriate text.

"Here you go." I place a latte on Samuel's desk. He's my paralegal partner in crime and busy on a phone call, so he mouths, "Thanks." I would've gotten a drink for Helen, too, but she's addicted to water.

"Ms. Jones," Axel barks. "In my office!"

He pivots on his large, shiny, black lace-up oxfords, expecting me to follow. I roll my eyes and set my latte down on my desk.

"Uh oh, Principal Cummings is pissed," I side-whisper to Helen. "Maybe I'll get out-of-school suspension today."

She winks, and I like her. She's much older and knows how to handle Axel's shit … while I just give it to him.

"Yes, Mr. *Cummings*."

Sweet sarcasm fills my voice as I enter his sprawling office with arched brick windows. His mammoth antique desk occupies half of the stately room, while a seating area with a tufted black leather sofa and matching side chairs takes up the rest.

Dark, leather-bound law books and literary tomes line the ornate bookshelves behind his desk. But it's his ebony leather executive chair that does something to me. It creaks every time he leans back in it, and I swear the sound zips straight to my clit.

She's not aware that we hate him.

Silently, I set his tray of espressos on his desk. Purposefully, I put them on his pristine, new copy of *Charleston Style & Design* magazine, hoping they leave stains.

Without a thank you, he reaches slowly for a paper cup, drawing my eyes to the ink on his big hand. The thick platinum ring on his pinkie. His fancy, gleaming watch. He's rolled up his starched white sleeves, revealing his corded forearms and even more dark ink and...

Uh-oh.

This happens every time.

The man is pussygrease.

Desire licks through me at the sight of his tattoos, and I hate that I can't stop staring at his hands while he deftly removes the white lid from the cup.

Then I loathe how my eyes flick up and meet his amused smirk, relishing my enraptured stare.

Because here's the problem...

I want to take a pair of rusty tweezers soaked in rubbing alcohol and stab this man a billion times. That's how I feel when he's chasing me.

But when I confront Axel's stare, it's not fair. This man has the most hypnotic blue eyes I have ever seen. They burn like ice. They cast a spell, freezing my logic and igniting my blood, all while he stares at me, smugly sipping his espresso.

Then he leisurely licks a drop off of his lush lips, framed

by a perfectly groomed dark beard, and I want to melt in the puddle he makes in my panties.

The man is a paradox of the finest tailored suits, fanciest shoes, and expensive tastes, while he's obviously covered in ink and sports a sexy nose ring and diamond-pierced ears.

You. Hot. Dickhead.

"Ms. Jones, what's this?" He flips open his black leather trial binder—the one I always prepare for him.

"My trial notes for you. That's Ms. Simpson's statement."

"Yes, I can read titles." Annoyed, he points to a piece of hot pink square paper. "What is this?"

"A Post-It note. They were invented by accident in—"

"For fuck's sake," he seethes impatiently, "what did you *write* on it?"

"My observation after preparing her statement."

"Do you care to use adult language, or are we texting like Gen Z again?"

"What?" I shrug. "It's my custom stenography."

"N. G. L. Capping?" He reads my note aloud. "Translate because they don't teach Slang at Carolina Law."

Here we go again. Him, shoving his damn degree down my throat.

Yes, I would have gone to law school, too, but I couldn't afford it. I needed fast income and paralegal was it.

"Not. Going to. Lie," I translate, "but *she's* lying. That's what it means, but I didn't think it prudent to note it in Michael Cummings, Esquire's trial binder as she sits beside you in court on Monday."

His eyes narrow. "Why do you think my client is lying?"

"She's not doing it on purpose. She says she needs to break her lease because the mold in her apartment is making her sick. Her landlord's statement says it's normal humidity around here, but when I listened to her statement, I could hear it in her voice: it's not mold making her sick; it's her landlord's harassment." Suddenly, the timing is too perfect, and I smile. "I kinda know how she feels."

His sexy face doesn't flinch. No, satisfaction ignites his icy eyes. "I see."

"Do you? Or do you need me to use more Post-It notes?"

"I need you to finish your text." He smirks, sipping his espresso.

"Huh, that sounds like a *you* problem."

"Ms. Jones, *you* work for me. My problems *are* your problems."

"Perfect: I'll outperform and add to them."

"You're sounding quite sarcastic today."

"If I sound sarcastic, you should hear what I *don't* say."

A smile ghosts his lips. "Which is?"

"This is a trap."

"This is your free pass."

I purse my lips, dying to say it, but I won't be seduced.

Then he raises a dark brow, waiting ... and something about his nose ring makes me blurt, "I just look at you sometimes, and wonder what you'd look like with a personality."

"Hmm." He fights a sexy smile. "I wonder what you'd look like fired."

I roll my eyes. "Are we done?"

"For now." He flits his hand.

Where are my tweezers?

Slowly, I pivot on nude heels I hate. I'm in a purple sheath dress I loathe, too, well aware it hugs my ass, but at least I can swish what Axel can't have for his gaze.

Then, I do everything possible to piss him off.

I leave his office door open and sit at my desk. I start typing my next report, loving how the clicking of my acrylic nails drives Axel insane. He's complained about it before. Once I finish, I kick my heels off under my desk and traipse, barefoot, back into his office.

"Here," I saunter toward his desk, "this is the exhibit tracking of the evidence submitted for Ms. Simpson's case."

His cold stare whips to my feet. "Ms. Jones," he snarls, "we wear *shoes* in this office."

"When you have to wear high heels, too, you can object. *That's* gender equality. But no, you get to wear expensive Italian shoes laced so snug, they're watertight, but at least they're comfortable. Case closed."

"You can wear oxfords. I'm not opposed."

"No, but every snob in Charleston is, and I take enough crap as it is."

"Crap for what?"

"You won't understand." I smile. "Carolina Law is where they teach the Oxford crap I deal with."

"So you prefer what?" He mocks, "Flip-flops?"

"Don't yuck my yum. Flip-flops are God's gift to feet." I push his buttons. "Want me to go to Walmart and secretly buy you a pair? You can wear them in private so your Carolina Law friends won't know."

"No." His face lights up. It's weird. "But you can go to Target and get a litter box and cat food. Not the cheap stuff. The good kind." He reaches into his jacket, making a flippant show of tossing his black card on the desk.

"Are you serious?"

"When am I not?"

"Once again," I fume, "it's *not* in my job description."

"Once again," he smirks, "this is me, *not* caring."

CHAPTER THREE
AXEL

This is me taking care of two pussies with one command.

I needed supplies for that damn cat, and I needed to douse Ruby's fire.

She implied that I harass her, that she doesn't like our love-to-hate game, so I tested her. I *love* testing her.

I gave her my address, gate code, and house key and instructed her to leave the food and litter box for Sparky, and she took the bait.

She could've said no. She could've quit.

Secretly, Ruby loves our game. She was born a queen: brave, strategic, confident, a fighter. And I see how she treats others in the office, too.

She brings them drinks. She works late so Helen can go home to her grandson. She collects the garbage every evening so Mr. Briggs, our elderly Custodial Manager, doesn't have to.

Ruby's fiery on the outside but has a warm heart, and she does something to mine.

She reminds me I have one.

Did curiosity kill her cat while she took care of mine? I mean, *mine* for the weekend?

Yes and no.

With cameras covering every angle of my house, I watched her on my phone app, entering my home with her pretty head on a swivel, scanning the place.

Instantly, Sparky went to her, purring against her bare legs. *Lucky cat.* For a moment, it looked like Ruby had forgotten her menial task. She talked to the cat, smiled, picked her up, and started cuddling the animal, and it pounded my heart. *Fuck, she's beautiful.* Until she glanced up and spotted the camera in my kitchen, and flipped it off.

I laughed. She was right. I was watching as she finished setting out food and the litter box. Knowing she was being surveilled, she didn't snoop. She left.

But now she returns, barging into my office, shouting, "She's pregnant! What are you going to do about it?"

"You mean my *cat*?" I growl, "Mind your words in my office, Ms. Jones, lest you start inappropriate rumors."

"Whatever." She swats the air. "She needs a nest, like a box."

"I'll get her one."

"Have you taken her to the vet?"

"On Monday, I'll ask the vet to find her a good home."

"Since you know everything, you should know when you're wrong," she snaps, reigning over my desk. "She needs a quiet space with no stress, and miraculously, she seemed content in your sterile home. You can't move her now. You need to—"

"Do not tell me what I *need* to do, Ms. Jones."

"Why not? I'm not confident you know how to take care of a pussy."

"Oh, I can take care of a *cat*, Ms. Jones."

She cocks a brow. "You sure? Because she seemed lonely. Like you don't know how to pet one."

"I know how to pet a pussy and—"

What the fuck?

Shut up!

Suddenly, she smirks. She won. "Whoops. Did I push your buttons, Mr. Cummings? My bad. I was just looking for MUTE."

Fuck, she's a wildfire.

Every muscle in my body burns to bend Ruby over my desk, rip her tight purple dress open, and spank her ass before I take brutal care of her sweet pussy. I'll make her come, screaming, and dripping on the floor. I'll stand in our puddle while I make her lick our cum off my shoe.

That's how I'll take care of her.

She makes my heart pound, my dick swelling rock hard as I clench my molars. "Ms. Jones..." I'm tempted to risk my career for her. My life for her. For just one hard, sweaty fuck with her. "Close my doo—"

"Knock, knock. Mr. Cummings." A deep voice accompanies a rap on my open door. In a lust-crazed stupor, my glare whips from Ruby to my brother, Nick, standing in the threshold. "Am I interrupting?" he asks.

"No." I'm shocked. "Come in."

Nick enters with his partner, Zar Rollins, and Ruby stammers, "What... What are you two doing here?"

Nick looks back at me, his eyes asking what she knows about us, and I barely lift my brows—*nothing.* Thanks to our father's violence, my brothers and I have a silent language of survival we can speak.

And Zar? He's one of our queens. He knows better than to reveal our secrets, too.

"We're clients," Zar explains, greeting Ruby with a kiss on the cheek.

For a moment, I'm confused about how they know each other; then ... *of course*. Zar is also partnered with Ruby's sister, Scarlett, and her husband, Luca Mercier.

This is a passionate small city.

"Clients for what?" Ruby's cute face twists. "Is everything okay?"

"Ms. Jones, it's inappropriate to question my clients." I stand, gesturing to my office door. "Give us privacy."

"But they're my *friends*," she debates. "They're more than clients to me."

And they're my family. But I can't tell her.

"*Now*, Ms. Jones."

If her eyes could fire bullets, I'd be dead.

"We're fine, hotness." Zar pecks her cheek again. "Mr. Cummings is helping us create a co-ownership agreement for my beach shack. You see, *that's* love ... since you don't do it."

Playfully, she backhands his biceps before pecking Nick's cheek, too. Then, she fires an eat-cat-shit-and-die glare my way before closing my office door behind her.

"You can cut the tension between you two with a hot butter knife." Nick sounds amused, settling onto my sofa. He reaches for Zar's hand as he settles in beside him.

"She hates me." I take the chair across from them.

"And you love it." Nick chuckles.

"And I know the Jones sisters," Zar adds. "For them, hot hate is a hair's breadth away from deep love."

"Enough." I wave my hand, exhausted by my passion for Ruby today. I need a break ... and sleep. "What's going on?"

They exchange a long look. "Do you want me to—?" Zar starts, but Nick says, "I'll tell him."

"Tell me what?"

"I'm being bribed." Nick's brawny shoulders sag. "Extortion, I guess, is the legal term."

"For what?"

Though I already know. I love my little brother too much. I'm too protective of him.

Nick is gay and deeply in love with Zar. Yes, he knows about Zar's bond with Luca Mercier and his role with Luca's wife. Nick joins them, and I've never seen my brother so happy. It's all I want. But Nick is also the leading tight end in the NFL, and it's career suicide if he comes out.

And it's lethal if anyone ever finds out who Nick really is.

"For being in love," Nick answers. "For going on a vacation last month. We rented a chalet in the mountains, and I'm being bribed for having sex with the man I love."

"What do you mean?" But, quickly, I figure it out. I have cameras in my house, too. "Someone took a video?"

"Yes."

The pained look on my brother's face fills me with regret and rage. Regret for the homophobic world we live in and rage that someone would threaten to out him. That's his choice. His right. No one else's.

"Did the rental listing say there would be cameras recording?" I ask. "Legally, they have to disclose them and say where they are. Most properties use them to monitor doors for security."

"We didn't fuck at the front door," Nick seethes. "We were in the primary bedroom, where we *should* have privacy and—"

"Regardless," Zar adds, "I checked the listing. It never mentioned cameras."

"So, walk me through what happened next."

"It's been weeks since our vacation, but yesterday," Zar explains, "I got a text. I had to give my number to rent the property, and I did it in my name, but I guess Nick is too famous. They recognized him and sent a twenty-second clip of our sex, demanding five million dollars, or they'll release it online."

"Jeez, they have so much on us." Nick drags his hand down his face. "It was our anniversary weekend. We hardly left the bed."

Zar leans over, kissing his cheek. "I'll walk through hell for you, baby. It'll be alright."

"But you're not ready to come out," I seethe. "And you deserve to do it with pride, not like this. They're trying to shame you."

"I have no shame, no regrets," Nick snarls. Like me, he can murder with his bare hands, but nothing can kill a viral clip. "But I have a career I love, a team I must protect, and a sport I've dedicated my life to. I'm not ready to leave."

"They can't make you leave," I insist. "The NFL has a policy that protects against discrimination of openly gay players."

Nick scoffs, "It doesn't protect me from everything else. Come on. Name a top-tier player who's out."

"So," I tent my fingers, itching to strangle necks, "what do you want to do? Take care of this legally or..."

We exchange a look, and Zar joins us.

"Both. I want justice," Nick sneers, "then I'll get revenge."

Spoken like a true son of Ruslan Kholodov.

When we escaped the Bratva, Nick was only five. You'd never recognize him now. But I guess he's like me. He's like our father. It's in his DNA, too.

I nod. "First thing: stall them. We need time and intel." I tell Zar, "Reply and say you'll pay one million every thirty days for their silence. As long as they stay silent, you'll pay *more* than five million."

"Fuck that," Zar scoffs. "I have a trust fund worth a hundred million. I can pay more right now."

"But they'll never stop asking for it," I explain. "So you supply it like a drug. You get them addicted and control them. In the meantime, Nick starts his pre-season, and we devise a plan." I take my phone out of my jacket pocket. "And we start now."

I call Nash first. He's the accountant, able to follow any money trail. Zar will email him with their booking information through the online platform they used, and Nash will find the source.

Then, *I hate to do this*, but no one in my office is better at it. "Ms. Jones," I open my door, "a moment."

With smirky satisfaction, Ruby joins our meeting.

"I need you to dig up all you can about a rental property," I order her. "No doubt, the owner is an anonymous LLC, but dig. Find out who owns it. I know you know how."

"Tell me what's going on," she insists. "It'll make my search faster."

I grin. *She's good. But not that good.* She wants to be in the loop with us, but I command, "The less you know, the better."

"Obviously," she blurts, "because you don't know shit, and you seem to be in hog heaven."

My brother laughs. Zar does, too. They're way too amused by my defiant employee.

"I'm not your goddamn Willy Wonka," I scold her. "I don't sugarcoat my orders. Do as I say or find another job."

Her nostrils flare. "Were you born this shitty, or did you take lessons from a toilet?"

Nick snorts, and Zar mutters, "Oh, no. Mom and Dad are fighting."

"Shut up!" We shout at them together ... and they laugh even harder.

Fire shoots up my neck, strangled by my tie. I yank at it, needing to murder. Glaring at Ruby, I relish the furious blush of her cheeks, the thrumming pulse in her neck, her ribs heaving under that mouth-watering cleavage in her V-neck dress.

I'm so furious I don't care if she catches me craving her tits.

This is what happens when you corner a beast. I *will* attack if provoked.

Then, I glance down at her rebellious bare feet with her toenails painted cherry red. Her feet are dainty and unmarred. They're perfect. They're the opposite of mine, and now, they're another fetish for me. I can't stop the growl up my throat, "Put your fucking heels on." My molars clench. "*Now.*"

"Yes, Mr. *Cummings*." She bumps past me, pushing ALL of my goddamn buttons as I slam the office door behind her, regretting it the moment I do.

This is what I mean. She loves to hate me. Or maybe I hate that I'm in love with her. Either way, she's fire to my ice. She's the only one who gets me this hot.

"Shit," Nick huffs. "Fall in love much?"

I whip around. "She can't know."

"Know about what?" Nick juts his chin. "Our family? The kings and queens? Or that you're in love with her?"

"Our family." I won't deny the rest. It's written all over me; I'm painfully aware.

"Why not?" Nick lifts his hand, holding Zar's. "She's one of us already. We're close with her."

I don't want to pry into my brother's sex life, but when it comes to Ruby? She's MY sex life. She's my future wife. I haven't fucked another woman since I met her because rituals don't count. I only *want* Ruby. And yes, it's been a year. It's another reason I'm ablaze, feral, and about to explode. "How *close?*"

Zar chuckles. "Not *that* close. First, her sister, Scarlett, will kill me. Then, you will."

"Touch her, and I *will* be the first to kill you."

Zar laughs even harder. "You haven't met her sister."

"Ruby comes to our parties," Nick explains. "But we're just friends."

"So," the logic hits me fast, "you three are just friends, but what about *your* friends? The other players? Are they all gay, or are some..."

Fuck, I don't want to know. I *will* kill for Ruby, and half of me relishes the instinct to do it.

"We're gentlemen," Nick answers. "If you want to know something about a lady, don't ask us."

"Exactly," Zar smirks, "if you want to know about your future queen, ask her."

CHAPTER FOUR
RUBY

Axel's future queen?

What the hell does that mean?

My mind races with a hundred questions while I sit at my desk, typing away. To my colleagues, I'm using my earbuds to listen to a witness statement. When really?

I *might* have bugged Axel's office.

Just a little.

You know ... as part of my stalking-the-stalker revenge.

I saved for a month to buy a high-quality WiFi audio bug, which I planted under Axel's desk. Every week, I sneak in and recharge it so I can use the app on my phone to listen to live audio or recordings triggered by the voice-activated technology.

I thought it would be exciting. You know—eat your heart out every *CSI* show.

But mostly, it's mind-numbing. All I hear are Axel's conversations with his clients, and I skip those. Or I hear him clicking and typing. Or flipping pages in his trial binders. Or doing God knows what while Tchaikovsky lulls from the speakers on his desktop. It's the cure for insomnia.

But when some random man disappears into Axel's office, I start listening.

Who wouldn't?

They're usually hot, tall, jacked AF, and hiding ink under their collars. They might as well walk in with a name badge stuck to their black jacket that reads:

HELLO, my name is...
Michael the Mobster

Yep, there's some mafia shit going on.

Axel and his men often talk about a job, a mission, or intel, and they have way too much style, ink, and money to be in the FBI.

That's also how I know "Michael Cummings, Esquire" is Axel's pseudonym. I heard his friend, Nash, use Axel's real name in their umpteenth fight about "kings claiming queens."

Though I have no idea what Axel's last name is or why they talk like they're British royalty, circa King Henry VIII.

But it's also how I know Nick is Axel's brother, and I love Nick and Zar too much to let them know that I spied on them.

They wouldn't understand—all's fair in The Stalker Wars.

I figured out the mafia thing months ago when Sire Rutledge came in for a "meeting." He's Charleston's hip pastor of a popular non-denominational church and like a God in this town with more ink than Axel. But damn, they have similar blue eyes. They must be brothers who always talk about "The Queen."

She must be their mafia queen.

But I don't know who she is.

Though I do know that hot daddy Nash is not Axel's blood brother, but he *is* a dad. He has a daughter named

Alena, who's apparently marrying Loch, another of Axel's brothers.

Yeah, I know.

I keep a journal on this with diagrams and question marks.

Because with each juicy meeting I listen to for more dirt on my boss, I only get more questions.

To be fair, I've never actually heard anyone say "mafia," but then again ... do they? If you were a mobster, you wouldn't go around referring to yourself as such. Then, you're not an organized criminal; you're just a dumbass loudmouth who breaks the law.

But I have had one question answered. I want to be a private investigator. I was born for this. But I don't have the ten thousand dollars this state requires for a surety bond to get my PI license.

So, I settle on investigating my boss.

And due to my snooping, my heart breaks for Nick and Zar. I didn't hate Axel when I could hear how mad he was about someone extorting his brother for being gay and in the NFL.

It makes me even more determined to help them, too. I've already gone online to confirm that the LLC was formed in Georgia, where anonymous owners are allowed.

So now I need to find someone I can persuade in the Georgia Secretary of State's office that they deserve one thousand dollars for giving me the name of who owns "Blue Ridge Mountain Escapes, LLC."

It made me hug Nick and Zar tighter when they left because I *will* find out. I'll help them.

An hour later, I tell Helen I'm going home and say it loud enough for Axel and Charleston to hear. Then, I take my time, walking back to The Mercier, where my car is parked.

More like my reliable hunk of bolts on wheels, but it gets me over the bridge to home and back.

And its rear-view mirror works just fine. I spot Axel's black Jaguar following me, five cars behind.

I park outside my modest two-bedroom apartment in West Ashley and swing the front door open. "Hey!"

"In here," Rose answers, so I poke my head into my little sister's bedroom and find her grading essays on her laptop.

"So, no hot date tonight?"

"Yeah, right," she scoffs.

"So, then...?" I chew my lip.

"Fine," she rolls her eyes, "but the next time you go sneaking around a sex club, I'm going with you."

"I'm not sneaking, I'm *spying*."

"Does your pussy know that? Because sometimes, Inspector Gadget comes home with real men and not a toy."

"That was over six months ago."

"He's going to bust you, you know."

"Not if you sit by the window and look like me." I wink. "As usual, he's waiting outside and will have no idea."

She slams her laptop closed. Rose works her ass off as a middle school English teacher. She's allowed to have no patience. "Why is this Michael-aka-Axel dude so obsessed with you?"

I shrug. "He likes the chase. That's all. I guess to him, I'm a glorified secretary that he thinks he owns, even after hours, and I hate him for it."

"Uh-huh." Rose tosses me a suspicious look. "You hate it when a hot-as-fuck, smart, and wealthy man chases your ass around? Yeah, rough life."

"It's annoying." We have this spat every week. "He's a rich asshole who gets custom suits on King Street and orders Beluga caviar with his afternoon tea while I shop at thrift stores and bring PB and Js on Wonder bread for lunch. He gets off being rich and smart, and me being poor and—"

"Um," she raises her hand like a student, "Ms. Bitch, please. Feel free to jump off the sexy, boujee boss train and let me ride him instead."

"Be my guest."

She laughs. "You'd lose your shit. You two are OTP, and you know it."

I scrunch my face. Rose teaches me all the slang from her students, but it changes on the daily.

"You're a One. True. Pair," she translates. "So stop running and let him catch you."

"Hell no. Stalking him back is way too much fun."

"Fun?" She raises a brow. "Or just another way of hating him so you won't fall for him?"

"Okay, Freud. Put down the ink blots. I don't see our father or stepfather in every other man."

Her face softens. "I do. And the more I work through it like Scarlett did, and like Cherry is, too, the more I heal … and so should you."

Cherry is our youngest sister, and she suffered the worst. After our dad bailed on us, my mom remarried the stepfather from hell. He was a predator, so Scarlett was our protector, I was our investigator, Rose was our nurturer, but Cherry was his victim. We used every trick to escape him, and it worked for a year until one afternoon, while my mom was at work, Scarlett caught him molesting Cherry. She almost killed him with an iron skillet.

So, yeah, we have legitimate trust issues.

"Come on, Rosé," I tempt with her nickname. "Just tonight. It'll be the last time I follow Axel to the club. I promise."

"There's a bull somewhere missing his shit." She throws a

pillow at me. "But fine. Go get dressed in your slutty cowgirl disguise, and I'll play Ruby for the night. *Again.*"

"Eeek." I clap. "Thank you!"

"You owe me, you delulu, stalking bitch!"

I shout down the narrow hallway to my bedroom. "I don't understand slang."

"Yes, you do!" she shouts back.

I am *not* delusional when I sneak out the back door and leave Rose sitting in the living room, watching the flatscreen with her long, red hair in a ponytail, her back facing the window to the lot where Axel is parked outside.

But I am impatient when I hide on the side of my apart-ment building because it takes him twenty minutes to leave. That's when I wait two more before I jump in my jalopy and follow him.

Almost every Saturday night, Axel follows me home, like he's curious if I'm on a date. Which I'm not, and once he leaves, thinking Rose is me, I sneak out and stalk him back.

Imagine my delight when I followed him to the sex club in the old naval yard. Of course, I knew the place. I'm a member. But so is my sister and Luca and their polycule of friends, and again ... lines ... and me not crossing them. I hadn't been back in over a year.

Besides, I've been content with Zar and Nick's beach parties. A few times, I've hooked up with some bi players, always two, never just one, or hearts get broken—theirs, not mine.

But even that was months ago.

Those last two Rose mentioned? I picked them up at the club the first time I followed Axel there, and we went back to my apartment. They were hot, and I'd finally scored the holy grail of dicks; a big pierced one. But I didn't join them. Oddly, it didn't feel right. I just watched them while all I could think about ... *was Axel?*

It surprised me.

And scared me.

The thought of Axel aroused me more than those men sharing one hot and beautiful coupling.

Rose is right. I have a problem. The more I work through my past, the more I see my lonely future, and the only thing that's been keeping me company lately are thoughts about how much I hate Axel.

Oh, and how beautiful he is, too.

Yes, Your Honor, I admit it—the man is clitmusic. I swear mine literally vibrates like a tuning fork in his presence.

"I.D. and phone." The mammoth security guard in the vestibule of the sex club follows procedures. I flash my credentials, surrender my phone, and get patted down by a woman before entering.

When I do, I scan the room, and it's unusually dark tonight. Only gold sconces and globe lights glow as music and moans fill the smoky, sandalwood-scented air.

Through the haze, I spot Axel at the bar. He's with his friend Nash and talking to some hulking guy covered in ink, too. I recognize him. He's a bouncer at Delta's, the sex store.

I try melting into the shadows, though I'm confident with my blonde wig, Daisy Duke fashion, and straw cowgirl hat pulled down low; Axel won't recognize me. He hasn't yet. And usually, I love wearing my micro jean shorts, knotted T-shirt, and cute red cowgirl boots, but...

Not tonight.

I scan the guests, and dread twists my stomach.

It's a Luxe Kink theme night. Everyone is dressed in high-end role-play. Most men and a few women wear expensive suits. Many women, men, and fluid bodies look ravenous in luxurious lingerie. I'm talking Agent Provocateur and expensive.

On the stage, there's a hulking man in a suit getting sucked off by three, elegant women.

The theme is supposed to be sexy and rich ... and suddenly I feel painfully insecure and out of place, my heart starting to race with anxiety.

I try to focus on my mission. I need to see who Axel talks to, if I know them, and if I can get more intel. I try not to let two women dressed in classy black silk gowns make me feel less than while they practically hiss behind their hands, their eyes burning a mocking hole in my country-girl clothes.

But ... they do.

They make embarrassment flame my cheeks. My bladder clenches under their scrutiny. Humiliation drops my chin. I chew my lip, feeling the crushing weight of being judged and powerless.

It's all I felt growing up: poor and worthless.

Clearly, their worth is far more than mine, and I can't breathe. I can't escape. I need to go to the bar and get a glass of water, but Axel still stands there, talking and scanning the crowd.

Three stunning women approach him. They're wearing matching pink lace bras, panties, and garters. Draped over him, they confidently wear heels and jut their breasts for his attention, and he smiles at them.

Axel. Actually. *Smiles*.

He's so breathtaking when he does it, and all I can remember is...

How he glared at me today. Like I'm trashy enough for him to chase but not worth enough for him to keep.

It's every insecurity I've had since middle school. It's every girl who bullied me, mocking my red hair and seizures. It's every boy who said they wanted me, then slut-shamed me afterward.

They didn't care about my tender heart, even when I tried

to be everyone's friend. They didn't care how hard my mom worked just to feed us and pay my medical bills. They didn't care that I have epilepsy.

They just knew I lived in a trailer park and didn't belong; they made sure of it. When I had a drop seizure, I'd hear them laughing about it later, calling me "Zombie Girl" and mocking my attacks. They wrote mean things on my locker. They trapped me in the stall of the bathroom, trying to give me a seizure. They threw stuff in my hair before I got on the bus. They...

"Excuse me." A velvet voice shakes me from my memories. "Darling, are you okay?"

My blurred focus finds the most elegant woman I've ever seen standing before me. "I... I..." I blink, and tears escape. "I'm fine."

Dressed in a black leather dress, she looks like a brunette Michelle Pfeiffer with stunning blue eyes and a face that makes age the sexiest thing you can wear.

Gently, she touches my arm. "*I'm fine* is what women say when they're breaking inside, but their pride won't crack. I should know."

Without introductions, I know who she is. Nadine Faye. She's the owner. A legend in this town, and none do her justice. In person, it's like you're meeting God, and she's a dominatrix.

"I, uh..." I glance down at my pathetic outfit, at my fists clenched nervously. "I just didn't know the theme tonight and feel out of place."

"Are you sure?" Like a mom, she sounds worried. "Did someone harass you? Because I can be as mean as a mama wasp. I will sic one of my men on them. You just say the word."

"No... no, ma'am," I stammer, mesmerized by her eyes. "I'm fine." She smiles. "Really, I am. I just don't belong here."

"Listen," she offers, "I have a private clothing collection on the second floor. I get so many samples sent to me; I'd be busier than a ceiling fan in July if I tried wearing them all. Come on." She wraps her arm around my shoulder. "I got something luxe for you to wear tonight."

"Uh... Thanks." Glancing up, I catch Axel standing alone, but—*oh, shit*—he's staring right at us, and I freeze. "But, I should go home. I have to work tomorrow."

"What kind of heathen makes you work on a Sunday?"

I turn away from his searching glare. "The kind who lifts his leg when he pees."

Ms. Faye laughs and leads me toward the door. "Can I have one of my cars drive you home?"

"No, thank you. I drove. I'm okay."

"Well, then, I'll tell you what," she says. "Next Saturday's theme night, in your honor, will be a Country Night. Hot cowgirls. Big bulls. Lots of whips and rides. Promise me you'll come back."

"Yes, ma'am. I will."

I don't know if I can keep my promise, but I'm so used to Axel's pursuit that I sense his approach. I'm too afraid to hug Ms. Faye and thank her for her kindness. I just wave goodbye and run across the parking lot.

I don't even look back, knowing Axel will be standing there, wondering, "Who was that?"

CHAPTER FIVE
AXEL

FIVE BLOCKS UP QUEEN STREET AND RIGHT ON KING Street—that's the route Ruby always takes.

So, what the fuck is she doing this morning?

I chase her until she darts right, disappearing into a parking garage, but I'm not dumb enough to follow. What if she busts me? So I run past, without stopping, as rage starts pumping through my veins.

I already felt off this morning because something was off last night.

I'd bet all my money that the blonde cowgirl talking to my mom at the club was Ruby.

The cowgirl stood out. The other women looked like plastic dolls and spoke like it, too. But for my mom's business, I'm polite to them. Sure, I appreciate the finer things, but I'm drawn to real women. Real strength.

Like those sexy, frayed jean shorts. Those red cowgirl boots. The faded T-shirt that read, "To Hell I Won't." Who could miss a real beauty like that?

But the club was darker than usual, and the cowgirl looked like she was crying. She seemed vulnerable, almost traumatized; I know that's why my mom spoke to her. She spotted a woman in trouble and tried to help her, but the cowgirl ran away.

When I asked my mom who she was, she had no idea. When I asked if the blonde hair was a wig, she quipped, "Son, it's a woman's prerogative to change her hair with her mood, and you'd be wise to say they're all beautiful."

As much as it felt like Ruby, it couldn't have been her.

Ruby doesn't cry. She doesn't cower or cringe ... but she does run.

At home, after my run and shower, I sit on my bed, yanking on my socks, and fuming to Sparky, "How fucking dare she run from me?"

Sparky nudges my elbow.

"And you..." I order, scratching her ear. "You're going to the vet tomorrow and won't scratch anyone. You understand? I need at least one pussy to obey me, and that's you. And the other one?" I grin. "Let's make her pay."

In my office, an hour later, I hear Helen arrive at her desk. I'm aware it's Sunday. I know my staff is working hard.

"Hey, Helen." I step out to greet her. "And you, too, Samuel." He looks up from his desktop. "Thanks for working this weekend. After these hearings tomorrow, take Tuesday and Wednesday off. Okay?"

They nod, smiling, as Helen asks, "What about Ruby? She's been working the hardest. Should I tell her too?"

I check my phone. "No, she's twenty minutes late. If she breaks the rules, she pays."

"But, she's..." Helen's about to defend Ruby when the elevator *dings*.

I glance up as the doors slide open and...

Holy.

Fuck.

No way that crying cowgirl last night was Ruby because

this woman, with her chin lifted, confidently stalks my way in nude heels, and a *very* fitting navy sweater dress with her hair in a polished auburn ponytail. Her sapphire eyes glare, brimming with power and...

Hell, yes, that's my future queen. My cock firms for her. But my heart warns, *She's not ready.*

"Good morning, Mr. Cummings." She arches a brow at me, looming by her desk. "Is there something you need?"

To fuck you six ways from this *Sunday, then three times, daily, for the rest of my life.*

"You're late, Ms. Jones."

"I was meeting with my brother-in-law to see if he knows the Georgia Secretary of State. You know," she brushes past me, "for the Barinov case."

Barinov. That's Nick's surname. We all have different ones. My mother didn't want us connected by name. Our blood with our father is already a lethal bond.

And like my father, I can be cruel.

"I'm putting Samuel on the Barinov case while you review my trial binders for tomorrow." I glare at Ruby. "Every punctuation mark better be correct, or you'll answer for it."

Ruby hates desk work. She wants the excitement, the investigations, the courtroom. This is the worst thing I can do to her today, and it feels good. It's her punishment for running from me, and yes, dammit, I hear the hypocrisy.

With a pivot, I calmly tell Helen, "Watch Ms. Jones please. She can run wild with commas and bullets."

"You better run from *my* bullet."

I smirk, hearing Ruby whisper it behind my back before I close my office door.

But she's right. And smart. And fuck. I should've thought about who I know, so I call a friend in the Georgia State Property Office and get the name of someone he says can be influenced.

Then I call Nick with the update, telling him I'll reach out to a "Liam Farley" and give him no choice but to tell me the owners of that LLC.

I also remind Nick about Wren's initiation tonight, though I wish I could cancel it. There's too much shit going on, but everyone is coming here, and Wren's too excited. I can't let our new queen down.

I'm sharing this with Nick when Ruby suddenly swings my door open, sashaying into my office, so I abruptly end our call.

"Care to knock?"

"Nope." She pops her lips. "You told me to care about commas, so here." She drops the binder on my desk. " That's everything for tomorrow."

I thumb the pages. "Will I find errors?"

"If you do," she demands, "fire me, not Helen. Or I swear to God I'll cut the brake lines on your fancy car."

Spoken like a true queen.

"Oh." I fake a bristle. "No need to get hostile. What did a Jaguar ever do to you?"

"Of course, you name-drop your E-type."

"I'm surprised you know my car."

"I'm surprised you haven't been murdered in your sleep." She smiles. "But hey, keep dreaming; that's what I believe."

If she only knew murder is what I risk daily.

"Look." She leans over, grabbing the edge of my desk. "I want to help Nick and Zar. Samuel is great, but he can't get what I want."

Ruby's putting her luscious cleavage on proud display, and she knows it. My thickening cock is well aware, too, drawn to one of the many places on her hot body that I need to fuck.

"And just *what* do you want, Ms. Jones?"

"Intel."

"And how will you get it?" I lean back in my chair, risking exposure.

It creaks, and her eyes widen before they sharpen. "I have *skills*."

"And what if your *skills* aren't good enough to get what you really want?"

I'm so furious; I'm finally flirting with her, letting my smile escape. I let her see how she thrills me. How she attracts me. How I'm fucking obsessed with her and...

"Oh, I'm *not* good, Mr. Cummings." She fearlessly flirts back. "I can be so damn bad, I make men drool to give me what I want."

Holy fuck, I can see it.

My hard cock aches for it.

I can see myself fucking Ruby so hard that when I come inside her tight, wet pussy, I lose control, even of my mouth. I'll have her spreading her cheeks, holding them open for me as I drool over her little pink puckered hole while my cock is buried so deep inside her sweet cunt, because I'll be fucking her ass next.

Good God, I want her. I'm tired of waiting for her.

Her eyes glisten, reading my filthy mind. She's a lust bullet shot right through my heart, and ... *she knows it,* smirking. "So, let me call Farley." She seduces me and—

Wait.

What name did she just say?

Farley?

I almost ask, but I have too much trial experience. Too much training.

My opponent just breached confidentiality. Her little secret.

"We'll see." I lean forward in my chair. "Good job on the binders. Finish the Walton case, and I'll call Ms. Alonso about hers, and then we're done for the day. Go home, and thank you for your hard work this weekend."

"Uh." She stands upright. "Okay."

She didn't expect that. I rarely praise her because it arouses me too much. All I can hear in my praise is me telling her what a good girl she is while she chokes on my cock. *Soon.*

"Tell Helen to please get our lunch. It's my treat today." I keep my voice calm. "Please have Samuel go with her and help her carry it."

"Yes, Mr. Cummings." Ruby looks rattled by my politeness.

But once she closes my door? Fuck, polite. I turn up the speakers on my desktop. Tchaikovsky's *1812 Overture* blasts as I start searching under my desk.

That fucking Wildfire bugged my office!

How else could she know the name *Farley?* The one I told Nick? And there it is—a little blue light blinking on a black box smaller than my palm, stuck to the bottom of my desk.

Usually, I'd kill someone for doing this. Slowly. Painfully. Lots of blood and salt is how I like it.

But with Ruby ... *this is too perfect.*

My cock stirs with all the power I have over her now. So, I let her overhear my call to Ms. Alonso as I find out even *more* damning evidence against Ruby.

My day just went from shit to shining.

"Ms. *Jones.*" I stalk toward her desk. "I just spoke with Ms. Alonso. She thanked me for the legal advice you gave without my supervision. She said—"

"Shh, Mr. Cummings." Ruby flits her hand. "The adults are talking."

The adults? Talking?

No, she's not even looking at me. She's wearing a shit-eating grin and scrolling on her phone. I glance and see hot men on book covers filling her screen. One shirtless fucker after another.

She reads smutty books on her lunch break, making me die to make her fiction fact.

But now she thinks she has the upper hand? That she can spy and get dirt on me?

Damn, I'm even more seduced.

Fuck, she's such a queen.

"Oh, I'll get very adult with your next paycheck, Ms. Jones, unless you put your phone away. They're forbidden in my office."

Phones are a considerable risk. I don't want my picture taken. All obey my rules about them except Ruby.

"Yeah, this chat?" She rolls her eyes. "We're done. I need coffee."

She shifts in her chair to go to the breakroom, but I lower my glare. "Move an inch, and you'll need a new job."

"Look," she huffs, "Ms. Alonso has a pervert for a landlord, so I just told her to buy a hidden camera to prove it."

"Uh-huh, and where did you tell her to put the camera?"

"I don't know where she'll put it," she scoffs. "Why? Is she going for a Golden Globe nomination in the 'Best Performance By A Son-Of-A-Bitch' category for her landlord? Because don't worry. You got that one on lock."

I clench my molars. Fighting my snarl. My smile. My truth.

You know that other saying about Karma being a bitch? She is. She's my mother, and I'm a proud son-of-a-beautiful-bitch. For my mother, my kind of karma kills, too.

"I advise our clients, Ms. Jones. Do you understand?"

I tent my fingers on her desk, and her gaze drops to the cryptic symbols inked on them. Her plump lips part, fixated, and inwardly, I smirk. *My tattoos get her every time.*

"When I have to represent Ms. Alonso in court," I lecture, "she needs legally obtained camera footage."

Besides, I don't need cameras recording what I plan to do

to Ms. Alonso's landlord. I know all about him. Any man who preys on single moms will be my slow, murderous entertainment for days.

"Did you consider that, Ms. Jones, when you played lawyer for a day?"

Ruby snaps, "Did you consider the color of the lipstick you can wear when you kiss my ass?"

I arch a brow.

"I mean..." She exhales calmly, setting her phone down. "She's a young, single mom, and that man is extorting her, and I'm trying to help her."

Again, spoken like a queen.

"Then help yourself and pick up my dry cleaning."

"Uh! That's harassment!" She huffs, "You're no different than the landlord. Fetching your tiny little suits is not in my job description."

Tiny? Hardly. I'm six-four and swelling larger around Ruby, loving how much I can test her, loving how much power I have over her now.

"That's cute." I wink. "Lecturing me on the law when you're the paralegal who engaged in the unauthorized practice of the law with my client. Let's tell that to the judge, too. Now..." I reach into my jacket and toss the claim ticket on her desk. "Fetch my suits. I have court first thing in the morning."

Fuck me, it's hot how Ruby grinds her teeth. "Mr. Cummings, why don't you—"

My smirk slides into a smile, craving our hating game and her next insult, but...

The elevator *ding* lifts my glare from Ruby to the brass doors sliding open.

Across my office, with its gleaming wooden floors, large arched windows, and stately antique desks I collect stands...

... my goddaughter?

Alena Allen steps out of the elevator, her big brown eyes frantically searching the room until they find mine, and *something's wrong.*

I've known Alena for too long, from when she was a toddler to a young woman now. *Very much a woman*, I made sure of it.

"Michael..." Alena marches my way, using my pseudonym. The one that hides my American name—Axel. It's one of my many lies, hiding the name I was born with—Aleksi Kholodov. "We need to talk, please."

"Ahem." I clear the sudden strangle over my throat. Turning to Ruby, I fight like hell to hide this from her. From everyone. "Ms. Jones, clear my afternoon."

"But," Ruby debates, "Helen's getting lunch. She knows your schedule, not me."

I grab a pen from Ruby's desk, quickly scrawling the password to my schedule kept on Helen's computer while the dangerously familiar aroma of Alena's perfume nears. It's powdery and innocent.

Just as she was ... before me.

"Do it," I order Ruby. "Ms. Allen is family, and I need to meet with her." My pulse triples. "*Please.*"

Ruby arches a brow at my pleasantry. At my plea. This time, it's real.

Politely, I hold my office door open for Alena. She brushes past me, fully trusting, and it's instinct—I barely touch Alena's back, always protecting her, before I glance over my shoulder and catch the look in Ruby's eyes.

They're searching.

They're suspicious.

They're ... *oh, fuck* ... jealous?

CHAPTER SIX
AXEL

Relief and dread barrel through me.

I'm relieved I found Ruby's bugging device and turned it off. She won't be able to hear my conversation with Alena.

I was about to make Ruby beg, on her knees, for way more than her job, but then we were interrupted ... and now I dread this.

Not that I don't love Alena. I do. But it's a complicated love, only Alena and I understand.

Once I close my office door, she falls into my arms, crying. "I have to tell him. Please, I love Loch so much and I can't lie to him. I can't celebrate our engagement tonight and feel like such a liar."

"You're not lying." I hold her. "You're protecting him. The truth will only hurt him. It'll hurt everyone."

"How can I regret something," Alena sighs, "but still be glad we did it?"

"I don't know." The weight of it crushes me, too. "But I understand."

"Just let me tell Loch," she begs. "That's it. Never my dad.

No one. I promise. But I just can't lie to my future husband. Please, Michael, I need to tell him about us."

If someone could die from guilt and lies, I would right now. In many ways, I want to. Alena asked me to take her virginity, and she didn't even know my real name.

She still doesn't.

To her, I'm Michael Cummings. I'm best friends with her father, Nash Allen. He's an accountant, I'm a lawyer, and Nash and I are so close; I'm her godfather, too.

Alena has no idea who I really am, who my family is, what we do, or how her father is family with us, too, and we do it all to protect her.

Nash was sixteen when he became a father and eighteen when he joined us. I was fourteen then, and we became best friends. I've known Alena for years, and all I've ever felt is protective over her.

So when Alena was twenty-one and cried to me on her birthday, sharing how she didn't feel like a real woman. How boys teased her about her weight. How no one had ever kissed her or asked her out. How she was about to graduate from college, still a virgin, and she felt so powerless, ugly, and unwanted, I couldn't fucking stand it.

Her tears were killing me.

I hugged her, but then...

She kissed my neck and sighed, "Help me."

And in a split moment, the kind that changes lives forever, I had to decide. Make this about myself, how I felt betraying Nash, and push his daughter away, making her feel even more unloved, and breaking her fragile heart? Or make it about Alena and, for one night, make her feel safe and taken care of? Make her feel like the woman she was? Like she's very beautiful because she is, and in some odd way, I loved her. I'll always love her.

It wasn't an impulse.

It was a decision.

Alena is one of our queens. Our *first* queen. Really, our princess. As Nash's daughter, a king's daughter, she was one of us, but she wasn't *my* daughter, and she deserved to be worshipped. She deserved my love and protection, and I gave it to her.

She asked me to be her first, and I did it as tenderly and carefully as I could. I went slow. I showed her how a man should always make her feel, and she was a changed woman.

Alena never pined for me. She wasn't in love with me. But she trusted me. She needed me. She asked for me, and I answered.

After that night, it was like she was free. Alena said she felt beautiful, powerful, and she was. She didn't cling. She didn't look back. She didn't even call me. Well, not all the time. Just once in a while, she'd tell me how happy she was with her new job.

Did she use me?

Sure, and we didn't regret it.

But then we'd see each other, always with her father around, and the guilt became suffocating.

It still is.

But now, it's worse.

Alena has no idea she's marrying my little brother. Nash arranged it. Loch was supposed to protect our queen, acting like a stranger and her co-worker when, really, he was her secret bodyguard until he fell in love with her. Until he wanted Alena as *his* queen.

Does he know about me and Alena? No.

Did I beat the shit out of Loch to make sure he really loved her? Yes. Because he fought back for her. Nash had to pull us apart. They thought I was being a protective godfather, and I was.

So, Nash and I insisted Loch had to marry her. We wouldn't let him break her heart, and it's not like he will.

Loch is madly in love with Alena, and she's madly in love with him. They're a perfect match.

But now?

If Nash finds out. If Loch finds out. If my mother ever finds out. This secret is so damning it will kill my family.

And why, more than anyone, do I suddenly care if Ruby ever finds out? Why is it her judgment I fear the most?

"Come on." I guide Alena to the sofa. "Let's sit down."

We sit with our knees brushing, but desire escapes me. It's not that Alena isn't a stunning young woman; she is.

But she was never mine; she's Loch's.

And the more I'm honest with myself, my cold heart belongs to someone else. It has for a year, and she's sitting right outside my office door.

"No offense," Alena wrings her hands, "but please don't come to our engagement party tonight. Okay?"

My smile is soft. "No offense taken, and I'm happy for you. Your fiancé is a lucky man."

"But it's so hard lying to him, and my dad will be there, too." She stresses. "I'm used to hiding it from my dad. It's easy. It's my body and my business. Fathers don't have a right to say—"

"But I'm his best friend, Alena, and if he ever finds out, he *will* have something to say about it. He'll want to kill me, and I won't blame him. I won't stop him."

She laughs. "My dad won't *kill* you."

She doesn't know her father like I do. Nash has already murdered for love, for Vale—Alena's best friend—and I helped him.

Yes, this is an ocean of secrets and lies, and I'm drowning.

"What about your fiancé?" I try another tactic. "I can be a

very threatening man, and I know he'll be angry if he finds out about us."

She laughs again, and it's bittersweet. At the mention of Loch, Alena's brown eyes sparkle, innocent and in love. But he's my baby brother. She has no idea how he'll feel betrayed by us.

"But it's not like he was a virgin, either," she says. "He knows what he's doing in bed and—"

"Does he think you were?"

My tone is gentle. I'm not rough with Alena. Never. But I need to know how bad this is as her glance darts to the floor.

"*Alena*," my tone drops, "did you lie to Loch? Does he think he was your first? Because, to men—"

"No, he's not like that." She confronts my stare. "Loch *respects* women. It's what I love most about him. I haven't met his mom yet, but she raised him right because he doesn't objectify me. He loves me. He didn't ask about my past because he only cares about our future. Besides," she shrugs, "I told him the truth, that I've never been in love." She winces. "No offense."

Softly, I laugh. "Alena, I'm okay. You can't ever offend me. You don't love me that way, and I don't love you that way. *We* know that. But no one else will see it that way. That's why no one can ever know."

"But Michael," I wince when she uses my fake name, "I worry about our secret and *you*. You've been an ass since your wife left you."

I bristle.

"I know you don't like talking about her," she says, "but Katya was beautiful. Your wedding was like a fairytale, and I don't know what happened, but you've been an asshole since she left. Even to me."

I drag in a deep breath because Alena's just skimming the surface of my pain.

If I thought Alena kissing me was a shock, Katya coming on to me was a bomb.

If someone had to write a perfect woman on paper for me, it would supposedly be Katya. Russian. Blonde. Breathtaking. Cultured. Demure and subservient. We met in an art museum, where she hung on my every word about the eighteenth-century paintings.

The only time she wasn't passive was in bed. I thought it was love, all the times she wanted to fuck me. We were so busy having sex, I didn't have time to realize ... it wasn't love.

But I felt so guilty after Alena, so worried I'd lose Nash, that I'd lose all of my brothers and our bond, that I made Katya my first queen. I hoped the bonds we built as kings and queens with our tradition would give us the strength to survive all the secrets and lies.

I still hope that.

And I still have no idea why Katya really left me.

I just came home one day to a note on my bed. She said I was a cruel man with a cold heart, and she couldn't take it anymore. She even made fun of my socks, how I always wear them, and how she never saw my feet. She wrote that she was going home to Moscow, the last place I'd ever go to find her.

And honestly?

I didn't want her back. I wasn't brokenhearted; I was betrayed. I was so fucking good to her. I spoiled her. I was a devoted husband, but once Katya left, I decided to be the exact man she said I was.

Cruel and cold-hearted.

"I'm sorry." I cup my hand over Alena's. "If I've been an asshole, it's not because of you. You know I'm happy for you."

"I just want you to be happy, too," she sighs. "It's hard getting married, but seeing you and my dad so lonely. No wonder you're miserable, best friends together."

"But Alena, we won't be best friends if Nash finds out. It's the same for Loch. He'll be angry with you. It's like you said, it was your decision and your body. I was honored you shared it with me, and you owe no man an explanation about it, so please." I squeeze her hand. "Keep our secret. Don't ever tell anyone."

Her face falls, not sadly, but convinced. "Okay, I won't tell—"

"Mr. Cummings," Ruby's voice calls outside my door, "your *caviar* is getting cold."

My caviar is served on a bed of crushed ice, we all know it, and she makes Alena giggle. "She's funny."

"She's a pain in my ass but the smartest woman I know." I wink. "No offense."

Alena grins, arching a brow.

"Don't," I tell her. "Don't focus on me. Go have your engagement party and be happy." I kiss her hair.

"Promise you're not mad about not coming?"

"I'm fine," I answer honestly.

Because I have far more to worry about.

I have a sexy wildfire of an employee spying on me, hating me. A woman who'll be my queen one day, but for now ... I need her to leave.

Tonight is our private, sacred ritual, and yes, it's quite taboo, too, so I need to clear my office for the next queen's initiation.

CHAPTER SEVEN
RUBY

My emotions have whiplash.

I woke up feeling vulnerable after my botched night at the club. So, I forced myself to find my confidence again. Escaping Axel on our morning chase was the boost I needed.

Then I felt accomplished, meeting with Luca and trying to figure out how to get the intel Nick and Zar need on that rental.

But Axel rained on my proud parade, giving Samuel my case. It made me so mad, I listened to his calls while I finished those reports. I'm dying to help with this, and I confronted Axel about it.

Did I use my tits, too? Hey, if men are dumb enough to fall for them, I'll serve up the girls any day.

But I didn't expect the icy heat in Axel's eyes staring at my cleavage, the throbbing thrill I felt when he finally flirted with me. It was intoxicating ... and *I* was seduced right back.

The name I wasn't supposed to know just slipped out.

I was in full-blown hide-my-panic mode when Axel stormed out of his office, also mad about my advice to Ms.

Alonso. So, I confessed to that while low-key freaking out inside, wondering if he found my bug, too.

But a sweet angel saved me. Alena Allen just interrupted my sure destruction.

Now, I have something on Axel because I can tell they're hiding something. Score a point for me because I know Alena is Axel's best friend's daughter.

Unfortunately, I can't confirm what they're hiding because oh-crap-on-a-kill-me-now-cracker...

Axel found my bug!

I sit at my desk with my earbuds in, and all I hear is white noise.

My heart is racing.

I'm sweating bullets.

Vomit is imminent.

And what's worse? I watched how Axel gently touched the small of Alena's back, politely escorting her into his office, and I suddenly felt ... jealous ... or hurt?

Why? Why the hell do I care?

Alena seems like a nice woman. Like she's my age and we could be friends. I bond with women; I'm not a bitch to them.

And I hate Axel. Right? I've got two strikes against me, and he's about to fire me, and I love my job. It's not like I can't find another one. I can. But I want *this* one. It's the highest pay I can find in this town, and I love my colleagues.

But I don't understand what I feel for my dickhead boss.

I just suddenly *feel*.

Everything.

What's usually numb inside me is alive. That man explodes every emotion through me, the good and the bad. And like an investigator, I want to understand them. Maybe once I understand what I feel for Axel, I can make it stop.

But I need a plan.

On his call with Nick, Axel mentioned "initiating Wren" tonight in his office.

Who is Wren? Why is Nick involved? And who initiates anyone into anything in a law office on a Sunday night?

Exactly. It's mafia shit.

So before Axel can fire me, I'll find out. I'll get the upper hand again.

He's still meeting with Alena, and honestly, I don't want him to see me flustered like this, that he made me feel *anything*, so I shut down my computer and tidy my desk. Taking my handbag with me, it'll look like I've left for the day. Then, I grab a bottle of water and some crackers from the breakroom before I go to the bathroom.

I have to be ready for a long night.

There's a utility closet in the boardroom. We use it for office supplies, but I'll use it for my stakeout. I turn off the light in the closet, close the door, and slide down the wall, getting comfortable and quiet in a spot on the floor.

My phone is silent. I am, too. Minutes pass until ... I must've fallen asleep as heavy footsteps and deep voices awaken me. I recognize some. Of course, Axel. Nash. Sire. Nick. And Zar, too?

Then there are other men's gravelly voices. And one woman with an accent. No, wait ... I hear *two* women.

Through the closed wooden door, I can hear them chatting in the boardroom like it's a cocktail party until finally I hear the voice I loathe the most say, "Let's begin."

Begin what?

It sounds like a wedding service, and Axel is performing the ceremony. It sounds like it's between Sire and a young woman. "Wren," they call her, and her voice sounds like a fairy.

Then they mingle like they're celebrating. Glasses *tink* in celebration. Flatware *clanks* over china plates. They must have food set on the sideboard in the room.

So, that was "Wren's initiation?" Her wedding to Sire, performed by her now brother-in-law, Axel, and a little reception with guests?

Where's the scandal in that? How can I bribe Axel with appetizers and precious wedding vows?

My ass, sitting on hardwood floors, is going numb like my mind. I'm bored to death until I hear Sire's pontificating voice. "My little angel. Are you ready to be made into my queen?"

"Yes, my lord." That's Wren's innocent voice.

"Then take your clothes off for your kings. Show them our beautiful new queen. Show them all that we will share tonight."

Oh.

My.

God.

The rush of lust through my veins is instant. I sway, not believing what I'm hearing.

"Yes, my angel. You're so beautiful. Now, lie on your back." Wood creaks. Wren must be climbing onto the boardroom table for Sire. "Now, spread your legs for us," he says. "Yes, angel, spread your lips, too. Show my brothers that sweet, wet pussy and that pretty little clit. Show them the queen they get to worship tonight."

I'm panting. I'm getting wet. I can't see a damn thing, but what I can hear is so damn erotic. So taboo.

It's quiet until I hear Wren's begging moans laced with Sire's deep growl of, "Fuck yes, come on my tongue, angel. Your pussy tastes so sweet, we'll kill for it."

She gasps, "Yes, my king!" and what follows sounds like Wren getting fucked by Sire on the boardroom table. Moans. Gasps. Grunts.

Those odd chairs I've seen when Axel leaves the board-room door open? They look more like thrones, half with black velvet seats, half with white velvet ones. They surround Axel's boardroom table, but now they scrape across the floor as if those gathered around are making room for the carnal show.

"Let them see how you take my cock like my sweet slut. How you love getting fucked." Sire sounds so Dom and debauched. Not at all like a pastor. "Aw, yes, angel. Play with your little nipples. Yes, good girl. Pinch them, baby, and look at my brothers while I fuck you. Yes, baby. Show your kings how much you love my cock. How you want my cum inside you. You want my baby inside you. You're *my* queen. You're *our* queen to kill for."

"Yes, my king! Yes!" The table's legs screech against the wooden floor. Sire must be fucking Wren so hard. "Yes, please make me your sweet slut," she cries out. "Let them watch. Please. Fuck me hard. Then, Nash, my second king," she gasps for him, "please fuck me, too. Share me. Then all of you, fuck me. Fuck your queen."

What the...

All of them?

Who? And how many?

Holy hell, I'm in a daze of confused lust. My panties are soaked. The need to touch myself is overwhelming. I need to see what's happening, too.

What is Axel doing?

I wait until it sounds like a full-on orgy. Whoever the other woman is, I can hear her getting railed, too. I definitely hear Zar and Nick's love; I know their sounds. Their beach house has paper-thin walls.

It's an erotic cacophony of spanks, gasps, groans, grunts, and screams, with the grinding wood of chairs and the table enduring the brunt of their force. The men sound like beasts, the women sound so lucky, and I have to see this.

Carefully, I reach up and turn the crystal door knob, praying the *click* of the latch can't be heard over the loud orgasm some beastly man is clearly having. Slowly, I crack the door open, risking getting busted, but I'm too aroused to care.

Let them find me.

Let me join them.

Through the narrow crack of the open door, the sterile fluorescent lights are off. Only candles flicker around the room. Tall silhouettes cast long shadows across the walls. Some bodies are joined. Others are waiting to have Wren.

She's lying with her back on Sire's chest. Together, they lay on the boardroom table, his arms hooked under her knees. He's spreading her open. I can tell by their position, by their left sides facing me, that he's claiming her ass, and by the look on her face, she's enraptured. She's entranced by this erotic ritual.

Two men, definitely brothers, I recognize them from the club last night—Delta's bouncer, who sat at the bar, and the man in the suit who was on the stage. *Good God, are they Axel's brothers, too?* They're kneeling over Wren's gaping mouth, their hard cocks teasing her panting lips. Her desire and demand, undeniable. "Yes, fuck me. Make me your queen."

The room is dimly lit, but I can see it's Axel's turn. He's still in his dark suit and shoes.

And the sight and sound of him dragging his zipper down makes me stifle a moan. He unbuttons his pants, too, letting them drape open. He's not wearing boxers as he reaches in to free his cock, and I hold my breath.

Yes, I've been hyper-focused on it, wondering about him for so long, and when I finally see what's in his hefty grasp, I cover my mouth, stifling my gasp.

Oh, my god, he's so hung!
And...
He's pierced!

His steel jewelry catches the candlelight, but it's not through his swollen crown or his thick shaft. It's not to heighten his pleasure.

No, Axel has a pubic piercing through the dark, trimmed hair at the base of his cock. It's a gleaming ring, the size of a quarter with a prominent captive steel bead, and my cunt clenches, throbbing in recognition, knowing his piercing is designed to pleasure a clit while he's deep inside you.

It makes my eyelids hood with lust, my breath shallow, my mind swimming in shock. I'm somehow so aroused, watching him roll a condom on before he's inside Wren. Before he closes his eyes and shares her with his brother.

I close my eyes, too, and can't watch.

Jealousy trickles through me, but it's nothing compared to the tsunami of lust rising inside my veins. My body is flooded with desire, my emotions so heightened that I'm dizzy.

Leaning my head back, I can't fight this urge. I need relief. I lift my dress and wedge my fingers under my lace panties. They're drenched, and it doesn't take me long.

My hearing tunes out all others but Axel. Listening to his heavy breath, to the strained sounds of his pleasure, of hearing him grunt so hard when he comes, that I come, too.

My thighs shake. My body convulses. My walls clenching. I choke down his name, wanting to escape my lips. I silence my voice, and it only leaves me aching and wanting ... *wanting him.*

Oh my god, yes, I want Axel.
I want him so much, it suddenly hurts.

I surrender to the warm flood of emotions, drowning in them, and I want to. I don't want to hear the rest. I just want to float in the sound of Axel's desire echoing in my ears. The memory of his pierced cock soaks me. The idea of him plunging deep inside me is all-consuming.

I'm alone in a dark closet, but I can feel Axel swimming through my veins.

It fills me with an emotion I can't name.

It leaves me panting and weak until it finally sounds like they're done and begin to leave. But with Wren's moans and Sire's dirty taunts, it sounds like he stays to clean her. He's getting off on it, and I don't think I can take much more. My world needs to stop spinning.

Finally, I hear them leave. I hear Sire call out, "I'm done." Then, a giggle tickles the air. It's Wren calling out, "Goodnight, my kings."

"Goodnight, our queen." I hear Axel reply, his voice booming from his office.

Quietly, while he's in there, I stand to collect myself, though my muscles are liquid from lust. With shaking hands, I smooth my dress and ponytail and collect my handbag. Carefully, I creak the closet door open to find the boardroom empty. I creep toward its door as Nash storms past it, aiming for the back stairwell, unaware I'm hiding.

But Axel's still here.

His office light glows.

What will I do with the intel I just gained? Who will I tell about what I just saw? How do I really feel about Axel? Why did he just consume every cell in my body?

I don't know.

I just need to run.

Kicking off my heels so I can be quiet, they dangle from my fingertips as I tiptoe across the open office floor.

I'm almost at the door to the stairwell, following Nash's path, when...

"Ms. Jones, step into my office."

CHAPTER EIGHT
RUBY

"Fuck It" is an official destination, and I'm walking straight into it with my head held high.

I've been caught spying, red-handed, so I proudly march toward Axel's office. If I'm about to be fired or have charges filed against me or god knows what else a mafia king masquerading as a powerful lawyer can do to me, I'll at least keep my pride.

"Please," Axel gestures calmly toward his sofa, "have a seat."

"I'm fine standing."

"Sit!" he barks.

Arrogant dickhead. Like he owns me? Like he can train me? Like I'll follow his command, so...

"Woof!" I bark back, letting my heels drop to the floor.

"Don't bark if you won't bite, Ms. Jones." He glowers with lust swimming in his eyes. "Fight me, and I will put a collar on your neck."

The zip of lust to my clit is sudden.

Me, wearing a collar for Axel?

Holy hounds of hell, I didn't know I had this kink, but I do, hiding it with a roll of my eyes. "In your dreams."

I turn around, hiding my blushing cheeks.

The thought of kneeling for Axel, of obeying his orders, rearranges my entire being, and that can't happen.

So, instead of sitting like a lady, all prim and proper, and about to be punished for breaking his rules, I recline like the Queen of Sheba, sideways and lazily draping my arm over his sofa ... because I don't give a damn about his rules.

But I do suddenly give a damn about Axel, and it's making me mad. All he made me feel watching him still thrums through my veins.

Casually, he sits across from me, leaning back and lifting his chin. Spreading his hulking legs, he slowly drums his tatted fingers over the arm of his chair as his icy eyes narrow. He licks his bottom lip, and ... okay, he needs to *stop* inducing orgasms when he seethes.

"Where do I start with you?" He coldly scolds, "You're like a wildfire burning out of control."

"Easy: you don't start and can't control me." I shrug. "This is the end. I quit."

"You can't quit."

"Okay, Ted Lasso, I don't need a pep talk."

"I won't *let* you quit." He smirks. "I have too much power over you now."

Breathe. Breathe. Do NOT freak out.

"What do you mean by 'power over me'?"

"Trespassing. Illegal use of electronic surveillance. Invasion of privacy. The unlawful practice of the law. But I must add my favorite: the intentional infliction of emotional distress." He says drily, "You finally saw my dick. Congratulations."

I nod, desperate to hide my hammering heart. "I'll give you that last one. It was distressing."

He cocks a brow. "That's not all it was, Ms. Jones."

No, it was big, hard, and pierced, and I will NEVER be the same. You wear dick jewelry for the woman you love. Lucky bitch.

"Okay, fine," I huff. "I was spying. So, how do we unfuck this?"

"Unfuck this?" He stifles a chuckle. "Oh, Ms. Jones. I haven't even started fucking with you."

"What's that supposed to mean?"

His pause is too heavy and long. *Like his dick.*

Oh my god!

Stop thinking about it!

"What did you see tonight?" he finally asks, and there are a dozen replies I could give. They're all salacious, and he knows it. Anything I say would expose me as much as he's been exposed, and it feels too intimate. Too vulnerable. I could get so hurt if I tell the truth.

I saw how beautiful you are, and you made me feel something for you.

I shrug. "Meh. I saw a little something."

"Little?" He raises his brows. "Lie to yourself but not to me. Now you know about me and my brothers. You know about our queens, too. You've been listening to my conversations for how long?"

I pick at non-existent lint on the sofa. "Only nine months."

"Nine? Fucking? Months?" he snarls through clenched teeth, veins popping everywhere. I'm hiding the coronary I'm having as he slowly shakes his head in furious disbelief. "Now you're a liability, Ms. Jones. You know too much, and I can't afford the risk."

"So what? You're going to make me an offer I can't refuse?"

Glaring silence.

"Or I'll wear cement shoes and swim with the fishes?"

Deadly silence. His eyes burn with a glacial stare. His sexy face is stone, and I can't grab a full breath. Yes, I hate the man. Sort of. But deep down, parts of me trust him, which scares me even more.

Usually, I don't trust men, and suddenly, with the lethal look in his eyes, this is why.

"Okay, Axel, you're scaring me."

He nods. "And ... you know my name..."

Hey, Mouth. Shut up.

I know you think he's hot and all. And he's smart. And he can't be entirely immoral; he does really heroic things like help survivors of trafficking. But right now?

Bitch, he's deciding where to bury your body.

"But I don't know your last name, so we're good. We're cool as cucumbers," I ramble, "though that's a really dumb saying because they grow in summer gardens and—"

"King."

"Axel King?" I snort. I can't help it. "That's your full name? Of course, it is. Even your ego wears a crown." It dawns on me. "Oh shit, you just told me your full name, so now you have to kill me."

"Have I killed people? Yes." He's way too calm. "Do you make me mad enough to kill you?" Pause for my murder. "Yes, more than any other human being from now and time immemorial. Every goddamn minute of my day, you make me mad enough to murder."

My breath thins, my mind racing.

How does the Lord's Prayer start?

I've joked with my sister that Axel is a "cold cuntkiller," so did I manifest this? Does he legit have to kill me now?

"But I'll never hurt you, Ruby. In fact, I'll kill anyone who lays a hand on you." For emphasis, he slowly rubs his hands together.

"Oh shit, you're not kidding."

"No, I'm not because ... you're mine now."

"I'm sorry." I lean forward. "What did you just say?"

"You're mine, Ruby Jones. Starting tonight, I own you."

Laughter bursts from my throat. "Yeah, right. You need to start a podcast called 'Axel Says Stupid Shit.'"

Silence.

"You? Owning me?" I shake my head, wiping away laughing tears. "I'd rather be jobless, penniless, and starving. Hell, I'd rather be dead before I let a man own me, Axel King."

"You may be cavalier with your life, but what about your sisters?"

I stab my finger at him. "Touch a red hair on one of my sisters' heads, and I will fuck your ass with a sword."

His eyes shock open. Then he laughs. "Well, damn. Someone's been watching *Se7en*."

"Exactly. And what deadly sins can I use to kill *your* brothers?"

He swipes his hand. "While I appreciate your penchant for creative violence, and seriously do hope it is purely fictional, I will never hurt your sisters. But it was you who spied on me, remember? If you want them safe, I have to keep you safe now."

"Safe from what? You?"

"No. Safe from the men who want to kill me and my brothers. And since you wanted to play Black Widow, looking hotter than Scarlett Johansson, I might add, you're one of us now. Hence, you're mine."

Wait. Did he just compliment me?

Oh shit. Did he just claim me, too?

"Hence what? I'm in the mafia now?"

"We're not the mafia. We're much worse." He sounds so relaxed about it. "The mafia wants us."

"You're wanted for what?" I quip, "Mafia fashion violations? They don't like your bling? It doesn't match your cliché black suit, white shirt, and evil ink? I keep meaning to tell you; very original. Visionary, actually."

He fights a smile, and it's really damn sexy, especially now that my murder isn't on his immediate agenda.

"You'll stay with me," he commands. "You'll prove I can trust you, and when I do, I'll answer your questions."

"Stay with you? Like, keep working for you?"

"That, and you'll live with me."

My silence. My shock. My heart, running like it's on fire and screaming down the street.

"It's the only way to keep you safe," he continues. "To keep you from being kidnapped and used as an asset against my family or yours. Apparently, you know too much about me, and they will torture it out of you." He calmly shifts focus. "You'll have your own bedroom. It has an ensuite. You'll have privacy and—"

"No way." I rebel. "I live with my sisters. We've always been together and kept each other safe. And the last person I trust to protect me is you."

That's not entirely true. Axel can protect me. He's so alpha and intimidating that he could've convinced Jeffrey Dahmer to starve, but hey, hyperbole wins arguments.

"Ruby..."

He leans forward, his arms resting on his elbows. He's taken his jacket off and rolled up his white sleeves. A golden tie hangs loose around his neck, and for the first time, I can see more of his dark ink and the cryptic story on his tan skin.

And for the first time, I realize...

Axel said my name.

He made it sound special. Like a gift on his tongue. Like he opened a ribboned box. Like he opened *me*.

"You're a very smart woman," he persuades. "I don't tell you enough how you impress me. How I trust your instincts and intelligence. You're strong and brave, and I've enjoyed our hating game, but we're not playing it anymore; this is fucking real. So if you can't trust *me* about this, then think for yourself. Ask yourself if I'm not deadly serious about the risk you're in now."

All the cryptic conversations I've overheard. All the money he has. The security, too. The gun he carries, holstered to his back. The odd things I've noticed. Like for days, how he'll disappear from the office, and we'll have to scramble with his cases. How he'll return with bruised knuckles, like the ones on his knuckles now. How he always wears black in a city of pastels. *Black hides blood.*

Axel may be heroic and use the law to help survivors, but he breaks the law and kills for vengeance. I've figured that much out. The man reeks of sexy, villainous power.

And I may be cavalier with my life. I meant it; I'd rather be dead than owned. But I'd never risk anything harming my sisters.

"Okay." I nod. "Promise me you'll keep my sisters out of this and safe, and I'll stay with you." I lean forward and mirror his stance. "But we have a problem."

"Which is?"

"If we're living together..."

His eyes gleam with triumph.

Yes, he's caught me.

So, I smirk. "How are you going to chase me every morning?"

And I've caught him, too.

CHAPTER NINE
AXEL

NINE! FUCKING! MONTHS!

Ruby's been spying on me? *And* she figured out I was chasing her, too?

Murder would be the punishment for anyone else, but what else do I expect from my future queen? It's what drew me to her in the first place. I saw Ruby's fire, and my cold heart wanted to play.

No one else noticed the closet door in my boardroom slowly cracking open during Wren's initiation. They were too distracted. But I clocked it and knew there was only one Wildfire brave enough to spy on me.

It made me close my eyes while I performed my duty, initiating a queen. I imagined it was Ruby's tight, wet cunt I was fucking. I imagined it was Ruby becoming *my* queen. The thought made me come so hard.

I've wanted Ruby for months. I've stalked and spied on her, too. I knew, eventually, I'd trap her. She's too stubborn to obey the rules, and now she's mine.

It changes our game because it's no longer one.

With all she knows about me, she's at risk.

With all I feel for her, I'm in trouble too. Yes, I've felt desire before, but this? This is a demand. An unrelenting need.

This woman is mine.

But is she ready?

I glance at her and...

Shit, she looks worried. Nothing close to ready.

She's unusually quiet as we drive to her apartment to get her things. I can see her scrolling on her phone, but her shaking finger swipes too fast, like her mind is racing.

There's too much tension between us. It's time to stop playing and be real. I need her to know...

"What you saw tonight," I clear my throat, "it wasn't love. I mean..." Fuck, that's not true. "We love our queens. We'll die protecting them, but each king has *one* queen, *one* wife, and Wren is Sire's wife. I know what you saw, but I don't love her. Not like I'll love *my* wife."

Like I'll love you, you beautiful, fucking, stubborn Wildfire. Put your phone down.

She does. She turns away, staring at the window. "So, you gangbang your brother's wife, and it means nothing to you?"

"It's not a gangbang," I correct. "It's a ritual from our people, our past, and it means everything to us. It goes way back to when a powerful man could die any day and needed his wife and children protected. He needed to trust another man to care for them. It does something to us each time we initiate a queen. We know she—"

"Zar isn't a she."

"He's an exception because we love our brother; we love the one he loves. But most queens are women. She belongs to our brother but is special to us, too. She's one of ours, and we'd kill for her."

"So you have to fuck a woman to care for her?"

Goddamn, she presents every argument like an ace lawyer.

"No," is my honest answer. "Believe it or not," my throat tightens, "I care for *you*, and yet, we don't fuck, but you've fucked us over by spying on me and—"

"Excuse me!" She whips my way. "You're the one who's been playing Stanley the Stalker for a year."

"Eleven months," I correct.

"Well, then let me give you eleven fuck-yous because you started this. I was only stalking you back. It's not my fault you do so much dangerous mafia shit; you have to have erotic orgies as life insurance policies."

"Erotic?" I smirk. "So you liked what you saw?"

"That's what you focus on in this Ruby-could-die mess? If I loved your pierced dick?"

My smirk explodes. "Oh, so you loved my dick."

"Please," she scoffs, "I have a strict two-at-a-time policy, so your solo jeweled jawbreaker doesn't impress me."

Fuck, I didn't want to know that. *I. Did. Not. Want. To. Know. That.* Now I'm going to have to find out who they were and kill them.

Rare jealousy torches through me, and damn, it burns the happy smirk off my face like napalm.

Suddenly, I can't even imagine our ritual with Ruby. I'd kill one of my brothers for initiating her.

Never did I feel this way for Katya. When we initiated her, she wanted it, and I didn't mind. She insisted that all but me wear condoms, and she seemed eager, no, ravenous for my brothers. Particularly Sire. He's dirty with his breeding kink, and Katya got off on it.

All the while, the only one I worried about was Nash. If he felt bonded, too. Not to her, but to me. That was a year after my night with Alena, and I wasn't jealous about my wife being initiated by my brothers, including Nash.

I was worried I'd lose Nash, my best friend, if he ever found out I had lain with his daughter.

But how can Ruby be my queen if I don't share her? It's one time, one night, one sacred initiation, and I believe in it. It's worked so far, and yet...

I will burn the world down if someone touches Ruby.

Past, present, and future; she's mine.

I feel her studying my profile, reading my raging silence. Does she care that I'm jealous? Does she know that hurt my heart, and it fucking surprises me?

"But I didn't love them," she softly explains. "Sort of like you and Wren. It wasn't love. It was sex, and honestly, it's been a minute. I've been solo for months." Huh, sounds like she cares. "Not like it's your business."

Sounds like she keeps her pride, too.

It's what I admire about her the most.

I don't reply. I let my rage evaporate as I park in front of her apartment and wait in my car while she gets her things. When she appears, tugging one suitcase behind her, I get out to help her.

"Where's the rest?" I'm shocked. Katya had a lot of baggage. Obviously.

"This is all I own."

"And your sister?"

"She's asleep. I'll have to come up with some story to tell her."

"Tell her you fell in love with your hot boss." I risk a tease. "I'm a very convincing story."

She scoffs, "My sister knows I'm allergic to love."

I arch a brow at that, setting her suitcase in my trunk, thankful she doesn't own much because it wouldn't fit.

On the drive back over the bridge, Ruby's silent again, so I play Tchaikovsky. When I pull into the reserved parking space by my row house, I inform her, "Your car won't fit with mine, so you'll have to walk and drive with me."

"I'm not your prisoner," she fumes. "I'll park on the street."

"It'll get towed," I snarl back. "It's a street of Land Rovers and luxury. Your car doesn't belong here."

She looks away. She looks ... hurt?

"What did I say?"

"Everything."

Her eyes blink like she's fighting tears.

Fuck. FUUCCKK!

I finally have Ruby trapped. I finally have a chance to make her mine, and it sure as hell won't happen if she keeps hating me.

The game is over. This is real.

"Ruby, I'm sor—"

"Next dictate from the dickhead, please," she interrupts, opening her car door. "Come on. Let's get this over with."

I get out and grab her bag before reminding her of my gate code and programming her thumbprint into the pad that controls my security. It automatically unlocks my front door.

"Meow!" Sparky comes prancing our way. She traps us by the front door, weaving between our legs.

"I got her a box." I point to it in the kitchen. "She's made her nest there."

"No, she sleeps in my room or yours." Ruby picks her up. "We have to be here when she needs us."

Closing her eyes, she nuzzles Sparky, but her soft body nuzzles mine. We're standing closer than ever, and I can feel Ruby's warmth. Inhale her lilac perfume. Admire the sexy constellation of tiny, faded freckles on her nose. Witness how breathtaking she is when she's loving and...

What just happened to my chest?

A heart attack?

No. No, it's fucking butterflies.

I love this sight. I love feeling like this damn cat is

suddenly our baby, and I might have a chance at domesticating this woman.

"Then come to the vet with me tomorrow," I gently insist, trying not to sound like an asshole. "We need to know what to do."

She nods, cradling Sparky, when my phone rings.

I take it out of my pocket and see TWO on the screen. It's Nash, and I answer, depositing Ruby's suitcase in her bedroom upstairs before I disappear into mine with fury spreading through my bones at the news...

Nash is being followed. He has Vale Monroe in the van with him, and he's trying to lose the tail. He knows what to do.

We've trained for this. Defensive driving schools. Black belts. Close-quarter battle training. Small unit tactics. Sharpshooter qualifications. That and six of us have violence in our DNA. While Nash? Sometimes, I think he has more. He has Alena, a daughter he fights for, too.

I'm pretty certain it's Claude Olan Turner the Fourth— the head of a sex trafficking ring we've been hunting for months—who's following Nash.

Turner found Nash snooping in his online accounts and tracked him down. But Nash can take the heat. He'll protect us. He won't lead Turner to us, and he'll protect Vale, too. Loch will protect Alena. The other kings and queens are safe; my mom's club is a fortress, and now I need to protect Ruby even more.

Yeah, I know.

That'll be as easy as putting a leash on a lioness.

While Ruby unpacks in her room and talks to Sparky, I call the others. For them, it's life as usual. Stay hidden. Stay alert.

For me? Time to change the plan. Again.

I knock on Ruby's bedroom door.

"What?"

I grin at her brashness. "Tomorrow," I push her door open, "you'll co—"

I choke on my orders at the sight...

Ruby's bent over her suitcase on the floor, wearing tiny jean shorts, a black cropped tank, and flip flops with her fiery mane tumbling in wild waves. Her peachy skin has no scars or tattoos, only light, sexy freckles. Her body has every goddamn curve I crave.

It's suddenly the real her, exposed and free, solidifying my maddening obsession.

Good God, that woman will be my queen.

"I'll what?" She rises, holding a hairdryer and turning around.

"You... uh..."

Fuck, she's not wearing a bra, either, and my air conditioner works. My dick threatens to harden like her pearled nipples. It really wants out of its cage.

"I, uh... what?" Her sapphire eyes sparkle, delighted that the sight of her stupefies me.

It's obvious.

I have to clear my throat before answering, "We go to court together, then go to the vet. Whatever. But you stick with me while I'm giving everyone the week off. They deserve it."

Ruby laughs. "Bullshit, Ebeneezer. You don't give people a week off. What's going on?"

Yeah, this will be interesting—a woman suspicious of everything I say because she should be. So, I give her this...

"One of the kings has been exposed, so the rest of us have to be careful. We'll stay away from my office until it's safe."

"Who's been exposed? Who's after us?"

"You have to earn my trust to know."

"How do you expect me to stay safe if I don't know? I could be ordering a latte from my kidnapper and have no idea."

"I meant it." My voice comes out cold. "I'll kill any man who puts his hands on you. You stay with me, and I'll protect you."

She chews her lip, her eyes darting to orange medicine bottles on her nightstand and a clear plastic package with something white inside.

"Listen," she sighs. "I really hate telling you this. I'm not vulnerable with anyone, but about someone putting his hands on me—"

Instantly, my blood boils. "*Who* put his hands on you?"

"Okay, calm down, killer. Murder is on your Google calendar next week." She points to her medication. "I have epilepsy, and I have it under control, but I've never lived away from my sisters. They know what to do if—"

"If you have a *seizure*?" I fume, "Jesus, Ruby, you work for me. Why didn't you tell me this before? I need to protect you."

She lifts her chin. "My disability is none of your business. I told Helen, not you. She knows what to do."

"Why wouldn't you tell *me*?"

"Because of *that*." She points to my face. "You look all caring and sweet. Like you actually give a shit about me, and it dangerously teeters on pity, and I'd rather kneel and kiss your feet than *ever* suffer your pity."

The image rouses my dick, a smile threatening my lips. I can't stop it. "Is that an offer?"

"Fuck you." A smile threatens her lips, too. "And that's *not* an offer, by the way. Just YouTube what you need to do if I have a seizure."

"I get atonic ones," she explains. "I drop like a wet noodle, so just learn how to put me in the recovery position, on my side, and count how long it lasts, and if it gets close to three minutes, use that nasal spray in that white plastic container." She points to it. "I keep one in my purse and one by my bed. It's deadly if I'm out longer than that."

As if I'd let anything happen to her. "What else do you need?"

"Um, I can't take baths or swim alone. It's not a good idea for me to cook. Oh, and when I'm out, I'm completely vulnerable. I wear a smart watch and hope it doesn't get stolen." She waves her wrist. "So no more GenZ sexting. I'll text with this if I need help, which I'd really hate because I'm fine, so don't mention it again."

"Fine." Goddamn, I love her pride. And holy shit, I'm falling so hard. "I'll keep harassing and stalking you and being a dickhead. No special treatment, I promise."

Again, she fights a smile, and it's so breathtaking, my fucking chest hurts.

"Do you have any allergies I need to know about?"

"I already told you." She wrinkles her nose. "Love. I break out in hives and can't breathe and shit."

I grin. "I think that's called 'blushing' and 'crushing on someone' and shit."

"Just so we're clear, roomie..." Her eyes sharpen. "How many of your dozen girlfriends will be blushing and crushing here?"

Oh, do I detect notes of jealousy?

Subtle hints of caring?

"A dozen?" I laugh. "Even my dick couldn't keep up with that much pussy. And just so *we're* clear..." I point between us, risking a step closer to her. "I'm a one-woman kind of mafia man. I won't fuck around on my queen; I'll worship her."

I'll worship you.

"Then tell me," she demands, "who's after us? Because I'm not a dumbass damsel for any man."

"Don't worry about it. I'll protect you."

She shakes her head. "I don't trust anyone to protect me but my sisters."

"And I don't need your permission. I've decided I'll protect you. *It's done.*"

"Spoken like a true stalker," she huffs. "So much for my consent, and just another reason not to trust you."

"Trust? You're the one who spied on me, so I don't trust you, either. You're smart as hell, but you take too many risks. You can't control your mouth, and you're too fucking stubborn to listen," I smirk, "unless it's with an illegal device."

"Fine. That's fair." She aims her hairdryer at me like a gun. "You say I have to earn your trust because I spied on you tonight and—"

"Tonight?" I seethe, "Try *nine months*."

"Okay, fine. Whatever. But my whole life, I've never trusted men. They've never protected me. They've only hurt me and my sisters."

My nostrils flare. "I will *not* hurt you, Ruby. No matter what. You *WILL* trust me on that."

Her eyes narrow. "Never."

I don't know how I'll ever win her over, but goddammit, I will.

"Fine." I turn around, leaving her room. "Six a.m., we're up. Eight a.m., we're out. We go to court."

She calls out, "And if I run?"

I grin, shouting back as I close my bedroom door, "Trust that I'll chase you."

CHAPTER TEN
AXEL

THEY SAY RUNNING IS GOOD FOR STAMINA, BLOOD FLOW, and moods.

No shit.

I've never been so aroused in my life.

Chasing Ruby is even more alluring when she *knows* I'm on her heels. She's running faster than ever through the park and making every part of me work harder for her.

My testosterone spikes. My heart races. My blood pumps, and it's all flowing straight to my cock.

I woke up alone, and so damn hard for her, knowing she was only a bedroom away. I desperately needed to jerk off, but I could hear her quickly getting ready for her run. It's like she wanted the chase, and I was up, literally, and running after her.

My black running shorts have a compression liner, but it's obvious I'm erect.

And I swear, it's like running with a charging lion in my shorts. It wants out. It wants her, and I'm trying to contain it, but I can't. I hyper-focus on Ruby's luscious ass in those blush pink leggings and follow my instinct.

I chase her.

Usually, she takes thirty minutes to run three miles, but not this morning. She's mad, and I'm on a mission. I'm only a block behind her, not two, and she can hear my breath, and I can smell her drug. Perfume. Sweat. Musk that lures a mate. She's my singular pursuit as dark urges pump through my veins.

She says she doesn't trust me. Not yet.

But does she want me?

Does she feel this maddening attraction, too?

I've kept it caged for a year.

By the time she's running back to my home, my watch says it's only been twenty-five minutes. Without a word, she opens my gate and races for my door, her thumbprint *beeps* it open, and she slams it behind her.

In no time, I follow and slam it behind me, too. Breath huffing. Body sweating. My instincts feral and hunting. I find her panting, sweating, and standing in my kitchen with her fists on her waist.

For a moment, we're silent.

Staring each other down.

Exhaling heavily.

Then...

Her gaze falls to my shorts, not able to contain my erection for her. Her eyes widen with surprise, and it only makes me harder.

I let her stare at it. I let her lick her lips at it, watching my cock swell even more for her.

I can't fight it. I get even more aroused at the lust in her eyes.

This is our truth—*I need you, and you want me.*

I'm fighting the urge to lick the bead of sweat trickling into her cleavage. I'm fighting so many urges when she demands to know, "What will you do if I ever let you catch me?"

Gone is the lawyer who's so careful, cold, and calculated. The one who's been waiting for her. Now, I'm an animal, a predator in heat; I'm hers.

And I can't hide it.

Last night, I was willing to wait forever for her. This morning?

I need to know ... *now*.

"Did you like it today?" I stalk toward her, and she steps back, but I've got her trapped against my kitchen table. "Trusting that I'd chase you? That I won't let you go? Did you *like* it?"

I hover close enough to swim in her scent. Like a king tide, the Earth, Sun, and Moon align, pulling me into her space, making her lips part and her eyes search mine.

This attraction is irresistible.

I won't go another day denying it.

"Yes," she confesses, "I felt like I was running from you and I liked it. It made me faster. Like you can't ever catch me."

I'm hot and sweaty and need to be unchained, so I rip my shirt off and toss it on the floor.

I stun her eyes with all of my ink, her stare drinking me in. Every flexing, glistening muscle on me is covered. Only my left leg is bare. The rest is all blacks and greys, all my pain and past, and I want her to see it. I need her to know...

"Then trust me when I tell you to *never* let me catch you because I will, Ruby, and you won't survive it."

My cock throbs, pressed at an angle against my abs, my swollen tip exposed, straining against my waistband. And I leak, remembering how she's seen my pubic piercing.

I got it for her.

When I finally catch her heart, I'll tell her. I'll make her feel how I got it months ago to please her. *Only her.* I didn't let Wren feel it last night. That was an initiation. Not love.

I'm saving myself for my true queen; I'm saving everything for Ruby.

I won't make the same mistake I made with Alena. I did that for her, not for me. And with Katya, I let myself be taken, instead of giving everything to her.

But for Ruby?

I'll give her everything because I recognize a true queen when I see one. Alena was innocent, and Katya was entitled. But not Ruby. Even when she falls, she gets up. She fights back.

That's a queen.

That's *my* queen.

She swallows nervously. "What do you mean I won't survive it?" But desire hoods her eyes. "You said I was safe with you."

I step even closer, licking my hungry lips.

"Your life is safe with me, Ruby, but your pussy is in danger. It won't survive how I obviously need to *fuck* you. *Hard.*"

I make her softly gasp as I let my burning gaze drop to the maddening outline of her sweet pussy lips in those leggings.

I want to rip them open with my teeth and devour her cunt.

I'm making her ribs heave, the sweat on her flesh driving me insane. Our lust. Our pheromones. Our bodies. Our breath. Our instinct to fuck is right here, demanding we do it.

"You say you don't trust me, and maybe you shouldn't," I warn. "A very violent man raised me. He was a cruel animal. It's my mother who made me human, but still. Yes, I'll protect you, but I feel it when I chase you and *only* you. I'm a beast who can't control what I want to do to you."

"What..." She stammers, glancing down again at my violent erection. "What do you want to do to me?"

Here I go, baring my fangs and heart for you.

"Everything," I growl. "I want you wet. Open. Taking. Shaking. Hot. Sweating. Squirting. Dripping and bloody. I want you covered in my cum, and screaming my name, and fucking loving it."

"Fuck," she sighs, her shaking hand grabbing my table.

"Yes, *fuck*, that's what I crave to do to every sweet, tight hole you have, Ruby. So fucking hard and so many times." We stand inches apart, my nose almost touching hers. "*Trust* that I'm being honest about how much I want you, so you've been warned."

"You're saying you're going to attack me?"

"Only if you want me to."

"I'm not afraid of you."

"You should be."

She scoffs, "Okay, my name's not Bella, and you're not Edward. We're not red flags and teenage vampires. We're adults. So, what are you saying, Axel? You have a primal kink, and you want my consent?"

Fuck, she's beautiful when she's blunt. "Yes, but I want your trust even more. I'll never fuck you without it."

"What makes you think I want to fuck you?"

"Do you?"

I freeze while she burns right in front of me. I don't want her to see how I'm holding my cold heart in my shaking hand for her. How this will hurt like hell if she says no.

The other women? They weren't a fight.

But Ruby is. She's a war I won't lose.

"Maybe," she teases, but it's tender. "But maybe you're not my type."

"Touché. A primal fuck is an acquired kink."

"How did you acquire it?"

"I met *you*."

I let her search my eyes and see it's not a lie. I hide so many truths, but my feelings for her are my most vulnerable ones.

"I met you," I confess, "and I met my equal. You stopped my fucking heart and you became mine—the woman I *will* have."

It's like she can't breathe, she can't believe it.

But she can feel it.

I brush my thumb over her plump bottom lip, making her softly gasp.

"But I want more than to fuck you, Ruby." I can't stop myself. I can't stop this feeling. "I want to catch you and for you to want me inside of you. I want your trust. I want everything you have because I'm not a man who settles for less. But you need to earn my trust, too. You're a wildfire. You get hot and burn out of control, and we can't *lose* control in my world. It's too deadly. But once we trust each other, imagine how we can burn ... *together*."

She softly shakes her head. "I'll never trust you."

"Maybe not. But you want me, don't you?"

Her body trembles, goosebumps blooming over her creamy flesh. Yes, she wants this. She's a runner; I'm a chaser. We're a true pair.

"So be my brave little Wildfire and tell me..." I urge my thumb against her lips, penetrating their seam. "Is your pussy wet from my chase?"

Her eyelids flutter. She falters for a moment.

And I hold my heavy breath.

Then...

She moans, obeying and shamelessly sucking my thumb. She nods her head; *yes, I made her pussy wet.* And I can stifle my groan, but I can't control my cock.

"Do you see how fucking hard I get chasing you?" With

my thumb in her warm, sucking mouth, I tilt her head down so she can stare at my tip, exposed and dripping for her. "Do you see how you're making my hard cock leak for you?"

A soft mewl escapes her throat.

"Every morning, after I chase you, I come home hard like this," I confess. "Then, I stand in my shower, stroke my cock and close my eyes, imagining doing so many goddamn dirty things to you. I come so fucking hard moaning your name." I lift her chin. "So tell me, do you want me, too?"

She's so stubborn, so good at being a rock wall against which so many men, I'm sure, have crashed themselves into pieces over. Ruby doesn't give her heart to men; I can see it in her dark blue eyes.

So, I step even closer and give my body to hers. Skin to skin. Sweat to sweat. My hard cock, its wet tip, touching the soft flesh exposed above her leggings.

She gasps over my thumb, at me, rubbing my hard body against hers. "Tell me, Ruby. Tell me if you want me, too."

My mind warns me to back away, and whip out contracts, demanding NDAs, and a relationship disclosure. I could lose my practice over her. I could lose my life and so much more.

But my heart pounds too hard for her. I need to know if, under our hating game and biting barbs that thrill me daily, does she feel this? Am I right? Have I made her hate me so much that she's falling in love with me, too?

Her eyes anchor to mine. Like a deep blue sea, something churns in them, and God, I've killed men, but this woman is killing me right now.

She won't answer me.

I've never felt this exposed before. I've never put my heart on the line. Maybe it's a big mistake. Maybe I should let her go and...

Her warm hand brushes my aching cock, squeezing my swollen shaft before dropping her grasp and I shudder. "Oh fuck." I press my forehead to hers. She made my thighs shake, my heart tumbling inside my chest. "This is your answer? You want me, too?"

She nods yes, and I close my eyes, letting something even more powerful than my desire for her release inside me. Warmth floods my heart. It's a new and brave feeling.

I pull my thumb out of her mouth, my lips slowly seeking hers, but she turns away, just barely, like she's afraid.

"Okay," I whisper, and I don't know why. I've never felt this willing to do anything for a woman. "We'll wait."

"No," she softly answers, "we'll be late for court."

She smiles, wriggling against me, so I silently step away and let her go.

Without glancing back, Ruby darts upstairs.

And I know, from this day forward, wherever that woman runs…

She'll take my heart with her.

CHAPTER ELEVEN
RUBY

For three hours, I sit on a hard bench in the courtroom gallery and stare at where Axel's dark hair meets the even darker tattoos hidden under his suit.

He rules behind the plaintiff's table, ruthlessly defending his client, while his cold water and bergamot cologne weave into parts of me I didn't know were open.

Or did Axel open them?

The case drones on, so I let my mind wander down "What The Fuck Lane."

I'm still processing this morning—what he confessed, what I felt, what we shared, but mostly ... what I fear.

I wasn't out of breath from my run. I was panting at Axel's desire for me. At his ripped body covered in ink. At his frighteningly hard cock in his shorts. At the smell of his expensive cologne and his feral, masculine sweat.

My god, he is a beautiful beast.

He let me see the tattoos on his chest, his abs. The child's hands clasped in desperate prayer. A crying Virgin Mary, a mother in pain, inked over his abs. He wanted me to see more of him, and I did.

I've never felt so desperate for a man. A need *he* created by chasing me, and with everything he confessed about how he feels? I felt so taken and controlled, so powerful and wanted.

Axel is wildly intoxicating. He's not always cold and cruel. He can burn hotter than I've ever felt with a man, and that scares me.

For a year, I was trapped in a trailer with a predatory man I didn't trust. So, now, can I trust being trapped in a life with a passionate one?

Because both are dangerous in different ways.

Yes, Axel can be ruthless and scary. But it's the flashes of his tenderness that lure me in.

How he wanted me to know he didn't love Wren. How he knew he hurt my feelings in the car. How he asked me to go to the vet with him. How he caught me unpacking and looked at me with such awe. How he didn't make me feel weak about my epilepsy. His erotic joke was sweet. And he swore he'd never hurt me. He confessed he wants more than to fuck me.

He wants everything with me?

That's the danger.

Because what do I have to lose?

Everything. My job. My heart. My life. I've never known a man worth losing everything for.

Besides, even if he gives me everything he has, what do I have to give a rich and powerful man like him?

All I have is my past, pride, and piece-of-shit car.

The judge berates the landlord, the defendant, Bill Ratcliffe, who turns to glare at me. He knows I work for Axel, so I glare back and subtly lift my middle finger to my lips, kissing it with a fuck-you smile.

I make him seethe and turn around.

I make myself chuckle and realize ... *wait* ... I do have

something to give.

I have skills and no fear. I can help Axel's brother. I love Nick and Zar, too, and something about my steamy morning with Axel inspires me.

While his third case against Ratcliffe is called, I sneak out of the courtroom and find a quiet spot in the marbled hallway to use my phone.

A text from my worried sister greets me.

> ROSÉ THE HOSÉ
>
> Where TF are you
>
> You better be alive and scaring the shit out of me and not dead in a ditch

I'm upping my body count with my boss

I'm staying at his place

> Are you faded

I'm not high and not 14

He's laying pipe I like

Nuff said

> I totally shipped this
>
> Told you he had rizz
>
> You're boo'd up

OMG you're not 14 either

> Right. We're adults so
>
> ...

I know what she's typing. I know what Rose worries about.

I have my meds and he knows

I'm fine

You TOLD him?????

Bish, you ain't fine

You in love

ICYMI I don't do love

Gotta go

I pause. I've never spent the night away from my sisters. They know the risks of my disorder. They worry about me.

Love you

I promise I'm okay

I end our texts, and after thirty minutes, I have a dangerous and dirty plan.

The judge bangs her gavel as I push the swinging door open to the courtroom. "This court is in recess," she rules. "You have your continuance. We'll see you in sixty days."

Axel offers his hand, helping Ms. Simpson to rise. By the time he escorts her to a waiting SUV outside the courthouse, we have one hour before our vet appointment.

With a flourish, he whips around, flashing a rare smile and an even cuter command, "Let's get Sparky."

I swear when it comes to that cat, Axel forgets he's a cold-hearted dickhead, and that we almost dry-humped this morning.

No complaints.

"Okay, but I'm kind of starving, too."

He waits for me to stride beside him, which is odd. I'm so

used to his chase, but now he flanks me. He walks on the streetside, protecting me while we walk back to his place.

"If I buy you dinner tonight," he asks, "will a protein bar get you through the afternoon?"

I'm shocked. "Are you asking me on a *date?*"

He stops in the middle of the sidewalk, looming over me, but somehow, the dickhead makes it tender. "Ruby Jones, will you please have dinner with me tonight?"

Oh shit.

Who is this man? Giving me ... what? Butterflies?

"I'd reach for your hand and ask," he doubles down, "but I don't want watching eyes to know you're more than my paralegal."

Yep, they're butterflies.

"Just so we're clear," I grin, "is this harassment or stalking?"

"Have dinner with me," he smirks, "and make it both."

"Only if you say yes to my plan to help Nick and Zar."

"Which is?"

"You have to agree to agree to it."

He laughs. "You need to start a podcast called, 'Ruby Thinks You're Stupid.'"

"Agreeing with me *would* be wise."

The hot dickhead keeps laughing. "The wisest way to my grave."

"So you don't trust me?"

"Nope."

"So you're chicken shit?"

"Never."

"Then agree to my plan, and let's earn some trust *together* ... for Nick and Zar's sake."

He licks his teeth, his glacial eyes hot with curiosity. "Fine. Have dinner with me, and I'll hear your plan."

"You'll agree to it."

"What are you? Seal Team Six?" Even when he mocks, he's sexy. "I don't agree to a mission unless I plan it. But you're smart and love Nick and Zar, too, so I'll give it serious consideration."

Okay, Axel didn't stay alive this long, evading the mafia for whatever reason by being stupid. He's super calculated and really looking like a yummy cuntsnack right now.

"Fine," I huff. "Give me the protein bar, and we have a deal."

Grinning, he doesn't take his eyes off mine while he unflaps his briefcase, fishes around, and presents me with a peanut butter and jelly flavored bar. "Your favorite."

"How'd you *know*?"

"I'm the Seal Team Six of stalking."

I laugh, munching on my bar for our afternoon stroll back to his place. Lucky for us, there's a veterinarian's office a few blocks from Axel's place, so he carries Sparky there.

And don't think I didn't notice how he secured his gun into a back holster under his jacket before we left his house. He couldn't carry it into a courtroom, but otherwise, he's always packing.

Yeah, a gun and that monster in his pants.

Walking down the sidewalk with him holding Sparky, I notice the threat of other pussies adoring the sight of him, too.

Axel turns heads.

Lots of them.

"Explain to me your fashion choices," I insist. "You wear custom suits from King Street, like so many lawyers, but yours are always dark. Like you wouldn't be caught dead in seersucker. You prefer conservative shoes and a briefcase but wear bling like a baller, carry a nine, and cover your body with dark ink under starched white shirts. So, what's your true vibe?"

"If I answer, you have to answer my questions, too." Sparky's getting fur all over his charcoal jacket while we wait at the corner for the pedestrian light.

"Deal," I answer.

Subtly, he looks over his shoulder, making sure no one hears before he turns and lowers his voice.

"Parts of me I hide to survive. I have to blend in, or I'll be found. But there are parts of me I can't deny. So, I wear them on my body and take the risk.

"Like my earrings. They're diamonds made from my mother's necklace. It's all she had from her family when she was kidnapped and raped as a child bride at fourteen. She's a strong woman, and I wear them in her honor."

I nod, stunned by the totality of his story, his beauty, his honesty. "You hide all of that from your enemies?"

"No," he answers, "I hide from my father."

The light changes, but we don't move. "Who's your father?"

Axel pauses, letting his eyes search mine with that same intense look he had in the kitchen when he was about to kiss me. When I was suddenly afraid of how I felt for him.

"This is me trusting you, Ruby. This is me, trying to earn yours, too."

I swallow. "I promise I'll never tell."

I won't. I'd never betray Axel. Hate him? Yes. Come for him? Obviously. But rat him out? I'm too proud to be that kind of person.

"It doesn't matter. My father has vicious ways of *making* you tell." His voice drops even lower. "He's Ruslan Kholodov, the head of the Russian Bratva."

"IT LOOKS LIKE YOU TWO WILL BE PARENTS SOON," THE VET announces. "According to this ultrasound, she's about fifty days pregnant."

"So, in about ten days?" Axel asks about Sparky.

"Yes. Congratulations," the vet proclaims...

But I'm still stuck on that whole Russian Bratva thing. That whole son-of-the-most-dangerous-man-in-the-world thing.

But like a worried dad, not an escaped Bratva prince, Axel is focuses on the cat. "Should we bring her here when she goes into labor?"

"You can," the vet answers, "but it's best not to move her."

"Can we get a carrier for her?" I ask. "In case she likes it better than the box we got her?"

In case we have to escape in a hail of Bratva bullets and don't want to leave Sparky and the grandkittens behind?

"We have everything you need in our shop off the waiting room," the vet answers.

But when Axel tries to put Sparky in her new carrier, one pussy to another, I'm impressed. She hisses, scratching him. She doesn't want to be trapped, either.

"Okay, okay," Axel huffs at her. "I'll carry you home."

And he does, all the way back to his place, where he sets her down. Together, we watch Sparky prance toward her litter box, and though she's pregnant as hell, that pussy has pride.

Yeah, I'm really growing attached.

"Ready for our date?" Axel turns to me.

A date? Wow, he's serious, and I've never officially been on one. Hookups and meet-cute-cocks at a bar don't count.

I glance down at my thrift shop score: an old Michael

Kors emerald sheath dress, and that deep vulnerability stirs inside. "Should I change first?"

His intense stare glides up my legs, lingering over where he touched me this morning, before his icy gaze heats every cell in my body. "Don't you dare change, Ruby Jones."

Oh, no.

This hot dickhead went from making me murderous to making me melt.

We drive to the restaurant in a dusky silence, his Russian music growing on me as a valet rushes to take his Jaguar. We enter, and Axel gently presses his hand to the small of my back.

Just as he did to Alena Allen.

I don't know why I think of it now or how I feel about it.

But holy hell, do I *feel.*

It's nameless and potent as we weave our way to a corner in the back of a blooming courtyard. The restaurant is a Victorian home turned famous spot for Charleston's elite. It takes months to get a reservation, but the hostess beams at Axel, silently escorting us to this table like it's his.

"Don't you worry, you'll be spotted?" I whisper when he pulls the chair out for me. Like he has manners. Like he's a prince, a Bratva prince.

Nope, I can't get past that part.

If I thought Axel was wealthy and powerful as a rogue South Carolina lawyer while running vigilante crimes as a side hustle, I was right.

But now I know he's also the missing heir to the second-largest crime organization in the world.

He makes me and my little spying on him feel like Dora The Explorer, not the Black Widow.

"I *want* to be spotted as Michael Cummings, the lawyer." He sits beside me. "I want the illusion of a normal life with nothing to hide, including very public dinner dates."

Jealousy stabs my heart.

Insecurity, too.

I'm not his special date; I'm a token cover story.

I hate that I care. I hate feeling this vulnerable, so I look away.

Women in fashion I can't afford cut their eyes at me. I can't face Axel and won't confront their judging glares, either, so I look down, twisting the linen napkin in my lap.

"Ruby," Axel's voice is low and pressing, "what did I say this time?"

"Nothing." I won't look at him.

"No, I said *everything* again, but I don't know what. Talk to me. What did I say that hurt you?"

Answering him would only hurt me more, so I don't.

I need him to read my mind. I need him to see my memories so I don't have to relive them. I need him to see the girl who lost control of her bladder during a seizure at school. I need him to know what it felt like to be bullied about it for years. I need him to understand what it feels like to be powerless, mocked, and shamed.

Axel could inherit even the darkest world, and I still wouldn't belong in it. He wouldn't understand and...

His hand reaches for mine. Hidden by the tablecloth, no one sees him gently hold it. No one but me hears him say, "I haven't been on a date since the day I met you." No one feels his warmth, but I do. "Is that what upset you?"

Oh, god, this isn't a game.

This is real.

"Why me?" I lift my trembling chin. "Why do you say you want everything from me when you come from the height of power, even the criminal kind, and I come from nothing? I have nothing but my..." I pause, remembering what he calls me, "my *wildfire* to give."

"Honestly?" He doesn't let go of my hand, and I *like* his

hold on me. "Because you remind me of my mom, and I don't mean it in a weird Freudian way; I mean it as the highest compliment. She survived horrible violence and escaped with six sons. A strong woman raised me, and I know when I meet one. When I met *you*."

"But you don't really know me."

"Yes, I do." He cocks a grin. "You flip off drivers who honk at slow pedestrians. You give lost tourists directions. You tip every busker and barista way too much. You threw a butter pecan milkshake at some boys who were picking on a girl waiting for the city bus, and—"

"You *saw* all that?"

"Stanley the Stalker strikes again." His thumb caresses my hand. "Yes, Ruby, I see you. The butter pecan was a guess, but I know it's your favorite ice cream."

"That's freaky."

"I prefer *impressive*, but hey," he smirks, "you know I like getting freaky, too."

He lets go of my hand, and I grab a breath because he's right. I was bullied, but now I'm strong. By the time I was a junior in high school, I'd had enough. I fought back. My sister, Scarlett, taught me her MMA moves, how to punch and choke, and I spent more time in suspension than in school. Honestly, fighting back helped to relieve the stress that triggered my seizures.

This is who I am now.

"So, since you like getting freaky," I let go of my napkin to twirl the knife on the table, "you'll like my plan."

He leans back in his chair. "Okay, let me hear it."

"Hear it? No, it's happening. I rented a night at the chalet where Nick and Zar were illegally filmed. I'm going tomorrow to give the owner's camera an erotic performance. Then, I'll wait for him to bribe me, too, and when I go to pay him, you can kill him."

Axel's speechless, then furious. "The fuck you are."

I silently mouth, "It's happening."

"It's a death trap."

I mouth again. "It's happening."

"Ruby…" He clenches his fist like he wants to pound the table, but won't draw attention. "You are *NOT* going alone to a criminal location where you'll expose yourself to be illicitly filmed, then bribed. Yes, I'll kill the man bribing Nick, but you're not going to find him that way."

"It's the *only* way." I keep spinning the knife. "I called Liam Farley while you were in court today. For five hundred dollars to his Venmo, I got the *three* names of who owns that LLC, so now we have to find out which one is the criminal.

"So," I sigh, "you can either come with me tomorrow and make it an even more convincing show for the camera or wait for me to get the intel on the man bribing Nick all by my silly self."

"We're *not* fucking on camera," he seethes. "I'd never let us be exposed like that."

I shrug. "I didn't expect you would. But you can sit out of range of the camera while you play my boss, and I'm your secretary. We'll pretend we're having a naughty affair and rented the chalet where I give you a dirty show until my husband calls, and we have to leave."

"You're *not* married." He grits his teeth. "And you sure as fuck won't give a dirty show to anyone." Pause for his smirk. "Except me."

"Come on," I huff, "think with your Carolina lawyer brain, not your jealous Bratva balls. The owner doesn't know I'm not married, and sextortion is the fastest growing cyber-crime in this country, and hiding adultery is a top reason for it."

I lean forward, hissing my whisper, "Nick isn't his first victim, and he won't be the last. Imagine how many rental properties this guy has, how many people's lives he's ruining because he's violating their privacy."

Axel fumes, but runs the calculations. He's tempted in more ways than one; I knew he would be.

"We go," he orders, "but we do it *my* way. There are loopholes in your mission, and I never operate alone."

"You won't. You'll be with me."

"No," he corrects. "Remember, you're *mine* now. You'll always be with *me* and another king."

CHAPTER TWELVE
RUBY

I'M DISTRACTED AND TRYING TO FIND MY SEATBELT WHEN I hear Axel's greeting.

"This is my brother, Grant. And Grant, this is Ruby Jones, my spying paralegal. She knows my name and way too much about us; don't kill her."

I glance up at two mountains of muscle, towering before me.

"Ms. Jones." Grant nods.

"Oh my god," I murmur, "you're Reacher's twin. Like the hot, huge Alan version, not the sad Tom one. Tom needs to stick to *Mission: Impossible* because you're *impossibly* huge."

Axel laughs coldly. "Are you *done* eye-fucking my brother, Ms. Jones?"

"It's a fact, not eye-fucking."

"I like her." Grant grins, taking a seat across the aisle from me in the private jet Axel insisted we take. "She's a very *factual* woman."

But Axel smolders, settling into his seat facing mine.

I've really messed up his plans with my daring one.

This morning, I snuck out earlier than usual for my run,

and when I got back, Axel was livid that he missed chasing me. He didn't speak to me all morning. Then he got a call and suddenly said he had a lunch meeting.

"Who are we meeting with?"

"*You're* staying *here* while I'm gone."

"Um, the only pussy you can order around here is *that* one." I stood in his kitchen and nodded toward Sparky, enjoying her Fancy Feast.

He clenched his jaw. "You'll stay here, pack for our trip, and wait until I get back."

"You know," I chomped on a banana, "I already know you can be a dickhead, so you don't have to open your mouth and prove it." His nostrils flared. "At least tell me where you're going in case hell freezes over, and I run after you."

"Delta's."

"The fancy *sex* store?"

At first, I was jealous, taunted by an irrational fear that he was meeting Alena Allen there.

Why do I keep getting these weird vibes on them?

Then I realized that one of Axel's hundred ex-Bratva brothers works there, so it had to have been mafia shit.

"Good," I chirped. "Get me a sexy blonde wig, some fake tattoos, a lipstick vibrator, and whatever you think would float a boss fucking his secretary's boat."

He shoved his gun into his holster. "Your plan is fucking crazy."

"My plan will work if you commit to your role. Just consider it your chance to help me win a 'Best Orgasm' Oscar."

"You're not *coming* for that man's camera," he barked.

"Yes, Martin Scorsese, I'm aware. If you direct me right, I'll act like I'm coming for you. I'll even let you keep the golden statue."

"Listen to me." Axel stalked my way, shocking me with

how tenderly his finger lifted my chin. "I'll never let you be exposed like that. I'm not talking about the sex; I'm talking about the sextortion. Even in disguise or whatever the hell game we play today, I won't let you get hurt. I *will* kill for you, Ruby, but digital files don't die."

"Between the two of us," my heart pounded at his threat, at his tender touch, "we can make it work."

Make what work?

Whatever this is, boiling hot between us?

Or my risky plan to help Nick and Zar?

I still don't know when the jet takes off on our short flight to some private airstrip in the Georgia mountains.

"I've created a fake marriage license," Grant informs me, clicking across his laptop. "Since you booked the place with your credit card—rookie mistake, by the way—he'll know your real name. But I'm creating a fake life for you. Fake address. Fake job. You're now the secretary for Carson Stewart and—"

"The idiot lawyer who chases ambulances?" I'm insulted.

"He deserves it," Axel grumbles. "He really *does* fuck around on his wife, and it's about time he's caught."

"It looks like the camera the owner used to film Nick and Zar..." Grant studies his screen, "is positioned directly across from the bed. So be aware of it as you two..."

Grant advises us while I sit stunned, admiring him.

He's beefy and tatted like Axel and his other brothers, and he seems smart like them, too. The only difference is the proud gold band gleaming on Grant's thick, inked wedding finger.

It's his only jewelry, like he's proud of his marriage, and I realize...

The other woman.

The other queen in the room during the taboo initiation must've been Grant's wife.

Because Wren is Sire's wife. Zar is Nick's partner. That hot daddy Nash always fights with Axel about Nash loving some woman named Vale. There was another brother, the bouncer from Delta's, who looks like Grant's twin, who was there, too, but I don't remember seeing a ring on him. And I've heard Axel say his brother Loch is marrying Alena. Their wedding is soon.

Though it still digs at the back of my mind, sensing there's more between Axel and Alena, as well.

What in the escaped Bratva hell?

This world I spied on, that I'm now trapped in, feels like a salacious soap opera cast with dangerously hot AF, inked men and their badass queens.

Oh, and don't forget the whole Bratva-prince part.

Oh, and don't forget their baller mom, either. Whoever she is.

Wait! That's one, two, three ... six? Or seven brothers? Seven Bratva princes? But Axel said his mother had six sons, and there were six men in Wren's initiation. I mean, six kings. But I'm counting seven total?

So, who was missing that night?

Jeez, I'm so confused and dying to ask Axel, but he said Grant thinks I'm just his paralegal.

"Don't let him know our secret," he warned.

"Our *secret?*" I scoffed in his fancy Jaguar on the way to the private airport. "Okay, Victoria, we're not a secret."

"Do you have to argue with everything I say?"

"I'm practicing for the Supreme Court."

"Practice supreme silence."

"God," I huffed, "when you're a dickhead, you make it hard to like you."

"No, Wildfire, *you* make my dickhead hard, and..." he winked, "you don't have to like it to *want* it. Not everyone has good taste."

"Taste my ass."

Yep, I served that up like a high set in volleyball, and Axel spiked the point with a sexy smirk. "If you want my tongue licking your ass, Wildfire, all you gotta do is moan for it."

He made me squirm in my car seat.

I think I preferred him *not* flirting with me to him attacking my senses like a frontal assault on my clitoris, so I changed the subject.

"Why can't all of your brothers know about me?" I half believed, "Are you ashamed of me?"

"No, I'm protecting you." He kept watching his speed. "We don't let anyone into our world because once you're in, it's deadly and there's no getting out."

"But you said I'm already *in*. You suffer the delusion that you own me now."

"I own your protection. It's my responsibility because I stalked you, so you spied on me. So, yeah, I fucked that one up, and here we are..." He took the exit to the private airport. "But you're not *in*. No one's in unless they're born into our world or initiated."

"Oh, you mean the gangbang."

"It's *NOT* a gangbang," he clipped. "Say it again, and you'll get a spanking."

I laughed. "Like you could catch me, Christian Grey."

"Like you're Flo-Jo." He laughed, too. "I'll catch you when you're ready."

"Ready for what?"

"Nothing. Forget it."

"Forget what? That you're into primal play?"

"Yeah, *that*," he mumbled.

Axel was focused on driving but acting odd, and I don't forget shit. I remember everything I've overheard, every tease he's revealed.

"Why do you have to initiate a queen?" I probed. "Why can't you just trust a woman?"

"Because trust doesn't mean shit when a knife is held to your mother's throat. Or you take a brutal beating for your brother. Only blood or a deep bond will die for someone else."

I turned to him, watching pain twist his gorgeous face. "Is that what happened to you?"

"A lot of shit happened to me. It happened to all of us, but we escaped because we fought back together. And we keep fighting for others because it has to be for a reason. If you give your pain a cause, it can't kill you. It only makes you stronger."

"Is that why you help trafficking victims or women like Ms. Alonso, who can't afford you? Because they're your cause?"

"Something like that."

"Well, shit, now your origin story makes it hard to hate you."

He grinned.

"But don't worry. You'll pull a dickhead move soon enough, and I'll remember you're Satan's shitstain."

He laughed. "You're *really* obsessed with my dickhead, aren't you?"

I blushed. "It really likes my leggings, doesn't it?"

Did he blush, too? It was tough to say because Axel's so tan and changed the subject.

"By the way, in my meeting today at Delta's," he shared, "I met with the owner, Stacey, and her husband, Ford. Their daughter is being bribed by this asshole. She's a young woman, a basketball player about to be drafted for the WNBA. She rented a beach house with her girlfriend, and now she's being bribed, too.

"So, don't let this go to your wildfire head, but..." He

looked at me with sincerity, with respect. "Thank you, Ruby. We're not just helping Nick today. This *is* a cause. We're helping others, too."

I turn from admiring Grant to find Axel admiring me the same way he did in his car, and I swear the man's intense stare is an ocular orgasm. All heat and ice rousing my senses.

"Time to get ready before we land." He gestures toward the back. "Your bags and disguise are in the bedroom."

My nipples get hard. I'm aroused, closing the door to the small bedroom in the back of the jet to slip on the role-play clothes Axel bought for me.

He's wearing his typical black suit and starched white shirt, like a boss, while he chose an elegant wrap dress, lacy bra, and panties for me. I think these red-soled high heels are worth a fortune, too, while I note how every luxe item he bought is blush pink.

It's the same color as my running leggings yesterday, which he splattered with his groan, and it heats my core.

I'm not afraid of this role-play because it's real. I want to give Axel an erotic show. I want the power over him. I want to see how much he wants me, too.

The stalking was a big clue, but I thought that was a controlling game for him. Like he just wanted the chase. But Axel said he wants much more with me. He wants to catch me. He wants us *together*.

But what do I want?

The answer terrifies me. I can't focus on it right now.

Adorning my upper thighs with fake tattoos, I give my body plausible deniability if a video is ever released online. *That's not me. I don't have tattoos.* I dust baby powder over them to make them look more realistic.

The new blonde wig helps. It's not a cheap one. It looks real, and with the heavier makeup I swipe on and a cute pair of black cat-eye reading glasses, I do look like a seductive secretary.

Opening the door to the jet's bedroom, I freeze when Axel turns his stare from the window to me.

Suddenly, his eyes soften.

I know he recognizes me from the sex club, and I shrug like, "Yep, that was me, the crying cowgirl. You see, deep down, I hide my vulnerable heart."

And here I am again, in another disguise for him. "Is this okay?" I ask aloud, inwardly teetering on insecurity.

"Is this strictly professional?" Grant replies instead, "Because, goddamn brother, you're a stronger man than me."

"Ms. Jones *works* for me." Axel ices his voice. "She knows this is a role, not romance."

I don't believe him. Or maybe I don't want to, and neither does Grant.

"Whatever." He arches a brow at Axel. "Just remember: stay off camera. Your paralegal is brave as hell, willing to be filmed for our op, but you can't be." Pause. "Not ever."

"Once we enter," I try to stay on mission, too, telling Grant, "give us an hour, tops, and then call my cell. Yell, and sound like a suspicious husband."

"An hour's not long enough," Axel argues.

"For two people escaping to have an illicit affair? Please," I scoff, "most would be fucking after two minutes alone."

"True that," Grant agrees. "I'm on my wife every chance I get, and it's perfectly legal."

"All are well aware your pecker has no OFF switch."

"Hey," Grant shrugs at him, "when a man loves his beautiful wife, he's always turned ON for her."

"Aw," I sigh. "What's your wife's name?"

Grant shoots Axel a look, and I hold my breath. I want the name of the other queen. I want as much intel as I can get on their world.

"I got the app loaded," Axel tells Grant, changing the subject.

I clock it, frustrated, but ask, "What app?"

"One that detects hidden cameras using your phone," Axel answers. "There's a radio frequency detector in my jacket pocket, too. Let me enter first and make sure the only camera is the one in the bedroom."

"But shouldn't I use it? I'm the one in disguise, not you."

"You're not entering first," Axel orders. "It's too dangerous."

"I don't know how to say this nicely, so I won't; that's dumb." I plop down in front of him and buckle my seatbelt. "Give me the detector, and let me enter first. Your face can't be on camera. And what if there's one at the front door?"

"She's smart and right," Grant agrees. "Besides, I got your six if there's real danger. I rented the chalet next door. I'll be watching the whole time."

Axel fumes but agrees.

THIRTY MINUTES AFTER WE LAND, WE ARRIVE AT THE chalet in our rental car. Silently, Axel hands me the detector to hide in my purse.

While he keeps his face hidden behind the open trunk, stalling while he gets our suitcase, I sashay toward the front door. The detector doesn't buzz. It doesn't detect a camera.

"Oh, my *king*," I call out, suddenly inspired to tease Axel with his last name. It's so Bratva and Dom, too. "I'll be inside waiting for *you*."

Quickly, I punch in the code provided by the rental app.

Opening the front door, I glance over my shoulder and startle at the sight.

It's Axel, holding our black suitcase and stalking my way.

But, oh shit, the look in his icy eyes.

It's a ferocious, pussy-wetting glare. Like I'm about to be attacked and *love* it.

I squeal, committing to my role...

But is it?

This feels too real as I race into the open A-frame living area with a view of the mountain valley below. The detector doesn't buzz in my purse, so I turn and quickly spot the primary bedroom adjacent to the room.

I rush in and find the king-size bed with fresh white linens tucked into a rustic cabin-like wooden frame. Thankfully, there's no footboard on the bed, so I sit on its edge, knowing I'm facing the hidden camera.

Arousal sizzles in my veins, noting the camel suede side chairs across from the bed, like a seating area set directly under the oil painting of a mountainscape. The art hides a pin-hole camera, disguised by the black paint of a shadowy valley.

The detector in my purse on the bed silently vibrates, but I force myself not to look at the illegal device.

Aware that the camera is there, too, Axel enters the bedroom. He stays out of range of the lens, leaving the suitcase by the door. Settling into a chair directly under the camera, all that can be seen are his legs in a dark suit.

"My, my, Ms. Jones." His performance begins for the camera. It records his voice as he sweeps his jacket open. "You're such a good girl, so eager to serve your *king*, aren't you?"

He spreads his legs and slowly unbuttons his shirt. "Now, keep being a good girl for me, and you'll get a reward. I'll give you a choice tonight." He smirks. "Anal or oral. Or does my naughty sub want both?"

Sorry, ovaries. It's time to burst.

He's going for the BDSM role-play, too.

"Both, my king." I cross my legs like a lady, trying to make my voice sound breathy, but it's not a stretch. My pulse races. My clit tingles. My birth control is battening her hatches. "I've been waiting months for you. Months to get away from my husband. He's such a little ... *dickhead.*"

Axel chuckles at my favorite word for him. But like a true Dom, he orders, "Tell your king the last time your sweet pussy was fucked."

You mean my wet pussy?

"It's been months. Over six months since I started working for you, Mr. Stewart." It's not a lie, but it's the fake identity Grant assigned to Axel.

"Good job, Ms. Jones." He taps his inked fingers over his thigh. "So your pussy is very lonely? Is it ready to serve me? *Only* me? Is it wet and aching for me?"

"Yes, my king." Good god, this is hot.

"Have you been my bad secretary and good sub, obeying my orders?"

Where is he going with this? "Yes, my king."

He cocks a brow. "Did you use the anal plug I left wrapped in a box on your desk?"

Oh.

My.

God.

Has this been Axel's fantasy all along?

He licks his lips, shamelessly confirming it, and the rush of lust between my thighs is instant.

"Yes, my king. Thank you for my anal plug."

"Did you wear it while shopping for that dress, like I told you to?"

I chew my lip. "Yes, my king."

"Did it get your pussy and panties wet for me? Feeling my toy in your tight ass? Wanting me to lick your ass tonight?"

He remembers my blurt in the car. And he's soaking my panties *right* now. All I want is Axel's tongue ... everywhere. "Yes, my king."

"Did you go into the dressing room," he taunts, "like I told you to, and get naked and play with your pretty pussy, sending me a video of you being such a dirty girl for me, and coming like you never do with your little *dickhead* husband?"

This is half-subterfuge, half seduction.

Desire crushes me. I'm finding it hard to breathe. It narrows Axel's eyes, too.

These fantasies come too quickly to him. Like they're the dirty things he said he fantasizes about in his shower when he jerks off and moans my name.

And how do I feel about it?

"*Yes*, my king," I sigh. *I love it.*

"Good girl, Ms. Jones. I love how you're so pleasing and passive for me."

The hell I am. My pussy is soaked, slick, and sliding from role-play into reality.

"But you were such a dirty brat the other day at work, tempting me." Because Axel's too convincing. Too controlling and taking me there. "You were wearing that pretty dress and rubbing your pussy on the corner of my desk and begging me to fuck you right there. Is that how you want to pleasure me, Ms. Jones? Making me bend you over my desk to fuck you?"

"Yes, my king." He's not lying. I'm not lying. I'm dying for him. "I want you to fuck me on your desk. I want to kneel under it, too, and suck your cock while you fist my hair and fuck my throat and—"

"*Fuucckk*, Ms. Jones," Axel groans like he's in pain, his

eyelids dropping heavy with lust. His hand slides from his thigh to stroke the thick erection in his pants. "Be careful, pushing my buttons. Don't make me punish you. Don't fucking tease me. Do you *mean* it, Ruby?" He's dropping our performance. "You want to *serve* me? You want to *kneel* for me?"

I've never done it before, and I don't care if Axel has been a Dom to other women; I suddenly want this too much. I've always wanted to be a sub like my sister Scarlett is to her hot husband, Luca.

I've always wanted this with a man, but never trusted any to do it.

But suddenly ... *I trust Axel.*

At least with this.

He's so goddamn Dom and dangerous, but he won't hurt me. Not my body, at least. Not unless I ask him to.

"Yes, my king." I want him to know I'm not pretending. "Please, I *want* to serve you. I *want* to kneel for you."

Axel lowers his glare. "Prove it. Prove you want to serve me and that I can trust you. Look me in the eye while you reach into your dress and pinch your nipple under that lacy bra I bought you."

Now I know why he bought me a wrap dress. It's so I can do this without exposing my body to the camera.

It makes half of me fall so hard for him, protecting me like this, while half of me wants to show how much I want him; I don't give a damn who's recording me.

I obey, just as I did when I sucked his thumb. I do this, too. Reaching into my dress, my nipple is already hard while I pinch it, staring at him.

The feral look in his eyes makes me moan, pinching and tugging, before I move my hand and reveal my aroused nipple, pebbled under thin fabric and lace.

"Good girl," he praises. "Now pinch your other nipple for

me, Ms. Jones. Show me how you can be so naughty and obedient for your king."

Oh, my God. *"Your king."*

Does that make me *his queen?*

That's what Zar called me, and Axel never denied it. The thought of it now feels fated, as if I was meant to stumble into his office. To work for him. To hate him. To let him chase me until I chased him back. To be so tempted by Axel that now I'm trapped in his dangerous world.

And with the possessive way he looks at me? It's like he planned it all along. I'm already his. I belong to Axel.

No, I belong *with* him...

And it feels right.

I leave my nipple aching and aroused, while I thrill my other one for his stare, while he lazily rubs his rigid shaft.

"Tell me, Ms. Jones," he demands. "Keep playing with your nipples while you tell me what you want your king to do to you that your little *dickhead* husband never does."

"Eat my pussy," I rush.

Axel licks his bottom lip. "He doesn't eat your sweet pussy? Is it aching for my tongue?"

"Yes, my king." It's all I want right now—Axel's bearded lips buried between my thighs.

"Do you touch your pussy, wishing it was me?"

"Yes, my king." I have. I've lain in bed so overwhelmed by how much I hate Axel that an orgasm is the only relief I can get from the thought of him.

"Do you have the toy I told you to buy?"

"Yes, my king," I remember the one I told *him* to buy me at Delta's today.

Reaching into my purse on the bed, I pull out the lipstick vibrator.

"Show me how you play with it, Ms. Jones, under your

dress and desk. Show me how you sit outside my office and wish it was me fucking you instead."

Oh, my god, he's doing it again.

Axel's protecting me. He won't expose me, but he wants to see this, and I want to show him.

I twist the vibrator on, its hum barely audible, while I slide my hand under the open slit of my dress.

"Good girl. Now, keep your legs crossed like *my* beautiful lady," he orders, "while you secretly play with your pussy like a dirty girl for me, too."

Oh fuck, is this secretly his kink, too?

His eyes look possessed, seducing me as I glide the smooth, buzzing tip of the vibrator under my panties and over my clit, its sudden sensation making me cry out, "Please, Aaaa—" I choke his name down, his real name. "Please, my king. I need to come for you."

He stares at me for a scorching beat. "No, keep looking at me and playing with your wet pussy, but don't you *dare* come until I tell you to."

Is he doing this to kill time or kill me?

I don't know, but it feels like I obey him for minutes, forever. I'm anchored to Axel's icy eyes and feel even more power obeying him than I've ever felt defying him.

I'm sweating and shaking. Moans keep crawling up my throat. I can't keep my eyes open; I'm edging so hard for him. It's sweet pain how I need to come.

And by the look in Axel's hypnotic eyes, the tightening grip of his choking stroke over his hard dick, he's fighting the urge to come, too. It's taking him over.

"Fuck, Ms. Jones." His lips shake. "You're so goddamn beautiful. I swear, Ruby, you're the most beautiful woman I've ever seen. You obsess *me*. You control *me*. You *own* me."

The scorching truth in his glacial eyes makes my thighs

quiver. No one has eyes like Axel, and it's like they only see *me*. They only want *me*.

"Please, my king," I beg. I'm soaked. "I need to come for you. Please. I'll kneel for you. I'll be your queen. Please, just—"

With a bolt, Axel leaps from his chair. Like a lion, he pounces on me, making me fall back on the bed. Crouching over me, he grabs my throat, growling with eyes feral and wild, "You *want* to be my queen, Ruby?"

Do I? Is that what I said? Is that what I want?

"Yes, please, make me—"

It's not a hard crash. It's my delicate destruction when Axel's lips, soft and tender, take mine in our first kiss while his hand gently squeezes my throat. Grabbing whoever I was before this moment, he pulls me into the only reality I want now.

His moan murders. His whiskers tickle. His body crushes. His tongue teases, brutally finding mine in a tender dance that plunges into a ruthless claim, dragging a moan up my choked neck. He tastes like the nectar of a beast, sweet power and savory seduction. I'm melding to him, my body rising for him. I'm opening and liquid in his controlling touch.

"Come, Ruby," he growls into our kiss. "Come for your king while I kiss my queen."

The instinct to let Axel inside me is overwhelming. His mouth. His body. His hand. It suddenly cups mine between my legs, pressing the vibrator over my clit. He touches my soaked sex, his heat the hottest I've ever felt, and I explode for him.

I scream into our kiss, my back arching with powerful release, my logic ripped away. He's my only anchor, keeping his lush lips sealed to mine, his ravenous breath swallowing the sound of my orgasm, taking it and taking me with him.

I want more. I need more. So much more of him. This is our beginning. I never want it to end...

But the phone in my purse on the bed chimes. It snaps us back to reality. He lifts from our kiss and freezes over me.

"Fuck," he pants.

He lost control. We both did, but at least his back is to the camera. It can't see his face.

"That's him," I stammer, trying to protect us. "That's my husband."

"Answer it," he growls.

I slap my hand over the bedspread until I find my purse and blindly reach for my phone.

Axel rises, kneels, and straddles me. He keeps his back to the camera, while I hope it picks up my audio and performance. I'm not giving up now. My plan has to work.

"Hello?"

"Get the fuck out of there!" Grant roars.

"Hey, honey. I'm fine," I chirp. "Just having drinks with the girls."

"Ruby," Grant's voice gravels low like Axel's, "this isn't about the camera. Tell my brother there's a man outside the house, scoping it out. He's got a gun and headed toward the basement door. Tell him I'm on my way."

CHAPTER THIRTEEN
RUBY

I don't need to tell Axel about the man outside with a gun. Grant is loud enough for him to hear it.

"I... I... I swear, sweetie," but I stammer to Grant on my phone. "I swear I'm just out with the girls." I'm not letting this mission go to shit, either. "I'll be home late. Don't worry."

I end the call, and Axel shakes his head. "We have to go before you're busted."

He doesn't turn around, trying to save our performance, too.

He keeps his back to the camera until he's out of range as I sit and subtly adjust my wig. Axel almost knocked it off with his primal pounce.

I touch my lips, too. They still tingle from his hungry kiss, but I don't have time to think about it.

"Let's get out of here." I shove the phone and vibrator into my purse. "I have to get home before he gets suspicious."

Silently, Axel nods and grabs our suitcase. Then, he holds his hand out, demanding mine, and I rush across the room to catch it.

He pulls me near, whispering, "Take the suitcase and stay behind me. Grab my shoulder and let me know you're there."

"Where are we going?"

"Out the front. There are no cameras there. Grant will cover the back."

We follow the same path through the house and reach the front door. Axel peers through the peephole as a gunshot rings out. I jolt, but he orders, "Let's go," reaching for the doorknob.

"I'm not going out there," I hiss. "You check first."

He turns to me, grinning. "I thought we were gender equal."

"In high heels, yes. In a high-noon shootout? Fuck that. Go be a cowboy."

He pulls the gun from his holster, teasing, "Someone's sounding like a damsel in distress."

"Someone's going to ice his balls later."

"Indeed, Wildfire." He opens the door. "You made them blue as fuck."

I'd be flattered if I weren't suddenly terrified with my shaking hand holding Axel's tense shoulder. He moves like a special-ops ninja, peeking around the door, his gun held down and ready before he declares, "Clear."

"Clearly, we're dead?"

"We're fine. Don't stop obeying me now. Get the suitcase."

I hold his shoulder and grab the handle, dragging it behind me. I follow Axel outside and freeze on the front porch, shocked as Grant appears around the corner of the fancy log cabin, holding his gun to the back of a man's head.

The man keeps his hands in the air as Axel aims his gun at him, too. "Name!" he demands.

"Brayton Jervis," I answer. "The quarterback for Tennessee."

Brayton pauses a moment before he recognizes me, even in disguise."Hey, doll." Terror shakes his voice. "Mind telling your boyfriends to holster their weapons?"

Axel swings his ferocious glare at me.

"You *know* him?"

"Yes, I *know* him," I whisper so Brayton won't hear me. "I know him in the biblical sense, so if you're going to fire jealous Bratva bullets over it, do it now. Otherwise, let's find out why he's here."

"I had to fire my gun to get him to put his down," Grant shouts, nudging his muzzle against Brayton's skull, making him walk our way. "He said he's looking for the owner."

They cross the front yard while Axel seethes over me, "Are you here for the owner, or are you stalking her?"

"The owner," Brayton answers.

"Who?" Axel tests him.

"Don't know yet."

"But you're carrying a Beretta and want him dead?" Grant interrogates him.

Brayton holds his hands in the air, his eyes frantically searching mine. He trusts me. He knows he can. Over a year ago, I shared a night with him and his husband at Zar and Nick's place. No commitment. Just trust and lust and one night of fun.

That's how I used to roll before Axel and his damn hypnotic eyes ran me off the slutty rails.

Now, apparently, I've lost my mind and pussy. They only want to kneel for him.

"He's being bribed." Instantly, I figure it out. The connections. The reasons. The crime. "Put your damn guns down. He's one of us."

Grant lowers his, but Axel is breathing hard with his muzzle aimed at Brayton.

Yep. I *might* have set him off with that whole biblical

knowledge thing. Maybe I should've kept that to myself, but how else can I explain this?

"Brayton is friends with Nick Barinov. You know, your *close* friend, too." *You know, your brother?* I try not to reveal too much. Just enough to turn the volume down. "I met Brayton at one of Nick's parties, and he must be here because he rented this chalet and..."

I pause, cautious and protective, but Brayton nods like he's desperate and caught, and my heart breaks for him.

"Can I?" I ask, and Brayton finishes, "Tell them."

"Brayton is married to a beautiful man named Jim," I calmly share, "and they must've rented this chalet. Probably heard about it through the NFL grapevine, and now they're being bribed. Right?" Brayton nods. "And these guys are helping someone being bribed for the same thing," I tell Brayton. I hope I'm right. "They can help you, too."

"Walk me through it," Axel orders.

"We heard about this place a few months ago," Brayton explains. "We spent the weekend here and thought nothing of it until a few days ago when my husband got a text with a video, demanding five million or they'll out me."

"See," I huff at Axel. "Put the fucking gun down, Good-fella, or you're going to shoot an innocent man."

Slowly, Axel lowers his weapon. "So, what was your plan? Come here and kill the owner?"

"I don't know." Brayton drops his hands. "I don't know what we're going to do."

"Have you arranged to pay him?" Axel asks.

"Not yet. We replied that we needed time to move that kind of money around."

"Get in your car and follow us." Axel holsters his gun. "Let's clear out and talk about this."

Reluctantly, Brayton agrees. He and Grant follow us in their rental cars, and I know better than to utter a peep lest I set Axel's jealous green giant off again, so I rely on his classical music to calm him.

Once we're safe at the airport, we talk. We get Brayton's details, and Axel and Grant let him go with a handshake.

You'd think all would be hunky-dory, but not in this ex-Bratva world.

Grant fires up his laptop after we're seated in the jet. I buckle up, remove my glasses, and slide my wig off before shaking my hair free. I'm trying to relax, but Mount St. Axel is about to blow in his seat in front of me.

"What?" I confront his spewing glare.

"Biblical?" he snarls.

"Yes. It was a religious experience. 'Oh god' was moaned several times while Brayton, Jim, and I shared a private night."

"What happened?"

"Um, you can open a business called 'None of Yours' because I don't fuck and tell."

Grant snorts, but Axel leans forward. "You *will* fucking tell me. It's my business when men you know *biblically* come looking for you with a gun in their hand."

"He wasn't there for *me*."

"We can't be sure."

"Look," I roll my eyes, "while I'll admit my pussy is worth dying for, that's not why Brayton was there. He's like Nick. He's trying to protect his career. His safety, too."

"I believe him," Grant adds. "You should've seen his jump scare when he saw Ruby on the porch. He was surprised to see her."

"See!" I swipe my hand toward Grant. "Why can't you be reasonable like your hot Reacher brother?"

"Watch out," Grant warns. "Of all my brothers, Axel can reasonably kill dozens and never get caught. Don't tempt him to lose his best paralegal, too."

"Oh, don't worry," I huff. "That ship has sailed the take-this-job-and-shove-it sea."

I close my eyes because I can't look at Axel for another second.

His stupid, sociopathic jealousy is making me catch way too many feels. Add those to the orgasm his hand has given me and his mind-scrambling, heart-melting kiss ... and I couldn't name my emotions if they wore a sticker like:

HELLO, my name is...
Bitch, shook over a Mafia Man

I don't want to see him. Talk to him. Keep remembering his kiss. Or that I called him "my king." Or that he said I was his queen.

I can still feel ... *him* ... swimming in my bloodstream.

And after today.

I don't think I'll ever stop feeling Axel everywhere.

CHAPTER FOURTEEN
AXEL

I watch Ruby fall asleep, and if blue balls are a thing, I've got a pair. And if I don't get another kiss from her soon, I'll lose my mind.

But Brayton fucking Jervis, the quarterback?

And his husband?

They know my queen in the biblical sense?

This is hell.

Yes, I'm a hypocrite. There's a room on the second floor of my mom's club, and years ago, if I met a woman or three I liked—okay, one time there were four—we'd go up there.

But that man is dead.

I want a different life with Ruby, and deep down, it's kind of fucking sweet.

Yes, she did *whatever* with bisexual NFL players, but she's protecting them, too. Most women would exploit them or out them. Fuck an NDA. The payoff for a sex scandal exposing a famous football player to the press would be worth it.

But Ruby won't rat them out. She won't hurt them. She's loyal.

She only told us when Brayton said she could. And it's not like my gun gave them a choice and—

"Hey, fuckwad." Grant snaps me out of my haze, staring at Ruby's long, fluttering eyelashes.

"What?"

He jerks his thumb toward the jet's bedroom, and I know what's coming.

He closes the door behind us and yells at me in a whisper, "She's your fucking queen, and you know it!"

"No shit, Reacher dick."

"Then what are you pussyfooting for?"

"Leave my feet out of this," I snarl.

Grant winces, remembering our childhood and clocking what he just said. "Sorry, man, that's not what I mean. It's just... Why are you waiting?"

"She's not ready." I move on. "And you won't say jackshit to anyone about her."

"Careful, brother. Play any game too long," he warns, "and you will lose her."

Like Jace, Grant's an inch taller than me, but I'm always his big brother. What I say goes, and he knows it. "I'm *not* playing games with her."

"Aren't you?" He points toward the door. "She's fucking amazing and perfect for you. I've never met a woman immune to your swagger, but *ta-da* ... there she is. She's a badass. She'll tell you to fuck off and which way you can go, even when she knows who we are and what we're capable of." He smirks, threatening, "If you don't claim her soon, I'll introduce her to Jace."

I laugh. "All those blow-jobs you get have sucked your IQ out through your dick because, one, I'll kill a brother for her. Two, Jace would never betray me. Three, neither would you. And a million times, I'd fucking die for her, so don't give me shit about her. Give me time."

"She's not Katya. She won't leave you." His voice softens. "Katya was cold and conniving. I never knew what you saw in her but blonde hair and big tits. She was never right for you, and she was *way* too into Sire."

I don't argue a moot point. He's right, she's gone, and I don't care.

"She never should've been your queen," Grant insists, pointing at the door again, "because *that* woman is."

"I know," I concede. "I knew it the moment I met her."

"Then what the fuck, man? Claim her. Don't let her go. Jesus," he throws his chin up, "she's just like mom. She's like the other queens—iron elegance and ruthless beauty. I'd be honored to be her second king."

"The fuck you will," I snarl. "Touch Ruby, and I'll make Delphine a widow."

"This again?" He rolls his eyes. "First, Nick. Now, you. And we know Nash will fight it, too. But ... it'll happen; we'll make sure the queens love it, and it's done. So, just start wrapping your jealous dickhead around it now."

"Uh, folks," the captain calls over the intercom. "We're on our final approach. Please be seated."

Minutes later, the plane lands, and Ruby's still asleep.

It's cute, the little drop of drool escaping her plump lips, so I smile. "Hey, Wildfire. Wake up, or your drool will douse the scorched Earth you've created in my life."

"What?" Ruby startles, wiping her mouth with the back of her hand. "Was I?"

"Drooling over me? Yes." I unbuckle my seat belt. "Come on. Sparky's waiting."

I stand and offer my hand to her, but she scowls. "Are your boxers still in a jealous wad?"

But she slides her palm into mine, and it flutters my chest every time.

"Jealous? No. Possessive? Until my dying day over you."

"Fine," she sighs. "Can you possess a pizza on the way home, too, because I'm starving?"

"Home?" Grant grins, sliding the laptop into his bag. "You two playing paralegal or house?"

"Both." We answer at the same time.

"Whatever you're doing together," he laughs, wrapping his arm around Ruby, and bending down to kiss her hair, "it's safe with me. Promise."

"Aw." Ruby punches his abs. "Thanks, Reacher. Can you give me a nudey butt-shot as you leave, too?"

"Not if he wants to live," I warn.

"He's just jelly," Grant whispers to Ruby. "It's kinda a cute look on him."

"Cute will be my bullet in your ass."

"Hah," Grant scoffs. "It's made of steel. It'll bounce right off."

"Go!"

I point toward the pilot, waiting by the open door, and Ruby practically holds Grant's hand, exiting the plane. Not like a couple. Like new besties bonding over how-to-make-me-murder.

We say goodbye at our cars parked side-by-side. Ruby gives Grant a big hug, and I flip him off.

But he won't tell our brothers about her.

Grant knows what losing my first queen did to me. I didn't grieve losing Katya. I grieved losing my pride and letting my family down. I wanted to give a grandchild to my mother. Or maybe it was the guilt over Alena that finally caught up with me, too.

Tough to say.

But I disappeared into a cold, dark hole until a wildfire with a skinned, bloody knee tripped into my life.

By the time we're home, the pizza delivery guy is waiting patiently at my gate. He's used to me. He knows I tip big.

While we eat at the kitchen table and Sparky purrs against our legs, Ruby goes on about what we should name the kittens, but I keep imagining Brayton Jervis and their threesome.

How many has she had? And did she mean it? She only does two men at once, never just one? So what does that mean? She'll never truly be mine?

I drop my slice, losing my appetite, and Ruby notices.

"You're getting jelly again, aren't you?"

I wipe my lips with a napkin, answering with silence.

"You know," she huffs, "I didn't order hypocrisy on my pizza. You give me reasons to be jealous, too. I've seen you at the sex club with all of those hot women. I bet you've been quite primal and Dom with many pussies."

"No one but you," I seethe, rage making me see red. "I told you the truth; I haven't been on a date since I met you, and I've *never* had a sub." I clench my fist, growling, "Only *YOU* make me feel this way," and slam it so hard on the table that my plate flies off, crashing into pieces on the floor.

It sends Sparky running away with a yowl.

"And *you* don't get to scare me like this." Ruby's hand suddenly shakes, shoving her plate away before she jumps up. "As a child, I lived with a terrifying man because I had no choice. But as a woman, I will *never* choose to suffer another threatening one."

She turns to race upstairs, but I chase after her.

"Ruby, wait. I'm sorry."

She whips around in the stairwell. "There are two sides to every story—in my life and in yours—but you know what, Axel? You're an asshole in all of them."

"So I'm supposed to be happy about your threesomes?"

She arches a brow. "Like you've never had one?"

I suck my teeth.

"That's what I thought. We're both guilty," she sneers. "And just where do you get off? We're *not* a couple. You don't *own* me. You just have me trapped with you and in deep, dangerous shit because of your escaped Bratva life, so thank you. My middle finger Hallmark card is in the mail."

"So, it was an *act* today?" *Why does this suddenly hurt so much? Why can't I breathe?* "You, wanting to be my queen. It was a *joke* to you?"

"No, it was..."

Her eyes search mine, and I see her fear. It's like I have her trapped in a corner. I'm her biggest threat but...

Growing up, I never let my father see my pain. I wouldn't give the devil the satisfaction.

But I let Ruby see it. I let her see it wasn't a joke to me. To be her king is all I want. To have her as my queen is what I live for. What am I fighting for if I'm not fighting for her?

"I don't know what it was." She stammers, tears welling in her eyes, "I ... I just... I just need to run."

It's what she does, but she can't leave. So, she dashes into her bedroom and slams the door, and I disappear into mine.

After a lonely shower, I slip on clean boxer briefs and socks and fall into bed, weighed down by something I've never felt. It's heavy and suffocating the breath out of me. I turn out the light and stare at the ceiling, but all I can think about is kissing Ruby, how she moaned over my lips, how I wanted so much more with her.

Minutes, maybe an hour, pass until I'm startled by a voice at my door.

"Hey, dickhead." Ruby sounds shaky. "Are you asleep?"

"No."

"I don't feel good."

Jumping up, I race to my door and yank it open to Ruby, staring up at me while she stands frozen in tiny pink shorts and a matching top covered in race cars. She's the sexiest thing I've ever seen, but the look on her face isn't.

Her eyelids droop as she blinks back tears. "I can't move my arms."

Without thinking, I scoop her up. "Let's go to the hospital."

"I don't want the bill."

"I'll pay it." I start down the hallway.

"No, Axel. Just..." She can't even wrap her hands around my neck. "Just lay me down with you. Put me in the recovery position, and don't leave me."

"Ruby, you're having a seizure."

"Not yet. Just... Axel, please. *Listen* to me."

"Okay." I won't stress her out. I won't make it worse. "Come on." I walk her back to my bed and gently lay her on her side in the center, feet away from any objects that can hurt her. I turn on the light and kneel beside her, cupping her cheek. "Ruby, are you with me?"

"Barely."

"Should I call your sisters?"

"Don't worry them." Her voice falls to a whisper, "It was too much today..."

"Okay, I got you." I nuzzle my forehead to hers. "I'm not leaving you."

Terror engulfs me as her stare falls blank. It's as if she's leaving me, her entire body sagging limp, and I watch, feeling rage that I can't do anything to help her, to bring her back and...

And...

And...

Love.

That's what this sudden warm urge is—a need to do everything, anything for her.

"Ruby?" I crouch over her. "I'm here, baby. I got you." I'm still holding her cheek and terrified by her blank stare, trapped in a void for seconds.

After Ruby told me about her condition, I watched dozens of videos of people with epilepsy bravely sharing their seizures, trying to spread awareness and compassion, all at the expense of their most vulnerable and sometimes dangerous moments.

But it didn't prepare me for this.

For this warmth flooding my heart, this fear and ferocity, too. *I will never leave her.* Not at her weakest. Not at her strongest. It's okay if she runs. I just need her to know I'll chase her. I'll catch her every time.

I'll be right here...

I count sixteen seconds before she slowly blinks as if she's breaking the surface of consciousness. Like she's finding focus, and I whisper, "Hey," gently stroking her cheek, "you're okay."

She stares at me like she's waking from a dream. It takes her minutes to speak, "I'm sorry."

The lump in my throat is sudden. A flood of emotions bites at my eyes.

She's apologizing to me? When I suspect this was my *fault?*

It's her compassion talking. She's focused on me. She's worried about me and how I feel right now, and if she only knew it's that one word I haven't said to her yet.

"Please don't apologize." I caress her cheek, hoping to make her smile. "It's my master plan. I finally got you in my bed."

Weakly, she chuckles, barely looking around. "Sparky?"

"She's here." I scoop her up from the floor. As if she could sense Ruby's distress, she was yowling by the edge of my bed. "You know she's the first pussy in this bed, and you're the second. And for the record, this is the only threesome I want nowadays."

I make her softly smile when I set Sparky beside her. But Ruby's hand trembles, still recovering control, so I pet Sparky while she nuzzles Ruby, making her grin until Ruby jolts. "Oh god."

"What? What's wrong?"

"Did I...?" She glances down her body, her hand patting the bed beside her. "Did I—"

"You didn't." Immediately, I know what she fears. "And it would be okay if you did."

"Oh god," she groans, closing her eyes. "Kill me now."

"Kill you? Never. Be a dickhead and scare you. Yes, and I'm sorry. But get you? *Always.*" I sweep an auburn tendril from her face. "I wet the bed until I was eleven. Childhood trauma, not epilepsy, but I understand."

"You understand?" She blinks back surprised tears. "What kind of trauma?"

"Too much to say. But the one that stays with me is my feet."

"Your feet?"

"My father would cut the soles of my feet so I couldn't escape. He only did it to me because I was his heir, and he feared I'd run away."

"Oh my god, Axel." Tears spill over her freckled cheeks. "I'm so sorry that happened to you."

"Me too," I huff. "I spend a fucking fortune on socks and shoes because no one can see my feet. I don't want their questions and pity. So, please understand why I sleep with my socks on."

"Oh..." She twists to sit up. "Sorry. I'll go back to my bed and—"

"The fuck you will," I say softly. "You stay with me, Ruby Jones. I'm not leaving your side. Not tonight. Not ever." I brush my thumb over her lips. Not sexy this time. Just fucking dying for her. "So either you start running faster, or you get used to me holding you."

CHAPTER FIFTEEN
RUBY

It wasn't a bad seizure. I've had worse. And my medication works. I felt it coming. I probably should've stayed in my bed where it was safe, so I wouldn't fall, but...

I wanted Axel.

I only felt safe in his arms.

With him by my side.

Yep, I'm falling in deep shit, aka. *Love*.

He tucks his sheets around me while I feel like the plug has been pulled on my body. It usually takes me hours to fully recover.

He stands by the edge of the bed, visibly concerned. "Do you need anything?"

"Water, please."

"Be right back."

He turns to go downstairs in his black boxer briefs and socks, and it's the first time I see the ink across his broad, tapered back. It's the melting face of a horned devil, dying with a knife through its skull, faces in anguish in its shadow.

It's his father. Axel's turned his back on him.

But flexing, snarling lions prowl up Axel's right leg, like an army, protecting him. But his left is bare. Why?

His body, muscles, and ink tell a story to fear.

But his feet?

They're heartbreaking.

He wears simple, black, half-calf socks, hiding what must be the most horrific scars. On his skin. In his heart.

Who would do that to a child? *Their* child?

It douses all the hate in my heart. Though, I admit ... I never hated Axel. I just never really saw him until now. And what he lets me see? What he shares with me? That he wet the bed?

I was right; he's beautiful.

When he returns, I have enough strength to sit up and sip the water he offers before he sets the glass on the nightstand.

But I can't help it. I let my eyes roam over his hulking, tatted body, and he grins. "See something you like?"

"Nope," I quip softly, "I'm blinded by annoyance."

"I get it. I *am* annoying with how hot I am." He lifts the sheets, making me chuckle, touched by how he crawls in beside me. "And let me add to the record: your sexy race car pajamas are annoying as fuck."

I fall back on his pillow, sighing, "I love NASCAR."

Resting his head in his hand, he props on his elbow beside me, making his bicep pop and my heart race. He gazes down at me, looking way too sexy and sweet. "You, loving dozens of men, racing fast? Shocker."

"Fuck you." I laugh. "I don't want the *men*. I want the car. I want to drive around a race track as fast as I can."

"Then do it." He grins. "NASCAR has no high-noon shootouts, so it's gender equal."

"Cute." God, I want to kiss him again. "But it's not about gender. I can't drive a race car or *my* car now that I've had another seizure."

"How long since your last one?"

"Over two years. Almost three. So, after a year without one, my doctor permitted me to drive. But now, I guess—"

"I'm so sorry, Ruby." Regret brims in his eyes. "It was my fault and—"

"Don't flatter yourself. You're not that powerful." He is, but in the best way. "It's not your fault. I pushed myself emotionally, and I should've known better. It's a long story I don't want to tell tonight." I poke his lips. "Just keep making me laugh. It helps."

"How?"

"Humor relieves my stress, so make a woman-driver joke. The timing is perfect."

"I'm smitten," he chuckles, "but not stupid. And for a daily blow job under my desk, I promise I won't tell your doctor about tonight."

"You need to stop being kinky *and* cute."

"Told you." He winks. "It's annoying."

"No, annoying will be me, riding the bus again."

"Fine." He rolls his hypnotic eyes. "For *two* blow jobs a day, I'll be your personal taxi."

"That *would* save your stalking from being utterly pathetic."

He laughs, and it reaches his eyes this time, making them sparkle like glacial ice in the sun. And that's Axel; all heat, all cold. He's everything I can feel.

"I didn't mean it tonight." I reach for him, brushing my shaking fingertips over his soft, groomed beard. "I might want to hear more about your new job offer to be your queen. You know, does my king offer sick days? Is it like mobsters with good benefits and—"

The laughter in his eyes suddenly burns into passion. "Damn, Ruby, I want to kiss you again."

"Not until you answer my questions."

"Oh?" He chuckles. "You finally let me kiss your mouth, and now you think I can *trust* it?"

"*How* can you know if you can trust me until you give me a chance?"

"Ditto, Wildfire."

"I trust you. I let you carry me like a damsel in distress. Trust me; that's trust."

For emphasis, I gently rub my feet over his, covered by socks, and watch it melt something in his eyes. I may never see Axel's feet, but I'm melting, too, finally seeing everything else about him.

"Okay," he sighs. "I'll tell you what I can. And if you tell anyone else, I'll have to kill you."

"You said you'd never hurt me."

"And I meant it. *I'll* never hurt you." He lilts, "Grant, on the other hand?"

"He adores me."

"Yes, he does. So quit making me fucking jealous about it."

"Okay, so answer this—how many brothers do you have?"

"I have five blood brothers, and Nash, he's like a brother, so that makes seven of us."

"Who's your mom?" I wince. "I mean ... if she's still alive. Sorry if she's not."

"Oh, my mom is alive and kicking ass. You've met her."

"Who?"

He blinks.

"Axel!"

He smirks, pressing his forehead to mine. "Once upon a time, there was a beautiful cowgirl at a sex club, but she looked sad, like she'd lost her little pink pony, so my mom tried to help her and—"

"Ms. Faye!" I practically shout. "The hot goddess who owns the sex club is your *mom*?"

"A goddess? I'll give you that. But please, don't call my mom *hot*."

"But she *is*. She's a badass. I want to be her when I grow up."

"Again," he winces, "not an image I want."

"But you said I remind you of your mom."

"You do. But in a ball-busting way. Not a dick shriveling one."

"Aw," I circle his nipple, "I don't shrivel your dick?"

"Reach down and find out, Wildfire."

The hot butterflies are instant. Axel sends a million fluttering through my core. Lying in bed beside him feels too perfect and right. And tempting.

I guess deep down, under our hating game, this was always here. We're so attracted to each other. It makes me want to reach for Axel and never let him go.

"But not tonight." He plays with a lock of my hair, confessing, "Yes, I'm hard as hell lying beside you. Hell, I get hard within two blocks of you. And I really want to kiss you, but then I won't be able to stop. I'll want to fuck you forever. So, just lie here, feel better, and drive me bat-shit crazy with your questions instead."

My muscles feel like a melted candle, but I want him more than I've ever wanted a man. He's not only hot, powerful, smart, and scary as shit; Axel can be tender. He's caring. He's fiercely protective and loyal ... but he's right. I don't feel up to it.

But I ask him an intimate question.

"What would it mean if I were your queen?"

He pauses, brushing the back of his inked fingers over my cheek. "It would mean everything to me, Ruby Jones, if you were my queen. But..."

He trails off. All conviction stolen from his eyes.

"But what?"

"But you need to think about it. *We* need to think about it. It would change your life, if not end it, and—"

"But you said I'm already at risk. That I know too much about you, your brothers, the other queens, and now your mom and—"

"But it's my father," he answers. "He's your greatest risk."

I shake my head, confused. "Why?"

"Because I'm his heir. Most men in the Bratva forgo a wife and kids. They're a liability. But *not* my father. He saw my mother; she was practically still a child, and he had to have her. He's that arrogant, powerful, and evil.

"Sire is my oldest brother, but from a young age, he wanted to be a priest, so the role fell to me, the second born. At ten, I was presented to the organization as my father's heir. I was named the next Pakhan, the future boss. I was supposed to take over when I turned thirty, but my mother saw the bloody writing on the wall: how all of us were at risk. To say nothing of his sadistic abuse, so she got us out."

My pulse skyrockets, hearing Axel's story. But I've heard of the Bratva. They're considered part of the most influential and dangerous people controlling the world.

"So, does your father think you're dead?"

"Fuck, Ruby." He winces. "This puts you at deadly risk. I didn't think this through. I just saw you and fell so damn hard for you and—"

"What do you mean?"

"I mean, I don't know what my father truly knows about us—me, my mom, and my brothers. A man helped us stage our deaths in a plane crash, but did my father believe it? I don't know. But I know him. He's looking, and he won't ever stop. And if he finds me and *my* queen, he'll torture you to kill me."

"God," I mutter, "no offense; but your father sounds like a real asshole."

Axel laughs. He actually laughs. "Yeah, he's the biggest asshole on the planet. So, I guess it's inevitable that I'm a big dickhead."

"Don't tell anyone," I whisper, "but I really like your big dickhead."

He pauses, breathing, "Only you make it this fucking hard."

"I don't believe you." My teeth grab my bottom lip.

"And I'm not falling for your beautiful mouth tonight." He grins, reaching to switch off the lamp. Turning back my way, he settles in beside me. "Now, let's start that whole Dom/sub thing, where you shut up, obey, and let me hold you."

Happily, I let him wrap his arms around me. Spooning me, he presses his hard, warm body against mine, making me gasp, "Oh, my god."

"What?" He tenses. "You okay?"

"No." I wiggle my ass against him. "Because you're fucking *huge*."

His chuckle is deep over my ear. "Told you: I'm always hard for you."

"Good God," I huff. "No wonder..."

"No wonder what?"

"No wonder you say dumb things to me all the time. Your poor brain is so starved for blood because it's all flowing to your giant dick."

"You're swelling my giant ego, too, talking that way." He grabs my hip. "Now, be still, dammit, or I'll paint your pink race cars white."

I giggle. Dammit, Axel actually makes me giggle into our hands clasped together, and if it weren't for my seizure, demanding that I sleep, I'd turn around in his arms and disobey him all night long.

Gently, he mumbles, "Can I ask *you* some questions now?"

This moment is too perfect, a first for me, letting a man

hold me while I sleep, so I sigh, "Later. If you kiss my ass and all."

"Noted: she's an *ass* woman."

His chuckle is soft. His skin, tight silk. His body, hot, hard, and feeling like my new home, so...

"Axel?" I whisper.

"Mmm?" He hums into my hair.

"Are we done hating each other?"

"Fuck no. It makes my dickhead too happy when you're a wildfire."

"Can we be each other's king and queen, too?"

He squeezes me tighter. "Till my dying day."

CHAPTER SIXTEEN
AXEL

MY MOM ALWAYS SAYS, "YOU CAN'T JUMP HALFWAY OFF A cliff."

As always ... she's right.

I'm falling all the way for Ruby Jones. Waking up to her in my arms, with Sparky curled on top of my white duvet, sleeping by our intertwined feet ... I'm done. This woman. This life. Even this damn cat.

This is all I want.

Ruby stirs against me, rubbing her warm ass against my hard cock and...

Okay, maybe I want *even more* with her.

Her auburn hair spills over my arm. Her lilac perfume owns my senses. Her skin is so damn soft. With her, I feel like a true king.

"Time to run," she mutters into my pillow. "And you have to give me at least a ten-minute head start."

"You can't run today." I sigh into her waves. "You'll come with me to a closing, then we'll go out on my boat, and—"

"I'm sorry. What?" She turns around and pulls away. "Did you just tell me I *can't* run?"

"Yeah. I *did*. You had a seizure less than twelve hours ago."

"Oh, hell no." She throws the sheets off and quickly climbs out of my bed. "I know my body, not you. Don't ever tell me what I can and can't do."

"You're not running today." I sit up. "End of story."

She turns and starts looking behind the paintings on my wall. I collect art, and I'm confused.

"What are you doing?"

"Looking for your know-it-all medical degree. It must be here, somewhere beside your dickhead Carolina law one."

"I don't need a medical degree to know it's a bad idea. You should rest. You should let me take care of you."

She whips around, her hair a fiery mane, matching the fury in her eyes. "Let's get one thing straight. No, five. One, I may kneel for you. Two, and I'll probably love it. Three, I'd be honored to be your queen. And four, I may want you to go all primal on me, too. But five, I will *never* let you trap me. That's not caring; that's controlling."

"So it's a good idea? You, running after your first seizure in years?"

"I've done it before."

"Before isn't *now*," I growl. "No more running without me because there *will* be a seizure. If not your epilepsy, it'll be someone going after me who seizes you. Sorry, Wildfire. But you spied on my world, and now you're trapped in it. You'll do as I say. Remember?"

She steps back with a frantic look in her eyes. Like I've suddenly triggered her. "Ruby, what is it?"

She shakes her head, something fracturing in her eyes.

"What did I say?"

"I'm trapped..." she stammers.

"But—"

"But that's what *he* did."

"Who?"

"My stepdad. He was a predator. After my dad left us, my mom was alone, and that man targeted my mother, a woman with daughters. While she was at work, he wouldn't let us go outside, so we'd hide in our bedroom, afraid of him, while all I wanted to do was escape with my sisters and run away, but I couldn't. I was trapped, and the stress triggered my seizures, so my sisters never left my side.

"We protected each other from him until one day..." Her chin trembles. "He got my baby sister. And my oldest sister, Scarlett, almost killed him, and I swore I'd always run. I'd never let a man trap me again and—"

"Okay. Okay." My heart races at the terror in her eyes. At her truth. I finally understand it. I kneel on the bed with my hands up. "I'm sorry. I didn't know. My father trapped me, too. He'd maim me and lock me in my room. I understand and—"

Tears escape with her whisper, "You understand me?"

"Yes, Ruby, I understand you. You can always run from me. I get it now. But I'll always chase you because I care."

"So, if I run this morning," her pretty eyes blink, half-believing, "you'll be there like Mafia in a marathon, but you won't *stop* me?"

I won't be her stepfather. I won't be her trigger. Laughter: that's her love language.

"Not gonna lie, woman. I'll chase your fine ass into hell and back."

She huffs a laugh. "Not gonna lie." Her tears stop, her smile blooming. "I kinda like your chase."

I kinda feel so goddamn in love.

I smirk. "Imagine how much you'll like it when I finally catch you." The promise stirs my cock again.

Cutely, her eyes sharpen. "Five-minute head start."

"Run beside me."

"One block behind me."

This woman is so stubborn; if I told her not to run through fire, she'd dance in it to defy me. Fuck, I love it about her. It takes a willful woman to be my queen.

"Half a block." I arch a brow. "Deal or no deal."

"Um," she eyes my rising erection, "your dick is making deals you can't keep."

"Ten." I smile. "Nine. Eight…"

"Eeek!"

I make her squeal, running out of my bedroom.

Of course, Sparky's on the pussy team. She jumps down from my bed and waddles behind her.

Quickly, I dress in running shorts, socks, sneakers, and a T-shirt. Because sure enough, Ruby's racing out of her bedroom, dressed to run, and dashing down the stairs three minutes later.

"Oh, it's fucking on, Wildfire." I chase behind her.

"You're supposed to give me a head start."

"Oh, one of my heads is *very* ready to start with you."

She laughs, and I'm relieved, but I note how she's not as fast this morning. Her usual run is an easy jog. Half of me is terrified that she'll collapse, that she's still too weak. And half of me is impressed because she's a fighter.

"Nice ass," I taunt, chasing only a half-block behind her.

She glances back, winking. "Nice hard-on."

This goddamn thing.

It loves chasing her. It loves how she races back to my house and slams the front door in my face before charging upstairs and locking herself in her bedroom.

I'm seconds behind and banging on her door. "Come out, Little Red Riding Hood. You afraid of this wolf?"

In a whirl, her door swings open. "You afraid to admit I'm right? You're sweet to care. Thank you. But I know my body. Deal?"

Fuck me, when she's all sweaty like that. "Deal." I step her way. My dick's rock-hard for her. "Now, let *me* get to know your body and—"

She slams the door in my face, making a laugh erupt from my throat.

"Are you playing hard to get?"

"Look down." I do. "You're the hard one."

She's right. Other women throw themselves at me. They're not a challenge. Of course, I fall for a goddamn Olympic challenge who gives me a gold-medal dick.

And bring it on.

"Alright then, Wildfire." I talk to her door. "Get dressed. We're going to a property closing in ninety minutes."

"I thought we can't go back to your office?"

"Not my office. The buyer's office. So get ready to be my paralegal, not the hot piece of ass I'll catch one day."

I follow my usual morning routine. Shower. Jerk off to Ruby. Dress. Think of Ruby. Eat breakfast. Hunger for Ruby. Grab my briefcase. And wait for-fucking-ever for Ruby.

And I know I should wait. Not just to fuck her, because once I do, she'll be my queen and that puts her life in danger.

If one of my many enemies, like this sex trafficker we're after, doesn't attack her, my father will.

Does he believe we're dead? I don't know. It's been thirty years since our mother staged our death, but my fear is alive and well.

I don't fear what he'll do to me. He's already done the worst, many times.

It's what he'll do to Ruby.

The queen of a king, the head king, is the biggest target.

Am I an asshole because I never worried about it with Katya? Maybe. Or maybe she didn't give us long enough for the threat to settle in.

If she had stayed. If she had borne my child, the grand-child and heir to the most evil man in the world, I can't fathom the danger. The lengths my father would go to get my queen and heir ice my veins.

It's all I want with Ruby: marriage and children.

But it would be her greatest risk, too.

It silences me on our drive to my friend's law office.

Ruby looks stunning in my passenger seat, professional and polished, humming as if she enjoys Tchaikovsky now, and I should've canceled this closing. But it's on a multi-million-dollar commercial property, and there would be hell to pay if I did.

Politely, I introduce us to the receptionist when we arrive. "Michael Cummings and Ruby Jones to see Ms. Sutton, please. We're here for the Calloway/Grover closing."

"Right this way." The receptionist stands. "Your clients are waiting in the boardroom."

"The Calloways?" Ruby side-whispers to me as we follow the receptionist.

"This was Samuel's case," I answer.

But he's not here since I gave my staff the rest of the week off. Samuel handles commercial property closings for me, but Ruby's my best paralegal. I put her on my pro bono cases. She's like a pit bull with a bone when she gets a whiff of injustice.

It's another reason my heart jumps off cliffs for this woman.

This woman, who startles at the sight of my clients when we enter the boardroom, but collects herself. I clock it, but focus on greeting everyone with handshakes. Then, I introduce Ruby.

"This is Ms. Jones, my paralegal."

"Nice to meet you." Harlow Sutton, the other attorney, shakes her hand.

"And this is John and Jessica Calloway and..." I start the greeting, but—

"Oh, we've met." Ms. Calloway sneers at Ruby. "We go *way* back."

"To high school," Mr. Calloway adds, shifting nervously in his chair.

Subtly, I glance at Ruby while we take our seats. She's silently lifting her chin, and *oh fuck*.

My Wildfire is raging.

Why?

I don't have time to address it. Harlow Sutton proceeds quickly on behalf of her client, sliding documents across the table for my clients to sign, accepting twenty-five million dollars for their family's land up the coast. I've been negotiating this deal for almost a year.

You'd think they'd be smiling as they sign, but Jessica Calloway keeps leering at Ruby while John Calloway won't look her in the eye.

I steal another glance at Ruby, but she's focused on the contracts, checking for anything missing before assembling the stacks and returning them to Harlow.

After twenty minutes, we're done and standing to shake hands again. But this time, Jessica Calloway hisses at her husband, reaching for Ruby's hand, "Don't you dare *touch* her again."

"Excuse me." My rage is instant. "Do we have a problem?"

"Ask your trashy paralegal," she hisses.

"I don't *need* to ask her." My pulse skyrockets, looming over my clients. "You will not speak to her that way; I don't care what petty reason you have."

Ms. Calloway twists her face. "We're your clients. You can't speak to us *this* way."

"Let me be clear." My tone drops to deadly. "I represent you, but you will not disrespect my staff. Apologize to her. *Now.*"

"I will not!"

"Mr. Cummings," Ruby touches my arm, "it's fine."

"Yeah," John Calloway fidgets, "we're fine. It was high school, a million years ago."

"It was like yesterday that you fucked her!" His wife fumes. "You and your best friend. The fucking whore!"

"I didn't know you two were dating," Ruby defends herself, "and you and your friends didn't have to jump me on the bus and cut my hair off and—"

Oh.

Fuck.

No.

My hand itches to pull my gun, but not here and not on a woman, even one who deserves it.

"Apologize to Ms. Jones," I seethe, "or we'll sue you for defamation."

"I'm your client," Jessica scoffs. "You can't sue me."

"No, but she can." I point to Harlow. "And we go way back, too, and Ms. Sutton *will* win on Ms. Jones's behalf. So apologize now, or you have a lawsuit on our hands."

Her husband begs, "Jessica, please, just..."

"Fine." Venom drips from her lips, smiling at Ruby. "Sorry for calling you a whore for having sex with my husband and his friend. And for then beating you up and cutting your hair and giving you a seizure. But you seem fine now. It seems you've seduced your boss into fighting your battles for you."

I snarl, "You fucking—"

"Alright," Harlow interjects calmly. "That's enough. I won't tolerate slander of anyone in my office. We're done here. Mister and Missus Calloway, you may leave."

"I'll return my fee." I glare at them. "You're no longer my clients."

"That's five hundred thousand dollars!" John Calloway gulps, "And you don't want it?"

"Not a fucking dime from either of you." I shouldn't swear, but it's either that or I start firing bullets.

Harlow escorts them out, closing the door behind her, and I turn to Ruby, taking her hand. "Are you okay?"

"I'm fine."

"She did all that to you?"

Ruby shrugs, but her eyes betray her pain. "I didn't know they were dating. John always flirted with me. He had asked me to the prom and made me feel special. Then, one day, he showed up at my house with his football friend, too, and ... I guess it's the price I paid for being curious ... for trusting men."

I'm sweating. I'm a dog on a chain, ripping my own flesh and growling to escape. "I want to kill her. And him. It takes everything for me not to."

"Why?" Ruby raises a brow. "I can sue her, right? And your very sexy, smart friend, Ms. Harlow Sutton, who you go *way* back with, would help me. So, I'm fine."

My heart pounds with rage at anyone insulting Ruby; I don't care why. I will put a bullet in their skull ... after I torture them with knives and salt.

But this?

It makes my heart hammer even faster. Deeper. Warmer. It heats my chest with something else.

"Wildfire, are you jealous of Harlow?"

"No," she snaps.

"Liar."

"Why would I be jealous of a beautiful, blonde lawyer who knows you *very* well?"

"Oh, so you're *very* jealous." I grin, pressing into her as she backs away, but I won't stop my pursuit until she's trapped against the wall. "And damn, it's hot."

"So you admit it." She glares. "You fucked her."

"So you won't tell me about your football threesomes,

but you want to know about mine?" I tsk, highly amused and falling even harder for her. "That's not very gender equal."

Her eyes sharpen. "I got your equal right here."

I grab her throat. "God, you make me feral when you're proud. I want to *fuck* you right *here*."

"Save it for Ms. Sutton."

"I don't *want* Harlow. Many men do, but not me. Not ever. Despite what you think, Ms. Jones, *you're* the first and only woman I've worked with who I plan to fuck on all fours until my cum drips down your thighs."

Lust lands in her eyes. "So, you're not judging me?" But she also doubts. "I did mess around with John and his friend. It was my first threesome, and they shamed me about it and—"

"And I'll shamelessly fuck every man out of you, Ruby." I brush my lips over hers. "Am I jealous? No. Possessive? Yes. I wish I were there. I could've saved you from assholes like him. I'll kill anyone who hurts you because you're mine now, and I feel the same way—I'm yours. No woman can hold a candle to my Wildfire." I'm hard ... and hungry. "Now, lift your dress and pull your panties down."

Her eyes widen. "What?"

"You heard me. You'll obey me. Lift your dress and pull your panties down and show me the pussy that belongs to me."

"What if we get caught?"

"Good. I want everyone to see my face buried between your thighs."

"Axel," she sighs, lifting the hem of her dress, "but Harlow's coming back in here."

"I don't give a damn as long as you come on my face, too."

I gaze down, watching Ruby lift her purple dress. It's a knitted one, so it stays bunched around her waist. My dick swells even more at her pulling down her emerald lace panties. They look perfect hugging her thighs.

But her pussy...

"Oh, fuck, Wildfire," I sigh at the first sight of it. At how she's not bare. At how she keeps her auburn hair trimmed, and it's a new fetish to drive me completely insane.

I fall to my knees and bury my nose in her scent, making her cry out.

"Shh, Ms. Jones," I tease, staring up at her. "Don't let them hear what a naughty girl you're about to be for me, aren't you?"

"Yes," she sighs

I nip her mound, making her gasp before I demand, "*What's* my name?"

"Yes, my *king*. My Axel *King*."

"Good girl." I lower my nose to her panties and inhale. "You smell so fucking good for me. Are you getting wetter, waiting for my mouth?"

"Yes, my king."

I unzip my pants. "Do you want to see how hard I am, just staring at your pretty pussy? Just smelling your sweet cunt?"

She mutters, "But Harlow may see it."

"Are you jealous, Ms. Jones? You don't want another woman to see how hard my dick gets for you? How it's yours?"

"Yes."

I reach through the slit in my boxers, fisting my swollen tip. "Yes, you're jealous? Or yes, you want to watch me stroke my dick while I eat your pussy?"

Her hand sinks into my hair. "Yes, to both, my king."

I smirk. "Such a jealous girl for me. Now, pull your lips apart and show me your little clit. Show your king his pussy to rule."

While Ruby reaches down with her other hand, obeying, I

free my erection, letting it proudly jut before me, bare, while I kneel before her gingery pussy, glistening and exposed.

"Fuck yes, this is mine," I growl.

Staring up at her, I let her watch as I gently kiss her clit for the first time. I make her shudder with a moan, and she makes me drip. Anchored to her eyes, I steam my breath over her tender hood before pulling it back, gently blowing cool air over her exposed clit, making her quiver and beg, "Axel, please. Lick it. Suck it. Please make me come fast."

Grinning, I slowly lave my tongue over her little pearl. I make her thighs shake harder before I tease, "Are you shy, my Wildfire? Do you want me to make you come fast on my face so we won't get caught?"

"No," she sighs. "I just want *you*. I've just imagined this so many times, please. Please, do it."

"Please do what?"

"Please eat my pussy, my king."

"Good girl. Now behave, and ride your clit over my tongue like a queen."

"Oh, my god." She shivers, but wants this.

Shamelessly, I offer her the pointed tip of my tongue while she starts rocking her hips, chasing the sensation back and forth, mimicking the furious flutter of my tongue over her hard clit.

It's an unusual method, but it fucking works.

It makes her act so desperate and damn naughty for me. She's raunchy, real, and raw with need, and it makes me hard as hell for her. I start stroking my swollen cock to her proud pursuit before finally flicking my tongue, eagerly matching her lewd search until she cries out, "Oh fuck, Axel."

"Be a good girl, and come on my face, Ruby." I dive in with my mouth, rubbing my nose against her clit, inhaling her maddening musk while I lick her entrance, spearing it and getting my first flavor of her.

Then, I taste something quite distinct and...

The door to the boardroom opens. I hear it, but I don't stop. *I won't stop.* It's Harlow, gasping, "Oh. Oh, my god. Excuse me. S... S..."

"Oh fuck," Ruby moans, shaking and fisting my hair. "Oh fuck, I'm coming."

I growl into her pussy while stroking my hard cock. *I'm going to fucking lose it.* It's making Ruby come—the sight we must be. Me, kneeling and jerking off while I eat the hell out of her pussy, and Harlow busting us, seeing us.

"I'm so sorry." I hear Harlow rush to close the door behind her, but I'm not done.

"Axel," Ruby pants, her thighs flushed and trembling after her orgasm. "Oh my god. We gotta stop."

I pull back, catching my breath, glaring up at her. "We're not stopping. You're coming again, and I'm coming, too."

"But..." She opens her eyes and gazes down at me. Suddenly, she flinches. "Oh my god. I... I... I started my—"

"I know, Wildfire." I lick my metallic lips. "Thank you. I can taste it."

"It's on your nose."

"And it's in my soul, and I only want more. I want everything with you, Ruby. You're fucking beautiful. Fuck those assholes who didn't worship you."

I rip her panties down, grabbing her ankle, and she steps out of them. "But, I've never—"

"And you won't. No one tastes my queen but me."

I grab her leg and swing it over my shoulder.

Yes, I have a primal kink. I want to chase Ruby down, catch her, and fuck her like a wild beast, taking every piece of her and making her mine, and that includes this. This is the ultimate reward for my obsession, my chase, my waiting.

Fuck yes, I want this woman this much. There's no shame, no taboo. This is her nature and power. This is what she can give me. Life. Love. It all flows from inside her, and I want every drop.

It's only slight, the metallic taste. She's barely bleeding, but it's enough to get me off, to have me gently plunge a finger inside her before I lick it off to her hooded stare.

"Oh my god, Axel," she marvels. "I can't believe you want me like this. This is so ... intimate and hot."

"Because you're so *mine*. Every drop of you belongs to me."

Carefully, I plunge two fingers inside her while gently sucking her clit.

"Oh fuck. Oh fuck," she moans, fisting my hair even tighter. "You're going to make me come again."

And I do. I kiss, lick, and suck her clit while I gently curl my fingers inside her slick, swollen walls, and her thigh shakes on my shoulder. Her moans drop into primal groans, and my dick aches for her, but I wait. I wait until she's about to fall over her edge, her gasps of my name, my sign and prayer.

I plunge my tongue inside her, taking what I can of her orgasm spilling into my mouth. She shakes over my face, and I moan as she holds me here. Taking. Relishing. Loving.

I don't need to breathe.

I only need her.

Plucking her panties from the carpet, I drape them over my dick and don't even have to stroke my shaft. Her wet silk on my sensitive tip. Her gazing down at me through a primal haze. Her tangy, metallic taste on my tongue.

Fuck yes, Ruby makes me come with a shameless grunt, my chest shaking as my dick pulses, over and over, saturating her silk.

Lightheaded, I catch my breath and look down at the evidence of my desire for her, and a wicked thought takes me.

I want this for her.

For us.

"Now," I lift her ankle, "put your panties back on and proudly walk out of this office like my queen."

Silently, she obeys. She lets me drag the soaked lace up her thighs, leaving creamy smears behind, before her panties settle in place, and I smooth her dress down.

She sighs, "The whole office knows what we did."

But I don't hear shame in her voice.

I rise, arranging myself, zipping my pants, and smoothing them down. Then, I fist her ponytail. "Do you want to be my queen, Ruby Jones?"

"Yes, my king," she sighs as my lips near hers.

"Then get used to wearing my cum between your legs."

I kiss her with warning, with warmth, with wanting so much with her, even if I shouldn't.

Even if it's dangerous.

Even if it's deadly.

CHAPTER SEVENTEEN
RUBY

For a week, Axel holds me in bed. We don't do anything but fuss, talk, cuddle, and laugh. And for a week, I'm on my period.

But for the rest of my life...

I'll never forget what we did in Harlow Sutton's office.

It felt like Axel erased all boundaries between us in one act, the most intimate act.

Then, he made the taboo tender by protectively putting his hand on my back while I proudly wore my panties soaked with his cum out of Harlow's office.

She blushed as we left but winked at me, too, and yeah, I like her. It doused my jealousy over her. I believe Axel, they're strictly friends.

So, why can't I shake this simmering jealousy over *something* with him?

It's odd because I'm not the jealous type. I've never given myself a reason to be jealous over a man or two, and I never stick around long enough for a man to be possessive over me.

But Axel brings the Bratva to his possessive party.

I know a lot of it is legitimate.

He's trying to keep me safe, and it *is* partially my fault that I'm in this hot mafia mess, that he's turned his charming historic home into our temporary fortress until his office is safe again.

When he says he's going to Delta's, the sex store, for another meeting and I have to stay here, I trust him. I know some of his brothers work there, hiding behind their roles. I know they're up to mission mischief.

But this morning, when I sit at Axel's kitchen table, and overhear him talking with Helen about moving his board-room furniture.

That's it.

I'm dying to know once he ends their call.

"What's going on? Are you moving our office?"

He refills his coffee, then holds the carafe over my mug, filling mine, too. "Don't ask, Wildfire. The less you know, the better."

"Um, ignorance is bullshit, not bliss in Bratvaland."

He grins. "I'm *not* moving offices. Everyone can work remotely for a while."

Pause for my frustration. "...*butttt*?"

"But what?"

"But tell me the rest. I'm your queen, right? So crown me with some intel."

He crouches to pet Sparky, who rarely moves. She must be due any minute. It's another reason I'm content to hide here, ready when she needs us.

And it's too sexy how he pets the cat but smirks up at me. *Tick. Tock.* So, I arch an eyebrow and lethally glare at him, making him chuckle.

"I'm not *moving* my boardroom." He stands. "I moved the thrones, the chairs in it. I found someplace safer to meet because I suspect we'll be doing another initiation soon."

"Another initiation?" My logic works too fast. "In Delta's,

right? I gotta say, it's brilliant—meeting in an adult shop. Now, people will assume you hide a sex addiction, not a rogue mafia operation."

"I prefer ex-mafia because there's nothing rogue about us. We have rules and follow orders. We have missions, and complete them."

"Whose orders?"

"The Queen's or mine, but all contribute. We all have skills."

"Which are?"

"Too much intel," he warns, refreshing Sparky's water bowl.

"I'll give you the silent treatment until you tell me."

He opens the fridge, laughing. "Don't threaten me with peace and quiet."

Silently, I seethe while he makes an omelet, smirking like a sinister chef, knowing that I'm bursting to know everything about him.

Until...

"Okay, fine!" I blurt. "I know Sire's a pastor. He's your divine cover story. You're the smug lawyer. Nick's the cute diversion, the athlete. Nash runs the numbers. Grant does your cyber shit, plus he's all beefy and cute." Axel cuts me a look. "But the other two? What do they do?"

He whips eggs with cheese and a silent smile.

"Tell me, or I'll start training for a marathon, and your ass will have to chase me." His smile drops. "That's what I thought. It's all fun and games being the king until you have to run behind me for twenty-six point two miles with bleeding raw nipples."

"Fuck me," he huffs, pouring the egg mixture into a skillet.

"Yeah, we're not doing that either until you tell me."

"We're not doing that until you *trust* me."

His back is turned, but I can hear the sincerity in his vow.

While part of me is dying for Axel. Like I want to pounce on him like a hellcat in heat and make him breed me to repopulate the world.

My heart needs to wait because this is too powerful between us.

The taboo teases he gives me along the way are enough to satisfy me temporarily. I assume they satisfy him, too, because it's like we both know if we cross over, there's no going back.

He wants me in his world, but it's lethal. And I feel him in my heart, but that's love.

Lethal love.

That's what we'd be together.

"Jace is my other brother," he finally answers, turning around. "He's the head of security at Delta's and practically Grant's twin. They look alike and are only ten months apart." He mutters, "My poor mom."

I swallow the sudden lump in my throat. I respect this most about Axel. All he's known is witnessing his mother's suffering, and now, he can see it in other women, and it enrages him.

He'll kill for a woman.

And I know he'd die for me.

"Jace is the big teddy bear who bashes skulls." He keeps going. "That's his skill. He's also an expert in surveillance and avoiding it. And then there's Loch, my baby brother. He wanted to join the Marines, but I convinced him to be a forest ranger instead."

"Loch?" My pulse doubles. "The one marrying Alena Allen?"

"Yes."

He turns around and flips the omelet.

But here it is again.

That feeling.

The one that doesn't have a name but wants answers.

"Why was Alena at your office a couple of weeks ago? She seemed upset."

Is it my imagination, or did Axel's broad shoulders just stiffen under his starched white shirt? Am I just new to this emotion, jealousy? Or does it normally make your stomach suddenly twist?

I don't know why I keep getting this feeling about Alena Allen, but I do.

He keeps his back to me, taking two plates from the cabinet. Halving the omelet, he quietly prepares our breakfast, garnishing our plates with berries.

Axel has a habit of cooking for me now, especially since I told him it's not really safe for people with epilepsy to do it, and I like his care. He seems to thrive doing it, but this feels unsettling, and I won't break his weighted silence.

Setting our plates down, he sits across from me.

Sparky waddles over and rubs my legs like she can sense that his silence is killing me. I reach down and pet her. It soothes me while Axel's fighting something tearing at his heart; it's obvious.

It's scaring me.

I stop petting Sparky, and it starts biting at the back of my eyes, making them prick with tears. Don't ask me why; I just need to know. "Axel, what is it? What is it between you and Alena?"

He picks up his fork but doesn't take a bite.

"She's my goddaughter," he answers, and I exhale. "And there's more to tell you, but it's trust, Ruby. It's a lot of trust you can't break, promise me."

"Okay," I murmur.

"Alena doesn't know about our family, our father. Nothing. *Her* father, Nash, joined us when he was eighteen. He became part of our family, and so did Alena when she was barely two.

Then, her mother died years later, and my mom became like a grandmother to her. But we don't tell Alena who we are or what we do. It's for her safety."

"I understand." I do. It makes me feel better.

"She thinks I'm Michael Cummings, the lawyer, and her dad's best friend, so he made me her godfather. But to *my* family, she became our princess. Now, she's older. She's a queen and at risk, just as you are, should someone go after you, so we assigned Loch to her."

"Assigned?"

"He was supposed to be her secret bodyguard. She's a forest ranger, so he became one. To act like her colleague. To keep an eye on her ... but then he fell in love with her. He's going to be her king."

"Aw." A thousand pounds lift off my shoulders. "That's so sweet."

"It's a fucking mess," he grumbles. "Because Alena doesn't know Loch is one of us. She doesn't know he's my little brother, and their marriage was arranged."

"Arranged?" Cue pulse rising again. "Um, I'm Team Alena on this one because I'd go on a rampage if I found out my marriage had been arranged."

"If it were you?" He quips, "We'd throw every gun in the ocean."

"Can you blame a woman?" I'm feeling the rage *for* Alena. "How dare you arrange a marriage for her? She deserves love."

"Loch *does* love her," he insists. "Trust me. I beat the shit out of him for defying our orders, and Nash had to pull us apart because Loch was willing to die for her. So, we said he had to marry her, but he said it was too late. He already had a ring for her."

Puzzle pieces move quickly in my mind, putting the picture together. "So Nash is hiding this from Alena? That

Loch's mission became love? And you're hiding it from her, too? That he's your little brother?"

"Yes. And this is me, trusting you not to break her heart. Please don't ever tell her."

"Oh," I pick up my fork, "I don't need to say a word. Karma keeps no secrets. Alena will find out one day, and I'll hand her the bullets."

Axel smirks, stabbing his omelet. "Spoken like a queen."

"What does that mean?"

"Our queens have a way of bonding, then bending our will until we break."

"Um." I chew my yummy breakfast. "Pussy has a way of doing that."

He grins, chewing his. "Don't forget Zar."

"Point taken." I aim my fork at him. "A big dick can be giantly persuasive."

His brows lower. "You've seen Zar's dick?"

"And Nick's." He glowers, and I chuckle. "Not biblically. Just their flaccid flap-doodles, jumping in the pool."

Axel spews his eggs, laughing.

It's cute, but...

"Hang on. If Zar's been initiated, that means you made him a queen, too, and..." Oh, the erotic image in my mind. "My god," I sigh. "It wasn't, was it? A gay gangbang?"

"Jesus, woman," he says flatly, "quit calling it that. It's not about sex. It's the vow. The bond. It's a king and a second king protecting their queen. And—"

"Wait. *What?* A *second* king?"

"Yes. A *second* king. Every queen has a king, and another man just as willing to die for you and your kids. That's how we got out: my mother's second king. He fell in love with her, and the tradition saved our lives. So, we do it in their honor because it works. I can't describe it, but it's a powerful bond. You just have to feel it."

"*Feel* it? Huh." I wonder, "So ... you're already a queen's second king?"

Why isn't this jealousy I feel this time?

No, it's something more powerful and bending my reality.

Am I *really* becoming Axel's queen? Is this how it feels to be one? I'm more concerned about what bonds *all* of us together than what binds two of us?

As Axel shared, it took seven, maybe eight of them, to escape his evil father. They did it together. It takes a group to protect a kingdom. Or, in his case, to escape one.

And if you're a true queen, you sacrifice your ego, even your jealousy, for the good of others.

You rule like a regal boss; you don't act like a little bitch.

Yeah, that's how this feels.

"Out of respect, we don't discuss our queens," he answers. "A king doesn't boast. He's brave and protects their privacy. He protects *every* queen."

But I already know Nash is Wren's second king. I overheard that part of her initiation. Still, I have no idea who the second king is to Grant's wife.

Or who's Zar's second king?

"Let me just say..." Yes, I feel like one. I want to protect the group. "If you're Zar's second king. If you're bisexual, I understand. I'd never be mad or jud—"

"I'm not—" he blurts before clenching his teeth. "I'm not *discussing* our queens."

I nod and finish my omelet. I let the dust settle on our first round of questions before I poke again. "So, who's being initiated next?"

Say me. Say me.

"Give it a few weeks," he answers, "and I'll show you."

"Show me? But I've already seen what you and your brothers do, and I liked it. I've done stuff before, and I'm ready now."

He sets his fork down, staring at me.

Seconds feel like forever while a decision rips at his soul.

I can see it in Axel's eyes. That's the power of them. You can see straight into his soul. Facets of good and evil glimmer like ice. Like a raw force you need to live, but it can kill you, too.

"Ruby," he finally speaks, "you liked that part of my world, the beautiful and erotic part, and I'll share it with you. Witness a full initiation and tell me if you really want it.

"But you need to understand there are parts of my world you haven't seen yet. The bloody parts." He's deadly serious. "You haven't seen the part of me that can be a beast, a monster if I have to. I gave you trust. I told you secrets; now give me this. Give us time."

My heart pounds. "Time for what?"

"Time for you to trust that even when I can be a terrifying man, I'll come back to you. The beast will leave, and it will be me." He vows, "I'm not your stepfather. I'm not always bad. I may kill others, but *you* don't have to fear me. I won't be a trigger for you. Not again."

This is the most respect a man has ever shown me.

Most give me minutes, maybe an hour or so, before they want something from me. Usually, they want in my pants.

But not Axel.

He says he wants more, and I do, too. I'm learning to trust him more than I have any man.

"Okay," I sigh. "And by the way; you didn't trigger me."

"Yes, I did."

He does this thing with his eyes. He melts me with honesty.

And I can't lie to him, or hurt him, so I move on. "And we have time. In two days, I'll leave for three weeks anyway."

"The fuck you are!" he suddenly barks.

"The fuck I won't!" I boldly laugh, surprised. "I put in a

vacation request with Helen over six months ago. Did you not see it?"

"No. A vacation for what?"

"With my sisters. Scarlett is taking us to The Mercier Hotel in Greece, then Bali, then the Seychelles and—"

"You're not going anywhere."

"This is cute." I wave my fork between us. "You, thinking I listen to you."

"This is cute." His finger mocks me. "You, thinking I won't chase your ass down, and sling you over my shoulder, and bring you back home."

"Aw, Male Jealousy." I crinkle my nose. "Such a ridiculous breed. Completely void of logic and known for its blindness."

"Oh, I can *see*," he seethes. "I can see your cute ass lying next to me in bed every night. You're not leaving me. It's not safe."

I take a raspberry from my plate and place it on the table between us.

"This is your brain cell about to learn that my sister, Scarlett, is a titled MMA fighter, bodyguard, and the head of security for a global hotel chain. You'll lose any fight with her." I wink. "And me."

I set another raspberry beside it.

"And this is your brain cell appreciating that my brother-in-law, Luca Mercier, is a billionaire Dom as possessive and protective as you are. You carry a gun. He carries a whip." I wink again. "Maybe he can show you a few things and..."

I drop another berry on the table.

"This is Zar, a badass queen you trust, who's coming with us. He can spy for you and report back that all I'm doing is staying drunk as Cooter Brown with my sisters."

"You're not supposed to drink with your condition."

I love how he's educated himself on my epilepsy.

"I don't. I watch my sisters get drunk and laugh my ass off at them."

He cocks a brow, and I'm starting to know Axel. Like *really* know him, too.

When he smirks like that? He's a beast, a lion who can't decide if he should pounce or purr at my pride.

I stand up.

"And this is me, going upstairs to pack while you seethe, slam shit, then get over it, and maybe call me a few times while I'm gone because I'll really miss your dickhead."

I walk around the table and give him a kiss to scramble the rest of his brain cells before rubbing my nose against the ring on his.

"And if you play nice with me, my king, your queen will always come home to you."

CHAPTER EIGHTEEN
AXEL

"WHY IN THE HELL ARE WE AT THE MERCIER HOTEL?" SIRE glares at me before turning on his heavenly smile, holding the door open for a gaggle of women.

"Why, good morning, ladies," he drawls. "Welcome to Charleston. Y'all have a blessed day."

They gasp and giggle, tittering their thanks for his Southern manners, and if it were the Victorian era, they'd be fanning their hoop skirts, too.

Sire knows he looks like God and the Devil spawned a tatted cover model. He ruins panties, and it runs in the family.

"We're here to meet with my future brother-in-law."

"What?" He freezes in the hotel's opulent, white marble lobby. "When did this happen?"

"While you were breeding Wren."

"I'm fucking serious."

"So am I." I lower my voice. "But it's complicated. We're going slow, but it'll happen. She'll be my wife one day, and I need your backup to get there."

"Complicated how?"

"Because she already knows about us. She spied on Wren's initiation and figured it out. And—"

His top lip curls. "If we can't trust her, you know what needs to be done because *nobody* puts Wren at risk. I'll ki—"

"We can trust her." I palm his shoulder. We're both wearing suits. We have a kings' meeting at Delta's next. We need to discuss our plan to trap the trafficker we're hunting, but I made a call this morning after my tiff with Ruby yesterday. We didn't go to bed mad about it, but I held her, worried. "She's close with Nick and Zar. She's earned their trust, and she has mine. *Mostly*."

His nostrils flare. "*Mostly?*"

"She can be a bit stubborn. A bit of a sexy, fucking wildfire and..."

Sire throws his chin up, filling the lobby with his almighty laughter. "Oh, so she's your *queen*. Has Mom met her yet?"

"Not really. I don't want anyone to know about her yet. Only you. And only Grant, because we're running a side mission together. Something to help Nick and Zar and—"

"Who's hurting Nick?"

Sire's as protective over our brothers as I am. We both took beatings to shield them, trying to defend our mother, too. Yes, we were young, but when your father's an animal, you learn to fight back like one, too.

"It's a long story. I'll fill you in later, but we're running late."

"Late for what?"

"We're meeting with Luca Mercier. He's the brother-in-law of the woman I..."

I stumble on the word. It's not that I don't feel it. No, I fear it. I fear what loving me will do to Ruby.

I don't give a shit about my risk, my pain. I've already suffered so much. But I will stop at nothing for her safety.

"The woman you *love*? That's what you were going to say?"

Sire's not laughing. "It's okay, brother, you deserve it. You never loved Katya, and she never loved you."

"Yeah, because she was pussy-crazed for you."

I'm not mad about it. It's true. Katya wanted me *and* Sire. She wasn't shy about it. She'd ask me to let him join our bed all the time. Of course, I said no.

"I never disrespected your marriage," Sire insists. "I always turned her down and told you about it each time. Only once. Only her initiation. Only that night and—"

"I know. I know you'd never betray me, and you're right. It wasn't love. But this is."

"So what's the problem?"

"She wants to go on vacation with her sisters and—"

"And you need to protect her." He nods, understanding; any time we claim a queen, we claim her protection for life.

The minute Sire saw Wren, he claimed her. He had to. She was a virgin, being trafficked and auctioned off, and he went through hell to get her out of it.

"So this is tricky." I lead us toward the golden elevator doors. "I need Luca Mercier to know the risk Ruby's in, but he can't know why."

"Ruby?" Sire smirks, joining me before the doors slide closed. "Isn't she your hot paralegal with those big blue eyes, fiery hair, and luscious tits like—"

"Shut up, holy fucker." He's trying to goad me. It's a wicked game we brothers play. "She's more than my paralegal now, and she's fucking *mine*."

The elevator doors slide open on the third floor to Zar standing there. Though I'm not into men, I see why my brother Nick is madly in love with him. Zar's tall, built, and tan, with dark hair and eyes. Zar drips with swagger, and when Sire's around him, the energy crackles between them, too.

"Mr. Cummings." Zar nods at me. "Pastor Rutledge." He winks at Sire. "Right this way. We're expecting you."

This meeting will be one of the trickiest situations I've ever negotiated.

The blood shared between some of us. The erotic connections between others. The dangerous secrets we hide. The powerful and interconnected worlds about to collide over one woman.

My woman.

All know Luca's protective over Ruby. He should be. She's his beloved little sister-in-law.

Some know Zar is fiercely in love with Nick. They'll get married when Nick retires from football. But only a few know Nick is our brother. He's a king, and Zar is his queen, and *our* queen, too.

However, Luca and Scarlett have no idea who we really are and how Zar is one of us.

A few know Zar is also partnered with Luca. Zar is his CFO, best friend, and loyal sub. Zar subs with Luca's wife, Scarlett, and Nick joins them.

I respect my brother's privacy. How ever Nick is partnered with them is his business.

But Ruby is *my* business.

And her protection is my vow.

"Mr. Cummings." Politely, Luca rises from his mammoth desk to greet me. "Pastor Rutledge." He shakes Sire's hand, too. "Please, come in."

As the CEO of The Mercier Hotels, Luca's office is impressive, but his rich Greek accent is inviting. He gestures for us to settle into the seating area, a circle of Grecian blue velvet chairs by the window in his office.

"My wife drove our daughter to school," Luca shares. "She'll be joining us momentarily."

As Luca's assistant asks for our drink requests, Scarlett

appears. She's obviously Ruby's sister, equally stunning with her long, auburn hair and fierce blue eyes. The Jones sisters are a force, I can tell.

I'll never stop feeling guilty, suspecting that I triggered Ruby's seizure. That I evoked the fear she used to have of her predatory stepfather.

But I note the jagged scar through Scarlett's eyebrow. The bruises on her knuckles like she's been sparring. The way she lifts her chin like her little sister. The way she glares suspiciously at me, and I see it now—how the sisters protected each other.

Like Ruby, Scarlett doesn't easily trust men, and I understand.

But it's reassuring how she sits lovingly beside her husband, Luca, and tenderly accepts his kiss before she glares at me.

"Why isn't Ruby here?" She demands to know, "That's who we're here for? Right? My sister works for you? Because I'm not talking about her behind her back."

Zar laughs. "Damn, Red, way to come out swinging."

"We're here," I answer, "because your sister is a wildfire who'd burn my world to ash if she knew I was meeting with you."

"Ah, I see." Luca rumbles a deep chuckle. "The professional has turned personal." He nods. "No judgment. We're just as guilty in this room."

"Fine." Scarlett softens. "This is personal. But why is Charleston's celebrity pastor here, too?"

"I'm here to vouch for Mr. Cummings," Sire answers smoothly. "We've been friends for years, and I can attest to his character in this matter."

"What matter?" Scarlett presses, and I can see why a powerful man like Luca Mercier married her. She's his equal. She's his soulmate.

Luca and Scarlett make me feel like I'm looking in a mirror. Like Ruby is my soulmate, she's as equally terrifying and tender as I can be.

I begin, "I understand that Ms. Jones is scheduled to go on vacation with her sisters."

Scarlett arches her scarred brow. ".... *and?*"

"And," I fight my smile at her ferocity. It's familiar. "And I need to discuss her security. Her protection."

I catch how Luca squeezes Scarlett's thigh before he glowers. "Exactly *who* does my sister-in-law need protection from, Mr. Cummings?"

"My business has its risks."

"But you're a property lawyer." Luca's not buying it. "How risky can that be?" But he plays along.

"We have some nefarious clients, some disgruntled ones, too. And as a member of my staff, it puts Ms. Jones at risk."

It's not a lie.

Disturbed clients have targeted legal teams before. I even clocked how Bill Ratcliffe seethed at Ruby in the courtroom. Like the predator he is, he was silently threatening her, too, and it's a matter of weeks before I kill that piece of shit.

"So you're saying my sister is in danger? From what?" Scarlett's equally calling *bullshit* on me. "A house sale that went wrong?"

"I also take pro bono cases," I explain. "I represent disenfranchised tenants to survivors of sex trafficking and—"

"And that's where I come in." Sire gets my back. He's not lying about this, either. "My church is a safe harbor. We have a rescue mission and offer survivor support. Mr. Cummings and his staff seek legal justice for the survivors we help, which puts them at risk of retaliation. I assure you he's a good man in a dangerous business."

"Does Ruby know this?" Concern grabs Scarlett's voice.

"Yes, Ms. Jones is the best paralegal on my pro bono

cases," I answer. "She's invaluable to our mission and at risk because of it. So, please understand my concern when she informed me that she'd be traveling out of the country and away from my protection."

Luca snarls, "Your. *Protection?*"

"Yes, my *protection.*"

Let him read between the lines.

Luca Mercier is no fool. Neither is his wife. Let them assume what they want about me, but don't let them doubt my loyalty to Ruby and my intentions to make her mine.

"Look, Mr. Cummings," Zar mediates. "Ruby is my ride-or-die. I love that little firecracker, and I'll be there. I'm crashing the Jones sisters' getaway, and I can assure you of her safety. Of everyone's safety."

"Ruby will be a target, which makes others around her a target, too." I don't fuck around with this. I tell Scarlett, "I respect you and your family. This is why I'm disclosing the risk. I have grave concerns about Ruby's safety."

Scarlett narrows her glare at me. "Like I won't kill *ANY* man who hurts my sister." It's a thinly veiled threat I respect.

"And like I won't help my wife," Luca adds coldly.

"I trust that's true." I nod. "Please, kill any man who puts a hand on Ruby." Scarlett cocks a brow. "Any *hurting* hand, because I will never hurt her. I've vowed to protect her."

"Listen," Scarlett warns. "We're not canceling our vacation, and you're not coming."

"Indeed, I can't. I have work here. So promise me that you'll spare no expense to protect Ruby. To appreciate the risk she's in now that..." Something grabs my heart, my voice. "Now that she *works* with me."

Now that I love her. Now that I'm fighting like hell to make her love me, too.

They nod, and with a few awkward pleasantries Zar uses to ease the tension, we rise to leave.

While Sire politely pecks Scarlett's cheek goodbye, Luca Mercier threatens me with his handshake, "Hurt Ruby, and you die."

I look him in the eye. "If Ruby is ever hurt, it *will* kill me."

The man can figure it out. I don't need to say who I really am for him to hear the truth in my voice. The love, too. I trust it's what Luca feels for Scarlett, too.

"Well, if that wasn't a meeting of the alphas, I don't know what was," Sire boasts in the elevator to the lobby. "We should make Scarlett Mercier an honorary queen."

"She's close enough. She's partnered with Nick and Zar." I worry. "Our worlds are colliding and fuck ... with this Olan Turner shit and our side missions, too; something's going to break. I can sense it."

Sire's quiet as we step into the sunshine, steaming the pavement over Meeting Street. We walk in stride for several blocks toward Delta's, and from behind my sunglasses, I catch the tourists craning their necks at us.

Maybe Ruby's right.

We should tone down our fashion. Dark suits. Sunglasses. Ink. Scowls. I could change more to blend in, but I won't be caught dead in Madras shorts.

I grin at all the shit Ruby gives me. What I wear. What I say. How I'm a smug, protective dickhead. How she said she *likes* my dickhead.

Then I glower about our conversation yesterday. I felt sick, not telling Ruby the whole truth about Alena.

But what if, as I fear with everyone else, Ruby leaves me over what I did for Alena? It's Ruby I fear losing the most, and that's if Nash doesn't kill—

"What in the hell is bothering you?" Sire has the uncanny ability to dive into my soul, any soul, and find your burden.

"Rewind the past hour, and you're up to speed."

"Stop lying." He stops in front of an artisan selling Palmetto Roses. "Long before today. Even before Ruby worked for you. What is it? What makes you act so damned. Literally. And don't say it's Katya because I'm not buying it."

God, if I could tell any brother, it's Sire.

As unorthodox as he may be in the bedroom, he takes confessions, vows, and prayers seriously.

I've kept this damning secret for so long, and he's my blood; he can sense it. It's been a lonely hell, suffering in silence, unable to tell anyone. Even Alena and I rarely speak of it.

I nod to my right, and he joins me in the park by a historic church. Seems a fitting location for this confession.

Once no one's in earshot, Sire guesses, "Who was she? Because you'd never cheat, so if you love Ruby, it's no one now. It's someone in your past because it's usually a woman who rights or wrongs a man's world, so who? Who did you get pregnant?"

"God, you're *obsessed* with breeding."

"Don't mock me." We stand, eye-to-eye, and Sire's deadly serious. "We're not talking about kinks and games. You know what heirs mean in our world. You know the blood that binds us, so is that it? You have a child with a woman we don't know about?"

"No," I sigh. "Thank god, no, there's no child. Though ... she'll be a great mother one day."

Sire steps back like he can sense it, like he knows this is my greatest sin. "Who?"

"Don't hate me."

"*Who?*"

"She *asked* me."

"Who? Wren? Delphine? Who the *fuck* did you fuck?"

My throat tightens. I almost can't say it.

I'll never forget that night. It was tender and sweet, but it was forever ago, so why does it feel like a curse that will damn me forever? Why do I wish I could take it back, but never would?

Alena needed me. She asked for me. I stopped her tears, and we shared something special, but like a rainbow, it faded in minutes. It was never meant to last.

Why can't people believe you can be with someone but not belong with them?

Alena belongs with Loch. I belong with Ruby. We know when we find our soulmate.

"Who, Aleksi?" Sire, born Sergei, lowers his voice, using my birth name, conjuring our past and pain, our bond that can't be broken. "Please, God, tell me who, brother, and I promise I will forgive you."

"Alena."

I say it and let the chips fall like Sire's jaw.

"She was twenty-one," I explain, "and she asked *me* to be her first. She felt ugly, like no one loved her, and she was crying. I couldn't let her feel that way and..."

I can't read Sire's eyes. They're as blue as mine and as piercing and murderous.

"Alena didn't love me," I assure him, "and I didn't love her. Not like I'm falling for Ruby or how you love Wren. It was different and—"

"And Nash is going to fucking kill you." He shakes his head.

"And I'll let him."

Sire seethes, "And I won't let him, and that's the problem, and you know it. This is going to tear us apart." He clenches his teeth. "Does Loch know?"

"Only me, Alena, and now you know. That's it, and the guilt has been making me sick for years, but I don't regret it. How is that possible?"

He looks away, his stare trapped by the church spire.

"Sometimes, we make deals with devils. Sometimes, we make deals with angels. And both are impossible bonds to explain."

"What in the hell is that supposed to mean?"

He turns back to me. "Just that I get it. I get how we do something for someone else with the best intentions, but the worst outcomes."

"Goddamn," I huff, "I hope you don't counsel your parishioners like this because I want to jump off the Ravenel bridge. So, you're saying to *expect* the worst outcome?"

"Nah." He huffs sarcastically, "Maybe Nash, your best friend and our brother, will be *perfectly* fine that you fucked his daughter and took her virginity. And Loch will *surely* love that you fucked his wife first and lied about it."

"You don't have to be so crass."

"Is there another way to spin this shit show?"

"What else can I do? You're right. This will tear us apart if anyone finds out."

If we pull this thread, our whole world will unravel, and Alena will know everything about her father, our brothers, my mom, and worse, *my* father. And nothing will destroy Nash more than if I put his daughter in harm's way.

The less Alena knows, the safer she is.

That vow I can keep to Nash.

"Look." Sire throws his arm around me. "I'll give them both five rounds with you. Nash gets to beat your ass into oblivion first. Then Loch. Oh, and then Mom. She'll fucking kill you. But let not your hearts be troubled. Believe in God; believe also in me. I'm here for you, brother. I'll help you fix your fucking mess, literally. Just make me the same promise one day."

"Why, holy fucker. Who'd you fuck? And you get a hall pass if it was Katya because I don't care."

It makes him chuckle. "I never touched Katya. Only for

her initiation. But if I touch Ruby when it's her turn to be tested?"

"I'll cut your dick off and boil it in holy water."

He smirks like the Devil. "Ah, but dear brother, my big dick would only rise again."

He makes me laugh, and I need it. "Fuck off, Sergei."

AFTER OUR MEETING AT DELTA'S, WHERE I GET AN EARFUL from the Queen of Snark, Vale Monroe, and the biggest confirmation that she will indeed be Nash's queen one day soon, I'm emboldened to talk to *my* queen.

Sire turns one way to go home to Wren, and I turn another to go home to Ruby.

I've trusted her with so much already. I can trust her with this. Right? She won't think I'm a perv or a predator?

If I tell her I had sex with my best friend's daughter, my goddaughter, and took her virginity because she asked me to ... Ruby will be *wonderful* with it.

Yeah, I'm wide awake.

I can smell the shit I'm shoveling, too.

But I have to do it. I'll tell Ruby and stand in her wildfire until it's burned out, and we move on.

Like Sire said: Believe.

It's an enchanting walk from Delta's to my home. Jasmine perfumes the air. The church bells ring with seven chimes. Pink azalea petals fall from their blooms, fluttering by on sidewalks where strangers say, "Hello."

I like this city.

My mother chose it as our new home because she's a history buff. She said if a city like Charleston can go from one with an evil past of trafficking enslaved people, into a city of churches, hope, and freedom, then maybe we had a chance here, too. Maybe it would be the last place my father would look for us.

It puts me in a pensive mood.

Then, a hopeful one.

Yes, then a little romantic when I spot purple lilacs blooming in my neighbor's flower box.

Sorry, Mrs. Aiken. I snap a flower stem off. *I'm trying to woo my woman.*

I feel seventeen again, about to ask a girl to prom, though I never did, as I reach to unlock my iron gate...

And find it unlocked.

What the fuck?

I race to the front door. It yawns, eerie and wide-open, with Sparky at the threshold, yowling because...

Ruby's gone.

CHAPTER NINETEEN
RUBY

"Turn around, you preppy prick in a bow tie. Come on. Let me get a good shot of you."

I aim my phone and pinch the screen to zoom in on the crowd gathered at the bus stop on Meeting Street.

From where I sit in the window of a corner bar across the road, I can scan the crowd of familiar faces waiting for the bus. Some of them work at Luca's hotel. Some I know from years of riding the bus, too.

I can easily spot who doesn't belong. Who I told to meet me at the bus stop so I could pay his bribe.

While Axel was gone all day, I got the text we were waiting for. It demanded one hundred thousand dollars, or a video clip of me "having an affair with my boss would be sent to my husband."

Did I bother troubling Axel's big, sexy brain with this small excursion?

Nah. He's got enough on his mind.

This is my mission. I'm not stupid enough to meet the man in person. I just need a picture of his face so that Grant can scan it and determine which of the three owners of the rental chalet is filming and extorting the guests.

It's obviously this preppy fucker.

Typical.

I don't trust men in seersucker suits. Okay, I don't trust *most* men, but any man with whales on his tie can blow my hole.

I hate them.

This is the man bribing Nick, Brayton, and the daughter of the owner of Delta's. This man, shifting nervously in his loafers, is the one targeting gay pro athletes.

A green city bus lumbers through the intersection, breaking in front of its stop and blocking my view.

I sip my iced tea and wait for it to move. When it does, my target is gone, but my mission is complete.

For now.

I signal my server so I can pay for my she-crab soup while I turn back and watch the bustling evening sidewalk outside.

It's almost summer, and tourists crowd the city, motivating many locals to go on vacation. I'm looking forward to mine with my sisters. We'll have fun. We always do, but I've never felt this...

I'm going to miss Axel.

Yes, the arrogant, smug boss who I loved to hate. The one whose executive chair I'd lower every night after he'd leave, just to piss him off the next morning. The one who made me so mad once that I changed the notifications on his desktop to sound like Tickle Me Elmo.

Yeah, him. I'm going to miss how he holds me at night.

I meant it; I hope Axel calls me. I hope absence makes the heart grow fonder ... and feral.

God, I'm so feral for that man. He's making us wait. Okay, I'm doing it too, and my pussy is not pleased with the stand my heart is taking, and quite frankly, I'm impatient with it, too. I'm almost—

"Well, well," a deep voice mocks over my shoulder, "fancy seeing you again."

Fancy? No. I turn around to meet the smarmy eyes of John Calloway. Standing next to him in Madras shorts and a yellow polo is his lanky friend, who he's told *all* about me; I can tell by the equally smarmy grin on his face, too.

"Fancy a fuck off," I scoff before writing in a big tip on my restaurant receipt.

"Why so mad, Rubes?" John sips his beer. "My wife's not here, so we have lots to catch up on."

"No, you have an unhinged wife, and I have a life. I have nothing to say to you."

"That's fine." He jeers, "Your mouth has better talents than talking."

"And my fists would have a lot to say to your balls, too," I smile, "if you had any." I grab my purse and phone, jolting to my feet. "Now, step aside. Life is short and so is your dick and I have other places to be."

He blocks my path. "You weren't complaining about my dick in high school. You were moaning on it and begging for more, so we gave you two."

"And yet," I bat my eyelashes, "I was still unfulfilled. But, hey, that's what I get for starting with the trial size."

"Damn, she's feisty." John's friend stares at my cleavage, barely revealed by my belted black shirtdress. "I bet she loves to have all that pride fucked right out of her."

It's instant, the spike of my pulse. The recognition of a predator. The pure disgust that floods my veins.

"Is your ass jealous of the amount of shit your mouth talks?" I try to push past them. "Because you couldn't fuck a hole in the ground if you fell in it."

But they don't move, and for the first time, I'm thankful for my high heels. I stomp on John's foot, stabbing my spiky heel into his Sperry loafer, and he yelps as I shove through their barrier.

In quick strides, I push through the bar's double doors, my heart racing like my steps down the sidewalk. With a glance over my shoulder, my stomach knots, spotting them. They're following me with lecherous scowls. They're after me.

I whip out my phone, thumbing through my contacts for SPITTING COBRA. He'll be furious with me, but I don't care right now.

With one ring, Axel answers, "I'm right behind you."

Relief floods me. "I've never been so thankful for your stalking."

"There's a graveyard on your left, just a half block up. Lure them there, and we'll take care of it."

"We?"

"Kings protect their queens, Wildfire. Don't ever doubt it."

A graveyard is always nearby in a city with over four hundred churches. This one is tucked behind an iron fence under a palm canopy, shadowing a neat row of weathered headstones dating back two hundred years.

"Kind of kinky," John sneers with his friend, stalking behind me through the open iron gate, "but whatdoyasay, Rubes? A threesome in a cemetery? I'm game."

With no fear, I turn and confront my predators. I let John approach. I let him reach out to fondle my breast before—

"No, Calloway, you're dead."

They whip around to face the ferocious wall of Axel, seething with his vow, and ... *that's not Grant*. But it looks just like him. Maybe just a smidge cuter, sweeter, sexier.

Oh, that's Jace—the big teddy bear who bashes skulls.

Good god, these brothers won gold medals in the

Olympic gene pool. Their father might be the world's deadliest asshole, but unfortunately, he's got to look like a *gigachad*.

Translation for all over fourteen: the ultimate man. Hot. Masculine. Muscular.

But they double down with the Mafia swagger, too. And I know how hot—sorry, Axel—how *stunning* their mother is.

Their beauty is distracting from the murderous show about to happen.

"What the..." John falters at the menacing sight of Axel. "What are you doing..." But he catches on quickly, throwing up his hands. "Hey, man. We were just having some fun with her."

Without a word, Jace drops a black hood over the other man's face and covers his mouth, muffling his shouts.

I look behind them, through the ivy-laced gate, to see if there are witnesses, but it's a quiet side street. I'm the only one watching as Axel muscles his way toward John, backing him into the deep shadows of the church, and Jace follows with his captive.

"Fun with her?" Axel snarls. "You dare to touch *my* queen? To even fucking *speak* to her?"

He pulls out a black tactical knife from his right front pocket, its automatic blade snapping with a razor-sharp reveal.

"Scream, and you die. Let me have a little *fun* with you, and you live." Axel trails the dagger's tip across John's neck, drawing a trickle of blood. "What's it going to be, Calloway?"

"Cameras." John glances around. "You can't do this. There are cameras everywhere."

"Not here, princess," Jace mocks. "This ain't our first knife party."

"But... but..." John trembles, "But I didn't even touch her."

"Oh, but you *did*." Axel towers over him. "And then you

shamed her for doing exactly what *you* did. For wanting what *you* wanted. For being curious like *you* were. You know, for such a wealthy man, you can't afford that double standard." He presses the dagger's tip to John's cheek under his shaking eye. "And you were about to assault her just now. That's not a double standard, Johnny-boy, that's deadly in my book."

In a slow, calculated cut, Axel pierces John's flesh, dragging the blade down his cheek while John whimpers, and I stand, shocked. Not horrified. Shocked at how I'm not appalled by what I see.

No, I want to applaud.

Maybe I'm not civilized. Maybe I'm too country. Maybe the only justice poor people like me get is vigilante justice, and it feels good.

In seconds, Axel leaves a weeping gash down John's face. It'll leave a scar. A permanent warning.

From his left pocket, Axel reveals a small, white paper packet. When I read the label, I see the beast Axel warned me about.

But unlike the nights with my stepfather, I don't want to run from Axel. I want to stay, right here, admiring him.

"You know the saying 'salt in a wound,' Johnny-boy?" Axel even sounds evil. "We say it now as an idiom for excruciating pain. And it is. Trust me, my father taught me well."

Blood drips down John's cheek, staining the blue cardigan draped over his shoulders. I glance down and note the wet stain on his Madras shorts, too.

Axel's made him piss his pants.

"But it originated as a medicinal practice," Axel keeps lecturing, and it's the first one I've ever enjoyed. "It cleanses a wound." He tsks, "But, oh, Johnny-boy, let me tell you. It burns like the fire of hell. It's a helluva price to pay for healing. So tell me..."

With his teeth, Axel rips the salt packet open. "How

many girls and women have you hurt? Other than *mine*, how many?"

"I... I..." Blood pools at the corner of John's blubbering mouth. "I haven't ever—"

"Don't fucking lie to me," Axel fumes. "Predators are made, not born. You were raised entitled. You were taught women are objects you can use and abuse. You became delusional about their desire. You think they *want* you when they actually fucking *hate* you. I was born to a man like you, so fucking say it. *How? Many?*"

Tears well in my eyes. Not for John's temporary suffering. But for Axel's. For his life.

To be born to a monster. Raised by a monster. Abused by a monster. And to be half a monster.

But Axel has a heart. The purest heart and mine breaks at the pain he's endured. His mother and brothers, too.

"I don't know," John quavers. "Only one. Maybe two. But she wanted it and—"

"That equates to eight, maybe ten." Axel pours the salt into John's gaping wound before slamming his palm against John's bloody mouth, stifling his scream. "And they didn't *want* it," Axel snarls. "They didn't want *you*. Because a real man knows. He waits. He asks. He gives, and he never takes. He doesn't hurt a woman, you fucking pathetic piece of shit. Stare in the mirror and know that's what you are."

John's screams turn into snotty tears.

And still, I'm not appalled.

The only regret I feel is for his victims. I guess I was lucky. If I had said no to him that afternoon, would my choice have been taken by the crime, too?

That's what makes me sick. The thought that a man like John ever touched me. There are so many like him, and Axel can't punish them all. But he tries...

"Now, I'm going to take my hand away from your mouth

so you can apologize to my queen." He pushes John, "Are you ready to act like a man for the first time?"

Frantically, John nods.

"Atta boy." Axel slowly pulls his bloody hand away. "You may speak to her, then never speak of us again, you or your little boy over there, or it won't be a cut next time. It'll be a kill."

I glance at Jace, easily wrangling the other man into submission.

Jace catches my shocked stare and winks, assuring me. He's super cute, and I fight my smile before swinging my eyes back to the threat of Axel. But I don't fear him. No, that's not this warm rush of emotions in my veins for him.

"I...," John stammers, "I'm sorry, Ru... Ru... Ru..."

Axel smacks the back of John's head. "Cat got your tongue?"

"I'm sorry, Ruby," John rushes. "I'm sorry for high school. I'm sorry for what I said. For what I did. And for Jessica being a bitch. And I'm sorry for today."

"...*and*." Axel twirls his knife. "Don't stop now, Johnny-boy. Cleanse thy soul."

"And... and..." John wavers, so Axel cocks a brow. "And I won't ever do it again. And I won't tell anyone about this. And..." he gulps, "and I'll donate a million dollars—" Axel smacks his skull again. "Five million dollars to a women's charity. And—"

"Enough." Axel points his bloody knife toward the gate. "Shut the fuck up and leave."

John hesitates, gesturing toward his squirming friend. "But what about...?"

Jace laughs. "I'll let Lankenstein go one minute after you leave. Best do it now."

Without glancing back, John runs out of the graveyard,

turning right, then left, as if he doesn't care where; he just wants to get the hell out of here.

"Now, I'm going to take your little pillowcase off." Jace engulfs the man, binding him with only one hulking arm wrapped around him. "And you're going to walk straight ahead, not look back, have a shitty night, and a horrible memory. But first..."

With a brutal punch, Jace hammers his beefy fist down over the guy's groin, making him grunt, double over, and dangle like a whining noodle in Jace's grasp.

"If I ever hear of you hurting a woman," Jace vows, "I'll cut it off, fry it up, and feed it to you. Shake your head if you think I'm lying."

The guy stiffens like a board.

"Good boy." Jace pats his head before ripping the pillow-case off of it. Then he smacks his ass. "Now, run along."

The guy obeys, grabbing his junk, whimpering with a limp out of the graveyard, turning right, and we don't correct his direction.

Axel sucks his teeth before swinging his glare my way. "Are you okay? Did he hurt you?"

"I'm okay." I swoon, "Thank you."

Axel shakes his head. "Wildfire, I swear, I'm going to—"

"I'm Jace." He offers his bear paw for me to shake. "And my brother's rude. It's nice to meet *you*...?"

His voice trails off for my name.

"Reacher." I shake his hand. "I mean... Ruby. Yeah, Ruby. That's my name. Sorry. You just look like that beefy actor on the show, but cuter and—"

Axel rolls his eyes. "Not this again."

"Nice to meet you, Ruby." The beard. The eyes. The lips. Jace looks like Axel's brother, with ink creeping up his neck and over his hand, too, but like Grant, he favors his mother.

So, Axel must favor his father. Not only in the face but with his ferocity.

"We good?" Jace asks Axel.

"Yeah, man." Axel nods. "Thanks."

"Can I buy you dinner to thank you?" I offer Jace.

One, because he seems sweet, almost to the point of loneliness. I just get the vibe from him. Two, I don't want to be alone with Axel. Not yet. I know I'll get a spanking for this, and like it way too much. And three...

I love this.

There's something about Axel, his brothers, and their world that doesn't feel like a trap. Not anymore. It feels like a treasure. It feels like I don't ever want to leave.

Even on my vacation tomorrow.

"Thanks, Ruby." Jace smiles warmly. "I'll take a rain check. I promise. But I have a date with a gallery opening."

"You mean *at* a gallery opening?" Axel sounds intrigued.

"No, I mean *with* an opening." Jace tucks in his starched white shirt. "They feature photography, and I never miss a show."

Axel and his paintings. Jace and his photography. Sire and his fashion. Nash and his numbers. I know Nick's into drawing, and I bet Grant's into woodworking. I'm not sure, but I'd guess Loch is into gardening.

Either way, these beasts are ruthless yet cultured, making me more curious about their world.

Politely, Jace pecks my cheek before leaving me to walk home with Axel. I'm expecting a lecture or for him to punch a window or roar like a lion at any moment.

But he's silent, so I fill it.

"I got pictures of the man bribing Nick and Zar. He texted me today and tried to bribe me, too, so I set up the drop to find out who he is. It was for *our* mission."

For three long blocks, Axel's quiet until we stop in front

of his iron gate, and he gently touches the small of my back. "Don't do that again. I checked my app and watched the video of you grabbing your phone and purse. You left so fast that you left the door open behind you and..."

The look on his face is haunted. It's new to me. "Did you think I *left* you?"

"I didn't know what to think. You didn't leave a note, call, or text." He swallows. "Ruby, I'll never trap you, but I must protect you. You need to tell me where you go, and hopefully, I can go with you and—"

That's so sweet, but...

"Wait. How did you know where I was? How were you only a half block behind me?"

"I tracked your location using your phone."

"How did you unlock my—"

"I watched you enter your code. Some stalking habits die hard, but I don't regret it, and tonight is exactly why. I saw where you were, and Jace was the closest king I could summon."

"Don't you think you should've asked me? Maybe I would've said you could track my location instead of you being sneaky about it."

"Would you have said yes?"

"No."

He laughs. "See. Wildfire, you can make it easy or make it hard, but either way, I'm protecting you."

I want to bark back. I want to fight with him, loving our tension. We thrive on it, but not now.

Not when Axel wears blood on his hands, and it was for me.

While he unlocks his gate, I start unbuttoning my dress. It makes him arch a brow, shadowing me to the front door. With a *beep*, my thumbprint opens it.

Once we're in his kitchen, I whip around and yank his golden tie, pulling his lips to mine for a hungry kiss.

His starving moan is instant. He cups my face, soaring the heat between us, his kiss as ravenous as mine.

"Thank you, Stanley the Stalker, for protecting me." I nip his bottom lip and reach down...

"Now, let your queen thank her king."

CHAPTER TWENTY
RUBY

"Fuck, Ruby."

Axel shudders when I squeeze his erection, trailing my lips down his neck, sucking and biting his flesh.

He lets me unbutton his starched shirt, his pecs heaving with anticipation. I kiss them and glide my tongue over his satiny, inked flesh to suck his nipple, gently biting it, too.

I make him groan before he fists my hair. "You think I forgot?" He tugs with the perfect pressure. "You think I forgot you were a bad girl today?"

"Let me make it up to you."

"Make it up to me?" He smirks. "No, you're going to let me punish you."

I knew he'd do this. And this is me, wondering what else I can do to get in trouble again.

"Bend over my kitchen table and lift your dress," he orders, and I obey.

Pressing my body against the cool wood, I rest my cheek on it and tug my dress up.

"Pull your panties down," he orders, standing behind me. "And give me a safe word."

"Michael," I answer, dragging my panties to my thighs.

"What?" He breaks his Dom role, sounding shocked.

"Michael," I insist. "That's my safe word because that's *not* who you are. This is who you are, Axel, and this is who I am for you. Punish me for being bad, for not letting you protect me, and please, my king," I beg, "don't ever stop."

"Don't ever stop?" His hand caresses my ass. "Oh, Wildfire, we're just getting started."

With a delicious smack, he spanks my ass, and I gasp. He smacks my other cheek a bit harder, and I cry out. He does it three more times, alternating cheeks, and the pain is instant but quickly chased away by the slick lust pooling between my thighs.

"I'll go easy, my queen." He smooths his big hand over my stinging flesh. "I'll go easy until you want more. Until you like it harder."

"I can take it," I rasp. "I want it."

"But I can't. I can't hurt you. Because..." His hands cup my ass, possessively pulling my cheeks apart. "Fuck, look at you, Ruby." For a long moment, he stares, and desire explodes through my veins, so exposed to him, so open to him. "You have no idea what I can do to you. What I *want* to do to you."

I gasp when I feel his spit land on my puckered hole, slowly rolling in a drip to my waiting pussy.

"Tell me, my king," I sigh against the table. "What do you want to do to me?"

"Everything." His finger glides through his spit, over my ass, and between my folds. "I want to chase you, catch you, and fuck you like an animal. It'll be savage, and we'll love it."

Slowly, he rims my wet entrance, making me tremble before his fingertip finds my clit.

He teases it and leans down, pressing his body over mine, his lips to my ear. "I want to fuck you in front of my brothers.

I want to fill your sassy mouth, your pretty pussy, and your tight ass with my cum. I want to show them how I finally found my queen. How you're *our* queen." He pinches my clit. "Is that what you want, Ruby?"

"Yes," I sigh. "Please, Axel. Please, make me your queen."

"Stay very still for me. Obey me."

His other hand, the one covered in dried blood from defending my honor, cups the back of my head, gently holding me, trapped against the table, while his hand between my thighs starts shamelessly fucking me.

Two of his fingers pump into my slick entrance while another dominates my clit, making wanton moans crawl up my throat.

For minutes, Axel holds me down like this, praising, "Mmm. Such a good girl." It's hot and humbling as he probes, pleasing my pussy while I'm passive, greedily taking whatever he gives me and mewling for more.

"You're soaking my hand," he coaxes. "You love it when your king plays with your wet pussy, don't you?"

"Yes, my king." I feel so lewd and loved; he's going to make me come. "I'll be a good girl for you. I want you in my pussy, my mouth, my ass. Please, Axel, make me taste you. Make me fuck you and—"

"Fuck, Ruby," he sighs. "Fuck, baby, I can't wait any more. Do it. Taste me."

Gently, he pulls his hands away and tugs me to stand. Turning me around, he grabs the open lapels of my shirtdress and rips the remaining buttons open.

"Take it off," he demands. "Take it all off for me and sit in your chair."

I shrug my dress off my shoulders, letting it puddle around my feet while I unclasp my bra and fling it across the room. Shimmying out of my panties, I keep my eyes locked on Axel's.

They're fiery ice while he commands, "Keep your heels on and sit on your chair. Spread your legs, and let me watch you play with your pussy while you suck my cock."

"Yes, my king."

Desire melts my muscles, my bones turning liquid with it as I settle on the kitchen chair before him.

He reaches down and lifts my hand, cupping it over the thick erection in his pants. "Whose cock is this?"

"Yours, my king."

"Try again, my queen." He traces his bloody thumb over my bottom lip. "*Who* do I belong to?"

In one moment, Axel's feral. In another, he's ferocious. Always, he's possessive and protective. But right now, he's open and giving...

And mine.

"Me, my king. You belong to me."

"That's right," he urges, unfastening his pants and dragging his zipper down. "This is yours."

As he reaches into his boxers, I lick my lips, relishing the reveal of what's mine, jutting so hard and swollen before me. The steel jewelry gleaming above his thick shaft traps my stare.

"Do you like it?" he asks.

"I love it," I sigh.

"This is the first ring I'll give you, Ruby. Kiss it. You're the only woman who ever will."

I'm surprised he hasn't let another do it, but I obey. I want to. I'm drawn to Axel's flesh. To his piercing. To his scent: bergamot, cold water, musk, and man. His dark hair is trimmed around his jewelry. It tickles my lips as I close my eyes and kiss his warm, metal ring—the one designed to please his partner.

The reverent moan from Axel as he sinks his bloody hand into my hair, pressing my kiss to his flesh, unlocks something inside me. Something I've never given to a man. I don't know what it is, but it's his.

In a daze, I lift my stare, and he surprises me. Bending down, his finger lifts my chin, his lips taking mine in a kiss that ignites from sensitive to salacious, his hunger obvious and impatient.

"Now." He pulls away, fisting my hair. "Wrap those stubborn lips around my cock, and let me finally fuck your throat."

But I defy him with a smirk.

Staring up at him, I slowly drag my tongue under his base, up his long shaft, over his turgid veins to his swollen crown, and lave over his sensitive tip until I make him lurch when I flick his salty, dripping slit.

"*Fuucckk*, dirty girl," he groans. "You want to play? You want to tease my cock, Wildfire? Go ahead."

I do. I want this power. I want to give Axel this pleasure. I feel it now: the warmth of his protection, the pride in his possession. I don't want this to end too fast.

I stare up at him and let my drool glaze his tip before I gently brush my wet, puckered lips over it, slowly kissing then gently sucking his crown.

His eyelids drop, his blood-stained grip on my hair tightening. "You're so fucking beautiful with my cock in your mouth, Ruby. With my tip sliding over those plump, bratty lips of yours. Do you like finally being my good girl and sucking me off?"

I moan, my eyelids fluttering as I take my first inch of his length, his salt blessing my tongue for the first time.

"Oh, *yes,* you do. Such a good girl," he praises. "Look at you. You like sucking your king's cock, don't you?" I moan again, and his lips part, relishing my obedience before he orders, "Touch your pussy, baby. Play with your pretty pussy and show me how much you love my cock fucking your mouth."

I wrap one hand around his base, pumping his shaft while my other sinks between my spread thighs. My pussy is soaked, aching, and wanting him while I rub my hard clit, moaning with his mass in my mouth.

"Oh, fuck yes, Ruby."

Slowly, Axel thrusts his hips, seeking more of my mouth. Lording over me, he looks too hot, he teases me too well, he tastes too good, finally demanding, "Now, be a good girl and sink your fingers into your wet pussy while you take every inch of my cock fucking your throat."

I start slipping into the orgasm he coaxes. I plunge my fingers into my sex, my palm thrilling my excited clit. I let him watch me take his length, as much as I can, relaxing my throat, and letting him fuck it as sweet tears weep from the corner of my eyes.

Axel groans, the ice in his eyes igniting, fiery and feral, "Such a good fucking girl. Suck it, baby, and play with that pussy." His pleasure looks so intense, so goddamn breathtaking that my orgasm hits me fast. I shudder, moaning with him in my mouth, my cunt and body clenching so hard, I have to fight not to clamp my jaw and bite him.

"Oh fuck, yes." He cups my head, his hips starting to thrust harder. "Oh fuck, Ruby, you're coming with my cock in your throat. Yes, baby, you're going to swallow every drop of me."

I'm ready. I'm willing. I want this. I moan for it and feel like I can come again, and he's about to, but...

A loud *YOWL* echoes through his house.

I freeze, and so does Axel, our locked stares widening in shock, in realization.

"Sparky," he rasps. "Oh fuck."

I pull back, my spit webbed from his tip to my lips, my breath huffing, "She's in labor."

He throws his chin up, roaring, "You've got to be fucking kidding me!" Letting go of me, he clenches his fists like he needs to punch something. Not me. Not ever. I trust him.

But Axel looks like he's going to blow a gasket, or blow something; he obviously needs to.

"Okay," he groans with the most frustration I've ever heard from a man. "Okay, goddammit, it's our cat and my karma."

It's so frustrating; it's funny.

I fight my giggle while he winces, wedging his angry erection back into his pants and ripping his zipper up with a muttered curse before he helps me rise, naked and in heels, my body tingling with the need to release, too…

But not now.

I run up the stairs, and Axel follows. Rushing into his bedroom, we find Sparky yowling with low grunts in the corner of her box on the floor.

"I got her." Axel drops to his knees, gently petting her before turning to me. His eyes brim with the hottest storm of frustration, humor, love, and excitement. "Get dressed, Wildfire. We're about to be parents."

I dash into my room and throw on jean shorts and a T-shirt, giggling when I overhear Axel lecture Sparky, "Listen here, pussy. Tomorrow, we're going to have a *long* talk about cockblocking and blue balls."

Quickly, I return to his side, and he takes my hand, tugging me down on the rug beside him.

"Should we take her to the vet?" he worries, carefully soothing her.

But I pause, letting the memory of this terrifying beast with a blood-stained hand, who tortures with knives and salt, disappear while I let the sight of this beautiful man, who cares so deeply, invade my heart.

"She's got this. We're made to do this. Just..." I cup my hand over his. "Just love her ... and don't leave."

He meets my eyes, his pause poignant. "I'll never leave you." The lump in my throat is sudden and sweet. "Do you want this?" He wraps his hand, caked in dried blood, over mine. "Life? Love? Lots of kids?"

"Lots of girls," I answer softly.

"God, that'd be my dream." His eyes light up. "Four of my little princesses? They'd worship me, be sweet daddy's girls, and never leave my sight."

"Clearly," I chuckle, "you weren't raised around girls." But I can see Axel spoiling his. "And one boy," I add, squeezing his hand. "A dark prince with icy blue eyes that'll happily trap my heart forever."

We can't say more.

We don't need to.

Axel reaches for my neck, wrapping his warm hand around it, and pulling me into a kiss. We can feel it, right here between us, and it's so beautifully overwhelming until Sparky yowls in pain, ripping our stare to her as the first tiny creature slips into this world.

For six hours, we watch between naps. I rest my head on Axel's lap. He plays with my hair, lulling me to sleep until we switch, and I do the same to him. We stay by Sparky's side until we have six grandkittens: four boys and two girls—all little golden lions.

While they nurse and Sparky sleeps, we crawl into bed as dawn blooms bright pink through the windows.

Axel pulls me to him, content to hold me as usual, but I turn around in his arms. Deeply, I kiss him, and as always, he kisses me back with more passion, more demand.

I leave his mouth, and with my lips, I memorize every

tattoo on his chest and down his flexing abs. When I tug his boxer briefs off, he groans, springing free and desperately hard for release.

I fist his base, and we don't need words or a tease this time. He lets me lavish him until he's moaning my name, fisting my hair, and pumping his hips. I try to take him, every inch I can, until he roars, his back bowing, his thighs shaking. With deep grunts, he fills my mouth with more than I can take.

I swallow what I can, but he spills over my lips, and he doesn't care.

No, it ignites his eyes. He pulls me up, gently tugging my hair until we kiss again. It's so erotic, so intimate, how he moans at the taste of him in my mouth.

Then, he's moving my body, silently lifting me and guiding me to straddle his face. He ruins my favorite race car pajama bottoms, ripping them open at the crotch seam, and I don't care.

I love it when he makes me ride his face and fist his hair, his mouth giving me what I gave him until I'm crying out, too. Until I'm coming with his name on my shaking lips, and he wants this kiss from me, as well—the flavor of us, together, in our mouths.

"I'm going to miss you," he sighs, cupping my cheeks.

"I'll miss you, too," I whisper, my throat tightening. "Protect our babies while I'm gone."

"Have them with me, Ruby." His eyes search mine. "Take my life and heart and have my future and our children."

Tears well in my eyes, gazing down at him. "Axel, are you asking me to—"

"Not yet," he insists. "Just give me hope. Tell me that no matter what, you'll be mine one day."

CHAPTER TWENTY-ONE
AXEL

"How long do we have?" I murmur, kissing Ruby's neck, then the tender spot under her ear.

"An hour." She giggles, tickled by my touch. "That's not long enough, and I need to shower."

"I needed to feed you lunch first." I wedge her against the kitchen table, wanting to spank her again. "And now…"

"And now I'm packed and ready, and you're getting me all hot in the biscuit," she sighs at my seduction. "But my sisters will be here soon, and I need to check on our kittens, then get ready. I can't fly to Greece with fuck hair."

"We didn't fuck, Wildfire." I grind into her, hard. "Not yet."

"But we did everything else and didn't sleep, and I'm not complaining, but you don't know my sister Rose. She'll drag me for looking high-key smashed and run through."

I nuzzle my forehead to hers. "I have no idea what you just said."

"Yours," she sighs. "I look like you made me yours."

"You'll wear much more of me when you're truly mine."

"Speaking of..." She glides her hands up my naked abs, making my cock hang heavy for her touch under my black pajama bottoms. "I'm wearing a lot of little dried Axel's on my tits right now, so your queen needs a shower and—"

The buzz from the button at my front gate startles us.

"Are your sisters early?"

"Never," she replies.

"Who the fuck?" I mutter, aiming for my phone on the counter. When I open the security app, checking the camera on my front gate ... dread twists the pit of my stomach.

"Who is it?" Ruby asks.

"Alena."

I feel sick. I haven't had a chance to tell Ruby yet, and I don't know why she's here.

"Does she normally stop by?"

I hear it in Ruby's voice, the doubt I'm giving her, the trust I'm gambling with.

"No," I answer honestly. "She never does, so something must be wrong."

"Oh, then let her in." She sounds relieved. "Make sure she's okay."

I press the button to open my gate before I set my phone down and turn, cupping Ruby's cheeks. Softly, I kiss her before I insist, "Go check on our kittens, then shower, and I'll speak with her outside. I'm sure it's wedding drama. Her father's probably pissing her off, and she needs me to intervene."

Ruby takes my next kiss, then rushes upstairs while I open my front door and meet Alena in my courtyard.

Violet wisteria drips from the oak, dappling the noon sun above, while a lion's head wall fountain gurgles, filling my Koi pond.

Alena's eyes shock open at my exposure. At my socked

feet, mussed hair, half-naked body and semi-hard cock in my pajamas.

"Oh shit," she gulps. "I'm sorry. I totally interrupted something, didn't I?"

"Don't worry. It's a not-fucking trend," I huff a laugh. "What's wrong?"

"Look. I'd never intrude on your life, but... You're a groomsman in *my* wedding."

"So, I've been told. Nash scheduled the fittings for our suits in a few days."

"But you can't *be* a groomsman in my wedding." Alena's tawny ponytail sways with the adamant shake of her head. "How can I stand beside Loch with you and my dad standing with him? It's like rubbing a lie in his face."

Here I go again, weaving lies to hold our lives together.

"Nash said he offered to be your fiancé's best man since his brothers can't do it," I repeat the plan Nash, Loch, and I devised. It's how we can witness Alena's wedding without her knowing everything. "And as your godfather, Nash asked me to be a groomsman, and I can't turn my best friend down."

"But it's all weird," Alena protests. "Loch said he has five brothers, and I haven't even met them yet, but he doesn't want to pick one over the other to be his best man, so he asked my dad for the honor? And my godfather, too? *You*. I swear, Loch is so trusting. He has no idea about..."

She trails off, upset.

"About us," I murmur.

I feel the weight of Ruby watching us from her bedroom window. I feel the burden of so many years and this suffocating secret. I see the tears brimming in Alena's brown eyes; she hates hurting Loch.

Tears from any queen kill me, and I need to be free, as does Alena. I will kill for her honor, but I'm tired of lying for it. I'm tired of lying to my baby brother. I heard his first cry when he was born.

"Tell him if you need to."

Alena's mouth drops open, shocked by my permission.

"I don't want you to lie to your husband. If you need to tell him about me, do it, and I'll take it like a man."

Because I need to be a man and tell Ruby. I need to tell her about Alena, about Katya, too. I need Ruby to trust that just as she has a past, I have one, too. But I want a future with her, and it starts now.

"What do you think he'll say?"

"Alena," I sigh, "I don't know. Like you said, some men only want a future with the woman they love, so they don't care about her past. But some men are jealous. They focus on her past and risk their future." Yes, I'm saying what I need to hear. "I can't tell you what your fiancé will do. But you love him, and that means he's a good man. It'll work out."

But ... I swallow the rocks in my throat ... *my baby brother will never speak to me again.*

And my best friend? *I'll lose Nash.* I'll lose the one man who always understood me.

My brothers love me, and I love them. But only Nash knows the inescapable responsibility of family. He's a father. I'm the heir. He always understood the pressure on me because he felt it, too.

"Do you think every wife tells her husband everything they did before their wedding?" Alena wonders. "Did Katya tell you?"

Come to think of it, I knew very little about Katya.

She was a blonde hurricane who blew through my life and destroyed my hope. Before her, I was a romantic. I believed in love, vows, and trust. I lost that piece of myself until I heard Ruby laugh for the first time.

Of course, it wasn't with me. It was with Helen, *at me*.

I sat in my office and overheard Ruby at her desk, laughing. I had just lectured her for thirty minutes about using commas and their effects on statutes. So, she told Helen, "Mr. Cummings can comma here and kiss my ass."

Ruby made me laugh at myself. She made my heart lighter. It's as if she found it, bruised and cold, and picked it up, and she's held it in her hand ever since.

"No," I answer Alena. "Katya didn't tell me about her past, and I didn't ask. Honestly, I didn't care."

"Because you weren't jealous?"

"No, because I wasn't possessive over her."

Ruby's the only woman I've ever wanted to possess. Not for control. For protection. For hope of a future with her.

"Loch's possessive over me, and I *like* it," Alena reasons aloud. "One time, we went to the sex club, and I wore a lace bondage hood so Ms. Faye wouldn't recognize me, and it was hot; how Loch wanted to have me ... you know ... in front of others. But he wasn't jealous. He was showing me off. How I belonged to him and..."

Yep, that sounds like my blood, baby brother, and everything I *don't* need to know about Nash's daughter. And if my mother, who's like Alena's grandmother, had caught Loch, her son, getting kinky with Alena at her club? My baby brother would be missing a pair of balls.

Sneaky fucker.

I'm kind of proud of him.

"Sorry," she winces. "TMI, but ... I get it. I get the difference between jealousy and possessiveness."

"It's okay. I get it, too."

Because that's how I feel about Ruby.

Do I want to fuck her in front of my brothers? Yes, that's my kink, my primal, possessive streak. Ruby's mine, and I want to prove my dominance. *No one else can have her.* It's in my DNA.

Do I want to offer her to another brother, to another king, so she can fully be my queen, *our* queen?

Never.

But—

"I'll wait to tell him ... *after* the wedding," Alena decides. "I know Loch has secrets to tell me, too. I can sense it. Besides, it's not a crime; I had sex before him. No big deal."

"Um, I am a very *big* deal."

I can't help it. I need to make us laugh, and Alena does, pointing to my front door. "Tell your paralegal I said hello."

"How did you—"

"Michael," Alena smiles, "it's obvious you're in love with her. And I'm happy for you. It's about time."

"It is?"

"Does she have a name?"

"Ruby."

"That's so pretty."

Yeah, I love the sound on my lips, too.

Glancing up at her window, I see her silhouette dart away. She couldn't hear us over the gurgling fountain, and all she just saw was me, talking to my goddaughter while I realized how much I've fallen so madly in love with her. With Ruby.

With Alena? She's free to tell Loch. I won't ask her to lie anymore. If she waits until after their wedding, it's her choice.

Either way, once Loch and Nash find out, I'll lose my brothers, my family.

But once I tell Ruby, will I lose her?

Fuck, how can I make her understand this? That yes, I'm secretly Alena's second king but Ruby's *my* queen.

"I'd better get going. I'm going to be late for a fitting." Alena adjusts her ponytail. "And again, sorry if I crashed your morning. It won't happen again."

Rising on her tip-toes, she pecks my cheek and turns to leave, just as she did after our night together, except I left because Alena begged me to. She never wanted me to stay.

But Ruby?

I turn toward my front door and don't want her ever to leave.

CHAPTER TWENTY-TWO
RUBY

"Arch the perkies, firecracker. Let's drive him crazy with your cherry-topped sundaes."

I laugh at Zar. "How many words for *tits* do you know?"

"Darlin'," he drawls, aiming his camera phone at me while I pose topless on my sun lounger. "A true Texan is a bottomless well of words."

"And adding to my big brother's spank bank." Nick sips an ouzo lemonade, grinning. "Axel's denied this for so long, but I knew you two were a thing."

"Not everyone knows," I remind him. "And we're not a thing. We're not official yet."

"Oh?" Nick lowers his sunglasses. "Not official? Tell that to the giant purple bouquets he's sent you every day, for six days straight since we've been here."

Here, at Luca Mercier's luxurious Mykonos hotel on the shore of the Aegean Sea. My sisters are in the spa, but I like it here on the beach, relaxing under the white umbrellas shading my cushy lounger.

Scarlett encouraged Nick to surprise Zar and join us before he starts summer training camp.

It's a sisters' vacation, and Nick and Zar fit right in. They're like our beefy brothers who don't judge when we lounge naked on the nude beach.

No, they join us.

No one recognizes Nick. American football isn't popular here, so seeing how free Nick and Zar can be with their love is heart-warming.

That's not Nick's life at home, where Grant has identified the photo I took of the preppy prick at the bus stop, the one bribing gay athletes.

His name is Blake Halstead. He's the owner, renting over ten vacation properties and sextorting countless victims. When I stood him up for our drop, he sent the video to "my boss," upping his bribe to a quarter million or he'd tell "my husband" next.

Really, Grant received the video and sent me a cute, standing ovation meme, all while Halstead's texts are irate and threatening. He wants more money, and I'm curious how far he'll go to get it.

"For every giant bouquet Axel sends me," I cup my breasts and pucker my lips, posing for Zar's camera phone, "I send him a boobie shot."

And every night, Axel calls me.

It's usually after we've been dancing at The Mercier's exclusive, bohemian beach club. The club doesn't have tacky flashing lights, making it safe for me. Rarely, they can trigger my seizures.

But here, I can dance all night. The bass still thumps in my veins while I laugh with Axel on our video chats.

He lies on his bed, surrounded by our newborn kittens, and I lie on mine, teasing him with dirty talk until we're both in pain, missing each other.

Then, he refuses to hang up on me, and I won't end our call, either, so we fall asleep together.

I had to leave too soon. We didn't really have time to say goodbye, and he didn't get to tell me why Alena showed up at his home.

That maddening feeling made me watch them talking in the courtyard. I felt guilty for doing it, though my gut told me I had to.

But all I saw was a worried Alena. She looked like a bride stressed about her wedding, and Axel looked like a godfather, able to help her with an overbearing father.

It looked perfectly innocent between them, and I felt like a pathetic, jealous fool, promising myself I'd never do it again.

I won't worry about Alena.

I trust Axel.

"I never thought I'd see the day." Zar flops on his lounger beside mine, done with our daily photoshoot. "My little firecracker is hanging up her spurs. Her Roman riding days are over."

"Roman riding?" I lather on more sunscreen.

"Like a gladiator, you stand on their backs, hold the reins, and ride two horses at once."

"Uh, reins were never involved in my threesomes."

Nick laughs. "But they will be with my brother. He'll bridle you, and be damn sure he's the only one ever riding you again."

"But..." This has been bothering me since the night Axel held me down, whispering his dark fantasies in my ear, and I moaned, sharing them. "But, if I'm going to be his officially, doesn't he have to initiate me and *offer* me to another rider?"

Why am I speaking in equestrian euphemisms? I don't know. Maybe I'm just trying to respect their secrecy. We're not alone on the beach.

"Isn't that what you did?" I ask Nick. "You let one of your brothers initiate Zar? He has a second king?" They exchange a look. "I'm sorry. I don't mean to pry. I'm just confused. I know how some of this works, but not all."

"It's alright." Zar winks. "It's for me to disclose. I'm the queen. I decide who knows."

Oh my god, I'm dying to know.

The little spy in me threatens to probe and get into trouble again. But now ... I love my trouble. I love this world, and I don't want to disrespect it.

I hold my tongue until Zar reveals, "It was beautiful. When I was initiated, I married Nick, his family, and his world. His brothers love me. They love *our* love. Men like us don't get that with every family." Nick reaches for his hand. "I was honored. I still am. There's so much more you'll learn about us, firecracker. So much you'll feel and protect and fight for."

I nod, swallowing. I didn't see that part of Wren's initiation, but I could hear it. It sounded sacred. It sounded like every soul was committed to their group bond.

"But we presented an unusual situation," Zar continues. "Of course, most queens are women. Of course," he winks, "I have more style than them all." I laugh. "The Queen and kings talked about how I could join them, and one brother said he'd be honored to be my second king. He's been with men before."

Who?

Jace?

Loch?

Grant?

The flash of images in my mind is so erotic. I have no doubt it was because I saw Wren's initiation. And if Axel initiates me like that, too? If they make me his queen officially?

"It's okay," I rush, feeling protective over everyone. "You don't have to tell me the secret."

"It's not a secret." Zar boasts, "I'm proud Sire is my second king."

Sire!

The celebrity pastor in a holy-rolling conservative town? The man who looks like he was sprung from jail then bought out a Gucci showroom? The man who breeds his young wife like a prize filly?

He's Zar's second king?

Why does that make Sire even more masculine and mysterious? Why does that make me love Wren, though we haven't really met?

This means Wren knows about Sire's sexuality and loves him. She's not threatened. She celebrates who he is and sounds just like me.

God, I want to meet the other queens. I'm sure I'll love them.

"Speaking of *your* king." Nick nods at me, answering his buzzing phone. "Sup, fuckwad?" he answers Axel, smiling, but instantly it falls, and I watch with my heart rate climbing.

"Shot?" Nick jumps to his feet in the sand. "Is he okay?"

"Shot?" I whip my worried stare to Zar. "Who?"

"Don't know," Zar replies, deadly serious. "But they've been running a dangerous mission and…"

He stops. He can't reveal more, and I get it.

Pacing, Nick listens to Axel, to whatever in the hell is happening before he says, "Yeah, she's here with me. I promise. I won't let her out of my sight."

The sweet football fucker.

That's why Nick's really here? Not to join Zar in a luxurious, LGBTQ-friendly vacation spot. No. He's here as a king, as my bodyguard. Axel assigned Nick to me, as he assigned Loch to Alena.

Why am I not surprised?

"Yeah," he says. "Here she is."

Nick hands the phone to me while I glare at him. He's busted. He knows, so he winks, looking just like Jace. Like he doesn't care. It's that whole always-protecting-his-queen thing.

"Are you okay?" It's the first thing I need to know from Axel, followed by, "Who's shot?"

"I'm fine, Wildfire." Axel sounds tired. "Just fucking obey me and stay with Nick. Promise me."

"Okay." I don't fight this anymore. "But who was shot?"

"Grant," he answers, and I grab my heart, tears immediately biting at my eyes. "But he'll be okay. He had on a vest, but it was at close range. It was a brutal impact, but he'll be out in a day or two."

"Of the hospital?"

"Yes. My mom is with him. So is his wife. He'll be fine. Just..." Axel falters. I can hear the pieces moving in his life. They match mine. "Just... It's best you're not here right now. We have a hostile on the loose; everyone's on alert until we find him again."

"Who is it? What did he do?" Axel doesn't answer, so I perk up, topless and determined. "Remember, my king. Ignorance isn't bliss in ex-Bratvaland. Give me intel if you need me to stay safe. You know I have good instincts."

He sighs, "Tell Nick he has my permission to tell you." I glance up, and Nick nods. He can hear him. "And this is more trust, Ruby," Axel adds. "More trust and more risk. It's getting deeper every day, and I have a bad feeling about it, so keep your head on a swivel. Think like my queen and stay safe."

"I promise."

Like the golden sand before me, I'm shifting. My world is changing, and I want it to. I want the storm of Axel's life to shape me into who I was meant to be.

"We'll stay together," I assure him about me, Nick, and

Zar. About my sisters, too. They're in this, though they don't know it. "We'll stay safe. Just..."

Why does my throat tighten? Why do I suddenly worry about Axel's safety when I never have before? He's always such a force. He's always so menacing and immortal, but he's not.

He can bleed. He can care. He's shown me.

"Just... stay safe, Axel. Please," I beg him. "Just stay smug and smart and safe like you always are. I trust you to."

"You *trust* me?" His tone softens from tired into something else. I can't describe it. "You finally trust me, Wildfire?"

I stare at the afternoon sun, dancing like diamonds over the cobalt ocean. Then, I glance at Zar and Nick, nestled together on their lounger, comforting each other in a time of need.

Nick holds Zar just as Axel held me, and my hand shakes. I'm worried, but my heart calms with my exhale. With my truth...

"Yes, my king. I completely trust you."

CHAPTER TWENTY-THREE
AXEL

"Lie down, you stubborn, fucking, mule."

I jolt from my chair, ready to shove Grant back on his hospital bed, but with one red lacquered fingernail, Delphine pokes Grant's pec, and he falls for her. Every time, and on his bed.

To ensure his compliance, she rewards him with an unblushing kiss, their lust obvious and not caring that we're in a hospital.

"All this passion," my mother sighs, "and still no grandchild."

I wince, feeling like I failed her, while Grant jokes, "Mom, we're not ready to lose sleep over a baby yet. Let Sire and Wren do it."

I was supposed to do it.

The heir is supposed to be the first to provide the next. But Katya never gave me that chance, and secretly, I'm relieved. I couldn't see her being the loving mother I had.

Even bruised and battered, my mother fiercely loved us. Like a lioness, she licked her wounds, held us close, and roared at anyone threatening us...

Except our father.

No one, not even her, could stop him.

Ruslan Kholodov would ruthlessly hold my youngest brother. First Jace, then Nick, then Loch. He'd grab the most vulnerable, making my mother plead through tears until she relented, and Sire or I would go with him.

He wanted us to learn, to watch him do his bloody bidding, until Sire started praying for him. Morality didn't sit well with my father, so he put his focus on me ... in every brutal way.

At least I learned how to torture, how to kill, and every time I do it, I see my father. I see my revenge and redemption. I only kill evil men like him.

"Or," Grant teases, pulling Delphine down to lie with him, "ask Axel. He's found his next queen. They can give you a *true* heir."

Even though he's shirtless, with hospital sheets tucked around his waist, and sickening bruises swell, dark and painful under the ink over his ribs, Grant's fucking with me.

I snarl, "You're supposed to keep your mouth shut."

"Oh, but he can't. He likes her." Delphine rests on Grant's chest, smiling. "He came home from your mission and told me how you found your true queen. You just need to stop playing games with her."

In her French accent, Delphine makes it sound torrid and teasing. She can't help it. But I'm not fucking around about Ruby. I'm serious and taking my time.

"Do my sons care to tell me who, or must I smack your thick skulls together?"

Mom never beat us. She didn't need to. She'd playfully smack the back of our heads or tug our earlobes until we whined and obeyed.

But with anyone else? My mother rules with an iron fist, a hellcat pistol, and a calculating mind that's a hundred steps ahead, anticipating your next moves—a skill only a survivor acquires.

She doesn't need to kill you, though she will. Wait a month, and you'll find your life in ashes and my mom smiling with a hot, gold lighter in her hand.

"Aleksi." My mother rarely says my birth name. We never speak Russian. We've perfected our American accents, some of us sounding Southern, too. We blend in. We survive. We thrive, though occasionally, my mother reminds me that though I'm King, she's The Queen. "Who is she?"

In an ivory Chanel bouclé dress and her long dark hair in an elegant twist, my mother sits in the chair beside me, demanding, expecting. She looks like royalty, because she is. The daughter of a wealthy oligarch, a descendant of the last Tsar of Russia, she became the stolen princess, the young queen to the evilest man. No matter how my father made her bleed, blue blood thunders in her veins.

She raised us with the same nobility.

"You've met her," I confess.

Do I keep things from my mom? Sure. I'm a grown-ass man into kinky shit.

But lie to her face? Never.

She arches a groomed brow while Grant stirs the pot. "She's beautiful. All fiery hair, fearless and feisty, and she doesn't put up with his shit. He can't bat his baby blues at her and make her swoon. She's a badass."

Oh, but I can spank her ass and make her obey.

I smirk at the memory stirring my cock.

"I've met this woman?" my mother asks.

"The cowgirl at the club." Finally telling her about Ruby does something to my chest. It's warm. It's promising. "She was the one, wearing a blonde wig, who you tried to help that night."

"The luxe night?" Mom nods, remembering, "But she was upset. Was it with you?"

Oh shit. Don't let my mom find out we've wronged a woman.

"No, Ruby wasn't mad at me. She was stalking me." Mom smiles, impressed. "Because I was stalking her. She works for me and knows about us. And now, I'm trying to protect her and go slow, but diarrhea-of-the-mouth over there is talking shit, so ... so much for that."

Delphine giggles and Grant beams like *Ain't love grand.*

"Where is she?" Instantly, my mom worries. "We have that sex-trafficking psycho on the loose now. He tried to shoot my little baby," she points at Grant, ignoring that he's six-foot-five, "and now he can go after everyone we love." She points at me. "Everyone *you* love."

"She's secure. She's with Nick and Zar." I love that my mom immediately protects whoever we love. "She's on vacation in Greece with them. Turner can't get her there."

"I want Turner's blood," my mother seethes. "I want him chained and bleeding. And I want every man who's ever bought from him. They'll suffer like they've made so many suffer and—"

"Yes, my Queen."

I understand.

My mother never got justice. She got freedom. She got us, but she lost the love of her life doing it. Still, she fights for others trafficked as she was.

The phone in my pocket chimes. It's Nash calling. TWO reads across my screen and I answer, "Yeah?"

"We'll stay at the marina until this system passes." Nash updates me on his status, hiding out on his boat in stormy weather with Vale Monroe. They're the ones exposed to Turner. Turner knows their identities, not ours.

Even while we held him captive after we trapped him,

luring him to us through a gambling golf tournament, Turner saw no faces and heard no names but Nash and Vale's. It's unfortunate, but by design.

We cover our faces, use numbers instead of names, and hide our properties behind anonymous LLCs—I make sure of that. We all have second and third hideouts.

And if we need to, any king will take the heat for others. That's the sacrifice Nash is making for us now, so we've got his back.

"And yes," Nash sighs, "I've found my queen."

I smile, relieved. "Told you."

I've watched Nash's secret love for Vale Monroe deepen. For years, she was just his daughter's best friend. Alena and Vale are close. But when Vale matured into a hot, snarking spitfire, giving Nash unrelenting shit? And *me*, I might add. He finally saw her as a woman, as his.

He's killed for her, and now, he's claiming her.

The irony doesn't escape me; Nash found his queen, and I found mine. Neither of us would ever share our queens, yet we know we'll have to.

I don't gloat about it.

I understand him.

"And you've found yours, too, you sneaky piece of shit." And Nash understands my silence. "Who is she?"

Too quickly, this is getting out of control. Grant, Sire, Jace, and now my mom know about Ruby. And Nash? I'd never lie to him, but I won't overwhelm him. He's got enough going on, keeping Vale safe and protecting Alena, too.

"Grant's in the clear." I change the subject. "No internal damage, just some wicked bruising." I glance at my mom and speak of Turner. "We're going to rip the last pieces of that fucker apart when we find him."

"We did so much damage already," Nash replies, "he could've drowned."

Nash took one of Turner's eyes out for disrespecting Vale. I let him, and then Jace, Grant, and I took turns interrogating Turner for intel—for his hideout and associates. We held him captive on my boat, and we were breaking him until...

"We don't operate on luck," I tell Nash while I glare at my brother. "*Clearly.* I can't believe Grant let his guard down."

Grant rolls his eyes while Nash defends him, "He feared we were losing our asset. We always check a pulse."

He's right. But that was a close call, Grant, getting shot at point-blank with his gun when Turner grabbed it while Grant checked his pulse. Thank god, my brother was wearing a vest.

I can't imagine losing a brother or a queen.

"Alena?" I ask. It's instinct. "The other queens?"

"Secure," Nash answers for his daughter and Vale. "The Queen?" he asks.

I nod at my brother, his wife, and my mom, hearing every word. "With Grant. And she wants blood."

"She'll get it," Nash promises, ending our call.

Tucking my phone in my pocket, I toss my chin up, blinking at the fluorescent lights, my heart torn in two.

I'm loyal to my family. I want to be here, protecting them. We have a vengeful predator on the loose.

But I *need* to be with Ruby.

Six days without her have been hell. Our calls and kittens are some comfort. But then she gets Zar to send me the hottest shots of her lying topless on a Grecian beach and I fucking die.

Hunger like I've never felt pulses through my veins. Like a starving man, the meal of Ruby is all I can think about. Like a dying man in a desert, she's my water, my survival. That's this maddening instinct to find her, to have her, to consume every inch of her and...

"Go." My mother's voice turns my heavy stare to her. "We're fine." She smiles. "Go get your queen."

"But we have kittens."

Shit.

The words fall from my mouth before I can stop them. Like a doting dad, I can't leave them, and Grant laughs. "Our family needs grandkids, not kittens, you pussy-whipped fuck."

I bark, "Says the man so pussy-whipped for his French wife that you cream for French fries."

"Hey!" Our mother glares. "Never forget where you came from. Don't you dare use that word as an insult. Honor it. Honor your women, or we'll smack your delicate balls."

Delphine laughs, Grant shuts up, and I shake my head, chuckling.

"I'll take care of the kittens," Delphine offers.

"Hell no," Grant huffs. "Then you'll want to keep one."

"And we will." Delphine trails her long fingernail down his chest. "Honor your queen, remember?"

My mother nods, surveying the proof of how she's raised us, then she reaches for my hand to calm me because I want to punch the shit out of my little brother.

Do I love him? Always. Do I care he's injured? Yes. Will I still beat the snot out of him? Hell, yes. We fight. We kill. We're alpha as fuck and will prove it.

But for our queens?

My mother squeezes my clenched fist, and I remember ... we were raised to love, too.

CHAPTER TWENTY-FOUR
RUBY

"WHAT DO YOU MEAN WE'RE STAYING ANOTHER WEEK?" I spew baklava flakes, challenging Scarlett, "We fly to Bali tomorrow."

"Change of plans. We stay in Greece," Scarlett answers, rubbing her belly under our dinner table, and I raise an eyebrow.

"Fine by me," Rose chimes in. "I met a lipstick last night. She's staying here all week and wants to smash, so I'm here for it."

"And that DJ is swole and giving me life." Cherry elbows Rose. "Think I can pull him?"

"He's totally DTF," Rose answers, and Scarlett cuts me a confused look.

It's like our little sisters are speaking a foreign language, but I'm so used to Rose and Cherry, I translate, "Rose found a femme pussy that wants to play and Cherry wants to spin on muscular DJ dick."

Nick and Zar laugh, but I clock how they're too relaxed, when I know Zar was excited about Bali. It's like they're behind this change of plans, and once they got Scarlett on board, I bet it was a done deal.

Usually, Scarlett would be like me, stubborn and fearless. We'd be in Bali tomorrow, *so...?*

I catch Zar sneaking a look at Scarlett. They've grown so close subbing for Luca, and...

"Oh, my god," I huff, my detective brain sounding the alarm. "He *didn't.*"

"He did." Scarlett doesn't lie to me. "Michael Cummings asked to meet with Luca and me, and he brought his friend, Sire Rutledge. And I don't know what kind of dangerous shit you're into at work, but I know that your boss is in love with you and asked us to protect you."

Axel went behind my back and risked exposing his true identity to meet with my family about my safety?

That's how much he cares?

That's how much danger I'm in?

It's my turn to cut Nick a secret look, and like an ex-Bratva prince, he subtly nods back, confirming my deadly suspicion.

My sisters can know about some of my new life, but not all of it. I understand, but I'm not used to lying to them—not ever —and it's awkward. My silence hangs heavy in the summer air.

"So, we stay here." Zar saves me. "Tomorrow, we'll sail to Delos on a day trip. The next day, Santorini and..."

Zar makes the most of Axel's command that we stay here in Greece, where he, Nick, and Scarlett can keep me safe.

The old me would feel trapped and angry. I'd want to run.

The new me feels ... like I wish Axel were here.

But I make the most of it, too. After dessert, we go up to Luca's lavish penthouse suite with five bedrooms, and I disappear into mine to change for the club.

Even with the sun down for hours, the nights are warm,

and the dance floor is hot. I tie the halter top of my white, gauzy minidress in place. It's paper-thin and toga-style, but I don't bother with heels. The dancefloor is smooth, with wooden planks scattered with occasional sand, and perfect for dancing barefoot until dawn.

For hours, we do. Dancing replaces my morning runs, relieving my stress. I smile with sweaty bodies pressed against mine.

I love seeing Rose happy and dancing with a hot brunette. Cherry is flirting with the DJ. He's invited her to stand with him, showing off his deck of mixers.

Scarlett lounges in the VIP section, catching up with Luca's security team. She's not drinking. She's not dancing. I know my sister is pregnant, and I love her. I understand her fears. I'll let her tell me when she's ready.

Nick and Zar dance beside me. They're drinking. I'm chugging water. They muscle all the men away from me while I laugh, rolling my eyes at their protection.

The DJ drops a new beat. It's erotica electronica, and what the Mykonos Mercier with its hedonistic vibe is known for. It's all primal tension building into a euphoric climax, like a musical orgasm for a hundred people.

Half-naked bodies—sweating perfume, cologne, and musk —writhe around me. Couples kiss. Groups touch. Solo dancers get lost in the carnal rhythm.

Closing my eyes, I feel the visceral beat, all the way to my lonely, wet core, and all I can think about is Axel.

I wrap my arms around my waist, like he did every night. My nipples pebble, missing his touch. My sex tingles, like he's near, but I'm shoulder-to-shoulder with strangers.

I'm surrounded and happy, though my heart aches alone. I'm in love for the first time, and it doesn't scare me. This raw, new mix of emotions keeps me company while everyone seems to have someone, but I don't. I feel so much, as if Axel's here with me, but ... *he's not.*

It's how I've felt every night, dancing alone, and—

A granite body crashes against my back, strong arms suddenly capturing me, trapping me and I gasp, trying to twist to smack the shit out of the man. He's obviously a big, handsy one.

My eyes snap open to see Nick and Zar kissing and not paying attention while I'm being mauled on the dance floor.

"Fuck off, you piece of—"

"Oh, we're fucking, Wildfire." A deep voice steams over my ear. "Trust that I chased you halfway around the globe, and I'm fucking you right here."

Axel doesn't let me turn around. He lets me melt into him, happy tears weeping down my cheeks.

I glance down at his corded forearms, bare and covered in ink, seizing me in his embrace. My back, bare in this halter dress, sweats against his naked chest. His muscles are like slick rocks, gliding over my flesh. His erection, thick and threatening, wedges against my ass.

He has to be wearing pants, and I know he always wears shoes, but he's not wearing a shirt. I can feel it. I can smell his intoxicating aroma—cologne and masculinity—and I glance around to catch eyes turned, admiring his menacing form.

Nick and Zar smirk, like they knew he was coming, and go back to kissing, their tongues dancing together, and proud.

Axel presses his bearded lips to the shell of my ear. "Are you going to be a good girl and obey? Or are you going to fight me? Just know, either way ... I'm about to fuck you."

I could be a good sub and kneel on the dance floor for him.

Or I could be a queen and make him kneel for me.

But I know him. I need him. Axel grinds into me,

surprising me with how he can dance, how he's melding his body against mine, my fire melting with his ice. We're elemental. One can't exist without the other. An undeniable attraction of opposites. A sacred alchemy.

He dropped everything. He walked away from his family. He flew in their jet. He gave up hours; he sacrificed all, I know…

To chase me.

"Fuck you," I hiss, trying to break free from his grasp. "You want a fight? You got one."

It's his kink, his primal play.

It's what he wants, and I do, too.

"Oh, fuck yes, Wildfire." His hand grabs my throat, squeezing. "Fight me. Scream for me. Bite me while I violate you, when I don't fucking stop taking your pussy." His other arm traps my waist, forcing his erection against my ass. "And don't forget your safe word."

My eyes flick up to the VIP section, to Scarlett and her security, two of them leaping to my rescue, but she grabs their arms, reading the look in my eyes. I bet it's the same one she gets when Luca straps her to his torture tower.

I want this.

I want him.

So she lets it happen.

Rose tries to shove through the crowd to intervene, but Nick grabs her and whispers in her ear while Axel gently chokes me, his body fused to mine. Whatever Nick says makes Rose grin, before she salutes us and returns to her new girlfriend.

Cherry clocks us, too. How I'm in the menacing clutches of a huge, beautiful, inked beast, holding me hostage on the dance floor. How Nick's not doing shit about it. How Zar's smiling … and she smiles, too, whispering to her new DJ friend, who glances up and notices our sadistic bond.

Approvingly, he nods, flicking switches on his mixer, and the song changes, thumping into an iconic, unrepentant, lustful, and animalistic grind from the nineties.

"You want to fight me?" Axel's hand moves from ensnaring my waist to my halter top, stealing inside it to palm my breast, his lips never leaving my ear. "Are you saying you don't want this, Wildfire?"

He pinches my nipple, his other hand gently choking me, and I sigh, "Fuck you." I squirm like I'm resisting him, like I want to be free, when really ... I'm rubbing my ass against his hard cock.

"Such a good girl, fighting me. This is what you get for being so sexy for me." He pulls my halter top aside, exposing my breast, my nipple tingling and aroused. "Such a good girl, when you really want to be bad for me, don't you?" He tugs the gauze aside, baring my other breast, too.

Nudity is normal on Mykonos. Half-exposed bodies surround us. But the way Axel does it to me? It's lewd, it's possessive, and perverse, and I love it.

He tugs, pinching my exposed nipples for anyone to watch, and many are. They lick their lips at our display, and the rush of lust between my thighs is instant.

"I'm getting your proud pussy soaking wet, aren't I?" He taunts, leaving my nipples hard and aching for his touch, before he reaches down my front, his grasp slowly bunching the fabric of my dress up to my waist. "Let's see what a good girl you can be for me."

In front of everyone, he plunges his hand into my white lace panties, his other hand still choking me while he rubs my clit, his lips teasing my ear, "Fight me, Ruby. Fight how wet I'm making your pussy. We're doing this right here, for everyone to see how you're mine no matter how hard you resist me."

Desire crashes into me, making me moan and throw my

chin up. Resting my head on his chest, I close my eyes and crane my neck for Axel's kiss. I desperately need it while he gets me off. While he's exposed my breasts, making them heavy and ache. While he strums my aching clit in public. While no one can see it, but all can watch him do it.

But he doesn't kiss me. He controls me. "I need you soaking wet for how hard I'm going to fuck you." Expertly, he scissors my clit, just enough tease, just enough torture. "So fight me, Wildfire. Fight, how I'll make your pussy gush and come right here, in front of everyone."

I shamelessly grind over his hand, seeking my pleasure as I reach behind me and grab his thick erection straining under his pants. But still I fight him, twisting and squirming in his grasp, "Fuck you, dickhead."

He kicks my legs apart, his deep voice hissing, "My dick head is about to be buried so deep inside you, I'll show everyone how your pussy was made to catch my cum."

His hand squeezes my neck harder. "Show them, baby." I open my heavy eyes to lustful stares watching us. "Show them how you make me like this. How you make me a fucking animal for you. You fight me so much, and I fucking love it." Ruthlessly, he strums my clit. "Show them how you're such a good girl for me. You want me to make you come in public. Your sweet, wet cunt is going to gush for me in front of everyone. "

He spanks my pussy and I obey. "Oh fuck." My bare thighs shake. My eyes roll. I sag against Axel. He has to hold me up while I fall apart, dripping over his hand. While I soak his fingers with shameless lust, and come, begging, "Oh fuck, Axel, please. Now."

I'm not supposed to say his name.

I'm not supposed to let him whip me around and hoist me up, making me wrap my arms around his neck, my legs ensnaring his waist.

I'm not supposed to take him in a ferocious kiss, but I do. I bite his lips, and he nips at mine. We get off on the taste of us, bleeding together.

With our blood on his lips, Axel growls at Nick and Zar, "Cover us."

They're in a storm of proud lust, too, following us as Axel walks me backward, through the crowd and past the DJ booth, until he slams me against the wall.

I catch the impressed look on my little sister's face. Cherry's gaze admires the animal I love. How he's about to fuck me right here.

Shadows cloak us, and our position does, too, but they're not enough to hide our indecent animal act. Bodies gather to watch, but Nick and Zar shield our space with their sheer size and shameless kiss.

Axel reaches down between my thighs, where I'm splayed open for him. Hooking his fingers over my soaked lace, he rips it, tearing my panties apart. With deft fingers, he unzips his pants, reaching in to free his hefty erection.

"Condoms?" I rasp, pressing my forehead to his.

"No condom," he snarls. "You trust me. I trust you. And when I fill your sweet pussy with every drop of my cum, and you have my baby, fuck yes, you will. You'll have every goddamn piece of me, Ruby."

I search his eyes and can't find the man who holds, protects, laughs, or even fights with me.

This is the man who cuts, who pours salt in wounds. The one who kills, and I want this death. I want Axel to kill every thing I was before and fuck us into something new, something together, forever.

He doesn't wait this time.

He doesn't ask.

He watches my eyes as I give my answer, crying out with his cock's first brutal thrust inside my waiting pussy. He invades with his size, shoving the breath from my lungs, stretching my ache away, and filling me with more than I've ever had before.

"Feel me burning, Wildfire?" He pins me against the wall, his fist tugging my hair, his other hand bruising my hip. His lips brush mine, taunting, "Feel where I belong? Where I'll live? Feel your tight pussy trying to take my thick cock? How you'll *always* take me whenever I want you? All the time, I'm going to fuck you so hard like this."

With his next thrust, he buries every inch of his cock inside me, to the hilt and I gasp, suddenly feeling it—the ring at the base of his cock, its steel metal bead rubbing against my clit.

His lips part, watching my eyes, amazed by the intense pleasure he's giving me. His size. His piercing. His grinding hips. "Oh fuck," I moan, my lips shaking at the euphoric sensation, at Axel, giving everything to me.

"Feel your ring, Ruby?" he growls.

"Yes, my king." I clench my legs wrapped around him and circle my hips over it.

"Good girl. Now take it." He starts thrusting, ramming his jewelry against my clit with sweet slaps. It's the most luscious thrill, heightening my pleasure as his cock... *God, it's too big and so good.* It pounds, stretches, and demands, and I want more. I need more. I need him.

I grab Axel's back, scratching his flesh with my nails, my teeth sinking into his hulking shoulder. "Oh, fuck yes, Ruby." He nips my earlobe before gently biting my neck; the pleasure and pain, perfect. "Fuck yes, baby, hurt me." He rasps into my neck. "Hurt me like I've hurt, wanting to fuck you like this for so long. I warned you; I'll mark you. I'll come inside you and make you mine."

"Yes, Axel," I moan into his ear, my body, my everything, completely his. "Yes, I am."

Dozens surround us. They're strangers watching a huge, inked man ruthlessly fuck a woman against the wall, her nails scratching his devilish back, her screams of ecstasy, *my screams*, carnal and only crying out for more.

But all I feel is Axel inside me. His pleasure. His pounding. His possession. His need, powerful and primal.

"Show them, baby," he growls loud enough for many to hear. "Be a good girl and let them watch your tight, wet pussy take my cock. *Only* my cock. This cock."

Sweat glistens over his skin. His eyes feral as he drags his thick, glossy length out of my weeping pussy. People on either side of us can see it, before he slams it back in, his metal piercing clashing against my tender clit. It makes me moan, the ecstasy harsh and heavenly.

"Show them how your pussy exists for me to fuck. For me to fill with my cum."

"Yes, my king," I vow with our gazes locked, and I love every moment of Axel's violation. Every second of his public claim. My every breath, his, as he grabs my kiss, too.

He's taking me so hard. So debased, debauched, and delicious. Our spectacle. Our sex. Our truth hits me when he buries himself deep inside, suddenly and ruthlessly grinding his piercing over my excited clit, his mass brutally stretching me and my orgasm shocks me.

It's intense, a sweet annihilation, a cataclysmic explosion of white light through my senses. I can't stop it. I can only cry out, convulse, and wrap around him as I come so hard, it hurts. My sweet flood doesn't end. It spills between us, making Axel grunt like an animal, his hips viciously hammering, chasing my release and his.

He groans into our kiss, like pieces of his soul release, and he's giving them to me. "Ruby, fuck baby, take me," he stammers over our lips, his brute body locking, trapping me as his icy eyes find mine and melt with his grunt, with his release spilling deep inside me. I can feel his thick cock jump, pulsing with his piercing, my ring, pressed between us. I can see the rapture in his eyes.

"Aw, fuck yes," he sighs, pressing his forehead to mine. "Finally, Wildfire."

The crowd evaporates. I don't care about anyone but the man I'm wrapped around. The man catching his breath, giving me a deep, fervent kiss, before he grabs my throat again.

"Run," he rasps, daring me. "Run to your room with my cum dripping down your legs and get on all fours, ready for me to give you more."

CHAPTER TWENTY-FIVE
AXEL

"Oh my god," Ruby groans into her pillow. "Who hit my pussy with a big Bratva truck?"

"*Ex*-Bratva." I chuckle, holding her, my cock hard and ready for another collision. "Need anything?"

"You."

"You got me." I kiss her bruised neck with a mix of pride and guilt at the marks I've left on her. "Need anything else?"

"For you to hit me again."

I laugh harder. "We *hit* it until dawn, and you just said you're sore."

"Just be tender next time." She turns around in my grasp, her fingers tracing the tattoos on my neck. "You know, treat me like a delicate virgin."

The mention of a virgin clenches my heart. There's so much I still need to tell Ruby. I kiss her shoulder and brace myself for a long talk.

"Let me get us some coffee first."

Crawling out of bed, I pluck my pants from the floor and tug them on. Of course, I never took my socks off as I open the door to Ruby's bedroom and follow the savory aromas.

Luca Mercier's penthouse suite in his Mykonos property leaves your jaw on the floor. White marble. Gold fixtures. Grecian blue furniture and a breathtaking view of the sparkling sea from every wraparound window.

But the sight of my brother sipping coffee and holding Zar's hand at the dining table on the covered terrace makes me smile.

"Goddamn," Nick shakes his head, "are you two finally done? The poor girl: it sounded like you broke her last night."

I rub my sore dick, smiling. "No, my woman broke me, and I love it."

"Speaking of love," Zar asks, "how long are you staying?"

"I leave this afternoon."

"Does firecracker know that?" He points to her room. "Because I don't want to be here when she explodes."

"She knows." I turn toward the credenza with its sumptuous breakfast presented on gold platters. Flipping over two porcelain cups, I pour two coffees. "She's my queen. She understands we'll go to war with Turner's men once we find him soon."

"But she's *not* your queen," Nick warns. "Not yet. And you know we'll always protect her, but you need to make it official."

I drop sugar cubes into our cups. "I'm not offering her to another king."

"How long will you disrespect her like that?" Nick challenges me, and I whip around, abandoning the coffees.

"What the hell does that mean?"

"We initiate our queens." Nick lifts his hand holding Zar's. "If they're not queens by blood, like Alena, every queen is initiated. No matter what. No matter if we don't want to share. It's our tradition. It's out of respect, and to make Ruby the only queen not fully initiated like the others leaves her out, when she should be included and honored. She'll be the first king's queen, *your* queen. And she'll be far more than Katya ever was because we all love her. And you love her. Ruby belongs with us, so make it right and—"

"Who's Katya?"

The gut punch is instant. I close my eyes, sick and not wanting to confront the voice asking.

"Axel?" Ruby sounds hurt. "*Who* is Katya?"

Dragging in a brave inhale, I open my eyes to confront my fiery beauty, wrapped in a white silk robe, standing at the marble threshold, and confess, "Katya was my first wife."

The truth smacks her face, making her wince. "Your first *wife*?"

"Yes, I'm divorced and was going to—"

Ruby shakes her head before spinning around, running into her bedroom, and slamming the door behind her.

"I take it she didn't know?" Nick mumbles, "Sorry, man."

"It's my fault," I answer, charging across the living area. Gently, I knock on her locked door. "Ruby, please let me explain."

"Explain this!" She opens the door and throws my travel duffel in my face. "You know. I'm not *always* a bitch." She tilts her head, her smile lethal. "Just kidding. Go fuck yourself, liar."

With a loud *SLAM*, I face her door again and drop my bag.

A bedroom door across the living area opens, and Rose pokes her head out. "Who lit Ruby's fuse?"

I raise my hand.

She laughs. "Good luck with that." Turning her chin, she tells someone over her shoulder. "Come have coffee and tickets to this show because when my sister blows, it's like the Fourth of July."

A brunette emerges from Rose's bedroom. Together, they aim for coffee and giggle at the deep shit I'm standing in.

"Ruby, it was over four years ago." I talk to her door. Seems to be a habit. "We were barely married a year, and I didn't love her."

Her door swings open again. My passport hits me in the face while she scoffs, "Way to plead your losing case, counselor. You married her but didn't *love* her? Sounds like the second thing on the list of dickhead things to do to a woman. Second only to lying about it."

"I was going to tell you ... *today*."

"Coincidence: I was going to tell you to fuck off ... *today*."

She slams the bedroom door again, and now another across the living room opens.

Cherry emerges, her hair mussed while she claps for me and the DJ follows her, laughing, "Man, you got ninety-nine problems and that bitch is *all* of them."

"Call my woman a bitch," I roar, "and I'll crack your skull wide open and piss in it!"

"I'm not your woman!" Ruby shouts from behind her door.

"The fuck you aren't!" I shout right back and could almost laugh at this drama. It's a goddamn Greek tragedy and a soap opera wrapped into one. But like hell, if Ruby ever doubts who she belongs to, "Get as mad as you want, Wildfire. Burn my fucking world to ash and I'll still be here, waiting for you to cool the hell off, because you're mine."

"*That's* how you handle her." Scarlett emerges from her room. In white silk pajamas and her auburn hair in a twist, she's elegant. She's calm.

"Keep fighting for her," Scarlett advises, padding with bare feet over the white marble, aiming for my audience. "Because god knows, she has a ton of fight in her, too. It takes a real man to love us."

"Ahem." Rose clears her throat.

"Or a real woman," Scarlett corrects herself.

"Ruby," I snarl, because I am a real man. A man about to really lose my shit for this woman. "Open the door and talk to me, or I'll kick it down."

"Kick it down and kiss your balls goodbye!"

"Wrong! Kissing my balls is *your* job." Fuck it. I know how to bait her every time. "Along with fetching my coffee and cat food."

"Uh!" Her door swings open again, her eyes wide and furious. "You better hope karma *kicks* you in the balls before I do."

"Trust me." I loom over her. "This *is* my karma. *You're* my karma. Because I fucking love you, and you're making me look like a goddamn fool in front of our family to fucking have you!"

Her eyes blink, unbelieving. "Did you just say you love me?"

"Yes!" My heart pounds.

"In the middle of a fight?" she scoffs.

"Yes! It's what we do, Wildfire; love and fight and yes, finally, we fuck, too."

"Do you mean it?"

"Yes, I fucking mean it," I swear to her wide blue eyes. "I love you. I have for a long time, and if I'm a dickhead to admit I never really loved my first wife, fine. Add it to my list. But when I make *you* my wife? My *real* wife? You'll let me love you until the day I die."

"Did you make her your queen?" She whispers so the others don't hear, but the pain in her voice is clear.

"I regret it," I answer softly, muscling through her door and slamming it behind me. Stalking her way, I make her walk backward toward the bed. "I regret everything about that woman. I got caught up in who I thought I *should* be, not who I am. *You're* who I am. *You're* the woman I want to be with."

"What happened to her?"

"She left me."

"Why?"

"She left me a note that said I'm a cruel man with a cold heart."

"No, you're not," she murmurs, shaking her head.

"Well, I guess she was the cruel one with a cold heart. She even made fun of my feet. How she never saw them. She never saw *me*, Ruby, and honestly, I didn't let her. I never really trusted her." I reach for her, but she steps back. "But I trust you, and I'm sorry I waited to tell you."

The back of her legs hit the bed, and she plops down, looking shocked.

"We played the hating game for so long," I confess, "until I finally got my chance with you and I didn't want to fuck it up. And now, I don't give a shit about our pasts, because I'm trying to have a future with you."

"If she was your first wife and queen, then what does that make me?"

I crawl over her, making her wriggle up the bed, so I grin and chase her until she's trapped underneath me. Too quickly, I grab her wrists, pinning them above her head. "That makes *you*, Ruby Jones," I swear to her eyes, "the first and only *love* of my life."

Something softens in her eyes, searching mine, but nothing is easy with this woman. I'd never want it to be. "I don't know if I believe you."

"Want me to prove it?"

"You better."

"My piercing?" I tell her, "I got it for you." The surprise on her face is cute. "I have the receipts to prove it, witness testimonies, too. Six months ago, I got a pubic piercing for you. And you're the only woman who's ever kissed it, who'll ever feel it."

"You pierced your dick for me?"

"Do you need a lecture on human biology?"

"Only if you want me to jump off the terrace."

I laugh. "I didn't pierce my dick. That would be for my pleasure. I pierced my body, right above my dick, to please *you*. Only *you*." Call 911. Or whatever it is in Europe. She's struck speechless. "I thought about piercing my nipples for you, but you can see them through shirts, and judges don't like that. And I heard you tell Helen—"

"You listen to me talk to Helen?"

"It's the best part of my day. I love it when you talk shit about me."

"Whoops," she murmurs. "Am I fired?"

"You should've been fired after your first day, when you made fun of my copy of *Moby Dick*."

"You made that too easy. It was low-hanging fruit."

"And *that's* what you said about my balls the next day."

She sighs, "You have very sexy balls."

I press my forehead to hers. "I stalked you. I got pierced for you. I never fired you, when goddamn, you deserved it, daily. And ... I'm saving my left leg for ink about you, about us." I lift, questioning her, "I've proven my love for you. So what have you done for me?"

She smiles. "Not put cyanide in your espressos. Not cut the brakes on your car. Not release killer hornets into your A/C unit. Not give your number to telemarketers." She pauses, letting tears well in her eyes. The sweet sight of them puts a lump in my throat. "Not fall madly in love with you, too, Axel King."

"Liar." I skim my lips over hers.

"I'm a big *bad* liar," she confesses. "Time to punish me with your piercing."

"*Your* piercing."

"Say it again."

"*Your* piercing."

"No, the L word."

"Litigation."

She laughs.

"Oh, *love*? That word?"

She nods.

I smile from my soul. "I love you."

"Say it again," she whispers.

I nuzzle my nose to hers. "I love you."

"Again."

"I love you."

"Again."

"I love you."

"What are you? A parrot?"

I laugh into our kiss, letting it melt our fight away. Remembering what she said when we awoke, I'm tender with her, as if it's her first time—*our* first time, and maybe it is.

I love her, and finally, she loves me. After I worship her nipples, then fuck her with my tongue, licking up my reward, I flip her over to ride me. To go as slow or as hard as she needs, and she kills me with the only death I want; my hard cock, buried so deep in her tight, wet pussy.

Every inch of me is hers while she pins my wrists above my head, and lets me gaze up at her beauty, her breasts bouncing and driving me insane. Grinding her delicious cunt over *our* piercing, she takes the pleasure I need to give her. She's the only one I've ever let feel this. The only woman I've ever let take me like this. *Fuck, she's so hot when she's aggressive and aroused.*

After she screams with her orgasm, after she makes my thighs shake as I roar, my back arching, my hips thrusting up, needing to come so deep inside her, I swear I hear Zar, Nick, and her sisters in the living room, clapping for us.

With gasping smiles on our faces, our gazes lock, and hers fills with tears, making them bite at my eyes, too.

"I love you," she whispers so softly, my heart explodes.

I swallow. "I love you, too."

Ruby falls on me, and I wrap around her, holding her. I have to leave soon, and I won't let it be with more heartache —not today. I won't ruin this moment for her, for us; our first *I love yous*.

I'll tell her more later. I'll tell her about Alena and all the secrets I hide. Life with me can be a lot to take, and I want to give her hope.

It's what she gives me.

"It's a little too late to ask, but are you on birth control?"

"Yes, I have an IUD," she sighs over my chest. "If I get pregnant with my epilepsy, I'm considered high risk, so I need to be sure, to be ready—"

"I'm ready." I press my lips to her hair. "I'm ready whenever you are."

"I think we have a few steps we need to take before that."

"You're right, so the next time I see you..." I'm still inside her as she straddles me. Pressing my thumb to her lips, obediently, she sucks it. She stirs my exhausted cock like only she can while I promise, "You'll kneel for me and watch another queen's initiation."

Her eyes light up.

"And if you want what you see," I vow, "you'll be next."

"Really?" she sputters over my thumb.

I nod.

"You'll share me?"

"Never," I swear. "But I'll honor you with an initiation. I'll officially make you my *true* queen."

CHAPTER TWENTY-SIX
AXEL

"So, where should I take her shopping?"

I question my mother, watching her blow perfect smoke rings and admire their form.

It's her one playful habit.

She smokes vanilla cigars, and seems to enjoy tapping her ashes on the back of the naked man, bound with his ass in the air when she answers me, "Chanel, of course."

"What if that's not her style?" I ask about Ruby but cock an eyebrow at our captive.

Wow, he's really hung and hard for this torture.

He's kneeling and bound in a BDSM device.

Vale suggested to Nash that we use it for interrogations. Though our next queen can fire snark like hollow-point bullets, especially at me, Vale's also getting her PhD in Sexuality Studies, and her knowledge *is* helpful.

This man, who Grant caught climbing over the courtyard wall at Delta's, ready to ambush us, has been a tough nut to crack. Literally.

This Humiliator device has him kneeling with his cheek on the ground, his ass in the air, and his ankles and wrists bound in chains to a bar behind his knees. The bar is two, locked together, and squeezed between them, in a vice, is the base of his scrotum. If our captive moves, he tortures his nuts.

Eventually, it'll make him crack.

Vale's a genius. A sex genius.

Because it hurts *my* nuts just looking at it.

Our captive has to be one of Turner's men, one of the sex traffickers, but he won't speak. He had no ID. No phone. No trace of who he is. He just silently stares at my mom with lethal admiration.

"She'll be your queen." Mom puffs her cigar. "Of course, haute couture will be her style. At least for our traditions."

Ruby flies home tomorrow, and I want to spoil her.

Her three weeks in Greece turned into four. Not that she didn't want to come home to me and our kittens. It was her sister Scarlett who delayed their departure.

Scarlett claimed she had a stomach bug and flying would be a special hell. But really, Ruby confided in me that she thinks Scarlett is pregnant and no one knows yet, not even her husband, Luca.

While Ruby's been gone, everything and nothing has happened.

Our kittens are cute, but I won't name them without Ruby. She has to meet them first. The furry little fuckers have distinct personalities, but all love to sleep in my shoes.

Nash will initiate Vale in two days. He finally relented, agreeing to let Jace be Vale's second king. And Vale passed her queen's test with orgasmic colors ... and a sex swing on the floor.

Of course, I did my part, but I barely touched Vale. I only tested Nash to make sure he'd allow her to be initiated and not murder Jace for it, as I'm sure Nash will also test the hell out of me when it's Ruby's turn.

The thought of Ruby's initiation makes me want to buy a twenty-five-pound bag of salt. For cuts. For bodies. For anyone who touches her.

I can't think about it without feeling psychopathic. So, I don't.

I focus on Turner, our escaped sex trafficker. We've located his men and hideout. We got that intel from a man who tried to kidnap Vale from my mom's club. That man cracked easier than an egg, not like this bound fucker with his ass in the air.

After Vale's initiation, we'll raid Turner's hideout, hoping to rescue his next cargo of victims.

But this guy? Watching my mom like a hawk? Like a hard-dicked hawk?

Something about him feels familiar.

But with all he's a part of? Trafficking women and children? He'll never make it out of this bunker alive. It's a bomb shelter in the old naval yard, north of Charleston. I bought it for us to use for weapons storage. For prison and torture. For cornhole on a rainy day.

"If I take her to Chanel," I'm bugging the shit out of my mom, "what color should I buy her?"

She puffs her cigar, smiling. "What have I always taught you boys?"

"Give a woman whatever she wants."

"Precisely. Take her shopping and let her pick. It's not her initiation; I like to buy our queens special gifts for that." She makes a face. "But I still don't understand why you want her to *watch* this one. It's not her turn yet. I still need to meet her."

"I want her to see everything before she agrees." I shrug. "It'll be different for her, more dangerous, being my queen, the heir's queen, and I want her to understand the risks."

"Ahem."

The bound man coughs. It's his first sound since I've been here, though he hasn't seen my face.

He can't look over his shoulder from where he kneels on the floor to where I stand. He can stare right at his rusty metal, threadbare bed, or he can stare left at my mom's black, spiked, red-soled Louboutin's.

All while I have a wincing, clear view of his very groomed asshole.

"He's someone's sub," Vale had guessed in an off-handed statement about him last week. Nash brought her here so she could see the darker part of our world. "He likes bondage and humiliation, and he's very groomed for it. Physically. Verbally," she said. "I don't know who he belongs to, but he serves someone."

I see what Vale meant.

This captive is way too compliant for a man so tatted and jacked. His body is honed for violence, not his passive pose.

Someone's trained him.

"Fine." Mom taps more ashes on his back. "Let your future queen watch an initiation. Yes, you need her full consent. But don't you dare do any rituals with her until she meets me."

"Why?" I smirk, leaning against the concrete wall, peeling with decades-old beige paint. "You afraid you won't like her?"

"No." Her face softens, answering me, "You love her and I'm afraid I'll love her, too, and I can't bear to see you hurt if you lose another queen."

"Katya never felt like my queen." I coldly huff, "She felt like my curse."

"Ahem."

Again, this fucker interjects? First, at me being the heir, and second, at a queen who left me?

Fuck this. Now, I'm suspicious.

Keeping out of range of his stare, I hunt, my shoes clapping over concrete until I stand behind him, just enough to step the point of my shiny black oxfords down on his trapped balls.

"Argh!" he growls, protesting.

"Oh, so this isn't your kink, ballboy?" I mock, "We finally found a torture that doesn't please your dick?" I step harder. "Care to contribute meaningfully to the conversation, or do you need a cough drop?"

"Fuck you, Aleksi," he mutters my birth name and my eyes widen. My mind, shocked. My pulse stutters as the hot blood in my veins turns to ice.

Then ... it's instinct.

I reach for my gun, and press the muzzle of my double-mag, Mossberg 9 mm to his asshole, and growl, "*What* did you just call me?"

"Aleksi Kholodov," he answers, laughing. "Nice to finally meet you, brother." I whip my murderous glare to my mom, my trigger finger itching to pull. "Half brother, I should clari-fy." He jeers, "We have different mothers, which is a good thing, because I *really* want to fuck yours."

I rage, "You fucking piece of..."

"Michael!" My mother shouts my fake name. "Leave! This man is delusional and my prisoner and the last thing he needs is a bullet in his ass. He wants me to fuck him there and I will for his intel."

What.

The.

Escaped Bratva.

Hell?

My half-brother? On my father's side? Somehow, in my cold bones and thundering heart, I believe him. It feels true. And if that's so, it means...

My father has found us.

"Leave!" My mother orders me again, pointing toward the

door. Outside, three of her armed guards await her orders. After that? Five more are stationed outside, with two snipers who keep the only door, in or out of our bunker, in their crosshairs.

This man will never get out.

My half-brother will die in here.

Did my mother know this all along?

"Not before he pays." I tuck my gun into my back holster and whip my knife from my pocket.

I'll obey my mother, our queen, but she knows who I am, too. Who I was born to be.

With careful precision, I press the blade of my dagger to our captive's hamstring.

If he truly is our father's son, he's seen this effective torture.

"You dare to disrespect *her*?" I want to call her my mother, to defend her honor, but I won't confirm our identity.

"You want to kneel for her?" I sneer, "Then let me help you. Do you know where the term 'being hamstrung' comes from, ballboy? It comes from slicing a man's hamstring. More accurately, your biceps femoris. Thanks for working out. I can clearly see yours." With a one-inch cut, I slice across it, making him cry out and taking his freedom of movement for months to come. "It comes from this revenge, you disrespectful piece-of-shit."

Then I pull out a salt packet. Now thanks to my sadistic father, I always carry one in my pocket. Pouring it over his weeping wound, he whimpers in pain while I jeer, "And now you'll live with no infection, but it'll be on your knees for her, you mother fucker, indeed."

I move my blade to slice his other hamstring, but my mom shouts, "Enough! I fight my own battles. Leave!"

It's with fierce love and something else in my mother's glare that she pleads with me to listen.

I have her eyes. We all do. And right now? She's trying to protect me.

From myself.

Without a word, I storm out of the room, letting the door slam behind me before I tuck my bloody knife into my pocket.

"Cover her!" I command her guards as I fight every instinct I have to kill my half-brother.

But with deep inhales, I pace the concrete hallway and get my shit together. We didn't survive this long by being impulsive and stupid.

Vale's initiation.

Alena's wedding.

Turner's destruction.

We have so much to do, and we'll get through it. We honor our vows and traditions. That's how we survive together.

While secretly I'll find out…

How in the hell did my father find us?

And I'll ask my mom how long she's known.

And I'll worry like hell…

What if he finds Ruby?

CHAPTER TWENTY-SEVEN
RUBY

"Where are we going?"

We're speeding down a dark road in a remote area up the coast from the city. Axel holds my hand over the console. His clutch is warm and protective, but he's making me nervous.

Do I trust him? Yes.

Do I know something's wrong? As sure as I have jet lag, there is.

"My hideout," he answers, turning down another road the state should've named "Creepy As Fuck Lane."

"Your hideout? Why?" I peer into the inky night. The headlights of this vintage Land Rover barely pierce the darkness. "And our kittens! And Sparky!" I whip his way. "Where are they?"

The first smile since I've arrived plays with his lips. "They're waiting for you there."

When Axel met me in baggage claim, his kiss was overwhelming. It was as if he didn't believe I was real, or he didn't want me to be. He kissed me like he wanted to whisk me away into a fairytale, not rush me into the airport parking lot with his head on a swivel while he pushed the luggage cart.

I'm happy to see him. I'm surprised by how much I missed him. How he felt like home when he wrapped his arms around me. It's been three weeks since we were together.

But he seems... Hurried? Harrowed? Haunted? I've never seen him like this.

"I won't play twenty questions with you," I sigh, "because when we get to your *hideout*, I know you'll give me answers."

He nods, looking relieved that I've turned a new leaf.

I mean, four weeks of nightly video chats and daily purple flowers, punctuated by the hottest night of sex in my life, followed by porn-worthy phone sex, and super cute kittens crawling over my jacked and tatted man would make any woman holster her pistol.

For now.

When he parks, I stare up at Axel's hideout, its flood-lights revealing it's a secluded waterfront cottage on stilts, nestled under sprawling, wide oaks dripping with Spanish moss. Though it's past midnight, I can smell the wide river, marshland, and pluff mud nearby.

Inside, it's a casual, coastal vibe. Axel locks the door behind him, apologizing for the "rustic accommodations," while they look five-star to me.

Taking my hand, we leave my luggage by the door before he leads me down a short hallway. Grabbing the door knob, he turns to give me another kiss, his lips brushing over mine. "Welcome home, Wildfire. We missed you."

When he opens the door to what appears to be his bedroom, a clowder of golden kittens wobbles our way.

"Oh my god, they're so cute!" I plop down on the plank floor and let them surround me.

"They just started walking." He sits beside me. "And now the cute little shits have started sleeping in my shoes."

"Yowl!" Sparky prances my way, and I scoop her up.

"Hey, Mama! Good job." She looks healthy, and the kittens are adorable. But Axel? He looks troubled, gazing at us with happy eyes under a heavy brow.

"Okay," I ease, petting one kitten after another. "Tell me what's wrong and I promise I won't run or slam doors or spit in your coffee or—"

"You spit in my coffee?"

"Uh..." I bat my lashes. "No?"

"Fuck," he fights a chuckle, cupping my cheek, "I've missed you."

With a hot kiss, that threatens to turn into our first fuck of a dozen in a day, I'm sure with how we've missed each other, I sigh over our lips, "Tell me, first."

Pressing his forehead to mine, he drops a bomb.

"My father has found us."

Blink.

Breathe.

Think.

Don't throw up.

"What... How... When... Oh my god, Axel."

"I don't know," he answers. "I don't know who knows, who betrayed us, or how he did it, but I know what he'll do. He'll go after my mom, then he'll go after you."

"Me? Because I'll be your next queen?"

"Ruby," he shakes his head, "I want to be smart and have your brother-in-law hide you in some luxury resort far away from me, for the rest of your life." He nuzzles his forehead to mine. "And I want to be a selfish, smug, dickhead who's in love with you and never lets you go again."

Heart thumping, I sigh, "I vote for option two."

He half laughs, half growls, "You don't know what you're agreeing to."

"The world's biggest asshole. Got it. If he catches me,

he'll torture me in unimaginable ways until he has you on your knees, agreeing to be the next Russian Pac-Man."

"Pakhan." He finally laughs. "It's *Pakhan*. It means crime boss, or gang leader, or—"

"Cunty stubborn brat. It means that's what your father will suffer every day if he kidnaps me."

"Wildfire, be serious."

"I *am* serious. You're a lucky man. You happened to hook up with a woman who's already suffered a terrifying abuser. I'm immune."

"You get seizures when you deal with men like him."

"No." Playfully, I flick his nose ring. "You've been giving me daily doses of dickhead so I've grown a high level of tolerance. Besides..." I match his softening gaze. "You've chased me this far, so don't give up now."

"For the first time in my life, I don't know what to do." He caresses my hair. "I've never been in love like this."

I swallow the sweet lump he just put in my throat. "And I've never been in love like this either. So..." my lips twist, fighting back tears, "don't make me leave you because I won't."

"If I made you leave," he searches my gaze, "you'd only run back, wouldn't you?"

"I'm sorry. Is that a question?" My tone softens, tender like my heart, asking, "Would you ever leave me?"

Warmly, he answers with no ice in his eyes. It's as if I'm the only one who melts him like this. "Ruby, I wouldn't know how to leave you. Not ever."

He does it again, seeking more than my lips with his kiss. It's our lives, hearts, and breath melding with our mouths together.

Kittens mewl, crawling over us. I want Axel and this life together, more than anything, so I grab a soft breath and say,

"So, we have a choice: live afraid or live fighting back. Wanna guess what I'll do?"

"I'm sorry." He smirks. "Is that a question?"

"Exactly. We fight and we stay together. So what's next?"

"We initiate Vale tomorrow night. Then we'll raid a compound. Then Alena's wedding is the following weekend. Then—"

"Oh, so normal ex-Bratva stuff."

"You could say that." He lets a kitten climb his shirt, not flinching at its tiny claws. "But *this* isn't normal. I can't believe it if one of my brothers has betrayed us."

"What do you mean?"

"I mean, it's a man who's found us. He's my half-brother. My father's son with another woman. Grant caught him climbing over the courtyard wall to Delta's a few weeks ago. Like he was about to ambush us, and we've been holding him captive, trying to get intel from him and he didn't say a fucking word until yesterday. Until *I* was there and he said my name."

"Aleksi Kholodov?"

"Don't, baby." He squeezes my hand. "Don't put that cursed name in your pretty mouth. That's not who I am. Axel King, *your* king, that's who I am."

I nod, agreeing. It felt wrong anyway. Like I was conjuring a deadly curse just saying it.

"So what does this guy want?" Two of our kittens nestle into my lap, cuddling together, their furry cuteness an odd contrast to our lethal situation.

"I don't know. Apparently, my mom has been interrogating him and—"

"Your mom knew he's your half-brother and didn't tell you?"

"Yeah." Axel aims his sharpening glare at the night outside. "He looks like me. Like Loch, too. We favor our father, and that sadistic man made sure my mother would *never* forget his face, so yeah ... I guess she knew."

"Well," I try to soothe him, "I don't know your mom yet. Not really. But she doesn't strike as a woman who would betray her sons. She strikes me as an Apache helicopter parent. Like she'd wipe out a village for you. So I'm sure there's an explanation."

He fights a grin. "You're right, and really fucking beautiful for defending my mom. I tried calling her about it this morning, but she texted back, saying she has it under control, and we'd talk about it later. But something's going on and I can't tell anyone else."

"Why not?"

He gets that same heavy look, fury tumbling with betrayal in his eyes. "Ruby, you're the only one I can trust until I find out which brother sold us out. You're right. My mother is innocent, and we'll fight back, but we have to be smart."

"But your brothers would *never* do that. I don't know them all, but I know that."

"How else did this man find us?"

I shrug. "A coinkydink?"

He fights another grin. "It's a coincidence that out of one hundred and ninety-three countries, he picked the U.S. and its seventy-first largest city to crawl over the brick wall of the one discreet sex shop where we meet?"

"Okay, Carolina Law, you can spout all the facts you want, but don't underestimate the power of a good vibrator."

I understand Axel's stressed to a deadly degree, so I at least need to make him smile.

It works. Then, he gets that hungry look in his eyes, aiming his lips for mine. "And don't underestimate how I'm about to fuck you for hours."

"Hold that thought." I smush my fingertip to his lips.

"This feels like the perfect time to tell you I'm running an errand tomorrow."

His pressed lips fume, "You *just* got home."

I drop my hand. "It'll only be for an hour or so."

"I'm coming with you."

"You'll ruin the surprise."

"We won't survive surprises, Wildfire. We have to plan everything."

"Okay," I sigh. "Somewhere between my lonely life before I knew you and my happy life of loving you, a wanted ex-Bratva PacMan, I need to be able to do things on my own sometimes."

He shakes his head. "Not without me or another king with you. At *all* times."

"Hang on. Dare I suggest that you think like your father? I will surely be a target if spotted with any of his sons. But shopping with my sisters, he won't know me."

He sucks his teeth.

"Good point, right?"

"Where are you going?"

"It's a surprise."

"What did I just tell you about surprises?"

"It was a lecture; I wasn't listening."

He lowers his brow. "*Where.* Are you going?"

"You can track my phone."

"I already do. From now on, we have to anticipate him, not react to him."

"Fine," I huff. "I'm going to Delta's with Scarlett and Zar."

"Fine." He nods. "Delta's is always secure. And after that, I'll take you shopping."

"For what?"

"A surprise. And you'll wear the new bracelet I bought you, too."

I clap. "From Tiffany's?" I might've been raised in a trailer, but I know those robin egg blue boxes.

He chuckles. "No. With a hidden panic button."

"Oh well," I sigh, "a country girl can dream."

Reaching for Sparky, I give her some attention, then turn to find his eyes sparkling at us. "You're loving this, aren't you? Me, letting you be in control."

"No, I love this." He plucks kittens off his chest. "Me, about to fuck you."

His lips aim for mine, and I don't interrupt. Not like I could. Axel gives me more than a kiss. He takes me hot and hard like an animal. Then he licks, devouring me like his last meal, and moaning at our flavor. But when he takes me again, deeply with our sweating bodies and gasping breath intertwined, he takes me...

Like I'm the only one he trusts.

"You should let your Dom choose your collar." Zar shakes his head, full of advice. "And your nipple clamps. Any of your bondage, he picks."

"But, I want to surprise ... *him*." Admiring a gold collar, I make sure not to say names. "I want to get a piercing for him." I turn, asking Vale, "Is your piercer here today?"

It's bittersweet for now.

I know who Vale is—the manager of Delta's, Alena's best friend, and Nash's next queen. But she doesn't know me yet. Well, not that I'm Axel's next queen.

She knows me as Scarlett Mercier's little sister and Zar Rollins's friend. As Luca's subs, they're here often.

And they're super close with Stacey Evans, the owner of

Delta's, who met us here to help Scarlett outfit the sex room in her new beachfront house. Not that Scarlett's in the mood for anything with her secret morning sickness.

But she and Zar promised they'd help me shop for my reunion with "Michael Cummings," aka Axel King, aka Aleksi Kholodov.

God, I have to constantly remind myself not to slip up with his name. I mean … *names*.

So, we're gathered as clandestine networks, half revealing our interconnected worlds, in the lavish showroom on the second floor of a sex store, while Axel patiently waits outside.

"Sure, our piercer is here," Vale answers, considering which lingerie set to wear tonight. I hope she picks the black lace one for her initiation. With her sexy Wednesday Addams vibe, it will look stunning on her alabaster skin. "But just know, whatever you pierce, you can't play with it for six to ten weeks. It has to heal."

"Spoken like Doctor Sex," Stacey adds.

"Six to ten weeks?" I huff, disappointed. "Never mind."

"Sorry." Vale smiles with a sweet shrug.

"What about kink jewelry?" Zar suggests, perusing the cock rings.

"Uh, that didn't go well the last time I wore it. Men asked how much I cost."

"That's right," Zar remembers, chuckling. "Who knew NFL players could spot fetish jewelry?"

"NFL?" Vale sounds intrigued, asking me, "Is that your new Dom, an NFL player?"

"No." I turn toward the display shelves featuring every high-end sex toy imaginable. I can't lie to her face while I confess a half-truth, "I dated a quarterback over a year ago. He was closeted, and I was sort of his beard. He took me to events, and I was happy to help him, but the poor guy tried too hard. He started buying me way-too-revealing dresses and kink jewelry. I started to look more like his escort and his teammates gave him shit for it. So we," I air quote, "broke up."

"It's sad he couldn't be out," Vale says. "A lot of athletes can't. But I get it. Sometimes, secrets are kinder than the truth."

Silence falls over the room.

I swear, you could hear a flea fart as all glance around, each hiding dark secrets for good reasons and no one asking about them.

There's too much respect in the room. Friendship, too.

"How about these?" Stacey breaks the awkward silence. She gestures toward a table of lingerie with accessories and suggests, "Vibrating panties: they're not just for Doms."

Zar nods. "Perfect."

"I agree," Scarlett adds before touching her lips. "Uh, excuse me." She rushes out of the showroom, and we exchange silent glances again.

Even with Stacey Evans, looking like she'll have her baby any second, no one breaks the compassionate code: Never ask a woman if she's pregnant.

Taking Stacey's suggestion, I select a pair of panties and wait downstairs for Scarlett. Zar joins me, clearly excited about the stainless steel cock ring he bought.

"Are you wearing that tonight?" I whisper.

His brows bounce. That's all he'll reveal. Zar's too good at keeping his secret worlds separate, and I guess I'll get used to it, too.

It makes my nerves sizzle with anticipation for tonight, because Jace sits on a stool at Delta's door. Wearing a fitted black suit barely containing his muscles, he greeted me as a customer, completely ignoring that I'm his brother's secret queen.

It makes me wonder who his queen is. I don't think Jace

has one. He said he dated gallery openings, not women. *Lucky galleries.* Still, it's sad because he's so sweet.

But when Vale comes downstairs with her racy selection in hand—she picked black lace lingerie—I catch their silent exchange.

Did Vale just blush?

Did Jace just fidget, grabbing his crotch?

Oh my god, I'm too good at this. Or maybe it's just obvious; Jace will be Vale's second king.

I know she belongs to Nash. They're madly in love, though it was forbidden for so long. Axel said he's known it for years.

Still, I haven't met Nash yet. I suspect Axel's hiding me from him. Not out of shame. It's something else.

Does Axel suspect Nash betrayed the family?

I'm not sure. I need to meet someone to get a vibe on them, and when I do, I'm usually right.

We leave Delta's, giving Stacey and Vale hugs, and I try really hard to ignore Jace while he holds the door open for us, but he's too cute. I cut him a glance, and barely smile ... and he winks back.

Nope, I don't get a bad vibe from him.

I get a "he's a huge man with a big heart, fist, and dick" vibe, like all of his brothers.

Speaking of...

Grant's joined Axel, standing with him on the shaded sidewalk outside of Delta's. They smoke cigars, stifling their smiles when I hug Scarlett and Zar goodbye, and aim their way.

"Good afternoon, Ms. Jones." Grant leans down, pecking my cheek.

"Hey, Reacher One."

"One?"

I thumb toward the door of Delta's. "Jace is number two.

I mean... not like shit... like he looks just like Reacher as well and—"

"We got it, Wildfire." Axel chuckles before cocking his brow. "What did you buy?"

"Another business of None of Yours."

Grant laughs. "Damn, I can never get enough of you busting his balls."

Axel licks his bottom lip. "She does something to my balls, that's for sure."

For our next shopping venue, we walk, weaving through the historic city using narrow cobblestone alleys, private parking lots, and hidden gardens.

I'm not surprised they've mapped every hidden inch of this city. But what does surprise me is how Axel reaches for my hand, holding it when he's sure no one's watching.

No one except Grant, who leads the way, and checks over his shoulder. When he glances down and sees Axel clutching my hand, he smiles.

But what surprises me is the love I feel with Axel, and the safety I feel with Grant, too.

I went from never trusting a man to loving one and caring for his six brothers.

I just can't believe one would ever betray another.

CHAPTER TWENTY-EIGHT
AXEL

Ruby wears French fashion; it doesn't wear her.

She stands with the Chanel fashion advisor, who's summoned their tailor. The three stare at the mirrors, the staff admiring how the brilliant navy bouclé suit highlights Ruby's sapphire eyes and fits her perfectly.

"Fuck," Grant huffs, sitting in the chair beside me, admiring her, too. "Brother, I mean this with all due respect; don't fuck this one up."

She's so beautiful, my heart hurts. It pounds, staring at my future.

"I don't want to initiate her," I admit. "I can't offer her to another king. Not even once. Even though I have to."

"I get it," Grant mumbles back. "I only like sharing Delphine because it's what she wants. She finally has control over her body. She decides who and how many, because we always choose each other in the end. And for too long, she had no choice."

My mother rescued Delphine from a high-class Parisian brothel—the most exclusive in Europe. Delphine was the young, chosen prize of some of the most powerful men, including politicians, to the point that she held powerful secrets. To the point that she was worth more dead than alive.

Mom brought her here to hide, like we do.

Or did.

Grant was the first man who wanted to talk to Delphine, not fuck her. He learned French for her and taught her English, using the show *Friends*, and somewhere between Ross and Rachel, they fell in love.

While the tailor adjusts Ruby's skirt hem to be shorter and sexier than usual, I ask Grant, "Has Mom been acting weird to you lately?"

He huffs, "You're asking her son who just got shot. Sort of. She texts me four times a day to remind me to put arnica gel on my bruises. You mean that kind of weird?"

"I mean like she's hiding something."

"Big brother, my king." He slaps my shoulder. "Our mother hides a lot. Like, I really didn't want to hear the rumor that she's the hottest dominatrix in town. But, that's what I get for secretly being her son."

"Hand me Clorox," I growl. "I need to bleach that image from my mind."

"Amirite?" he mutters.

It can't be Grant. He's the third oldest. He remembers too much about our father, too. He'd never sell us out.

"Michael?" I stare at Ruby. "Michael? Hello?"

Oh shit. She's talking to me.

"Yes?"

"Can I speak with you, please?"

I rise and smooth my dress pants, remembering to play the Southern lawyer, not the suspicious Bratva son. As I approach Ruby, the Chanel staff retreat, leaving us by the mirrors.

"Yes, ma'am?"

"Can I speak with you? In private?" She nods toward the lavish dressing room, and I follow, hoping this is about to be a naughty sub moment.

"You know," I tease, "that suit pairs perfectly with the black lace bondage hood and blindfold you'll be wearing tonight."

She blinks, batting her thick lashes, processing before she frets, "But this suit doesn't have a price."

"Because you're priceless."

"Axel," she huffs, "I can't let you buy this for me. Because no price tag means it's more than my annual salary."

I tsk. "Reminds me; I need to give you a raise."

"I need to punch your balls."

"Promise? You know I love a good fight."

"I'm serious."

"So, am I. This suit is one of many that my queen will wear. Because you look breathtaking in it and because I said so."

She lifts her chin. "I'd rather be naked than bought."

"We can play that kink, too, Wildfire. Whatever my queen wants."

"I'm not wearing this."

"Well," I say, "not all night. I'll take it off when I fuck you. It *is* expensive as shit."

I'm pushing her buttons, and she's spewing lava.

It's so hot when she's hot.

"Listen." I cup her cheek. "I'm giving you everything, Ruby. Everything I have, body, soul, and wallet, is yours. I've already signed the contracts, making it very real. You're sexy as fuck in Daisy Dukes. You kill me in NASCAR pajamas. And you're my goddamn queen in Chanel.

"And tonight, you'll see what that means to me, to *us*. Most of our queens wear Chanel, Prada, whatever. We dress formally for our rituals. But you'll be *my* queen, the first queen in ranking after my mother, so wear whatever you want, as long as you wear it for me."

She blinks. "Wow. That was some speech."

"Mic drop."

"Okay, I'll wear the suit. It's pretty. Thank you. And you had me at blindfolds and bondage hoods, but I have a question."

"Yes, you may kneel and suck my cock in this dressing room."

"Axel." She slaps my chest. "Who's going to be Vale's second king tonight?"

I hate where this is going. "I can't say. You know that. Only a queen can tell you or ... show you."

"Because the queens pick their second kings?"

"Yes."

"If you make me queen and—"

"*When* I make you my queen."

"Okay, *when* you make me your queen, can I choose Grant as my second king?"

MURDER must flash in neon across my face.

"Axel, I trust him, too," she explains, "and you know that's hard for me. No offense to the other kings, but if..."—I glare —"I mean, *when* I become your queen, I would be honored if Grant is my second king. Like you, he makes me feel safe."

Suddenly, it's not about petty jealousy or primal possession. Since my father has found us, it's about protection with Ruby.

This is why I fell in love with her. Fuck yes, it can happen at first sight. With her bloody knee, proud chin, fiery hair, jeweled eyes, and plump lips that wouldn't stop talking, she blazed through me. I was done. I was hers.

Now, together, we'll fight back. We won't live afraid of my father.

I'm tired of running and hiding. His tyranny is over.

Will that make me stupid? Careless? Fuck no.

I'll sharpen our defenses. I'll find out who betrayed us. It makes me sick if it's one of my brothers, but I'm sure there are two, so far, who never would.

One, Nash. He's my best friend. He's proven his loyalty through actions, not blood. Besides, my father doesn't know him. He'd be the least likely.

Two, Grant. When he was nine, he went on a hunger strike after he witnessed our father beat our mother. For three days, he refused to eat. He hated our father that much. He wanted to shame him by dying in front of him.

But I couldn't watch him suffer, so I snuck him pelmeni, Russian dumplings, his favorite food and he was too tempted by hunger. He finally ate.

Would Grant spit in my father's face today? Certainly.

Would he starve to protect Ruby?

"Alright," I answer. "When you're initiated, Grant can be your second king."

She rushes, her curiosity pure, "Does that mean we like DP or—"

"Jesus, Ruby." I half-laugh, half feel homicidal. "Don't fucking push me on this. Just let me get used to not murdering my brother for even touching you."

"Okay. Okay." Gently, she palms my chest, caressing my pecs. "Thank you. I just... For the first time in my life—don't laugh at me for saying this—but I know why they call it 'making love' because that's what it feels like between us. And I want to be your queen no matter what and—"

"Goddamn," I press my forehead to hers, "I want to take you home right now." I urge her against the wall. "Or have you right here."

"Not yet." She grins. "Tonight, I'll prove I can be your queen. I'll be quiet and support Vale. This is her night. Just as long as you promise, I get my night, too."

"So you just sit here and watch?" Ruby trails her fingertips over my throne, worrying, "You won't *initiate* Vale, too?"

"No." Her tender jealousy turns me on. "Nash will barely let her second king touch her. We all did for her test, but tonight—"

"Her *test*?"

"Yes, it's the first ritual. It's your chance to decide if it's what you want before you agree to be a queen."

"When will I be tested?"

"Tonight will be one of them." I gesture toward the black leather tufted platform. "Kneel."

I had it custom-built for our new throne room. The boardroom table was kinky but uncomfortable. We also couldn't style my boardroom to honor our history and rituals.

But then I saw this room on Delta's third floor, with its high ceiling and plaster walls, all black with ornate gilded gold leaf designs.

So, I made an agreement with Stacey Evans, Delta's owner, that if I helped her step-daughter, the female athlete being bribed, I could have this lavish room for my private use.

I moved the thrones here, along with antique tables and golden candelabras, and it felt like our new home. All it needed was this large, padded platform, a comfortable place for bodies to forge bonds.

We can enter Delta's, looking like curious customers. We can meet in privacy with Jace or Grant, guarding the door. We can conduct our rituals without moans or shouts, drawing attention. We have extra guards posted outside; a team we've trusted for years.

We're safe here.

I hope.

"Kneel?" Ruby asks. "You're testing me right now?"

"I'm testing you all night." Something about Ruby in my throne room thickens my cock. It feels like I've been waiting forever for this. "So, before the others arrive, I need to prepare you."

Gently, I fist her hair, guiding her to face me on the platform. It's centered between our row of black velvet king's chairs, facing our white velvet queen's thrones.

Obediently, Ruby kneels, watching as I retrieve a gift box from the antique Russian credenza. Soon, the caterer will arrive with full platters to serve on it, though only the kings and queens may enter, so I'll meet them at the door.

For now, I planned this time alone with her.

"I bought this for you." I open the box and present Ruby with a dainty, black collar, its gold chain leash very Chanel and chic. "Will you honor me by wearing it?"

"Yes, my king." She lifts her hair as I wrap the leather around her neck, my cock aching for this.

I've never wanted a sub until I met Ruby. What was the point? Every woman submitted to me, but not her. That's why this feels special, locking a collar around her throat. I finally have her trust, long after she claimed my heart.

"Now, bend over," I command. "Rest your cheek on the platform."

"But... but..." she stammers, complying, "you're about to see my surprise for you."

"My surprise?"

She lifts her navy skirt, revealing white lace panties, tied with ribbons over her hips. "They're vibrating panties and—"

"Vibrating panties?" I've died and gone to Dom heaven. "My *dirty* girl."

"There's a little bullet that goes in them and you hold the remote and—"

"Fuck, Wildfire. You're the one testing *me*."

"No, my king. I wanted to show you how I can be good for you. How I'll edge all night for you."

"That makes two of us," I mutter, kneeling behind her to untie her panties. "I'll put them back on, but for now, I have another surprise for you."

She giggles, all throaty and aroused. "This feels like kinky Christmas."

"Exactly." I give her ass a playful spank. "Now, reach around and hold *my* gift open. Let me stare at the pretty ass and cunt that belong to me."

I love making her do this. I watch for minutes as she submits, swelling and glistening before my eyes. Her breath labored with lust, her will fighting to stay silent.

"You should see how good you look right now." I finally praise. "Such a good girl, showing me her sweet ass, so let me give you this." I circle my tongue over her tiny, puckered hole, making her gasp fall into a wanton moan. "This is how you've always wanted to be bad for me, isn't it?"

"Yes, my king," she sighs.

Using my spit, I tongue and tease, rubbing her clit, too, until she's begging, "Axel, please. Do it now."

"Hot, little brat." I smirk, spanking her other cheek. "You're not in charge. I am." From the same box where I kept her collar, I raise a purple, crystal rose butt plug. "Now, look over your shoulder," I order. "I want to watch your eyes while I prepare you to be a greedy little sub for me."

"Yes, my king," she sighs.

"This little bottle of lube?" I show her the tiny, palm-sized one I bought. "I'll use it now and keep it in my pocket for later."

"Later?"

"If you're a good girl, I'll fuck your ass tonight."

Drizzling the lube, I mix it with my spit. She trembles as I tease and probe with the plug, confessing, "I wasn't lying at the mountain cabin. This has always been my fantasy with you." Slowly, I press it inside her. "When you wear my collar, you'll let me dominate you any fucking way I want. Do you consent?"

"Yes, my king."

I secure her panties and smooth her prim skirt down. "Now, stand up and be my good girl. Prepare your pussy for me to control, too."

"Yes, my king."

Her teeth grab her bottom lip when she sees my erection for her. With hesitant steps, her body adjusts to the erotic intrusion, reaching for her handbag on my throne. I lick my lips when she lifts her skirt and tucks a little silver bullet into her panties, right over her clitoris, before she hands the remote to me.

"Good girl." I slide it into my pocket before grabbing her leash. "Now, all night, I'll test you. I'll make your pussy drip but you can't come. No matter what you feel or what you hear." I tug her chain. "You don't come for your king until I fuck your ass."

CHAPTER TWENTY-NINE
RUBY

Axel blindfolds me.

He said he wanted me to watch an initiation, when really, he wants me to feel it.

I kneel on a soft pillow while he caresses my head in his lap. A lace bondage mask and silk blindfold hide my hair, face, and eyes. Only my ruby lips are revealed.

But I get the impression through whispers that all are intrigued by our display.

I can feel Axel's erection pressed against my cheek. I sense the poignant moments and passion in the air. I hear every reverent and erotic word said. And I fight the maddening buzz of the vibrator against my clit.

In holy moments that sound like the wedding of Nash to Vale, officiated by Sire and Axel, he clicks off the vibrator and lets me breathe.

In hot moments, like when Nash tells Vale, "Show my brothers what's mine to fuck," Axel tortures me, igniting the luscious hum against my aching pussy, my panties soaked, while the toy in my ass only intensifies the sensation.

I hear Nash spanking Vale, taunting her while she sucks

his cock. I hear the other queens admire some toy he's torturing her with. Then, Vale begs him to fuck her ass, and I hear Axel bark at him minutes later, "She needs to come like that," he orders. "If she doesn't like it, stop."

God, I love that about him.

Axel was born to dominate. He will stalk, chase, claim, and kill, but he will never take.

"No, I love it. I love Nash." Vale's consent is demanding: "Don't stop. I want it."

I bite my lip at the lust in her voice and fight mine. But when she says, "Yes, Daddy, fill my ass with your cum," I shudder, stifling my moan with a dangerously close orgasm.

Axel clicks the bullet off, and I pant against his thigh. Holding my lace-covered cheek against his thick cock, he's taunting me with what he'll give me tonight.

Finally, their sex ends, their breath panting as murmurs of approval fill the room. Then it sounds like some rise to get more drinks. Like that was the wedding, and the reception is next.

But Axel doesn't rise, and obediently, I kneel.

My legs and back are starting to cramp, but I'm too stubborn to protest. There's something about this ultimate submission that gives me supreme power. I can feel the praise in Axel's touch, loving our bond.

A heavy knock raps on the door, making me jump. Voices fall silent as thudding, booted feet enter the room.

Who is it?

Who wasn't here before?

I don't know. I just hear Sire clear his throat, proclaiming, "Now that all are present, let us continue."

It sounds like another ceremony, but it's between Nash, Vale, and Jace this time. My ears strain to hear this part since Axel said he'll allow Grant to be my second king.

At first, it sounds like Jace is so serious and sweet, agreeing to protect Vale, too.

But then Axel chimes in, "Each queen decides how to receive a second king. A queen may receive more than two kings if that is her or his desire, for we are here to honor our queen's flesh. Be it tonight or any other, we always serve our queens."

But Axel's hand, caressing my head, holds it even tighter, not cruelly, with jealousy. No, his hand feels warm and fierce with protection, almost shaking with ... *with fear?*

No. Fury.

Only Axel and I know about his father finding them, and The Queen isn't here. I haven't heard her, so it's only the kings with their new queens gathered.

But one of them is a traitor?

It doesn't sound like it when Jace expresses his deep respect for Nash and Vale. It doesn't feel like it when Grant playfully teases Jace about it like they're thirteen.

There's no betrayal amongst the kings.

Since I can't see, all I can do is hear, smell, and sense the love in the room, and a shared lust so powerful for their queens that it soaks my thighs. So when Wren, in her fairy-like voice, says of the kings, "I like it when they're beasts."

I sigh, "Hmm," into Axel's thigh because I agree.

I love it when he's a beast. I'd love all of them if they're beasts. I trust them. They'd never hurt another king or queen.

But the room falls silent at my first sound until Nash barks, "Will you lift that sweet woman off of her goddamn knees?" Me? It must be. "Let her sit on your lap." He's fussing at Axel. "She's at least passed *this* test."

After a rumbling growl, Axel gently tugs my arm. My legs shake as I rise, then I hear him pat his thigh, guiding me to sit on his lap.

I listen to what sounds like Nash going down on Vale. Then it sounds like he's thrusting inside her, swearing to fill her before Jace's turn.

The sound of Nash's possession and Vale's pleasure perfume the air like an opiate, drugging me. Without thinking, I grind my hips over Axel's erection, and he grabs me, like *hold still*.

This arouses him.

Greatly.

I can feel it.

Greatly.

As much as Axel hates the idea of sharing me, he craves the public spectacle of claiming me. He did it like an animal at the dance club in Mykonos. He dominates me almost every time we fuck, and I love it.

The threesome between Nash, Vale, and Jace fills the air. Their taunts and moans building to where I can hear Nash slipping from fighting their union ... to getting off on it.

Vale's pleasure is obvious, and Jace's restraint is touching. It's like he respects his role but can't deny the pleasure of filling it, of filling Vale.

Axel said each queen decides how she'll receive her second king. So, how do I want Grant? How can I receive him in order to become Axel's queen, without hurting Axel?

For the first time, I care.

I've shared nights with two men, so I'd feel nothing for either. So I'd never get hurt.

But this time, I only love one man and want to respect him. I don't want to hurt him, but how? How can I truly be Axel's queen?

And will we even make it to my initiation if his father has found them?

And then there's the secret of Alena and Loch. How she doesn't know about their arranged marriage.

I don't hear her. She's not here. It's too taboo. Nash would never allow his daughter to witness what he's doing with Vale and Jace.

They protect Alena from this, from so much. But how will everything change once she finds out? I wouldn't blame her for being hurt.

If Axel lied to me like that? After he's fought so hard to earn my trust? I can't imagine the pain. I've protected myself from it for so long. But now?

Axel's the first man I've loved.

The last man I'll love.

It makes me nestle into him, resting my head on his shoulder. With strong arms, he wraps around me. "I got you," he whispers tenderly.

Then he shifts underneath me, his erection unrelenting, his lips urging over my ear, "Wildfire, I want to fuck you so hard right now, I'm in pain."

I grind over him, lust and love storming through me, too. The sounds of the others in the room, sharing the same desire, drip through my veins.

It sounds like Vale comes, Jace finishes, and Nash takes another turn with her while I hear the others.

Zippers drag. Chairs creak. Moans beg. Dirty whispers taunt. Slick skin slaps. The kings sound like beasts, and the queens sound like their ready mates.

It's a sacred orgy and I'm dying to join them, to have Axel.

"In the bathroom down the hallway," he whispers in my ear, "look under the sink. I put your shoes there."

"What?" I whisper back. "My shoes?"

"Your running shoes." He tugs my collar. "Because you're going to run, my queen, and I'll finally catch you."

CHAPTER THIRTY
RUBY

"But your father," I warn, standing on the side porch of Delta's.

"Fuck my father," Axel seethes. "We're not living in fear of him. He's not taking who belongs to me. Again."

"So, you want to chase me? Tonight? Why?"

I'm a flood of emotions. Lust, love, fear, and fight: they collide through my senses. My mind still reels from Vale's initiation. My body is overwhelmed, too, and now my feet wear familiar shoes to run away.

"This is part of your test. *Our* test," Axel reveals. "Do you want what you heard up there?"

"Yes."

"Do you want it with *me*?"

For a moment, his ice cracks. It's in his eyes; Axel's holding his heart out for me.

"Yes," I step toward him. "I'll never run from you."

"But you're worth the chase, Ruby." He cups my cheek. "And I won't ever stop until I catch you. I don't give a fuck who's chasing us, too."

"But how?"

"You put one foot in front of the other, but real fast like they're on fire and—"

I slap his chest, grinning. "Axel."

"You have your new bracelet on." He grins, pointing to the gold charms around my wrist. One is an SOS beacon. He can track me using GPS through an app on his phone, and I can double-click it if I ever need help.

I always wear my smart watch, too, but this jewelry is covert. No one would know it's a tracking device.

"You have thirty minutes to run to the pineapple fountain." He loosens his tie. "If you get there first, you get bragging rights, and can name our kittens—"

"And I pick your next tattoo."

"Deal." He smirks. "But if I catch you first—"

"You pick my first tattoo."

"No, Wildfire." He pauses, his tease evaporating. Reaching into his jacket pocket, he pulls out a blue velvet ring box. "If I catch you, I get to keep you forever."

Who knew ice could melt you? Because that's what Axel does to me. He's sincere. He's serious. He's my future. He's willing to risk everything to have me. But he doesn't open the ring box. He puts it back in his pocket, making the weight of this even more heart-pounding.

"What if I don't say yes?" I tease.

"Don't." Gently, he grabs my neck. "Fight me. Say *no* and make me fight for you."

With his other hand, he caresses my hair. I left my heels, blindfold, and mask in the bathroom of Delta's. But I still wear his collar with its chain tucked under my posh jacket. I can feel his plug inside me, and the toy in my soaked panties.

This is going to be the most erotic run of my life.

We left the other kings and queens moaning in the throne room. It's just us while Axel reminds me, "Use your safe word and I stop, or use your panic button, and I'm there. I promise."

"There?" I smile, shoving his granite chest away. "Where, dickhead?"

With a lightning pivot, I laugh, racing down the stairs, then turning up the sidewalk.

Axel will give me thirty, maybe forty seconds before he chases me. Inertia will pull him down the block, thinking I darted onto a quiet side street, so immediately, I duck into the next dark space, a cobblestone parking area beside a row house. Crouching behind a Range Rover, I'm so thankful for these big-ass, fancy cars tonight.

Holding my breath and body still, shadows cloak me. The gas lantern flickering by the hospitality door of the home I'm hiding beside barely illuminates the summer night.

With heavy steps, I hear Axel thundering right past me but I wait. Ten. Thirty. Sixty seconds before I strain my ears until I'm sure he's not there.

From Delta's, the best way to the famous pineapple fountain in Waterfront Park is up Meeting Street, then down Broad, then Exchange Street. The wider sidewalks of the main roads make it the fastest way.

But no.

First, a woman running in a Chanel suit like her hair is on fire in the middle of the night would draw way too much attention and ruin our game.

Second, wouldn't Axel expect me to do the most obvious, gambling on my speed versus his?

Third, that's no fun.

Fourth, it's not smart.

Axel's chasing me. And if his father is, too?

Good luck catching me, Bratva boys.

I sprint through a side courtyard and cut through an empty church parking lot. Peeking around a front gate's brick pillar, I scope up and down a quiet, residential street with its renowned homes. It looks empty.

I suppose as I run, at any moment, Axel, his asshole father, or some rando could jump out and grab me but somehow...

It makes this even more thrilling.

Sweat moistens my skin. Desire has long since soaked my panties. My thighs are slick with both, my ribs heaving with bated breath.

But it isn't from exertion. My body's too trained for this.

It's from the thrill of the hunt. The drug of the chase. The rush of being loved.

Axel bought me a ring.

"Yes" beats through my veins.

My feet pound like my heart.

Thirty minutes is more than enough time to race directly to the fountain, but Axel knew that. The extra minutes allow for extra subterfuge.

Which way would he go?

Glancing over my shoulder, I make sure he's not already there. That somehow he didn't double-back to trail me.

But the street yawns, eerie and empty on the sultry night with parked cars sleeping by the curb.

Bolting left, I tread over the undulating cobblestones of Church Street. It's a running hazard from hell and a risky place to race, so of course, I take it.

For blocks, I run, only turning a couple of heads at the odd spectacle of a woman running like the goddess Nike in a Chanel suit and sneakers through Charleston after midnight.

It's laughable.

Then it's odd.

Then...

It's scary.

Where is Axel?

Based on my pace, it's been at least twenty minutes. He should be following me by now. I should hear his familiar footfalls or his husky voice taunting, "Nice ass" from a half block behind.

Glancing over my shoulder again, the gas street lamp glows, defeated by the night veiling the road, shrouded by oak trees and flanked by stately homes. It's empty except for a white utility van, oddly parked in an area of luxury cars.

Shit, I hope that van's for a remodeling job nearby.

No way could Axel's father track me, anticipating I'd be here and use that white van to nab me.

God, I've watched *Silence of the Lamb*s too many times.

That's impossible.

Then I remember what Axel warned—anticipate his father, don't react.

How long could Ruslan Kholodov have been watching Axel King? His son. His declared heir and the next Pakhan? To what lengths would he go to reclaim his honor?

His blood?

Could he already know about me? Maybe he's been watching Axel's office. His home. Maybe he already knows about Delta's and is somehow tracking me, too.

I'm not sure, but I'm fast.

Instinct makes me whip right, turning down a slender, historic alley, famous for its secluded approach to the waterfront. Its cobblestones narrow to only six feet wide, flanked on both sides by white star jasmine spilling over tall, brick walls and ornate iron gates.

It's a charming alleyway, offering cool shadows on a humid summer's day.

But by night?

I stop in the middle of the alley and spin around, gasping at a shadowy figure stalking my way, his heavy shoes clapping over cobblestones.

Tall, wide shoulders, dark suit, dark hair: that's all I can ascertain about the threatening silhouette.

I whip back toward the mouth of the alley, facing the river, and there stands another silhouette. A man with a pooched belly, smoking a cigar.

What the fuck?

I'm trapped?

My pulse skyrockets. Stress attacks my nerves. I feel like a caged animal. A feeling way too familiar and dangerous for me.

Which way do I go? I don't know, so I turn back to fight the silhouette, slamming its palm over my mouth, about to scream.

"You're okay, Wildfire. I got you."

The relief is instant.

I nip Axel's hand and he laughs, yanking it away before I pull him into a relieved kiss, then turn to see the man and his cigar, leaving with a dog on a leash behind him.

"You good?" Axel rasps over my lips.

"Very good." I shove him away, fighting. "Now, fuck you."

He smirks. "No, I'm fucking *you*."

He moves too fast, whipping me around. Pinning my back to his chest, he yanks his chain to my collar, his other hand fisting my skirt.

"Put your hands on the wall, but don't spread your legs," he commands. "Keep them together. Keep your ass really fucking tight for me to fuck."

He's sweating. So am I. His cologne and my perfume waft through the night jasmine air. The low rumble of an occasional car drives by. Pedestrians are absent. Perhaps another resident out for a nightly walk will catch us, but they won't stop us.

Axel's too hungry. "Such a good girl, trying to hide your naughty ass under this tight skirt." He yanks it up, leaving it around my waist. With his lips to my ear, I hear him dragging his zipper down. "I warned you what I was going to do to you tonight, didn't I? Are you afraid?"

"Yes," I lie.

Sort of.

My mind still registers the primal fear of a chase. But now … my fear bleeds into desire, soaking my muscles to relax.

"You know you can fight me, but I can have you any time I want." He reaches around, his hand diving into my panties, his fingers skimming my slick lips. "Um, and your wet pussy sure knows it, too." Teasing, he pulls the bullet out of my lace. Pressing the toy to my lips, he demands, "Taste what your pussy does for me."

I lick my tangy flavor from the warm metal.

"Hmm, such a good girl, licking her cum for me," he praises, tugging the bows free that hold up my panties. With a rude yank, he rips them off.

"Go to hell," I hiss.

"Hell?" Holding my panties to my mouth, he taunts, "Yes, I am going to fuck the *hell* out of your ass. Do you have anything to say before I shut your bratty mouth up for it?"

"Fuck you, dickhead," I hiss, letting it side into my command. "Go ahead. Be a man. Fuck me like you hate me."

"Oh, Ruby." His bearded lips tickle my ear. "I could never hate you, baby. Not when your pussy exists for my cock. Not when your ass needs my cum."

Gently, he presses my wet panties to my lips. "This is for your screams. Taste how they're a lie. Taste how you really want my fuck."

I let him stuff the lace into my mouth, leaving the ribbons to dangle over my chin. He does it just enough so I can breathe, just enough so I can crave my delicious degradation, tasting my desire for him on my tongue.

"Now be a good girl," he growls, "and hold still."

Fabric rustles. It must be Axel adjusting his pants. Quickly, I glance up and down the alley, making sure we're still alone.

Not that I care.

Not that I wouldn't want anyone to watch how much he wants me.

Not that I don't want him, too. Anywhere. Any way.

I tremble when I feel a cool ribbon of lube, drizzle between my cheeks. I moan when Axel turns the crystal plug in my ass, teasing and tugging at it, too. Letting go of my collar, he rubs my aching clit as he gently pulls the toy out, leaving me open, raw, and ready.

A bottle cap *snaps* closed. He must be putting the bottle and plug into his pocket before he presses his lips to my ear.

"You make me like this, Ruby. You make me an animal who wants to fuck you all the time." His wide crown slowly urges into my slick, gaping entrance. "You make me want to do every filthy thing I can to you, for anyone to watch me fuck your ass, because you're so fucking beautiful and mine."

Slowly, Axel thrusts inside me, stretching me even more. He doesn't make it brutal, but he's not tender either. Spanking my tingling clit, he pushes right through the luscious burn in my ass, making me scream into my soaked lace, my thighs trembling, my hands shaking at his invasion.

Quickly, he yanks the panties out of my mouth, dropping them on the cobblestones. "Sorry, baby. Say your safeword if you need it."

"Fuck you," I rasp, jerking my hips, giving him the fight we crave. "And fuck my ass."

"Such a brat." He tugs the chain to my collar, his other fingers circling my clit. "I need to fuck your tight ass and take care of this little attitude you have."

Take care of me?

Axel does.

With lewd, long thrusts of his cock, he drags his thick length out, before driving it back in. Over and over, he pumps into my ass, the pressure luscious and heightening every sensation in my body. My nipples ache. My pussy, too. Every part of me wants him like this.

"Look at you," he praises, his voice husky. "Such a good girl, taking my thick cock in your tight ass. You love it, don't you, Wildfire? All open and gaping for me. Your pretty, pink pussy's dripping for me, too."

"Yes, my king," I sigh, shamelessly arching my back, taking more of whatever he gives me, and Axel's taking me fast.

I don't know how long I can resist the high edge he's fucking me to. My hands find purchase against the brick wall, braced for his force, but slick lust streams down my thighs, wanting to slide into the waiting storm of pleasure.

I don't want to fight Axel.

I want to fall into him and never return.

Like he senses my need, his fingers glide to my aching entrance. Plunging them inside me, his palm grinds over my clit. "So full of me, aren't you, my queen?" He groans, "Your sweet cunt is dripping over my hand. Your tight ass clenches, loving my cock. Fuck, Wildfire, you can fight me all you want, but you have me. All of me. Always."

"Axel, please," I beg, abandoning our roles. "I want to come for you. Only you."

He squeezes my neck. "Only me?"

"Yes," I rasp. "Always, only you."

"Good girl," he praises. "Now, come for your king." With a brutal thrust, he makes me take every thick inch, and I see stars. I feel his piercing, our ring, pressed against my tightest entrance, and I can't find logic. The pressure and pleasure are too intense.

I can only feel his fingers, claiming my cunt, his palm,

exciting my clit, his lips to my ear, his heart pounding with mine.

Axel's everywhere inside me.

With another brute thrust into my ass and his gruff command, "Come, my queen," pleasure bursts through my core, cracking my walls. I cry out, and he covers my mouth, my shaking screams against his palm as savage as the blinding orgasm tearing through me.

It's in control. Not me. It rushes over his hand, streaming down my shaking thighs. All that I've been holding back for hours won't stop squirting from my cunt and Axel loses his mind with me.

"Oh, fuck, Ruby. Fuck, you're squirting for me." He sounds primitive. In pain. Unstoppable and unleashed. "Oh fuck, baby, I love you."

He pumps into me, ruthlessly, cresting another wave inside me. He feels it, my walls pulsing around his fingers. It almost hurts, making me mewl into his hand, so he pulls them out, his slick fingers barely teasing my clit. That's all it takes with his feral thrusts.

"Axel," is all I can moan, think, or feel while I convulse, coming again with a splash over the cobblestones.

"Oh, fuck, Ruby, you're making me come." He uncovers my mouth, reaching to hold my hand, grasping the wall. He grabs my other, too, his hand dripping with my release.

With our hands clasped against the wall, his hips hammer, his cock claiming whatever is left of me. With a groan, he bites my neck, his thighs shaking against mine. Burying his face into my flesh, he grunts over my skin as his hulking body locks, and he spills inside me.

I can feel it. Pulse after pulse. His cock jumping with his next grunt, and I'm still pulsing and panting, too.

But suddenly, I sort of remember where we are, who we

are, and for a moment, I fight for my focus. My hooded eyelids part, and I glance one way, then the other.

Thank god, we weren't busted.

But still.

"Axel," I sigh with his head on my shoulder, his hands still clutching mine. "We need to get somewhere safe."

"I don't care." He exhales. "I want to live and die with you, Ruby. Only you. You're all I care about."

I feel it, too. I didn't know I could feel this much ... but, "You care about more than that." I sweet-talk, "And you're kinda buried deep in my ass in a public space, so imagine the look on your mom's face if she has to bail us out for lewdness and indecent exposure."

He chuckles into my shoulder, but won't let my hands go. "At least laws against sodomy are unenforceable."

Softly, I tease, "You really want to test that case right now, counselor?"

Gently, Axel leaves my body before smoothing my skirt down. I'm dripping and shaking as he asks, "Are you okay?"

"Never been better." I mean it, turning around with a wobble. "But I don't think I can walk." Instead, I sag against the brick wall.

"I got you," he assures. "Just hang on. I'll text Jace to pick us up."

He gives me an adoring kiss before I can protest Jace seeing us like this. And his kiss doesn't stop until he's finished arranging himself.

It's June and we're dressed for a fancy church wedding, though I'm sure we look like sweaty, fucking hell and it makes me laugh.

"What's so funny?" he asks, taking his phone from the pocket of his rumpled jacket to fire off a quick text to his brother.

"I never thought we'd be here," I marvel. "Chanel. Collars.

Cum down our legs. Panties on the ground. Butt plugs in pockets and—"

"And don't forget a ring in my pocket." He cups my face. "I always knew I'd finally catch you."

Is everything about to change? Yes, I want it to. My heart flutters, happy and not afraid to ask…

"But can you not ask me three minutes after our first anal? I need more romance than that."

When Axel smiles, I swear his eyes are my rising sun.

"Oh, so my queen wants a royal proposal?"

"At least throw in a Burger King crown."

"She wants a whopper of an engagement." He aims his smirking lips for mine. "Noted."

CHAPTER THIRTY-ONE
AXEL

"Are you sure this dress is okay to meet your mom?" Ruby smooths the front of her lilac Chanel frock.

"You look beautiful, Wildfire."

It's not a lie. Ruby takes my breath away.

She's twisted her hair up with fiery tendrils falling free. Her lips are painted blood-red, the contrast with her blue eyes mesmerizing. Her curves in that dress are sinful, but it's that color. It makes me a better man.

"You know, you wore lilac the first time I saw you, and it was love at first sight."

"Insta-love?" she questions. "That's only in romance novels."

"The ones with or without shirtless men?"

"Both, and it's pure fiction."

"Your honor, if I may introduce my beating heart as evidence." I hold her hand to my chest, her warmth seeping through my shirt. "Because you sat in front of me in a lilac dress with a bleeding kneecap, and wouldn't shut up about how incredible you are, and my heart agreed. This damn thing hasn't stopped beating for you since. This is insta-love, Wildfire. Case closed."

She swallows, and I'm dying to know, "Did you get insta-love for me, too?"

"No." She shakes her head. "I felt insta-hate. Like white hot and obsessive. I couldn't stop thinking about how much I hated you."

"Why?"

"Because I saw the posters on the front of your office before my interview. That's why I tripped. I'd never seen a law office do that; warn about the signs of sex trafficking. I was touched and impressed. But then I met you and you shot that all to hell."

She makes me laugh. "How?"

"Because you look like an orgasm of muscles and ink with ice blue eyes that would make God marry the Devil. And don't get me started on your nose ring and bling."

"Wow," I smirk, "my ego's growing bigger than my cock."

"That, too," she confesses. "I clocked your bulge when you stood to shake my hand. I hated every thick inch of it."

"Yep, that's growing to hate you, too."

Cutely, she rolls her eyes. "But then you stalked me for so long, and I finally figured it out."

"This should be good."

"This is fact: the opposite of love isn't hate. It's apathy. It's when you don't care. Because hatred requires the same passion as love. But I didn't trust love when I met you, so I hated you."

"And now?"

"Now?" Her eyes soften, her hand on my chest gripping it harder. "I love hating you, Axel King."

Good God, this woman. If this is what romance feels like, hand me a shirtless man book. I'm in.

"Oh, so you still hate me?" I aim my mouth for hers, hoping to wear her lipstick tonight.

"Yes," she sighs over my lips. "You're the first man I've hated. The only man I'll ever hate. The man I'll die hating. And I'm going to live, every day, hating you so much that your heart will grow bigger than your cock and ego combined."

"I'm going to need more evidence."

I take Ruby in a kiss that proves more. It's every sunrise we'll share. Every night she'll be mine. Every stupid fuss and stubborn fight. Every child and every memory I will have with her.

Jesus H. Christ, this woman had me at first sight.

"Wow," she gasps, grabbing a breath. "I really hate your kiss, too."

"Um, I agree. Your bratty, soft lips are abhorrent."

"Oh shit," she gasps, "my lipstick."

Licking the pad of her thumb, she reaches for my mouth.

But I gently grab her wrist. "Is that your spit you're about to clean my face with?"

"What?" She laughs. "Your tongue will play tonsil hockey in my mouth, but I can't use spit to wipe my lipstick off your face before I meet your mother? I don't think so. Hold still. I need to make a good impression."

"This is impressive, alright," I mutter, letting her groom me. "I'm fucking five again."

"Small price to pay to impress your mom."

"I don't need to impress her. She *has* to love me."

I touch the small of Ruby's back, guiding her past the guards at our bunker's double, metal doors. We just gave them a helluva show, and I give zero fucks about it.

I didn't want Ruby to meet my mom here, but The Queen insisted.

"But *I* want to impress her," she whispers nervously. "What should I call her?"

"Most call her Ms. Faye. Or Nadine. Or The Queen." I take her hand, leading her down the corridor. "And, you'll call her Mom one day."

The rare ring I bought for Ruby burns a hole in my pocket. I'll propose to her, but I'll do it as she requested. An intimate, romantic moment. Lots of lilac flowers and tears. Then a royal party where I can show her off to family and friends.

But the timing is bad.

We just ambushed Turner's compound last night. The sadistic fuck hid his human trafficking empire in an old church. We took out his men and rescued the victims, but Turner was MIA.

He's still on the loose.

Add that to Halstead, the irate rental property owner bribing Ruby, Nick, Stacey's step-daughter, and countless others. Grant pays Ruby's weekly bribe for his silence while Nash follows the money trail.

Our payments are a trap. We're figuring out how Halstead operates, who he's extorting, and where he hides.

All while we have Alena and Loch's wedding to celebrate this weekend.

And then ... there's this.

My captive, half-brother.

My mother won't share the intel she's getting from him, and I understand. She doesn't want to talk about it until she's sure—until she knows which of her sons betrayed her.

"What if she doesn't like me?" Ruby worries.

"She already loves you."

"How?"

"Because I do."

She pauses, tugging our held hands. "You can't be so sweet when I have to be serious."

"Should I be a dickhead instead?"

She grins. "You're really good at it."

"You really *love* it..." I smirk. "In your mouth."

"Axel." Her eyes widen with her smile. "Not here. Good impressions, remember?"

"Here?" I glance around. "Wildfire, read the room. We're in our hidden bunker full of recently used guns and weapons. You're about to meet my mother, the owner of the most exclusive sex club in the South. She's a dominatrix who'll shoot men's kneecaps for grabbing women. And you're about to meet our captive, too. My half-brother, whom we'll kill once we get the intel we need. By comparison, you're tracking just fine. Don't worry."

"That's easy for you to say."

"No, it isn't easy," I say softly. "It's serious, because I'm serious about you. I want you to meet my mother. For her to see why I love you and to give us her blessing, because after Alena's wedding, it's our turn."

Her eyes sparkle. "Who said we're getting married?"

"Me."

"Hmm." She lilts, "Better ask me nicely or I'll say no."

"Better say yes, or I'll spank you."

"Not in front of the kittens."

"Nah." I tsk. "All of my pussies need to see who's boss."

"They see me every day."

I laugh. "You wish."

"You *know*." She laughs back.

"Care to share the joke?" A velvet voice echoes down the concrete corridor.

My laughing eyes swing in my mother's direction.

With one hand on her hip, she holds a cigar in the other.

With her toned body and long, dark hair in a chignon, she doesn't look a day over forty, wearing a black leather sleeveless dress and blood-red spiked heels.

Smoke curls around her. Armed guards stand, ready for her command. The heavy door to the captive's room is closed as Ruby's mouth falls open.

"Oh my god," she mutters at the lethal sight of my mom. "Big fan. Like, huge."

"Mom," I tug Ruby's hand, leading our steps and the introduction, "please meet Ruby Jones, my future queen."

"Well, you sure look like one." With open arms, Mom pulls Ruby into a hug. "Dressed like a cowgirl or in Chanel. My dear," Mom gushes, "you are *stunning*. No wonder my son is so smitten."

"Is he smitten?" Ruby jokes, meeting her eyes. "Or smug? It's hard to tell."

"Both, darlin'," Mom drawls, beaming at her. "That's what happens when God gives them balls *and* brains. But don't worry. They've got nothing compared to ours."

They laugh, their ease instant. I never doubted it. They're a lot alike.

And God, help me.

"It's nice to meet you, Ms. Faye," Ruby says. "For real, this time."

"Please." Mom waves her cigar. "Call me Nadine, and call me impressed." She winks at me. "I approve. She's whiskey in a teacup."

I laugh. "You *just* met her."

"Bless your heart," Mom sighs. "Shall I wait another minute to draw the same conclusion, or can we move on?"

"Yes, ma'am."

It's what every wise man says to survive.

"Now," Mom takes Ruby's hand, "before you say yes to my

handsome second-born, you must know what you're agreeing to. In our world, we have great days and gruesome ones. Do you understand?"

Ruby nods. "Yes, ma'am."

"My boys and I do good work in evil ways," Mom explains. "The victims we help don't need prayers and patience. They deserve pissed off women who won't put up with this shit anymore. You must be one of those women, or my son wouldn't be so in love."

"Yes, ma'am. I am."

Ruby nods, not intimidated. She's in awe. Most are when they meet my mom.

"Good." Mom nods back. "Now, I have a situation in this room. What I must do to get the information I need may make you uncomfortable, so you can leave, but it would help me if you stay. This man wants an audience for his pain."

With dread, I exhale. "Mom, do I have to watch this? I'm fine with blood, but not your BDSM."

Mom tsks just like me. "Quit clutching your pearls. I ain't getting naked or fornicating. I'm just using whips. Nothing to permanently scar your mind."

Ruby snorts, cutting her eyes at me. "It's not like you're an angel, either."

"I'm sure he's quite the devil, and I don't want to see it." Mom puffs her cigar. "Just as long as my boys never hurt a woman, I don't need to know how they love her."

"He does love me," Ruby rushes. "Thank you for raising a good man. Axel cooks me breakfast and gives me foot massages and—"

Mom looks at me, sharing the memory of what only she's seen. My scarred feet. But that was thirty years ago, and no one has seen them since.

Yes, it's why I massage Ruby's feet. It's not a fetish. It's love. Her feet are perfect with no marks of pain, and that's how every inch of her body will remain.

Touch my queen, and you've taken your last breath.

"She loves me, too." I want Mom to know, "Ruby likes shining my shoes, and she bought me six pairs of these." I lift the hem of my dress pants.

"Are those…" Mom trails off, laughing.

"Dickhead socks!" Ruby chirps. "I got him a pair in every color."

Yeah, Ruby took my soul with these. She understands why I won't let her see my feet, so she makes sure my shoes are spiffy and my socks are well … cocky.

Fuck, I love her.

"As I said," Mom brags, "if she ain't the jam to your jelly, no woman is."

"She is," I say. "And I really want to get this over with and take her home." *And fuck her all night.* "So, what's next?"

"Alright then." Mom hands her cigar to a guard. "I'm going to need your help."

Oh, fuck.

"Mine?"

"No. Hers." Mom turns to Ruby. "Have you used a feather tickler before?"

"Uh…" Ruby stammers, nervously looking at me. "*No?*"

Mom laughs. "Okay. Good. You're a pro. So, when I tell you to, tickle my captive's dick and—"

"The fuck she will!" I bark.

"You tried it your way." Mom's calm. "He's hamstrung, remember? And it didn't work. And I don't have time to go around my ass to get to my elbow. He's someone's sub, and I know how to break him. To get this intel."

What just happened to my life?

The love of my life, my future wife, is about to help my

mother, a famous dominatrix apparently, use BDSM pleasure to torture intel out of my half-brother?

This is a Freudian hell.

I'm just glad Nash isn't here for this. Or Sire. Or Grant. Hell, any of my brothers. I'll never live this down.

Then again.

Maybe this is the only way to find out if one sold us out.

"Prepare yourself," Mom warns. "I've held him captive for almost three weeks with no relief."

I arch a brow. "Relief?"

"Don't make me paint a picture."

Oh, but Mom just did. She hasn't let him come in three weeks. I'd almost feel sorry for him if I didn't pity myself more for knowing it.

"Does he have a name?" Ruby asks.

"That's the only intel I have so far," Mom shares. "Roman Kholodov. That's his name."

With her signal, a guard opens the heavy metal door. Instantly, I'm hit with the smell of sandalwood incense and notice that the harsh overhead fluorescent lights are off. They're replaced by candles glowing around the room and floor lamps in the corners.

I know what she's doing.

She's relaxing our captive. Seducing him.

We enter the room, and I keep my face emotionless, noting how she's added a pillow and blankets to his iron bed. How she's taken him out of his humiliating position on the floor. With the help of her guards, she's strapped him, naked, to a padded Saint Andrew's Cross propped against the wall.

"We have guests, my toy," Mom tells him, aiming for her table of whips and gear while Ruby stands dutifully by my side, across the room from him.

But Ruby doesn't seem afraid. Hell no, she's fascinated, and I fight the roll of my eyes.

"Oh my God," she mutters to me. "It's genetic."

She means *that*. His big, erect dick, jutting before him. I can't avoid it, and she's right. Size runs in the family.

"Greet them," Mom commands him.

"Yes, Domina," he answers, proudly standing spread-eagled with his ankles and wrists bound to the X cross. "Good ... *evening*," he guesses the time of day, looking me dead in the eye.

"I told my guests," Mom picks up a leather flogger and a feather tickler, "what a bad toy you've been. How I play with you, yet you still won't please me with answers."

For minutes, she flogs him, one lash after another across his bare thighs, leaving angry welts behind. But he doesn't cry out in pain. His lips part with euphoria. Though his muscles tense at her stinging flogs, his face is relaxed, his smile satisfied by her torture.

He loves this.

And why do I get the feeling...

He's falling in love with my mom.

I'd be disgusted if my mother hadn't raised me as an open-minded adult. I don't judge kinks, and I want this intel.

"I'm not pleased, my toy. You like my pain too much," Mom scolds him. "You like them seeing your discipline, don't you? How you can't be broken. So what if..." She crooks her finger at Ruby. "We break you in the softest way?"

On cue, Ruby approaches my mom, and every muscle in my body tenses. Though our captive is bound, if he escapes. If he lays a hand on her or my mom, I'll slice his neck open and pour salt down his throat.

"This is my princess," Mom says of Ruby. "Isn't she beautiful? I'm training her, and you're going to like it too much, how her feathers feel."

She hands the tickler to Ruby, who glances back at me for permission, and I nod.

Fuck it. I trust Ruby, and my mom knows what she's doing. And I want to know how Roman Kholodov found us.

"Show him, my princess," Mom speaks regally to Ruby. "Show him how a woman can break a strong man like him with a feather."

It's the last thing a man like him wants. Me, too.

With a wicked grin, Ruby tickles red feathers under the shaft of his soaring cock and he groans, his left thigh suddenly shaking.

"Please, Domina," he begs, dropping his head. "Don't make me."

"But we can't make you, can we?" Mom gestures to Ruby to do it more. "We can't cut you or beat it out of you, so what if we show you how easily you can be broken by the simple touch from a woman?"

Inspired, Ruby barely dusts the feathers over the swollen head of his cock, making Roman grunt and me snarl, "Come on my woman and I'll cut it off."

Fuck, I'm going to punish her tonight for this and we'll both love it.

Then again, Ruby's never looked more beautiful to me. Ruling like my mother. Ruthless in her protection for us. No matter what it takes, feathers or fights, Ruby would start a war for us.

"I think he's going to come, my queen." Ruby taunts him, dusting his tip. "He can't fight us. He's too weak. He's dripping for us."

"No…" Roman huffs. "Not like this. Please, Domina." He lifts his desperate eyes to my mom. "You know how I want it. How I *want* to serve you."

Unfortunately, I do.

The strapons on my mom's gear table leave nothing to the imagination, and I wonder if I shampoo with Clorox if I can bleach the image from my mind.

"Then tell me," Mom coaxes. "Be my good toy, and I'll play with you. I'll give you what you need. Tell me how you found us, or my princess will make you come, and you won't get to lick my heels."

With huffing breath, he stares at her, his brows bent for her. He's fighting it, but then Ruby starts tickling his balls, and his other thigh shakes, too.

"Please, Domina," he begs.

"Tell us," Mom commands. "Or come."

"*Yebat',*" he groans in Russian. *Fuck* is what it means and what he's desperate for.

"Tell us," Mom urges. "How did you find me?"

Stepping so close that her leather dress brushes his naked flesh, she whispers something in his ear. A promise to fuck him, I'm sure, and he groans, tossing his chin up.

"Your son," he heaves.

"Who?" I growl, demanding a name, and fearing it, too.

*Please don't say Lyov, Nikifor, Jasha, o*r any of my brothers' Russian names. It will destroy me.

"Yours." Roman lifts his glare my way. "*Your* son."

Ruby stops, shocked like me. She steps back while I step toward him.

"What did you just say?" I demand.

"You have a son," Roman confesses. "With your Katya. She was my wife before she was yours, and *that's* how I found you."

When everything you know explodes, it's silent. Chaos claims your mind while the fragments of your life fall into new places. You stand numb in its destruction.

I can't even feel my heart pounding in my chest. I can't see. Tears blur my vision. I'm blind. All my senses leave me, while my mind can only focus on...

My son?

I have...

A son.

"Don't do that." The smacking sound of Ruby slapping his face brings me back. "Don't lie and hurt him like that." She's crying. She's defending me.

"I'm not lying," Roman insists, his cock deflating at the heavy truth in the room.

I glance at my mom, and she's in shock, too, shaking her head.

But then it hits me: the primal instinct. "Where is he?" I sneer. "Where's *my* son?"

"In Moscow," he answers. "With her and our father. They're married now. He took her from me and sent her to you. To get pregnant by you and then return to him. To give him his true heir."

It makes so much sense, I feel sick, worrying, "Is he okay? My son? Does he *hurt* him?"

With tears biting at my eyes, it's my only thought. I'm a little boy again, remembering my father's abuse, and all I don't want to imagine is my son being hurt, too.

"No." Roman sags against his cross. "He treats him like a princess, not his prince. Not like we were raised. Our father is weak with age and cancer. He dotes on his grandson. At least," he exhales, "the last time I saw him."

"What's his name?" Mom clenches her teeth. "What is my grandson's name?"

Roman looks at me, answering, "Lev. His name is Lev."

"Lion," I mutter, though my heart pounds. "Of course, he named him *lion*."

"But how?" Ruby questions, "How did Katya find Axel?"

"I don't know." Roman tugs at his wrists. It strikes me how he barely speaks with an accent. "Just..." He yanks at his chains again. "I hate him as much as you do. Just let me sit down and explain."

Mom looks at me, and I pull the gun from my back

holster. "Wildfire," I order her, "step back." I keep my aim on him, not wanting Ruby near while my mom unfastens the buckles and leather straps restraining Roman.

"Sit." She points to his bed, and limping with a bandage on the back of his thigh, he obeys.

"Tell us everything from the beginning," The Queen demands, "or today is your last."

CHAPTER THIRTY-TWO
RUBY

I can't take my eyes off Axel while tears spill from mine.

He has a son.

And he didn't know about him.

God, it would break my heart into a million pieces if that happened to me. Of course, it's a virtual impossibility for a woman. But for a man?

What a cruel punishment.

All Axel wants is marriage and kids. He'd be a great father.

But now, all I can see is his focused rage and pain, the muzzle of his gun aimed at his half-brother, while Roman explains, "My mom was your maid's daughter." He looks at Nadine. "Remember her?"

"Polina, my lady-in-waiting?" Nadine looks appalled. "Her little girl, Eva? She's your mother? Oh my god, she's too young."

"She was," Roman snarls. "She was fourteen, just as you were when you had Sergei."

Sergei?

Oh, he means *Sire*, Axel's oldest brother.

"I grew up hearing about you," Roman continues. "All of you. You're mythical back home. The six lion princes who escaped with their mother, the lioness. The mother who'd rather be free and die with her sons than live as Ruslan Kholodov's captives. The queen who escaped with the love of her second king. You're legends."

"So what?" Axel fumes. "Our father sent you to kill us?"

Roman shrugs. "That's how he raised me. American English. Martial arts. Tactical and weapons training. He tried to make me into his *boyevik*." Roman looks at me, translating. "His warrior, but he neglected one thing."

Nadine nods. "How much you hated him, too."

"For what he did to my mother?" Roman answers, "What he wouldn't stop doing to her? Yes. Then, I got older, and fell in love with his *Sovietnik's* daughter and—"

"What's a Soviet Nick?" I ask.

"Like a *consigliere*." Axel glares at Roman, but answers me, "His advisor."

"Oh my God." Nadine shakes her head. "Viktor's daughter? Katerina? I hadn't seen her since she was a baby, but I see it now. She was Katya?"

"Yes, and she was my wife," Roman answers. "We were young, and I thought we were in love, but she used me to get close to the Pakhan. She started flirting with him and making other plans. I was his bastard son, and he wanted a true heir. His only heir. And Katerina was very eager to provide one."

"So he didn't force Katerina—" Nadine pauses. "I mean, *Katya* to leave you and seduce Axel? My son? She wanted to do it?"

"How did he know I was here?" Axel seethes.

"I don't know." Roman holds his hands up. "Honestly, I don't. One night, Kat was with me; the next day, she was gone. And all I got were orders from our father to never speak about her again, or he'd kill my mother. My grand-mother, too."

"Then how did you find me?" Fury twists Axel's handsome face, and I can imagine everything he's questioning.

Every moment spent with Katya. Every day since she left him, pregnant, with his son. Every year he's missed so far.

"When she came home a year later," Roman answers, "she wouldn't speak to me. It was obvious she was pregnant, and all she wanted was power. Was to be Ruslan's queen, the mother to his heir, and I was dead to her. But one night..."

He trails off, and suddenly, I have sympathy for him, too. When he's not bound and highly aroused, Roman is a beautiful man. Black wavy hair. Brown eyes with thick lashes. He has Axel's perfect nose. Straight and proportioned over full lips with a defined bow. Like him, he's covered in ink and pain.

Roman's not Axel's enemy. They have too much in common.

Including betrayal.

I swear, if I ever meet Katya, I'll cut the bitch. I'll do it country style in the kidney with an Arkansas toothpick.

"But what?" Nadine encourages him. "What happened?"

"But one night, I went looking for answers," Roman says. "I broke into their sleeping quarters, and saw Lev sleeping in his crib and—"

I glance at Axel.

Anguish pours down his stunning face.

"By his crib," Roman continues, "by the lamp and baby stuff, there was a green rose made of twisted, dried grass in a vase. It wasn't Russian, and it didn't belong. It was my only clue."

"A Palmetto Rose," Axel fumes. "It's what I gave Katya on our first date, and she kept it."

"So..." My heart starts racing, oddly afraid. "So Katya still *loves* Axel and kept his rose and—"

"No." Roman sharpens his eyes. "That woman only loves herself. She's driven by ego, power, and money. But I guess somewhere in her cold heart, she knows who the father of her son is. She keeps one piece of him alive, the Palmetto Rose, and it took me a year to figure out what it was and where it came from."

"So you came to Charleston," Nadine presses. "Did you tell anyone?"

"No," he answers. "I was on a mission. *My* mission."

"To do what?" Axel won't drop his gun.

"Kill you." Roman shrugs. "Join you. Get revenge. I wasn't sure. I wanted to find you first."

"How'd you do it?" The investigator in me demands to know, "How, out of hundreds of thousands, did you find Axel?"

"I didn't." Roman meets my eyes. "I've been here a while and finally found Pastor Sire Rutledge. He was on the news, doing a humanitarian relief drive for his church, and I went."

"Fuck," Axel mutters. "I told him to stay off camera."

"Yeah," Roman agrees. "He looks like Ruslan. All of you do. Or maybe, because I have a mirror, I know what to look for."

"So you followed Sire," I push, "and then what?"

"Then, one day a few weeks later, Sire Rutledge walked down Meeting Street and met a man who looked even more like my father before they entered The Mercier Hotel."

Axel shakes his head.

Roman's talking about him.

"Then, they came out an hour later and walked straight to Delta's," Roman concludes, "where they met two more men who look like my brothers, too."

CHAPTER THIRTY-THREE
RUBY

"We need to name them." Axel pets the kitten prowling up his chest.

I lie nude on my side, nestled against him. We've been cuddled in bed all day, watching movies. Then, he brought Sparky and the kittens to bed for some comfort, too, and I understand.

For two days, he's been quiet, processing the shock of his son.

"But they all look alike." I pet another golden fur ball. "I can't tell them apart yet."

"This one has white sock feet." He pets the one on his chest. "And this one," he reaches for the one, climbing his thigh. "Ouch. With sharp claws, has a white face and—"

But I feel this for him too much. Axel's hurting, and I want to help him talk about it.

"What did you want to name ... *him?*"

I'm not asking about our kittens.

Axel's moved us to a villa at a golf resort on Daniel Island. He said Alena's wedding is here in three days, and the kings own this resort. They have it locked down and covered with security. And he said he wants me to come to Alena's wedding.

No hiding behind a lace hood this time.

I'll join him as his future queen.

"Max," Axel answers me heavily. "I always wanted to name my first son after my real father, Maxim. My mom's second king. The man who helped us escape."

"Maxim was good to you?"

"He was good to all of us. He was a Vor. A *vory v zakone*. It's an elite status in the Bratva. They're leaders. They settle disputes. They're connected to politicians, and that's how we got out. Maxim used his connections. Burned them, actually. To get us out, knowing he'd never go back. He crashed his plane into the Baltic Sea and died for us. My father thought we were on that plane." He pauses. "Or so *we* thought."

"I believe Roman," I say warmly. "He was hurt just like you. I don't think he's a threat."

"I don't either. So that means…"

"That means it was someone else who told your father and Katya where you were."

Axel nods, silently rubbing Sparky's chin. She sits beside him, loyal and purring.

"Do you want to talk about him? Lev?"

The hinge of his jaw flexes. "I'll kill him if he's hurting him."

"Roman said he's not. He said your father is old and dying. Maybe after losing his sons. Maybe he's changed. Maybe his grandson is too precious to him. He won't hurt him."

"If age doesn't kill that man first, I will. I'm going to rip my father's throat open for what he's done."

I kiss the black skull on his shoulder, believing him.

After a moment, letting his rage pass, he says, "I wonder what he looks like."

"Like you," I answer tenderly. "You've got all that alpha

DNA. I bet he has dark hair and brows with a perfect nose, perfect lips, and blue eyes that melt your heart and—"

"I want one with you," he interrupts, turning to me. "Ruby, I swear I'll get my son back. I feel sick, worried about him, wondering about him. I won't rest until Lev is home, safe with me. With *us*. I'll never give up on him, and I want one with you, too. Daughters and sons. A real marriage. A woman I love and trust. Old age and rocking chairs and—"

Heat blooms in my chest.

"Axel, are you asking me—"

"God, Wildfire. You're so predictable." He finally smiles. "I can't propose after anal, but you want your engagement to begin with me in boxers and covered in kittens? No, I'll propose the right way."

He has no idea how *right* he looks *right* now.

Domineering. Doting. Lethal. Loving. A killer covered in ink and kittens.

No time like the present to commit to my future.

But I worry, "You need to know what you're asking for. I understand your world now, but you have to understand mine."

His brows furrow. "I do. I see you, Ruby. I always have."

"No." I exhale, sharing what I hide from most. Even him. "You see a lot about me, but not my epilepsy. It's an invisible disability. Most of the time, I'm fine. I take my meds, manage my triggers, and take care of myself. But it's always there, waiting for me like a bomb that can drop at any moment. And if I want to get pregnant, I have to change my medications, and that changes everything."

He reaches for my face. "I'll do whatever you need."

"But Axel, we'd have to plan it. What if I have a drop seizure while I'm really pregnant or holding our baby? I worry about having a seizure all the time," I confess, tears welling in my eyes. "I just don't like talking about it. It owns enough of my life as it is. I won't give it more power."

"Okay." He nods. "How do we plan?"

"We'd need a new house," I explain. "No stairs. No sharp corners. All soft carpets. It's dangerous for me to cook by myself, or even take a bath by myself, and what if I have a seizure while bathing our baby? I can't do some things on my own, and if I'm a mom, what if—"

"It's okay." He cups my cheeks. "I'll be there the whole time. We'll baby-proof *and* Ruby-proof our new home."

His smile is assuring, but...

"You can't be there the whole time."

"I can be there as much as I can. I *want* to be. And when I'm not? Have you met my mom? She'd love it. Or Wren. Or Sire. God, he'd make the best uncle. You should hear him sing. And Jace? He's a teddy bear. Kids love him. And then add in all your sisters? We're not alone. For better or for worse."

"What if you resent me one day? For needing you?"

He shakes his head, as if he's in on a secret I'm just now learning.

"Wildfire, you needing me is all I've been waiting for."

He pulls me into a kiss. His lips soft. His beard tickling. His tongue tempting. His breath promising, "Because I need you, too."

I search his piercing eyes and see our truth. Our future together.

"Okay," my voice eases, "but we're getting way ahead of ourselves." I nuzzle his nose. "There's no ring on my finger."

"Such a feisty woman." His lips quirk. "You want to fight me for it?"

"Fight you? For my ring?" With the way Axel looks now, I'd kill for it. "You may be primal, but I have pride. You know the drill. Get on your knees for me."

"Yes, ma'am," he smirks, plucking kittens off him. "Come on, Sparky. You know the drill, too. No more cockblocking and blue balls."

Axel corrals the kittens, exploding my ovaries when he holds all six, mewling in his inked arms. "Listen here," he orders them, aiming for the ensuite bathroom. "Play with the toilet paper. Make a mess as usual. I don't care. Just give us an hour or three."

Once he sets Sparky in there, too, he closes the door and stalks toward the bed.

"Now, someone was talking about me on my knees with my blue eyes and alpha DNA, and—" He yanks my ankles toward the edge of the bed, making me squeal. "I think we need to practice spreading it." He smirks. "Like your thighs."

"You're already ready for me?"

Slowly, he wedges his boxers to his ankles, his eyes locked to mine as his hefty cock springs free. "Look down and find out, Wildfire."

I lick my lips, my heart lighter now that Axel's smirking again. It's been a rough couple of days for him, and this isn't about me. I need to take care of him, too.

"Lie down, my king, and let me serve you." I tease, "Any way I please."

His eyes narrow, intrigued. I move aside so he can stretch across the bed with his head on a pillow.

"It's my turn to kneel." I fist his thick base, lifting his heavy shaft. Gazing into his eyes, I wrap my lips around his tip and take what I can of his length into my mouth. Loving it. Loving his girth. His taste. His pleasure. Bobbing my head up and down, I moan, giving him a show, letting his crown hit my throat each time.

"*Fuck*," he rasps, "look at you. So fucking beautiful choking on my cock." He fists my hair, licking his lips at the sight. "But this isn't how we practice making our babies."

Spit webs from my lips to his swollen tip while I grin, "Shut up, dickhead," and flick his sensitive frenulum with my tongue, making his eyelids flutter with his moan.

"Now, let me give you something you've given me." Leaning over, I open the nightstand. Of course, I brought toys and lube. We're here for a wedding after all. The mood is perfect.

I turn back and present him with the purple anal plug he used on me last week. "Can I please you with this, my king?" I ask, teasing it over my hard nipples.

Axel grins. "You want to take my virginity?"

"You mean you've never?"

He shakes his head. "But I will for you. I meant it, Ruby. I'll do anything for you."

"But do you *want* it?"

When he spreads his muscular thighs, opening himself to me, it's so sexy, my clit ignites. "I'm sure my Wildfire will *make* me want it." He fists his shaft. "Are you going to pop my cherry with your fingers first?"

"No, rookie." It's my turn to smirk. "Not with fake fingernails, I won't."

"Hmm." His eyelids hood with lust. "Then keep your nails natural for our wedding night, so I can feel you inside me then."

Our wedding night? I can see it.

And tonight? I feel this inside, too. It's so erotic. It makes me so wet, covering the smooth toy in lube and pressing it to Axel's virgin entrance.

He grunts, shocked by the sensation, but doesn't fight it. For the longest time, I don't push it in. I tease and probe him, relishing his moans while I lavish his cock, stroking it and sucking it, making him writhe until he lifts his hips off the bed, demanding, "Fuck, Ruby. Do it, baby. Put it in my ass."

Gently, I press, slowly stretching him until the plug is at its widest part, about to breach him. "Exhale," I tell him. "Exhale while I push it in."

Axel obeys and it's the hottest thing ever, taking his ass for the first time, while I plunge my mouth down his swollen cock, gagging on it for his pleasure, too.

He fists my hair tighter and roars, *"Fuck!!"*

I open my eyes to see tremors shaking his inked quad. With his leaking tip salting my lips, I ask, "Do you like me in your ass, Axel?"

"Oh fuck," he huffs, staring down at me. "Oh fuck, yes. It feels weird and good and fuck, baby. Fuck. Fuck me."

"Yes, my king." I leave his shaft, covered in my spit, and straddle him, rubbing his tip over my excited clit. "Like this? Is this how you want me to fuck you?"

I barely seat his wide crown inside me. Circling my hips, I make Axel grab them while I please him, control him, his lips parting, his stunning eyes anticipating, needing.

"Fuck, you should see how hot you look right now," he rasps. "Fuck, Ruby. Your hair. Your eyes. Your tits. Your pretty pussy. Don't ever shave it bare." With his thumbs, he parts my lips, staring at where we're joined. "Look at us. Look at your little pink clit."

He fondles it, and I moan, taking another inch.

"Good girl," he praises. "Just like that. Take my cock. Let me watch it stretch you open."

He's right. Taking Axel all at once can make me see stars. Sometimes I like it. But not on top. I like riding him, teasing him, slowly taking him inch by inch.

"That's it. Such a good girl for me." He circles his thumb over my clit, his other hand reaching to tug at my nipple. I love it when he's rough with them—slapping them and biting them. But tonight?

"Ride me," he demands. "You know what I want. Ride me and make your pretty tits bounce for me."

"Yes, sir," I sigh, loving it when he makes me give him a dirty show. And I do. I arch my back and use my thighs, bouncing on his generous length. "Like this? Am I your good girl fucking you like this?"

"Oh fuck, yes." His lush lips part in awe, his stare drinking me in. His strong hands guide my hips to move faster, harder. "You want all this cock inside you, don't you, baby?"

"Yes." Just the sight of Axel takes me. But then his warm touch. His maddening stretch. His taunts and dirty desire. The way he watches me, wanting me. "Please, my king," I start trembling.

He grabs my throat. "Now, take me. Take every fucking inch of my cock in this tight, wet pussy."

I obey, sinking to his base, moaning when my clit hits Axel's piercing. Every time it hits my soul, too.

He got it for me. Only me.

I grind over it, and Axel groans, buried so deep inside me.

"Can you feel me?" I lower my lips to his. "Can you feel how wet I am for you, rubbing my hard clit on you? On our piercing? Can you feel me in your ass, Axel? Do you like it? Will you let me fuck your ass one day?"

"Oh fuck, yes, baby." He holds my neck, pressing his other fingers to my mouth. "Spit on them," he demands. "Because your ass is mine, too."

I suck his fingers, drooling over them before he reaches around, and slowly sinks them inside me, making me cry out, my back arching open for him. "That's it, Wildfire. Burn for me," he demands. "Take me pounding your ass and pussy."

Suddenly, he hammers his hips, fast and hard, slapping his piercing against my clit, and pounding his cock into my pussy while he rams his fingers in my ass. His brutal possession takes me everywhere, claiming every excited nerve, exploding pleasure through my body, my pussy clenching for release as I cry out, "Axel, I'm coming!"

"Fuck, yes. Come on my dick, baby." He stares up at me, his neck straining, his eyes not believing. "Fuck, you're going to make me come so hard with this thing in my ass. Fuck! Fuck!"

I buck with my release and he seizes my hips, locking my body to his with his grunt, making me take all of him while I convulse, my pussy clenching so hard it hurts.

My orgasm won't stop. More convulsions hit me when I feel his cock jump inside me. I shudder at the sight of Axel coming so hard that he throws his chin up, his sexy body shaking, his neck straining as he groans, *"Fuck, Ruby.* Oh, fuck yes, baby."

I collapse over him, shaking like him, our breath huffing for a minute, before he wraps his strong arms and legs around me. "Goddamn, Wildfire," he pants. "You made me see stars."

I grin against his neck. "Wait until I take it out."

"You keep fucking me like that and I'm keeping you barefoot and pregnant for the rest of your life."

"Again," I softly joke, nuzzling my forehead to his, "I don't see a ring on my finger."

He stares up at me, lacing his fingers through my hair. "I'm going to give you more than a ring. *My* queen will have everything."

After a night like this. After every time Axel's inside me, making me feel completely his, I wonder, "But will you really do it? Will you really let Grant initiate me, too?"

"Pop," he mutters, "meet the bubble."

"I'm sorry." I wince. "I don't mean to ruin this. It's so perfect. *We're* perfect together, and that's why I ask right now. We can't keep avoiding it. You said after Vale's initiation and Alena's wedding, I'm next. But will you really let it happen?"

Sweetly, he smacks my ass. "You're aware my dick is inside you as you ask this question?"

"And my toy is in your ass. Seems like the perfect time."

"You'll be my queen." His voice sounds thick with resolve. "You decide how."

"Does it have to be both you and Grant ... you know ... double dipping me?"

"Be specific, Wildfire. You use too much slang, and *double dip* could mean a lot of things."

"I mean..."

Why am I suddenly shy? I've never been shy about sex.

Oh, I know why.

Because I've never been in love while having it.

"I mean, I want to respect you. I only want you, so do both you and Grant have to fuck my vagina? One after the other? You know, with your penises until you both ejaculate inside me?"

"Well, shit." He chuckles. "Way to get *real* specific."

"Uh! You said to."

"I know. I know," he grumbles, laughing. "And yes, that's what the other queens have done. It's like receiving two husbands on one wedding night. That's the tradition, but now we do it with condoms and consent."

"But not Zar," I plead my case. "He doesn't have a vagina, so on his wedding night, his ass received Nick, then Sire, right?"

"Damn," he marvels. "When I said take a specific inch, you took a very vivid mile."

"Answer my question, your honor. Are asses up for initiation?"

"Apparently, so. Yes."

"Then let Grant initiate my ass so I can save my pussy for you. Only you."

"Again," his laugh is so deep, I feel it inside me, "you're

aware my penis is still inside said pussy while we're having this conversation?"

"I'm very aware *every* time your penis is inside me, and it seems apropos."

"Oh." He winks. "Objection. That's a Carolina Law word."

"Answer the question, please, and settle this case. Can we do it that way so I don't have to worry anymore?"

"Were you worried?"

"Yeah, I was."

Silence. Heavy, unlaughing silence.

"Ruby, we won't do it if you don't want it. I'm the first king. If you want, I'll insist we make you a queen another way."

Here we go again: Axel melting my heart with his icy eyes.

He'd rearrange his world for me when all I want is to be in it.

"But I want to be like the other queens. It's like what Nick said when we were in Greece. I don't want to be different. I grew up that way. I was bullied for it. And I trust Grant. I've done it before. I heard how much Nash and Jace made Vale like her initiation, her DP, and—"

"They didn't DP her," he explains what I didn't see. "That's not what they wanted. Nash held Vale while she was on top of him, rubbing her clit on Nash's cock while Jace initiated her pussy and I think they got off on rubbing their cocks together, too, and—"

"God," I sigh, "that's hot."

"Not for me. Nash and Jace aren't brothers. But I'm not doing that with mine and—"

"I get it. And I only want you in my pussy. So let Grant DP me with you, and I know it will be special." Yes, I hear myself. "As special as a DP can be and—" I sigh, "You get the idea."

"We'll stop," he assures, "at any moment, if it's not what you want. I promise. I'll kill a brother if he hurts you."

I believe him, and I'd never let him do it. Axel's family means too much to him. To me, too.

"It *is* what I want." Gently, like a mouse to a crouching lion, I kiss him. "Because I kind of *really* love you."

"*Kind of?*"

When Axel smiles at me like that, he's the sky, embracing my entire world.

And I smile back, wiggling my empty finger in his sexy face. "There's this song by Beyoncé…"

"Oh, I'm putting my ring on it." He laughs. "But first, let me get *your* toy out of *my* ass."

He holds my face and gives me a kiss better than any ring before he leaves my body and climbs out of bed.

Cutely, he covers his cut ass with his hand, making me laugh. "Like I don't know what you're hiding."

"Like a man needs his dignity." He laughs back, swinging the bathroom door open before exclaiming, "Holy hurricane of toilet paper! What the fuck? It's everywhere!"

I roll on the bed, holding my stomach, laughing so hard. "You told them to do it."

"Since when do my pussies listen to me?" He shouts from the bathroom. "Jesus H. Christ, it looks like it snowed in here!"

Axel's so angry, I'm laughing with tears, hearing him softly cuss at the kittens while he grumbles, resolving the situation in his ass and the bathroom.

When he returns, naked and crawling into bed beside me…

I've never had this much hope.

I've never felt this much love.

Then Axel's phone rings.

And everything changes.

CHAPTER THIRTY-FOUR
AXEL

"She *knows*," Loch fumes. "And she hates me now."

"What do you mean she *knows*?" I bolt up from the warm bed I was sharing with Ruby, seething into my phone, "How the fuck did she find out?"

"Her best friend, Vale, Nash's queen; she figured it out." Loch barks right back at me, "I told you this would happen. We never should've lied to her."

"Where are you? Where's Alena?"

I say her name with my back to Ruby, the reality hitting me like a truck; *I haven't told her about Alena yet.*

Fuck, I forgot. I've been so overwhelmed.

My half-brother.

My father.

My son.

For God's sake, I can't catch a break or a breath.

"I'm with Mom in her villa, and Alena's in her bedroom with Nash, talking to him. It's his right. He's her father. He's telling her everything, but goddammit, it's my right, too," Loch rages. "I need to talk to her. She's going to fucking hate me."

That makes two of us.

"What are you going to do?"

"Fight like hell for her!" He roars. "And you're going to own this shit. You and Nash. You'll look Alena in the eye and tell her what you did. Don't you dare pull rank on me now! Do you fucking hear me?"

Damn, he's mad.

Loch may be my baby brother, but he's got more grit than the rest of us. I prefer guns, knives, and salt. I deploy power with precision. Yes, I was raised to be merciless, to rule, while Loch doesn't even remember our father. His power is American-made. He was raised here. He fights hand-to-hand, raw and ruthless. It's why he wanted to be a Marine.

I convinced him otherwise. I told him his duty was to our family first. To Alena. To protect her, and he did.

He does.

"Tell her," Loch growls at me, "that I already had a ring for her. I was going to ask her, before you and Nash told me I had to marry her. Don't let Alena believe for one goddamn second that I don't love her!"

I turn around and look Ruby in the eye.

She's clutching the sheet to her chest, her eyes wide and worried, hearing my half of the shouting match.

"I'll tell her," I answer Loch, but swear to Ruby's eyes. "I promise, I'll tell her everything."

"You fucking better," he snaps. "Here's The Queen. She wants to speak with you."

Please, everyone.

Pile on the Fuck Axel train.

Last stop: Hell.

"You know when you boys fight it makes my ass twitch," Mom fusses at me on the phone and Loch, who must be standing beside her. "My youngest baby's mad. My grandgirl's crying. Nash is trying to make her feel better, and we're fixing this. I want all the kings at my club tomorrow morning. We need to meet."

"What about the queens?"

I stare at mine, her hair tumbling in dark flames.

"Where is Ruby?" Of course, Mom worries about her, too.

"With me. In my villa."

"While you're gone," she replies calmly, "I'll put more guards on her and all the queens."

"My Queen, shouldn't our queens join us?"

Instinct tells me not to leave Ruby. But my mother's pause is long, and waiting for me to think with my head, not my heart.

"We have too many unknown variables, my son," she answers wisely. "I won't expose our queens to risk. I want this meeting just between the kings until we know ... *everything*."

Until we know which brother, if any, betrayed us. Who sold me and my son to our father?

My mom's still keeping Roman captive. Now that she has his intel, I suspect they're getting everything else they want from each other.

"Yes, my Queen," I answer.

"What's going on?" Ruby asks when I end the call.

"Alena just found out about Loch." I sit on the edge of the bed. The edge of my truth. "Vale figured it out. She's Alena's best friend, and I don't blame her for telling Alena. So now, Nash is telling Alena everything about our family and—"

"Oh, god," Ruby sighs. "Poor, Alena. And it's three days before her wedding? But then again, I'd want to know everything about my husband before I got married."

I wince.

"Loch loves her." *Like I love you, dammit.* "He'll try to explain. He just needs her to give him a chance." *Like I hope you'll give me.*

She reaches for my hand. "So, what can I do to help?"

Damn, just when I can't love you more.

"You can help by letting me tell you something I should've long ago. And when I do, don't run away. Stay and fight with me about it."

"Well…" Her face falls. "That's ominous as fuck."

My heart pounds, way past anxious. I'm afraid to say this. And it's fucking insane.

Am I afraid to die? No. Why fear the inevitable?

But am I afraid I'll lose Ruby? Yeah. I don't want to live without her.

"It's about Alena."

She swallows. And when she doesn't speak, it only makes this worse.

"When Alena was twenty-one, she asked me to take her virginity." Her eyes widen. "And I did, because she was crying and saying she felt ugly and unloved and—"

"Is she in love with you?" She blinks fast, like she's fighting back tears.

"Never. She used me, and I could say it was a mistake, but it's not. She needed my help, and I felt sorry for her. I know it's a dickhead thing to say, but it's true. Alena's one of our queens, and I couldn't stand to see her crying and feeling so unloved and—"

Her bottom lip trembles. "Do you love *her?*"

"No. Not like I love you."

She flinches.

And…

Fuck!!!

Goddammit, we need more than one fucking word for this.

"I mean… Ruby, despite my reputation, I'm not a total dickhead. I'm not going to take a woman's virginity and say it meant nothing. Alena's one of our queens, and helping her felt right. It felt loyal and like love, I guess, but it's the love I feel for Wren, Delphine, and Zar, too. Hell, even Vale, though she lives to hate me. It's how a king feels for the other queens." I pause. "It's how I guess you'll feel for Grant. You'll love me, but you'll feel loyal to him, too."

Tears spill over her lashes. The shock makes her shake her head. "Why did you wait this long to tell me?"

"I needed you to trust that, yeah, I *can* be a dickhead, but I'm one who's madly in love with you. Only you. And I worried that you'd judge me and hate me."

"Because she's marrying your brother?"

"Hopefully."

"And she's your best friend's daughter?"

"Yes."

"And she's… She's your *goddaughter?*"

That one felt a tinge of judgment.

"I never felt that way. I'm not her father figure. She was like a friend. I'm only twelve years older than her. Hell, she's almost the same age as you. And all I've ever felt is protective over her, and all she's felt is trust in me. It was never more than that. Please believe me."

Tears fall from her raging blue eyes, streaming down her flushed, freckled cheeks, pooling in the seam of her pink lips, and dripping from her dainty jaw.

Fuck, Ruby's tears kill me.

All the silent ones I saw my mother shed. I swore I'd never be a man like that; a man who makes a woman cry.

And here I am. Realizing how you don't have to hit someone to hurt them. Words. Lies. Betrayal. They can wound, too.

I've hurt Ruby. More than anyone, I know. But I can't break her. I don't think any man can.

Because she clutches the sheet to her chest, her fist blanching white with fury while she lifts her chin, making me witness the pain pouring down her face.

The pain *I* put there.

Tinker Bell with auburn hair—that's who Ruby looks like.

Tinker Bell with a loaded Uzi—that's my queen staring back at me.

Her silence seeps into my skin like the heavy humidity outside. I let her study my face and search my eyes while her tears dry.

I don't know what else to say except, "Please believe that I've said the word *love* before, but I never felt it until you. Until you let me take care of you, and I will. I'll love you until my dying day."

She lifts her chin even higher.

Such a goddamn queen.

"That'll be soon once Loch and Nash find out."

Her tone is growing cold. It scares me, but I deserve it.

I nod. "I'll tell them next, but I wanted to tell you first."

She purses her lips, ordering, "No. Don't tell them. That's Alena's right."

"But what about my rights? That's my brother. That's my best friend. I should look them in the eye and tell them."

"You want a perfect world, go live in a fairytale. But in this one? Men take too much from women as it is. Their bodies. Their safety. Their secrets. Their lives. Fuck that. Alena will tell her father and her husband, not you. You and your dick head have done enough."

Now she's raging hot. *Good.* I'd rather have her wildfire than her ice.

And fuck me; she truly sounds like a queen, defending another one.

"Do you have any questions for me?"

"Yes. Do you prefer cremation or burial after I fucking kill you for lying to me?"

"Is that a question?" I grin. "I love your fire."

"Don't fuck around, Axel. I'm going to be mad for a long time. Are you man enough to handle it?"

"Like I'll ever leave you."

Her eyes sharpen. "Like I'll ever leave you, either. I'm too damn stubborn. I meant it. I love you and I'll stay. I'll be your queen. And you'll be my king who puts up with my rage with a goddamn smile on his face until I'm done."

Pain and pride swirl in her deep blue eyes. They're a raging ocean of emotions I've caused. I just hope our love doesn't drown.

"I'm sorry."

I feel it in my bones. My soul. My heart that's pounding, but will never give up on our love.

"And I don't know what I feel." She flips the sheet open. "So, sleep beside me in case I feel like murdering you in your sleep."

"That was your dream. Right? Me, being murdered in my sleep." I slide in beside her.

"Oh, no," she mutters. "You're going to live long and hard over this."

She's not raging. She's not running. I almost wish she would, because this new version of Ruby? It's impressive. It's terrifying. It's seductive.

It's my queen.

I turn off the light and roll her way, needing to hold her.

But she turns her back on me, cuddling her pillow.

For minutes, I stare at her curvy silhouette and fiery hair. I'm respecting her boundaries. The last thing she wants is for me to touch her.

"Axel?"

"Yes?"

"Did you kiss her?"

"No. I mean…" Fuck, no more secrets. "Not on her lips. Just enough to—"

"Was she good?"

Shit. This is fucking with her head. It would fuck with mine too. Hell, I'm tempted to murder every man Ruby's ever been with, while she's just asking about one woman.

"I'm trying to be a gentleman here. I don't want—"

"Just tell me. Was Alena better than me?"

Jesus fuck.

That's what she's worried about?

I have to catch my breath. I have to speak through a strangled throat. I have to fight my own tears.

"Ruby, you bring me to my knees. Only you. Every goddamn time I touch you."

She doesn't answer. She doesn't move.

It feels like forever passes, and I know she's not asleep.

But when I hear her muffled crying.

Fuck respecting boundaries.

I wrap around her and hold her tight.

"You lied to me," she whispers, "and it hurts so much."

"I know. I know, and I'm so sorry."

"I need time."

I swallow. "And I need you. Take all the time you need."

Please, don't need long.

But she does.

Days become weeks that bleed into over a month, which almost kills me.

CHAPTER THIRTY-FIVE
AXEL

"You look like holy hell."

My pastor brother sounds like a divine dick.

"No, shit. He looks like shit. Like *royal* shit."

And Nash has to triple down on everything.

"Are we grilling burgers tonight or me?"

Sitting on the patio beside Nash's pool, I sip chilled vodka in the September heat, but it's nothing compared to my sweltering misery.

"Quit giving him shit, y'all." Jace reclines in the Adirondack chair beside me. "All he's eaten for a month is his heart out."

"They're just *friends*," Nick stresses it for the umpteenth time but I don't give a fuck. "It's just a show for the press. To keep them distracted until we make our big announcement."

"And yet..." Grant grimaces for me. "It's a big fucking knife in his heart. Face it. Colton Hawke is the NFL's finest, and he creams panties. Delphine sure is a big fan."

I wince, groaning, "Fuck off. All of you."

"Colton Hawke loves Beau Bronson and Blair Monroe."

Nick sits up, pointing his beer bottle at me. "They're a loyal throuple, and Ruby's just helping them. I've fucking told you this a million times. She's Colton's beard, or whatever the fuck you want to call it, until we all come out together and—"

"Damn," Nash huffs. "It's brilliant. You have to admit it. A group of NFL players are forming a movement and coming out together so that one won't be targeted? Fuck yeah, leave it to our queens to come up with that middle-finger to homophobic Americans."

Am I proud of Ruby for helping the closeted NFL players who've decided to come out together before the Super Bowl? With half of them being bribed by that irate, piece-of-shit rental owner, Halstead?

Yes. I'm so damn proud of her it hurts.

Everything about her hurts.

Does she still love me? Yes.

Does she sleep with me and let me hold her and want to fuck me sometimes, too? Thank fucking god, yes.

Do all the kings and queens know about her now? They've started a Ruby fan club.

But is there a distance between us?

Yes. It aches, maddening and silent, and I don't know how to fix it.

Like the strong woman who captivated me at first sight, Ruby's proud. She said she wants to put it behind us. That it's for Alena to reveal the secret and for us to move on.

But I know Ruby thinks about it every day, and it's haunting our future.

I won't propose to her like this. I won't make her my queen officially. It feels wrong, and I'm desperate to make it right.

I asked Ruby what I could do, and she said to let her run this mission. This one with Nick, Zar, and Vale, Nash's queen.

Because of course, put strong women together and they'll figure out a way to help others and fuck over the assholes.

Assholes like the homophobic and biphobic fans and press keeping NFL players closeted. Players like Beau Bronson and Colton Hawke, who, yes, are in a loving throuple with Vale's twin, Blair.

Vale and Ruby formed an alliance and a plan, and got my mother on board.

Did my mother jump at the opportunity to help her son, Nick, a closeted NFL player, and anyone else being shamed?

Does a dominatrix crack a whip?

The queens have identified every player being extorted by Halstead, the vile rental owner. Nash is watching Halstead's accounts and tracing the deposits back to the parties being bribed. And one by one, Ruby makes contact with them, inviting them to join the movement being led by Nick and backed by us.

They even meet about it. The queens, including Ruby, walk right past me, standing at the bar in my mother's club, and go upstairs into my mother's office to hold their weekly strategy meetings.

Are the kings involved?

Nick is.

The rest of us? We're on the sidelines.

We tossed the body of the sex trafficker who was chasing Nash and Vale into the Atlantic. It's my favorite graveyard.

But The Queen still doesn't know who betrayed us, and I still don't know who sold me and my son out. Though I've got eyes and ears on Lev now.

Roman's mother and grandmother, my father's terrorized staff, are on my payroll, too. They're sending me pictures and videos of him. They're the sweetest torture. Ruby was right; Lev looks just like me. So I'm getting maps of my father's new compound. Schedules of their movements. All the intel I'll need to get my son soon.

In the meantime, my mom ices me out of her meetings with the queens.

Why?

Because my mom can sense a woman's pain a mile away, and she knows I hurt Ruby.

To Ruby's credit. To her soul-crushing loyalty and heartbreaking love, she hasn't told my mom what I did.

She hasn't told anyone.

Ironically, she's protecting me.

And it's killing me.

Ruby's professionalism is regal. She doesn't bitch or fight. She still works on my staff. For safety reasons, she agrees with me—all work remotely, while none of them have any idea that she lives with me in my hideout by the river.

Her loyalty to my family is noble. She's grown so close to the queens and The Queen. She loves helping Nick and Zar, and now the kings adore her too.

And me?

I love her too much.

It kills me when I see the paparazzi photos of Ruby "dating" Colton Hawke.

Nick can insist it's fake. That her double dates with Colton, accompanying Blair Monroe with Beau Bronson, the NFL's number one quarterback, are really a disguise for Colton's relationship with Blair and Beau ... but you can't convince my heart.

Those pictures of Ruby with Colton? The man is a hot, inked mountain of NFL muscle. And the way he hugged Ruby, protecting her, shielding her from the throngs of paparazzi cameras waiting outside an Atlanta restaurant?

It broke something inside me.

Something that probably feels almost as broken as what I did to Ruby.

I deserve it.

It's my karma.

"Come on, man." Grant nudges my shoe. "It's lady ballsy as fuck what Ruby's doing for us. So, when are you gonna make her our queen?"

"You can't force a queen to be ready." Jace jumps in. "Sometimes, all you can do is wait for her."

Curious glances dart, including mine. All of the kings wonder who Jace is talking about.

Jace has been so cryptic about his love life, but I know he spends a lot of time with Nash and Vale.

Funny, how Nash fought so hard against Jace, or any king, being Vale's second king, but now, the three seem close. It's like Nash and Vale bring Jace some warmth while he's waiting in the cold for some mystery woman.

Everyone thinks Ruby's not ready to be initiated because of Katya. That she's still getting over me not telling her about my first wife.

Only Sire knows the truth.

And he's taken Ruby's side. He agrees that I shouldn't tell Loch and Nash. That Alena should.

Which is odd for a man so devoted to the truth, but I guess he fears what it will do to our family.

Normally, I'd do whatever the fuck I want. I'm the first king. But since I've fallen in love and fucked up, my instincts are off. I can't tell when I'm being selfish or selfless.

I just know I'm so goddamn in love with Ruby and I need her back, fully. I don't want a show of her standing by my side, like it's her duty.

I want her heart, body, and soul.

As much as she has mine.

"Tell him she'll be ready soon. Right?" Nash asks Nick.

"Ruby's going to your parties with Zar. She's recruiting more closeted players. She and Vale have some big meeting planned and—"

Nick shakes his head. "We don't talk about our queens. Period."

"Come on. Give him a hope and a prayer," Sire insists. "The meeting is soon, right? Then the mission will be done, and Ruby will be ready. We're all ready for her to be a queen. Wren fucking loves her."

Yeah, I love her, too, and Nick and Zar's parties are my hell.

Because deep down I know that Ruby's imagining my one time with Alena.

And without intention, she's giving it right back to me.

Because all I can imagine is how she's the fiery seductress, the only woman allowed at Zar and Nick's intimate parties for closeted players, and it makes me sick with jealousy how some of those men want to score with her, too.

But I trust her.

I know she'd never cheat.

Still, I can't shake this feeling that something bad is going to happen.

"Why is everyone so damn worried about Axel and Ruby?" Loch huffs. "They'll be fine. She fucking loves him. She kneels for him, and he worships her. In the meantime, Alena won't even talk to me, and it's not my fucking fault."

He glares at Nash, then at me.

"What, man?" I answer him. "Nash was just trying to protect his daughter, and I apologized to her, like you asked. I told Alena the truth; you love her. You weren't forced to marry her. You already had a ring. So, did we order you to protect her? Yes. But you can't make a man love a woman. So now, fucking fight for her."

Like I'm secretly fighting for Ruby.

What will it take to win her trust again?

For now, Ruby insists that I stay out of this drama between Alena and Loch, and I understand. Alena's hurt and angry, and I won't pour salt on her wound by telling Loch and Nash about us.

I'm too focused on how I hurt Ruby.

"Don't give up on her," Jace urges Loch. "We're all here, alive and well as brothers, because we've seen how love can conquer all."

"Good God in heaven." Sire rolls his eyes. "Who the fuck has you talking like a goddamn Hallmark movie?"

"What?" Jace booms back. "Don't preach as if you don't worship Wren more than God."

"At least my woman has a name."

"At least mine is none of your goddamn business."

"Aha." Nick grins. "At least we know it's a woman."

"Who is she?" Grant grins, too. "Come on. Give us a name and we'll shut the fuck up."

"Goddamn. Leave him alone," Nash defends Jace. "We've all hidden secrets until it was time to tell them."

"No." Loch shakes his head. "We should know better by now. Secrets can kill us."

"And yet," I finish my vodka, "they've kept us alive, too."

When you spend most of your life hiding who you are. When secrets and lies have kept you alive. When the truth is your greatest threat.

You have to hang on to one thing that's real.

That's always been my brothers, our mother, our family.

Blood and bonds have kept us together.

But now?

It's Ruby. It's our love. It's the only thing I can trust.

Because I stare at the wide, inky water, snaking beside Nash's new home with Vale. He chose this place for its strategic location, just as I chose mine. We live by the water for rapid escape.

It affords a sense of safety.

But now all I can wonder is...

What if one of those yachts, anchored for the night on the river, is our father or one of his henchmen, who's been watching us the whole time?

And who in this circle helped him find us?

CHAPTER THIRTY-SIX
RUBY

"What do you think our kings are talking about?"

Delphine peers through the second-story window of Nash and Vale's bedroom. And I swear, her French accent could make grocery shopping sound clandestine.

"Us." Vale holds up the fourth dress, considering my wardrobe for my next date with Colton. "Their minds are like drunk babies. They wander off, distracted by business, but they always stagger back to us."

"When they're all gathered like that?" Wren stands beside Delphine, admiring the view of a circle of seven inked men gathered around an unlit fire pit. "Why does it make me want to go down there and do naughty things?"

Delphine laughs. "Because your husband has trained you well."

"Sire didn't *train* me," Wren scoffs, but it comes out as a giggle. "I'm the bad influence. Not him. I'm the one who tempts him into breaking the rules."

"Breaking or breeding?" Vale chuckles. "You know, your guest bedroom has Swiss cheese for walls. We've heard Sire's kink. How he's madly in love with breeding his *horny little bunny*."

"Oh, okay, Daddy," Wren teases Vale back. "We've heard how Nash, *yes, daddy*, makes you his dirty little girl, too."

We're all laughing as Delphine turns to me. "Speaking of shared kinks and kings. Ma chérie, what are you waiting for? You're one of us and deserve your initiation, too."

"I want to finish this mission first," I answer, taking the emerald dress from Vale, silently agreeing that this is the one to wear on my next date with Colton.

It's elegant. It'll look great in paparazzi shots. It's all strategy for me. No romance. I've locked that part of me away.

Yes, I love Axel. Yes, I need him to hold me, to wait for me. But I don't know what it will take to get back to trusting him.

And I know he feels it. I know he loves me. He's not pushing me.

So, in the meantime, I thrive on this mission.

Once Stacey James, the owner of Delta's, and Vale, one of our queens, came to me with a request to help Blair Monroe, Stacey's employee and Vale's twin?

You had me at *a woman needs help*.

Is it serendipity or strategy that Vale and I devised this plan? A way to help our king, Nick, and our queen, Zar, while also helping Vale's twin and her partners?

Hell yes, it's both when women are involved.

And it's the perfect distraction for me until...

Until something shifts inside me and I can fully trust Axel again.

"I can't believe that was you the whole time at Vale's initiation." Wren fills the silence, praising me, "I'm impressed. I don't think I could've knelt for hours."

"Darlin', you underestimate the power of a good Dom." Zar sits on the sofa in Vale's bedroom, swirling his whiskey. "Their reward is worth the pain."

"It wasn't painful," I confess. "And yes, Axel made my reward *very* satisfying."

"I bet." Wren grins like my co-conspirator.

"I have never seen Axel do that; be so loving," Delphine shares, while gazing down at him from the window above. "He was not that way with Katya."

"You *knew* her?" Suddenly, I'm riveted. I didn't know this.

"For a month or so." She shrugs. "But then she left him and *au revoir*, bitch. That is the right word. Yes? *Bitch*?"

"Yes. Bitch." Zar laughs. "It's not my habit to use the word but from what Nick's told me about Katya, it fits like a bitchy glove."

"I never met her," Wren adds. "But Sire told me he never trusted her. That she was cold to Axel. It's like Sire hates Katya and now, she's coming between you and Axel and..." Wren sighs, "It sucks he didn't tell you about her at first. I get it. I'd be hurt, too, but I hope you can forgive him soon."

Forgive him?

I did that months ago about her.

Now, like Sire, I hate Katya, too.

No one but me, Axel, The Queen, Roman, and one unknown traitor knows about Katya's plan with Axel's father, to get pregnant by Axel, then leave and take his son with her.

The whole heartbreaking betrayal is still a secret and I will kill that bitch if I ever meet her.

It's Alena I can't forget, and it's not about forgiveness with her.

She did nothing wrong. She's innocent and hurting over Loch. The other queens talk about her. They worry about her, particularly Vale, her best friend, but I won't tell them what I know about Alena and Axel.

True respect is respecting someone's privacy and letting them tell their truth. I won't rob another woman of her story.

Because mine is...

A deep insecurity, hidden inside the girl who sat alone at the lunch table. The one with a disability. The one who was bullied and mocked.

She can't stop imagining Axel with Alena. She's flawed and vulnerable and worried she's not good enough. She was shamed and used and treated like trash, though...

I believe Axel.

He doesn't want Alena, and she doesn't want him. I'm starting to feel that in this group.

How the kings love their first queens above all, but they'll never forsake another queen.

I see it between Nash, Vale, and Jace. I see it between Nick, Zar, and Sire. I even see it between Sire, Wren, and Nash. There's a silent regard. An unspoken respect. A duty and protection that's understood.

I know I should be a boss-bitch and move on. That's what I tell Axel, and I've moved on with everything else.

Because half of me isn't that bullied girl anymore. I'm a strong woman. Only I can heal my pain.

I just don't know how.

"Is it true that you spied on my initiation?" Wren plops down on the bed beside the suitcase Vale and I are packing for my next trip to Atlanta. That's where the paparazzi stalk Beau, Blair, and Colton, and that's where I come in to help. "Sire said Axel told him about it. How you spied on us."

"Guilty." I wink at her. "That was me, hiding in the board-room closet. Sorry. I didn't know what I was about to see. I just wanted more intel on Axel."

"I think it's hilarious," Wren giggles.

"And dayum, that took lady balls." Zar raises his glass to me. "I'm proud."

"I would give my lady-balls to have seen Axel's face!" Delphine laughs, too. "He was pissing. Yes?"

"Pissed." I laugh with her. "And yes, he was so mad that he said he owned me and made me live with him."

"Aw, lucky you," Wren sighs. "I had to beg Sire on my knees to take me."

"Poor man," Zar deadpans. "Pastor Sire Rutledge, lured into sharing his bed with his hottest young parishioner. I'm sure the struggle was real."

"It was real kinky." Wren blows him a cute kiss before aiming her big brown eyes at me. "So, whenever you're ready, do you know who your second king will be?"

The light catches the diamond Monroe piercing above Wren's lip. All the queens have one, except Zar. He has a diamond barbell through his nipple. They're gifts from The Queen, marking them as queens, and I'm next.

"I guess." I glance nervously at Delphine. I've avoided this topic. "I don't want to disrespect or—"

"He will be honored." Delphine toasts her wine glass toward the circle of kings seated outside. "My husband is a beast, but a very loving man. They all are, and Grant likes you. He likes how you help Nick and the shit you give Axel. He says you are Axel's true match."

"And you won't be mad?" I worry. "If Grant ... *initiates* me?"

"I loved my initiation!" Wren blurts.

"Oh, we know, darlin'," Zar drawls. "You cute, greedy little bitch."

He makes Wren smile proudly because there's no judgment in the room. Just fun. Just love.

"I will not be mad or jealous. I share Grant." Delphine turns toward us. "I am free because for too long, I had no control, no choice. I was bought and sold, so please, not to offend, but I am not a puritanical American. I do not own anyone, and no one owns me. I love freely, and my husband loves me, Axel loves you, and we love our bonds. *All* the kings and queens."

"Yeah, but I worry about some of them." Vale tucks a pair of heels into my suitcase. "The last time I saw something like this, I flushed it."

"What?" Wren laughs.

"This shit," Vale says. "This shit between Loch and Alena. She's devastated. She was so in love with him. They were like the hottest romance. You should hear her stories, but now *this shit*. They were lying to her. And yeah, I love Nash. I always have. So he can handle it when I speak Cuntanese to him about it."

Delphine scrunches her nose. "Do you mean Cantonese?"

"No, darlin'." Zar laughs. "She means Cuntanese. It's what a queen speaks when we're raging and right."

"Ah, a cunt." Delphine nods. "Yes. I speak Cunt to Grant when I am mad."

"Do you think Alena will love again?" I pack my bra and panties, secretly trying to get some intel and feeling guilty about it.

"If you count Smokey the Bear, yeah," Vale answers. "Other than that, the only bear Alena loves is Loch. It's him or no one. He just needs to grovel enough to get her back."

Grovel?

Is that what I want Axel to do?

All the nights we spend together in bed with our kittens and...

No. I know he's sorry.

I need something else.

"And then there's Jace," Vale sighs, joining Delphine at the window. "He's in love with some woman he calls Mary. It's not her name, but that's what he calls her because she's married and he's in love with her."

"Married?" Wren's shocked. "I mean, some of us like to share, but Jace?"

"He's not sharing her." Vale gazes down at the kings. "He's waiting for her to leave her shithead husband or something."

"Damn," Zar huffs. "And I thought my situation was complicated."

"It is," I jump in, zipping my suitcase closed. "Nick wants to come out. You two should be free to love. No more bribes or closet. And we've secured every player in the group except Colton and Beau. They're not sure if they're ready to do this, and honestly? Nick's movement won't be as powerful if we don't have them. I have to make this work."

"Blair's *so* ready," Vale says. "She's tired of having to hide their love."

"Firecracker," Zar rises, "you're a true queen." His hug is warm. "Thank you for doing this for us."

"A chance to fuck with a fucker? It's my favorite thing." I squeeze him back. "So, I'm off to another Atlanta game as Colton's girlfriend, and hopefully I'll convince them to come to our meeting."

"Our meeting?" Zar scoffs. "Darlin', we won't merely *meet* at my beach house. We'll have a meeting of the minds, then we'll have a meeting of everything else."

Oh, I know.

The first floor of Zar and Nick's palatial beach home is for casual entertaining. It's the perfect place to meet and share our plan.

But after their meeting downstairs?

Upstairs, red ties will hang from doorknobs to bedrooms where privacy is wanted, while black ties will hang from door-knobs where partners are wanted. Where anyone can watch or join.

But me?

Zar and Nick have dedicated a bedroom to me. A red tie

hangs from my doorknob while I sit alone on my bed and gaze at the sparkling night ocean, watching it churn, unsettled and seeking.

Like my heart.

Seeking a way back to Axel.

CHAPTER THIRTY-SEVEN
RUBY

"You know it's just an act."

I nuzzle my nose to Axel's, teasing his nose ring. Yes, he knows the truth, and I don't want to hurt him. I want to reassure him that my double dinner date with Colton, Blair, and Beau tonight is business. It's part of our mission.

"It's just hell watching you with another man," he brushes our lips together, "when all I want is for you to be mine."

"I *am* yours. You know that. It's just..."

We stand at the bottom of the boarding stairs to Axel's jet. The clock is ticking down. I need to get to Atlanta before the kick-off, but I don't want to leave him.

"Baby, I need to fix this." Axel wraps around me tighter. "I need to fix *us*. What can I do?"

With everyone else, Axel's a cold, ruthless king.

But with me?

"I don't know." Tears well in my eyes. "I want to trust you again. Believe me, and I'm trying. But I don't know how and..."

I trail off and let him take me in a deep kiss. Most of me is here, forever with him, but a piece of me is distant.

"Be careful." He sighs over our lips. "Be my queen and stay safe."

"Always," I promise.

Reluctantly, he lets me go.

As the jet taxis down the runway, I peer out of the window and blink back tears at Axel, still standing there, watching me leave.

He's waiting for me.

And I'm waiting for ... something.

In a haze, my quick flight to Atlanta passes. Using the small bedroom at the back of the jet, I change into the emerald dress Vale picked out, while all I can remember is my first flight with Axel. The trip that started this whole thing.

Our first kiss.

Our love.

Our partnership as king and queen.

Our mission to help another king and queen.

It feels like a lifetime ago. I don't recognize that wild woman anymore.

I'm still fearless, but now I'm focused. Now, I'm helping others, and I understand how Axel's addicted to this, too.

Justice is a powerful drug.

"The maître d' says there's at least a dozen waiting outside for us tonight."

Beau Bronson, Atlanta's quarterback, sits with his arm around Blair, but glances toward the restaurant window, worried about the paparazzi waiting for us when we leave.

"We got this." Colton elbows me, winking.

And I wink back.

Is Colton Hawke a tall, blonde, inked skyscraper of muscles with a sexy hair knot? Yes. And he's all Blair and Beau's, he just can't show it.

"Are you wearing your touchdown panties again?" I tease Blair about our last double dinner date when the paparazzi swarmed us.

When one aggressive photographer heckled Blair, causing her to trip and fall in her cute dress, exposing her TOUCH-DOWN panties, which were meant only for Beau and Colton's eyes.

But instead?

They went viral.

"Yes." Blair bounces her raven brows at me. "I took your advice. I'm spinning the whole panty scandal to my advantage. I'm wearing BALLER panties tonight, and selling copies on Etsy, and donating everything to charity."

"Smart woman." I point my fork at her. "If they're going to call us *sluts*, at least we'll be charitable ones."

"Speaking of proud sluts." Blair lowers her sexy cat-eye glasses at me. "When are you going to confess about your pussy pact with my twin? That you and Vale are in a three-decker with Nash Allen?"

Blair's smart.

She knows there's a connection between me and Vale. Obviously. Vale's the one who asked me to help Blair and her partners.

But Vale's a queen, who can't even tell her identical twin everything about her king, Nash Allen, the man she loves.

All Blair can know is that Vale has fallen in love with Nash, her best friend's dad.

But like me, Vale has to hide the kings and queens from her sister. Except I'm under more pressure, hiding Axel's ex-Bratva life from three sisters.

So, I understand Blair's natural curiosity.

And soon, hopefully next week, Blair, Beau, and Colton will at least meet Nick, Zar, and the other closeted players and understand more.

Until then.

They have no idea who the mastermind behind our plan is.

The Queen.

And they don't know who I love. The Queen's son. The Bratva prince, whose evil father won't stop cutting at him, body and soul.

"While I support all love," I answer Blair, "my heart is taken and not by your sister and her best friend's dad."

"Oh?" Colton swigs a Hennessy on the rocks. "Do tell. You know all about our love. Seems only fair we know about yours."

Why am I blushing with warmth?

Why does it feel good to talk about Axel?

Even though I can't say his name.

"Fine." I smile. "You want an intimate detail?" They nod eagerly. "I'm learning to be a sub for a Dom, which is saying a lot if you knew how hard it is for me to trust a man."

"That makes total sense," Blair says. "It's liberating. It's the ultimate love, even, to trust someone to bind you, to control you totally."

Huh. I guess I've been taking that for granted.

Sexually, I still trust Axel. Even though my heart struggles to trust him again, my body sure doesn't.

We've been experimenting with nipple clamps, clit suckers, spreader bars and bondage rope.

As my Dom, Axel's trying to make it up to me. He's torturing me into the most orgasmic submission. I even trust him to chain me to our new sex bench. He likes to leave me there, with my dress hiked up and my panties around my thighs, my pussy and ass exposed to him until his icy, silent stare makes me so hot and wet that I'm begging for him.

"Really, kitten?" Beau raises his brows at Blair. "You'll be our sub, too?"

"Baby," Blair coos at him, then at Colton. "You know I'll role-play *anything* with my men."

"Careful what you wish for," Beau teases her.

"So, when do we get to meet your Dom?" Colton's sweet and not judging me.

"One day soon, I hope. I have lots of people I want you three to meet. We have a plan we want to share with you."

They nod, and I know better than to push.

We finish our dinner, drinks, and dessert over comfortable laughs before we run the usual gauntlet of cameras, flashes, and shouts hurled at us when we leave the restaurant.

Like a pro footballer, Colton blocks for me, shucking away the wall of obnoxious men and their cameras shoved in our faces.

Once we're safe inside the limousine, Blair pops open a bottle of bubbly to celebrate their win tonight. I sip water and enjoy the music. I'm not fazed by Blair kissing Colton, then Beau, or Beau passionately kissing Colton and palming his erection with a moan.

If Axel could see their love, he wouldn't worry about me.

They can hardly keep their hands off each other as we pull into the circular drive in front of Beau's massive home on the outskirts of Atlanta.

"You're staying the night, right?" Blair asks.

It's what I usually do. Beau's lavish home has more than enough bedrooms, but suddenly...

I want to wake up in Axel's arms.

"I think I'll fly home," I answer, giving her a peck on the cheek, then Beau, before they crawl out of the limo.

"Call me tomorrow, sugar lips." Colton teases me, kissing

my cheek as a show to the limo driver, not that I think he cares.

Hell, he doesn't even turn around.

They wave goodbye and stumble through their front door before the driver pulls away.

"Where to?" he asks gruffly.

"Peachtree-Dekalb airport."

I take my phone from my purse and text Axel.

Flying home tonight

I want to wake up with you

SPITTING COBRA

I'll tell the pilot to ready the jet

And I'll pick you up

I'll do whatever it takes

…

I chew my lip, always baited, waiting for Axel's reply.

I don't do heart emojis

But you always have mine

Same, my hot dickhead

BTW

Is this harassment or stalking?

It's everything with you Wildfire

See. I'm not afraid of emojis and loving you

And don't pick me up

Sleep. I'll take an Uber

You'll let me take care of you

Now shut up and obey

Safe flight

...

Again, I wait with baited breath for him and he replies...

Wow. Axel's first emoji.

Why is it so silly and simple and flooding me with love? I don't know what flipped my switch, but something's changed.

Maybe it's what Blair said.

Deep down, I do trust Axel. I need to get out of my head about it and listen to my body.

My body that starts to tense, when I glance out of the tinted window, and I don't recognize where we are.

"Excuse me," I ask the driver. "Where are you going?"

"I need to pull over. Tire pressure problem." He slows the car, pulling to the side of a remote road, not the interstate where we should be. "Just a minute."

I watch from the back seat while he appears to text someone on his phone, maybe roadside assistance, before he turns around, aiming a gun at me.

"Phone," he barks. "Right now."

Oh my god, it's Halstead.

I didn't recognize him without his dumbass preppy clothes.

"Now, bitch," he hisses, waving his gun. "And that smart-watch on your wrist, too, or you can eat my bullets. You've been fucking with me for too long. Cooperate or die tonight."

With shaking hands, I take off my watch, then pick up my phone.

With the press of a button, he rolls the window down beside me.

"Toss them out," he orders. "No one's tracking where we're going."

Yes, they are.

The tracking bracelet Axel gave me, I never take it off. I use my other hand to toss my smartwatch and phone out of the window, not wanting to draw attention to it.

"Put these on." He tosses a pair of metal handcuffs. They land on the floorboard in front of me. "And keep your fucking mouth shut."

"I'll put these on," I say, securing one metal cuff, then clicking the other closed. "But good luck shutting up my mouth. I've come to a point in my life where if you don't like what I have to say, fuck off. Problem solved."

"You fuck off, you dumb slut," he snaps.

"Hey, Einstein. You're the one kidnapping me. So, the only off I'm going is on you. And you know, the only people who shame sex are the ones who don't have it. Or don't have it *good*."

"Shut. The fuck. Up," he sneers.

"Point made. The truth hurts." I smile. "And so does looking at your face."

"Keep fucking talking." He turns around. "It'll make it fun to choke you on my cock later."

"Please," I scoff. "I wear heels bigger than your dick."

The doors and windows are locked. He controls them. The road is isolated. This psycho thinks he can kidnap me, but I know I'm worth far more alive than dead. And while I'm alive and avoiding heaven for now, I'm going to give him hell.

"I love that you record innocent people having sex. Is that

because you're taking notes for when you finally do it? You were confused about which hole? Don't worry. With you, they won't feel a thing."

He starts raising the partition.

"I promise," I shout to the rising glass. "One day soon, someone will pity fuck you ... *over*."

Then I'm left in silence, frantically searching the back of the limo for anything I can use as a weapon, and I tug at my hand, making sure I left enough slack in the cuff to pull it out when I need to.

Wherever Halstead's taking me? He's planned it.

This whole night, he had to have planned.

Shit, did I make it too easy? All the pictures of me with Colton in Atlanta at the same restaurant. I've been all over social media.

But wait. How did Halstead recognize me? I was disguised in my video with Axel at Halstead's chalet.

Unless...

Unless at the drop on Meeting Street, when Halstead was waiting at the bus stop ... he was secretly clocking me, too. I was sitting in the corner window of the bar. It was like a giant fishbowl, and I guess... I guess I stand out.

Damn, I've never cursed my curiosity and flaming hair before.

But maybe that's it. Maybe Halstead saw me watching him, and somehow he followed me and Axel that night? The night Axel cut Calloway?

I'm not sure, but it's my best guess.

Either way, even with my hands cuffed, I'm able to double-click the charm on my bracelet. It's my SOS beacon. Axel will get it.

The only problem is, will he find me before it's too late?

THE ISOLATED ROADS HALSTEAD'S TAKING HAVE HIGHWAY markers, all of which read 'East'. I try to stay calm and focus on where we are. Not what he'll do.

I'm not trapped.

I'll be okay.

I can always run.

But when Halstead parks the limousine in front of an abandoned one-story roadside Georgia motel, half-eaten by kudzu vines and the perfect place for zombies ... or my murder.

I'm not so sure.

The door beside me swings open.

"Ankles." He tosses leg cuffs at me, the black muzzle of his gun eclipsing his face. "Now."

"How will I walk?"

"Bitches like you should be dragged."

"Jeez. Someone's been trolling the Kardashians."

I force myself to joke, to find my next inhale and exhale, obeying with trembling hands.

With my wrists and ankles bound and a gun in my face, I'm utterly defenseless except for my mouth.

I could scream, but it would only be swallowed by the empty night and cicadas. So I hold my fire.

When he waves his gun for me to crawl out of the back-seat, fuck yes, I lift my chin. When he reaches to grab my arm, I jerk it away.

"I can walk and you can kiss my ass. Every time you touch me is every stab I'll put in your dick."

He laughs. Sick and twisted and amused.

"I have lots of plans for your ass tonight." He presses the

cold muzzle to my temple. "And I'll record it. And send it to the fucking bogus email you gave me and who ever it is that you work for will pay me a million dollars not to fuck your ass again." He smirks. "But I will. Off camera."

I'm okay.

I'm okay.

Shuffling in my heels over broken pavement, I let him shove me toward a blistered, red door. Behind a tattered curtain, yellowed with age, a light glows inside the creepy hotel room.

"In," he commands, so I reach and twist the rusty door-knob, opening the creaking door.

Immediately, I'm overwhelmed by the smell of mold and stench attacking my senses. It retches my stomach when I see the old bed, its bare mattress covered in gross stains.

There's no power in here. The light that glows is from two camping lanterns he must have brought earlier.

"On the bed," he orders, and with every ounce of strength I have, I make myself sit and not shake into a million pieces.

Do not drop.

Do not drop.

Breathe.

Stay here.

"I like what you've done with the place." I glance around. "It's giving me *The Walking Dead*."

He doesn't answer. He leans against the cinder block wall, texting something.

"I was always Team Daryl on that show. You had me at a hot, red-neck MC with a motorcycle and a crossbow. Though Rick was hot," I chuckle, "his accent was not. We don't sound like that. Do we? Go ahead. Say something Southern and I'll tell you if it sounds like your mouth is full of syrup."

Silence. Texting.

"But I gotta say. Your new limo driver look? All black? It's way more snatched than your belt with whales on it. That thing is Moby Dickless."

"Shut up," he mutters before lifting his phone, its camera light practically blinding me.

"Cheese." I smile for his kidnapping photo. "Anyway. Let's talk about your seersucker suit. Ain't no dick getting sucked in one of those. Sorry, but I'm keeping it real."

I'm keeping myself sane and talking. I don't want to slip. I don't want to drop.

With a *ping*, my picture's sent. Probably to the email that Grant checks. I don't know, but I'm sure my kings will come for me, but what if it's too late? What if I have a seizure?

Stay here. Stay here. Breathe.

"So my advice is to stay away from nautical fashion for men. Pussies go dry at sailboats and whales. Ain't nothing wet about them. Stick with the black. Maybe mix it up with some kicky greys and sick whites and—"

In two steps, he's backhanding my mouth so hard he splits my bottom lip open. The taste of blood spills over my tongue while my ears ring from the impact, my head spins to the side while I force my focus on the moldy carpet.

But it keeps me here.

Fuck him. Fuck him.

I lick the metallic taste off my lips and face him with a bloody smile.

"Thank you," I smirk. "Red is my signature color."

Purple. No, it's purple and the first color Axel saw me in. Where is he?

Charleston is hours from wherever in the hell we are.

"So, enough about fashion." I glare up at him. "Let's talk business."

To anyone else, Halstead looks like a Vice President. You know the kind, looking so godly and conservative, he's hiding the sickest secrets of all?

"What do you want?" I ask. "A million? Three million?"

"Who do you work for?"

"Oh, I don't work for him. I kneel for him."

He blinks, shocked.

"And when he finds you with me, whether I'm dead or alive, he will cut off your hand, salt it, and fuck it up your ass … while you're alive." I bat my lashes. "He's so hot and sadistic like that."

"Your boss?" He sneers while tucking his phone in his pocket, his other hand still aiming his gun at my face. "The one who looks like a thug, covered in ink."

"Okay, you're not understanding the assignment. His ink is hot. Your bow ties are not."

"Hot?" He tilts his head, his gaze dropping to my braless breast under my emerald slip dress. "This is hot."

With the tip of his gun, he slides the silky strap off my shoulder. It dangles over my arm, the fabric barely exposing my breast.

And I lift my chin. *Stay here. Stay here.* I don't flinch when he rubs the gun over my flesh, tugging my dress down more, exposing my nipple next. *Stay here. Stay here.*

"I think we should make a video for your inked boss," he jeers. "You can kneel for me while I shut that mouth up and fuck it with my cock."

"Got any mustard?" I ask. "I like it with my little Vienna Sausages."

"Fuck you." He yanks my hair, dragging me to the floor. "On your knees! On your fucking knees!"

"If you insist." I fall hard on my kneecaps before him, the carpet slimy against my flesh. "Just know. If you put that inchworm in my mouth, I will bite it off. I'll take death over your dick any day."

He stares down at me. And with every minute as a girl, I

cowered, afraid of a man like this—*no more*—I fire my rage back at him.

"Go ahead," I taunt. "Eventually, every man meets his match and this bitch is yours."

Fuck him. Fuck him. Stay here. Stay here.

"You think you're my fucking match?" He presses the gun to my temple, its metal warming against my sweating flesh. "You think I can't handle a bitch like you?"

"You've never met a bitch like me," I sneer. "Stubborn is where I start and stabbing your little dick is where I'll end. Here or in hell, mother fucker. Bring it on."

I see him. I see my stepfather. I see Calloway. I see every boy in high school who grabbed my ass. Every man on the street who thinks his catcall is game, when it's really his little dick energy calling card.

I meant it when I told Axel I'd rather die than let a man own me.

I'm staring down this rapist psycho with his gun pressed to my temple and in life or death, *fuck you*, I'm proud.

And I'll make Axel proud.

This man will not break me. He won't have me.

I only belong to Axel, even if it's in his memories. Even if that's all I'll leave behind for him; I was his proud queen until the end.

I won't even close my eyes while I wait for the trigger to be pulled.

But instead...

The door is kicked open.

CHAPTER THIRTY-EIGHT
WILDER

ONE CAP TO THE ANKLE.

The fucker falls.

One cap in his thigh.

Okay, that was just target practice.

When Axel King calls, I answer.

I'm supposed to leave this fucker alive and protect Axel's woman, but who says I can't entertain myself until he gets here.

"Hey, little Bo Peep." I kick the gun out of the bleeder's hand, get in his face ... and smile. "Baa. Can I fuck you like a sheep?"

Aw, shit.

Really?

I hate that smell.

"Goddammit." I kick his ribs with my boot. "You just pissed yourself and I ain't cleaning that shit up."

Carefully, I help the hot redhead stand.

"Here, darlin. Ain't no weatherman calling for golden showers tonight. You don't wanna be kneeling in that."

I'm damn sure I'm not supposed to be staring at her gorgeous goddamn tit with that pretty, pointing, pert, nipple.

Like a Georgia peach, I bet she tastes sweet.

But I'd like to keep my filthy vision, so I lift the strap of her dress and pat it in place.

"There, there. It'll be okay."

This is how you comfort a woman, right?

Fuck if I know.

I usually bring the terror. Like the DoorDash of Death.

But I owe Axel and Jace.

Ahh fuck, that's right. And I owe Pastor Sire, too. He snuck a shank into a Bible for me the last time I was in the cage.

"Who are you?" The redhead jerks away from my warm, caring touch.

Can't blame her.

Stranger Danger and all.

"Wilder." I tip my non-existent cowboy hat. "A friend of Axel's."

Her glance darts to the bleeder, balling in pain on the floor.

"Aw, don't worry about him." I swipe his gun off the floor and tuck it into my back pocket. "Fucker won't live to see dawn."

I mock, laughing down at him. "Gunshots hurt. Don't they, piddle pants? You watch *John Wick* too much. You thought they're like bee stings but FUCK NO. They're like bombs to your bones. You probably wanna shit yourself in pain, too. But do it, and I'll shoot your ass again."

"What? What are you doing here?"

This redhead is full of questions.

I'm not in the habit of answering them, but...

Shits and giggles.

"I live in the neighborhood. Got a ranch, slaughterhouse,

and brewery down the road. I was balls deep in my second pussy of the night when your man called and needed me to make a house call." I glance around. "Scratch that. A skanky hotel call, and here I am."

"Where's Axel?"

"By my guess?" I scratch my scruffy chin. "An hour or so out. He told me to come here, secure his woman and keep any fuckers alive so he can kill them."

"No," she raises a brow, "I'm going to kill him."

"Well, damn, kitty, kitty." I wink. "I see why my man's in love."

She steps away.

Probably from me.

I'm out of deodorant.

But definitely from that spreading puddle of piss on the floor. No. Wait. That moldy shit is carpet.

"How do you know Axel?"

I tsk. "Not sure I'm supposed to say. And damn sure I ain't gonna answer."

I'm bored.

"How do *you* know him?"

"Damn sure you can figure it out." She lifts her chin.

And...

Ahh, fuck, her pretty plump bottom lip is busted.

"Hey, piss ant." I kick the man's loafer. "Did you hit her?"

"What? Who... Who gives a shit?" He groans, "You fucking shot me."

"Come on now. Give me some credit. I shot you *twice* and that ain't gonna be shit compared to what her man's gonna do to you for hitting his woman. You wanna run, Forrest, run?"

I glance down at his exploded ankle. "Aw, shucks. You can't. Hollow point bullet to the ankle. Sorry 'bout that."

"Fuck you," he whines. "I'll pay you more. Whatever he's paying, I'll double."

"I may be a psycho country boy, but I ain't dumb. Your money ain't got nothing on what my friend will do." I lean down and whisper to him, "Rumor is, he's Russian and sick as fuck. He'll go all Bolshevik on your ass. Ever heard of the Red Terror?"

I hear it.

The shocked gasp from Axel's woman.

So I rise and turn her way, shushing her with my finger. "Just a little rumor I heard about him, darlin'. Don't worry. Axel's more myth than man."

Seriously, though.

I've been meaning to tell him about that Russian oligarch's superyacht in Savannah.

But I've been overwhelmed by pussy, beer, and bullets.

CHAPTER THIRTY-NINE
AXEL

"Did he do this to you?"

I gently brush my thumb over Ruby's busted bottom lip. I sweep the auburn tendrils off her beautiful face. I'll be careful with her...

Before I cut that man into pieces.

"I'm fine, dickhead, and thank you for being such a stalker." She smiles as if she's damn happy to see me, her lips seeking mine in a kiss that confirms it.

She's okay.

We're okay.

But I'm not.

"Which hand?" I softly murmur over her lips.

"Hmm?" She wants more of our kiss.

"Which hand did he hit you with?"

She pulls away, her smile resigned. "You're going to go all Axel on him, aren't you?"

"Fuck yeah, he is," Wilder crows over my shoulder.

I raise an eyebrow at Ruby, and she answers, "Right."

I signal Grant and Nash, standing in the doorway of the motel room. "Cover her."

I don't give a shit that Wilder has this fucker, Halstead, tied to a rusty metal chair. Even though he's been shot twice, I won't risk my woman.

Nash and Grant enter, and Grant reaches for Ruby. As if to comfort her for this, but she pats his pecs. "I'm fine, Reacher. Just stand there, look pretty, and grunt."

Grant laughs but the fuck if this is about to be pretty.

"Hold him down."

Wilder knows the drill. He grabs Halstead's right arm and pins it, holding it over the top of a decrepit table strewn with beer cans, cigarette butts, and shit I don't want to know what it is.

"No. No." Halstead resists, but he's no match against Wilder. Against any of us.

I take the tactical knife from my pocket, pressing the automatic blade. When Halstead sees it, he blubbers, "What do you want?"

"Your phone and laptop," Nash calls over my shoulder. "And passcode."

"In my pocket. In the fucking limo. Six sixes but please," Halstead begs, "Please, fuck. I'm sorry."

"Not yet." I grab his right hand and smash it with my leather-gloved one over the table. "But you will be fucking sorry. You ever heard the saying 'Taking the law into your own hands?'"

"Yeah," he snivels.

"Good, because I'm about to take yours for touching my woman."

"Told ya," Wilder snickers into Halstead's ear.

"Then I'm going to shove it in your mouth to stifle your screams while I kill you for hitting her."

"Fuck," Jace mutters from the doorway. "Goddamn, I don't want to clean up a mess in here."

But I make it as neat as I can, though cutting through a

wrist joint is a bitch. I give Halstead a long lecture on the controversial history of the term that once legalized vigilante justice in America while he screams.

Grant yawns. Jace rolls his eyes. Nash hacks into Halstead's files. Wilder laughs, and Ruby stands there, with her chin lifted.

I keep worrying about my Wildfire. That this is too much for her, but she's stone-faced and watching me.

Some people see red and explode when they feel rage. That's what I've been told.

Not me.

I've been too exposed to this, seeing the woman I love hit. First, my mom. Now Ruby. I go right past rage and get ice-cold revenge.

I keep my word and take his hand. The fucker passes out but that's why I carry salt *and* smelling salts in my GO bag.

When he's startled awake, Ruby insists, "Hand me your knife."

Because I'm a gentleman, I wipe the bloody blade clean on Halstead's shirt before handing it to her. "Are you feeling stabby, my queen?"

She winks at me, and I'm expecting her to slice his face or arm—some simple shit.

But she sneers at Halstead, "What did I tell you I'd do to your dick?"

His dick?

What the fuck did he do to her with his dick?

I don't have time to ask.

I watch, shocked, as Ruby stabs his junk!

Three times!

Goddamn, like a queen!

"Fuck yeah." Wilder claps. "Y'all are like mister and missus Smith, except without the whole Brangelina ugly divorce shit. You're fucking soulmates."

Yeah, I could propose right now. Hell, I'd live on bended knee for this woman, but I have a better plan.

"I'm in." Nash leans on the wall, tapping through Halstead's phone.

He'll delete every video he finds. We'll end Halstead's life and hopefully his reign of terror, bribing innocent people after recording their most private moments.

And soon, after Ruby, Vale, Nick, and Zar enact their plan, and the athletes come out? There will be less to bribe people about.

"Take her outside," I order Grant.

Ruby's fists land on her waist. "I told you I'm fine."

"Yeah, but I'm not fine, Wildfire. Why'd you stab his dick? Did he touch you anywhere else?"

Okay, now I'm starting to see that whole red thing.

"No."

"Don't protect him or me," I warn. "Tell me the truth."

She raises her chin. "If any man touches me the way you worry about, I won't just stab his dick. I'll cut it off and feed it to him."

Ruby stands there like a siren of death. Flaming hair. Piercing eyes. A bloody knife in her hand and a wicked smile.

"Fuck, no wonder you're in love," Wilder sighs.

"Alright, Killer." Grant reaches for her arm. "Let *our* killer finish up in here."

She doesn't resist. She hands me back my knife and pecks my cheek.

Okay, so Halstead didn't touch her anywhere else.

Still...

Grant takes her outside while I turn to Halstead, pressing my blade to his throat. "When we meet in hell, I'll kill you all over again. This is for her, my brother, our queens, and all the people you violated."

"Fuck." Jace surveys the mess when I'm done. "What do I

keep telling you fuckers about plastic drop cloths? The damn things only cost five fucking dollars."

Jace is our best cleaner. Thankfully, Wilder is here to help him.

I leave Nash with them, too, before I climb into the back seat of Grant's Tahoe.

I pull Ruby into my arms, and now my heart starts beating. All the feelings no one else gets from me belong to her. I let every fear I have of losing her flood me, and she lets me kiss it away until she sighs, "I need to lie down."

"Are you okay?"

"Yeah." She stretches across the back seat and rests her head in my lap. I smooth her hair as she gazes up at me. "I need to tell you something about Wilder."

"That he's batshit crazy?"

"Yes, and..."

But her hand goes slack along with her jaw, her eyelids drooping, her stare, blank.

"Okay, baby, I got you." I reach for her handbag that Grant grabbed from the limo, sighing with relief when I feel her emergency meds in there. "I'm right here."

And I count. Ten. Twenty. Fuck, thirty seconds.

"Come on, baby." I stroke her cheek. "Wake up. Come back to me."

"Is she okay?" Grant worries from the driver's seat.

"She's having a seizure. It's the stress from today."

I keep my voice calm, but not my heart.

"What... What does she need?" Grant almost panics for me.

"For me to be right here, waiting for her to come back."

After forty-two long seconds, Ruby blinks and stirs. After two long minutes, she finally speaks, "I'm sorry."

I can't fucking hold it in.

After fearing I'd lost her. After seeing her busted lip?

After knowing the terror that fucker put her through? Like she was a trapped little girl all over again? After imagining what he could've done to her?

I fight a tear. "Baby, it's okay. I'm right here. I'm never going anywhere." I smooth her hair. I smile down at her. "Besides, it's a precious moment when you finally shut up."

She barely smiles. "Fuck you."

"If you're lucky."

I keep trying to make her laugh. She said it's her medicine. It brings her back.

But once we're home, and she's safe, sleeping in my arms, and our kittens surround us, and Sparky sleeps by our feet?

I bury my nose in her hair and vow...

I will burn the world down for my Wildfire. I'll take so many lives to have this one with her.

I will have more than Ruby sleeping in my arms.

I will have my queen. My wife.

And I'll give every part of me to make it happen.

CHAPTER FORTY
RUBY

"So, Wilder killed them?"

"He and his cousin, Remi, yes. They're contract killers," Axel answers. "And their cousin Bishop cleaned the superyacht in Savannah when they were done."

"So, who were the men they murdered?"

Once I felt better after my seizure last week, I told Axel about Wilder knowing he's Russian. It took a few days for Axel to investigate, more like to track the crazy cousins down and get to the bottom of this.

"Probably the men my father hired to watch us," Axel explains. "But someone wanted them dead, too, and hired the cousins to do it. That's when Wilder heard my name. My birth name. Right before he slit a throat."

I turn in my passenger seat. We're parked in Axel's Jaguar outside Zar and Nick's beach home, and I'm running late to join them, but I need to know.

"So, is your father dead?"

"No. We have eyes on him in Moscow."

"So, who was it who wanted his men dead? Who hired the cousins to do it?"

"They don't know. It was an anonymous contract."

"So, what does this all mean?"

Yes, I hear myself. I'm a parrot full of questions.

"It means that my father has known where we are for a while, but for some reason, he's waiting. All while our big advantage is that he doesn't know that *I* know. That *The Queen* knows and we're going to keep it that way until we know more."

"Until you know how he found you?"

He nods. "And until I get Lev, I won't risk my son being used as a pawn."

Axel reaches for my hand, lifting my fingers to his lips. "Now, enough of my father's bullshit. Go make me proud as usual, and finish this mission, my queen."

"I'm not officially your queen," I tease, but finally...

I'm ready.

After Halstead's deadly threat. After watching Axel brutalize the man who hurt me. After watching most of the kings descend upon that creepy hotel to rescue me, and all the queens comforted me afterward?

I'm ready to be initiated.

"So impatient." Axel grins, brushing his kiss over my fingertips. "And so late." He nods toward Zar's front door. "Go do your meeting."

"You know, after our meeting, Zar and Nick have an erotic party planned."

"Don't remind me," he growls. "I saw Brayton Jervis, your Tennessee quarterback, and his lovely husband, Jim, go inside an hour ago. I'm sure they'd love a replay night with you."

"But you trust me."

"With my life." Something cracks the ice in his eyes. They search mine. "Do you trust me? Again?"

I lean over, wrapping my hand around his inked neck,

pulling him into a kiss. I find his lips, his tongue, his moan, and I make them mine before I pull away.

It's my answer when I can't say *almost*.

"See you in the morning," I sigh.

The plan is, after the meeting, I'll stick around for the guests. Particularly for Beau, Colton, and Blair. They're here and I'll stay to answer questions in the morning after their long night, I'm sure.

It'll begin the next phase of our plan—the PR campaign. Vale and I have it all mapped out.

And Axel will pick me up tomorrow after everyone leaves.

"YOU BEHIND ALL THIS?" COLTON ASKS ME, IMPRESSED after our long meeting, where Nick and Zar convinced them to join their movement.

"In a way, yeah," I answer, peeling a shrimp. "But it's not just me. I'm like a representative."

The sun is setting. The low-country boil picnic on the patio is a hit with the players, and my friends are glowing. Relieved and excited to be free soon.

"So you work for someone?" Colton's full of questions, and I understand. He's about to risk his entire career for love.

"Work? Fuck? Love?" I answer. "It all comes together, right?"

"Any minute," Blair says, "I expect to see my sister walk through the door. That plan? That's something she'd come up with. She studies this for a living. I know she's in this other mysterious group."

But I can't answer her.

I just smile and know they trust us.

The mysterious group. The kings and queens. My friends can't know about us. They think I'm friends with Nick and Zar through my sister Scarlett and her husband Luca, and it's not a lie.

It's just not the whole truth.

As we finish our dinner and all refresh in the restrooms, I catch my friends eyeing the other guests, disappearing upstairs. They're curious. I can tell, and they've never had a chance to be free like this.

"I've prepared something for you," I share, escorting them upstairs. "The room at the end of the hall. It has a red and a black tie on the door handle. Leave the red tie on if you want privacy. Hang the black tie if others can join you."

They're excited. They're in love. They finally have hope, and I'm happy for them.

I stop in front of my bedroom with a red tie hanging from it. "This one's for me." I flit my hand, shooing them down the hallway. "So y'all have fun."

Me? I'll work on my laptop and prepare PR statements. Then I'll investigate the rental properties. The ones Halstead's LLC used to own. After his deadly, freak boating accident on Lake Tobesofkee, where he lost his hand and life, the rumor is his rental properties will be put up for sale, and I'll help The Queen buy them.

Yep, everyone else is having an orgy tonight but me.

Typical.

Pushing the door open, I'm greeted by the familiar darkness and the night ocean beyond the wall of glass doors.

I reach to flip on the switch that turns on the bedside lamps, and when I do, I jump at the man sitting in the corner chair.

CHAPTER FORTY-ONE
RUBY

"W HAT ARE YOU DOING HERE?"

I glance around the bedroom, my eyes shocked by the vases brimming with lilacs, irises, hydrangeas. Every purple flower you can imagine. They're everywhere.

Even lilac petals blanket the bed.

"I couldn't leave you alone on a night like this," Axel answers. "I meant it. I'm proud of you. I want to celebrate you."

"Okay... But... But..." I stammer, smiling. "You could just buy a cake or something."

"And what would it say?" He beams, rising in his dark suit. "Marry me, Ruby Jones? Be my queen, Ruby Jones?" He reaches me, his hand cupping my cheek. "Please trust me again, Ruby Jones. There's so much I need to ask you."

I blink back tears. "I *do* trust you."

"I need to earn it," he says. "You gave me something no man has ever had. Your heart. Now, I want to give you something no woman has ever had."

I don't know what he means as he shrugs off his black

jacket. Unbuttoning his white shirt, he commands me softly, "Please, sit on the bed."

Flutters hit my heart. Those beautiful butterflies only Axel can give me. They alight in my chest as I sit on a blanket of flower petals.

After he peels off his shirt, letting me admire the spectacle of his inked body, Axel leans over and unlaces his shiny, Italian shoes. Toeing them off, I watch silently as he stares at me and takes off his pants.

Standing in his black boxer briefs and usual black socks, he's always a breathtaking sight. If it's not his stunning, muscular body that has me in awe, it's his sexy face or his mesmerizing eyes, their ice burning bright tonight.

But he's not hard. Not like he usually is when he takes off his pants for me.

"I don't know quite how to do this," he says. "I've never done it." I'm confused, watching him sit beside me on the bed. "I guess... Um... Let me..."

He maneuvers around me, such that he's sitting in the center of the bed and I'm on the edge, turning toward him, not knowing what he's doing until he reaches for his socks.

And that's when I notice.

His hands are shaking.

It makes my heart start to beat so hard.

"Axel, you don't have to—"

"Yes, I do." He tugs a sock down. "I want to give you something I've never trusted anyone to have. This side of me..."

He pulls off his sock, revealing a wicked web of scars over the top of his foot. Like white faded ropes, they wrap around to his soles, where flesh-toned gashes and deep lacerations long since healed, crisscross his flesh.

It hurts just looking at them. My senses. My heart. My soul.

"He liked to use a razor blade," he shares. "One cut a week. He started the night of my seventh birthday, and this is what made me wet my bed."

Oh my god.

All I can imagine is Axel, what a beautiful little boy he must have been. Innocent and with big blue eyes. Eyes that cried in fear of his father. Fear that turned into rage. Rage that became revenge, hardening his warm blue eyes into ice.

I know that journey, too.

The coldness.

Sometimes, to survive abuse, you have to stop feeling anything for a while.

But now, I've never heard Axel's voice so choked. I've never seen his hands shake while he pulls off his other sock, revealing more scars he's hidden for years.

I wipe at my tears.

They won't stop spilling down my cheeks.

"My mother was the last person to see this. Once we escaped him, I never looked back. I put this part of me away, and *I* couldn't even find him. Not for years."

He takes my hand and places it on his right foot.

His skin, like everywhere else, is hard, warm silk, inked and stretched tight over muscles, but on his feet, it's soft, almost tender, and so marred to the touch.

"I didn't feel my heart again until I met you, Ruby." He presses my hand to his flesh. He lets me see the tears brimming in his eyes. They're not ice. They're warm and looking at me. "Please trust; there's no woman, ever, who can touch me like you do."

I choke back a sob. For his sake. For his pride, I won't do it. I swallow the lump in my throat and say, "I love you." I lean down and kiss his foot, one then the other. "I trust you and I love you, too. Always."

This is why he rubs my feet. He cherishes how they're unmarked. How I have no scars on my skin, and I trust Axel will die to keep it that way.

He pulls me to lie down in his arms, my cheek against his chest. I can hear his heart pounding under his flesh. I touch it. I kiss it. I catch my breath while he catches his.

"I'm so sorry," I whisper.

"Don't," he whispers back. "Don't apologize for him."

"I'm apologizing for me."

"You did nothing wrong."

"I've been distant."

"I understand why."

"But I've made you wait."

"I'd wait forever for you."

When he holds me this tight. When he's shown me everything. When I trust Axel more than any man, I smile against his skin.

"Liar," I softly tease.

He chuckles. "Okay. I waited until I couldn't. Until I had to chase you tonight."

"And you caught me."

"Every damn time." He lingers his hand down my back. "It's what we do, Wildfire." He kisses my hair, his voice getting husky. "And you know chasing you is my kink."

"So now what?"

"So now we can lie here and listen to dozens of men fucking," he says, rolling on top of me. "Or I can make you scream louder than them."

"I vote number two. I mean, the second one. Not shit. But you and me fucking and—"

He smiles, nuzzling his nose to mine. "I want to do something first."

"So you *did* buy me a cake."

"Not quite."

He climbs off the bed, aiming for his jacket on the chair. When he reaches into the inside pocket, my heart starts racing.

"Are you about to—"

"So impatient." He grins, pulling out the blue velvet ring box.

I chew my lips, forcing myself to shut up. To not ruin this as he lowers to one knee by the edge of the bed. I sit up and let him take my hand, but it's burning inside me.

I have to investigate. I have to ask.

"Are you about to propose to me in your boxer briefs?"

He smirks. "I can take them off if that makes it more romantic."

I consider it.

But he's the impatient one now. "You're lucky. I was tempted to put this ring on the one I already wear for you."

"On your penis piercing?"

"Hmm, but then you'd be too distracted by that ring to see this one."

He cracks open the box, and I gasp.

It's the most unusual, precious sparkling stone I've ever seen, set on a thin gold band.

"It's a rare antique, Russian Alexandrite gem, rarer than a diamond and circa nineteen hundred," he explains. "It changes color from blue like your eyes to purple like your favorite color, and under certain, rare light, it's the most beautiful ruby..." He pauses, gazing up at me. "Like my wife, if you would please marry me, Ruby Jones."

"Yes." I nod. I cry. I let him slide the ring on my shaking finger. "Yes, I'll marry you."

He cups my wet jaw, pulling my lips to his for a kiss...

But of course, I have to investigate.

"Does this mean you'll make me your queen, too?"

When Axel smirks, he makes the Devil swoon and God nervous. He makes grown men shake in terror and me tremble with excitement when he teases, "So impatient."

CHAPTER FORTY-TWO
AXEL

"What do you think she'll like?"

I consider a black latex bodysuit.

"Not that," Vale scoffs. "That's so Dom and all you."

She swishes across the showroom floor of Delta's, wearing her usual Wednesday Addams fashion. Pulling open an ivory lacquered drawer, she says, "Yes, Ruby's a badass. She's always tough. So let her be your soft, beautiful sub tonight."

She purses her lips, considering the options in the drawer.

Vale and I have come a long way.

Naturally, she hated me at first, and I hated that she didn't fear me. Hell, Vale doesn't fear any of us.

It's the mark of a queen—a woman not intimidated by men.

"What's her favorite color?"

"Purple. Or lilac."

"God, she's going to look stunning in this."

With her fingertips, Vale lifts a lilac lace bra. I'm sure it costs a fucking fortune for less than a foot of fabric.

"They have matching lace ouvert panties," she says.

"What in the hell are *ouvert* panties?"

"Elegance in the front." She lifts a pair, flipping them around. "And party in the back."

"Crotchless?"

"Sort of, but prettier. See..."

She hands me a pair, and this is how much I love Ruby. I'm getting schooled on French lingerie.

"The lace covers her pretty mound, but then two thin straps leave her perfect pussy exposed and wrap around to the back, leaving her gorgeous ass exposed, too, and—"

"I get the idea," I growl.

"You're getting jealous." Vale smirks. "It's ironic. All the shit you gave Nash about him not wanting to let me be tested and initiated by the kings, and now the shoe is on the other not-mafia-mafia foot. How's it feel?"

My shoes.

My socks.

I've stopped wearing them around Ruby. I climb into our bed, completely naked and totally hers.

"Like everyone changes," I answer Vale.

"Ahh." She pats my arm. "I'm so proud. Have I ever told you how handsome you are when you aren't being a big dick?"

"Oh, I'm always a *very* big dick." She rolls her eyes. "And you're always even prettier when your mouth is shut."

Vale always gives me shit and I give it right back. It's what we do. And I will kill for her and die for her, too.

She's a queen, so I give her a quick hug.

"Thanks." I peck her raven hair. "Now, point me in the direction of the hottest nipple toys."

"Do you want the magnetic balls like Nash used on me?"

I can't help it. The memory of Vale's initiation stirs my cock. Probably because Ruby's cheek was resting on my stiff erection that was dying to initiate Ruby, too.

Finally, it's tonight.

"No, I want something I can use with her collar."

"I got your kink covered."

Vale hooks her finger, and I follow, spending an entire hour shopping for Ruby's initiation before I disappear upstairs into our throne room.

Usually, I prepare the room for initiations, but since tonight is for me and my queen, Sire is taking over.

I find him in the throne room, rearranging things.

"What are you doing?"

"Time to change it up," he says. "Instead of the queens sitting opposite the kings, let's sit in a semicircle, surrounding the platform, but we'll leave The Queen's throne opposite and at the top of the room." He centers her red throne, before scanning the others, the black and white thrones. "See? This way, everyone's included."

Never does our mother attend an initiation or a test. She only sits on her throne for meetings.

And forever will Alena's throne, the seventh queen's chair, remain empty on the other side of Loch's.

Alena doesn't know about this room. She'll never be initiated like the other queens. She doesn't need to be. She's a queen by blood, and hopefully, Loch will get her back. He's dying without her.

But when we grow and Ruby gives me my four little princesses, we will definitely change our traditions. I'll find a convent for our daughters, and no one will ever touch them.

And yes, I know Ruby, my beautiful future wife and mother of our girls, will teach our daughters how to rebel under my rule.

I'm ordering the Xanax right now.

But this tradition?

It means too much to me and my brothers.

It's the foundation for our families to grow.

For some reason, our father is showing mercy and

restraint. Not like we won't fucking kill him if he comes for us.

But it's this tradition that gave us a fighting chance against him in the first place. A chance to be more than the beasts he raised.

We're men.

We're kings.

We're free.

"Thanks." I deadpan, "Because that's exactly what I want tonight. For *everyone* to be included."

"It is more blessed to give than receive." Sire chuckles. "And Ruby's earned it. We need to give her a royal initiation."

My cock stirs.

"So, you'll help me?"

"Always," he vows. "Tell me your boundaries and I'll respect them."

"Let's see what mood strikes me."

Sire smirks, nodding, but he knows. Nash knows. All the kings and queens know.

There's something that takes over during an initiation. It's powerful. The sacred becomes sensual. The bonds become boundless. The devotion to another erotic. It's anointed and animalistic. Pure and profane.

Of course, we have lines that brothers never cross.

But with the queens? We share. We worship. We're beasts dedicated to their pleasure.

"And tomorrow?" Sire sets out crystal glasses for vodka shots. "Wren's inviting herself to your place for lunch. All of us. We'll bring the food, and you'll give away the kittens."

A pang hits my heart.

What the fuck? Already?

From finding Sparky, our pregnant pain-in-the-ass cat, to watching each kitten born, to them pouncing on our bed, or shredding toilet paper, and lately, purring against my bare ankles when I brush my teeth ... it's time to say goodbye?

Not like we won't see them. Not like we're giving all of them away. We're keeping Sparky and one kitten.

But it's what Ruby wants.

It's another bond for our family.

Everyone will take a kitten home. Everyone except Mom, who says she's waiting for grandkids, not grandkittens, and Loch. He has dogs that won't play nicely with a little golden lion.

Sire sees my face fall, like Ruby and I are about to be empty-nesters, and he shakes his head. "Wow, she's really got you."

"My cat?"

"Yeah, her too. But I mean Ruby, and I'm happy for you. Relieved actually. Damn you're a dick when you're miserable."

"Like you're a fucking ray of sunshine."

"Oh, but I am, dear brother. For the Lord is a sun and a shield."

"God, when will you stop quoting scripture?"

"When it stops annoying you." He laughs, setting Ruby's throne beside mine.

I guess from now on, she'll sit between me and Nash.

Nash is second in command. He's earned it, and Sire never wanted it. He accepted the third king's throne out of obligation.

I think Sire fears how savage he can be. That he's worse than me, so he doesn't want the power.

Instead, he prays.

"So after her initiation tonight, when's the big day?" he asks.

"She wants to get married next month in Mykonos. At The Mercier Hotel. It's the first place we—"

"Oh, I heard. Nick was impressed." His smile crinkles the tattoo by his eye. "And you give me shit for *my* kink."

"Hey, every king has his kink. No judgement. As long as it gives us kids, too."

"Yeah." He gets that distant look. "Give us kids."

"Hey, man. I didn't mean to—"

"It's alright."

I know Sire is bisexual. Since we were teens, he never hid it.

And I know he loves Wren above all. All the judgment some people give him as a pastor who's now married to his parishioner. One who's twenty years his junior. Though Sire looks perpetually thirty; it must be all those prayers and shit keeping him young.

Either way, he refuses to be shamed for loving Wren.

If the uptight haters only knew how they met. What he did for her. What he sacrificed.

Besides, they don't know Wren, either.

Just because a woman is young, it doesn't mean she doesn't know exactly what she wants. That she can't make that choice for herself.

And good fucking luck trying to argue with Wren that an older man knows what's good for her when, hell no, she'll tell you what's best for herself.

So it's none of my business how Sire's sexuality plays out in their marriage. I just know he'll be devoted to Wren until his dying day.

"I'm trying to get her pregnant," he adds, "and yes, fucker, I need it kinky, too, so Lord willing, we'll have a baby one day soon."

I nod. I smile. I hide the ache in my chest over Lev.

I want to tell Sire about my son. How I'm going to get him back. I share so many of my secrets with him, but not this one.

I promised my mom I wouldn't say a word, and I know it's killing her too, fearing that one of her sons betrayed us.

Though Sire?

He endured so much abuse from my father, too. His ink covers his scars. If anyone knows what a threat our father is, it's Sire.

"What do you think?"

He gestures to the room in a sweeping motion.

"I like it."

I do. The new arrangement is more fitting with the queens sitting beside their kings instead of opposite them. It feels more intimate and connected.

It's like a new era has begun. Our queens share our power and missions now. Particularly mine. They don't just sit by and watch, and our throne room should reflect it.

Arranged like this?

For tonight?

Every king will be able to watch how I love my queen, how I'll claim her for them to witness, while he enjoys his queen, too.

And fuck.

It stirs my cock even more.

I check my phone.

It's almost time to get Ruby.

For our new life to begin.

CHAPTER FORTY-THREE
RUBY

"So, like," I whisper. "How's Roman?"

The other queens gather around the bar across the room in my hotel suite at The Mercier. They're not listening.

I've been spoiled by their attention and my sexy lilac Chanel tweed bustier top, matching jacket, and mini skirt. My top lip still stings a bit from the diamond The Queen gave me for my new Monroe piercing, too.

But nothing can distract me from wanting this intel.

Okay, this *tea*.

I'm dying to know. "Is he more than your captive now?"

Nadine cuts her eyes at me before slicing her gaze toward the others.

Vale has them laughing over champagne and the new prostate massagers she brought them from Delta's as gifts.

And I don't mean to pry, but I worship my future mother-in-law. I worry she has no one else to talk to.

"I've enjoyed many subs." Her voice is hushed. "But I've never felt this before."

"Felt what?" I whisper back. "Love?"

"No, I've felt love. Love saved my life. It saved my sons. And after Maxim, I swore I'd never love again, but…"

She trails off, trying not to wring her hands dripping with royal jewels.

"But what?" I lean toward her. "I promise I won't tell. But every woman needs another to talk to. I have the queens, you, and my sisters, but who can you talk to about him? I swear I won't judge."

She sighs, "What can a man his age see in a woman like me?"

I jolt back, shocked. "You can't be serious. You're the hottest woman I've ever seen. And it really pisses off Axel when I tell him that."

She chuckles.

"And Roman's no boy," I whisper. "He's a very grown man. It's obvious he wants you. Like…" I gesture with my hands, approximating his length. "Like really big and obvious how much he wants you. So why not?"

"Because I'm covered in scars," she shares, and it hits my heart. *Just like Axel.* "I hate that my sons saw them when they were boys. Poor Jace. They made him cry. And Axel? He knifed a wall, over and over, after he saw them. My scars are horrific, and I hide them because I hide so much more inside. And if I ever let myself be with…"

She glances, making sure we're still not overheard.

"If I let myself be with Roman," she whispers, "he'll see them. The ones on my body and the ones on my heart. I can't hide them."

I reach for her hand. "I feel like Roman was a gift. To Axel, so he could find out about Lev. And to you, so you can stay safe from your ex-husband. If any man can understand the scars Ruslan gave you, it's Roman. I don't think he only came searching for Axel. I think Roman was meant to find you."

Her blue eyes go from soft to a smirk that plays with her lush lips.

God, I see where Axel gets that look from.

"I'm sure my sons would be so pleased." Nadine chuckles low. "Their mother, a dominatrix and a cougar to a man who's their age?"

She tosses her chin up, laughing.

"A cougar?" I shake my head. "No, my queen. You're a lioness."

She winks back, squeezing my hand. "It takes one to love one. So, thank you for loving my son. I know it's not easy. I know he's not perfect. But no woman has ever had his heart like you, so thank you for guarding it like a lioness, too."

"I promise, I will."

"I know. Mess with one of us and you'll kiss the business end of a pistol."

A knock raps on the door.

"It's time!" Wren claps.

"And that's my cue."

The Queen stands as Zar lets Axel into the suite.

And I don't care how many times I've seen that man in a black suit, a white unbuttoned, starched shirt, shiny black shoes, and sexy bling; he's never looked hotter than he does tonight.

It's his eyes when they see me wearing purple. When they spot my new Monroe piercing, marking me as a queen. *His queen.* They're hungry, hunting, chasing, and claiming.

Me.

On sight.

There's a predator in his glare, and I press my bare thighs together, the tightening tingle in my core sudden and intense.

God, what does he have planned for me tonight?

"My Queen." Axel kisses his mother's cheeks.

"My son." She gently grabs his bearded chin, warning, "*Don't* go crazy with your new queen."

It's cute. If anyone else were to put a hand on Axel like that, they'd lose it.

But his mom? He only smiles back with respect, teasing, "But she likes it when I go crazy with her."

He winks at me, and Nadine swats his arm before raising hers. "My queens, give me hugs. I have other places to be."

When it's my turn for her hug, I whisper, "Make him kneel for it."

She laughs, and after she leaves, Axel asks, "What was that about?"

I arch a brow. "You really want me to tell you?"

He searches my mischievous eyes. "Will it shrivel my dick?"

I nod.

"Jesus fuck," he huffs, chuckling. "Why did I ask?"

We wait an hour for the others to leave and join their kings in the throne room at Delta's.

While I sip sparkling cider and Axel sips chilled vodka, he glances around.

"I have a crazy idea we're going to do."

"Oh." I laugh. "Thanks for considering my opinion."

"You'll agree because it's smart. Here." He gestures to the four-bedroom penthouse, which boasts a terrace view overlooking the city. "Let's live here while you're pregnant and we have our babies."

"What? At The Mercier?" I shake my head. "No. I'm not taking my brother-in-law's money. Never have. Never will."

"We won't. I'll pay him."

"Exactly. *You'll* pay him."

"Wildfire, my millions are yours. That's marriage. I've already signed it over to you."

I blink.

"Think like a queen, not a stubborn sister," he says. "Between Luca's security and mine, this is the safest place we can be. You'd be surrounded by family. Your sister, Scarlett, and her new baby. And Zar has a suite here as well. We can outfit this penthouse to ensure your safety. It has no stairs. We'll install plush carpets. Buy new soft furniture. Help can be seconds away and—"

"But your father, Axel. I won't expose my family to him."

In three steps, he's pulling me into a hug. "I'm sorry, but they're already exposed. Just as easily as Katya found me, my father has found you, too. That means he knows about your sisters. About all of us."

"Why hasn't he done anything? Like a high noon, Bratva shootout?"

"I don't know. But I know this hotel is a fortress."

"What will we tell Luca? And Scarlett?"

"Like they don't have their guesses about me and wouldn't want you and our babies to be safe."

I grin. "So impatient to knock me up, and we're not official yet." He lifts my hand with the rare gem sparkling on my wedding finger. "Okay, so I have a ring, but I'm not Ruby King yet."

"Fuck," he sighs into a growl. "Fuck, Wildfire, if you take my name *and* my heart? You better let me do everything I can to protect you and our family."

"Sparky, too. And a kitten," I whisper before his kiss.

As always, Axel's kiss quickly burns with passion, seeking more from me. He's getting hard and hungry, but I rasp, "We're going to be late."

"Tell me your boundaries tonight."

"What are yours?"

"No, my queen." He caresses my neck. "This is your initiation. I honor you tonight. Tell me what you want and don't want."

"You know I want you, and I want Grant to make it official. To be my second king. What else is there?"

He licks his lips.

Oh, my god, there's that look in his eyes.

I see why lions are his family crest. His symbol. Axel's an apex predator at the top of the food chain, and I'm his meal.

"I can do so much with you tonight," he warns, squeezing my throat. "And after everything lately, I will. You've done so much for us; I'll give you the initiation you deserve."

His thick erection twitches against my belly, clearly aroused by his plan.

And I start breathing hard.

My nipples harden.

Wet heat rushes my core, spilling to my sex, when I ask, "What are you going to do to me?"

"Me?" He smirks. "You mean me *and* the kings."

CHAPTER FORTY-FOUR
AXEL

THERE'S THE FIRST TIME I SAW RUBY, SITTING PROUD IN the purple dress she couldn't afford, and ignoring her bleeding knee while she told me I'd be a fool not to hire her.

And there's now.

Because I'm no fool.

I knew then she was a queen.

And I can feel it now as she becomes mine.

The other queens and kings sit on their thrones while I stand before Ruby, just as I will during our wedding.

Sire performs the sacred ceremony when I usually would have.

But not tonight.

I'm speechless, anchored to Ruby's gaze, and she's committed to mine.

We've heard these words before, but their meaning isn't lost. I glance down at my hands, holding hers, her engagement ring sparkling with promise, *our promise*.

We keep smiling at each other.

And yes, dammit, I'm fighting tears.

But like fuck if I'll ever let my brothers see it.

Finally, Sire gets to the last part. "Do you, Axel King, with a free and unconstrained will, claim Ruby Jones as your queen?"

I nod and lift Ruby's ring to my lips, kissing it. "My *true* queen, and I do."

"Will you guard her, above all, with your life? Will you love her, above all, with your heart? Will you die for her, with no hesitation, leaving her your soul?"

"Forever," I vow.

"Will you, Ruby Jones..." Sire smiles. Yeah, he approves. "With free and unconstrained will, accept our brother, Axel King, as *your* king?"

She smirks, and I brace for what my Wildfire will say.

This is why I love her.

But her smirk rolls into her chewing her lip, her eyelashes fluttering, and fighting back tears.

"Proudly," she vows, and I swallow the lump in my throat.

"Will you love him, above all, with your heart? Will you give him, more than any other, a life worth fighting for? Will you honor him, even in death, as his queen?"

A tear spills down her cheek. "I was born Axel's queen, and I will die as Axel's true queen."

"Fuck, Wildfire."

I need to kiss her now.

Hurry up.

But Sire must continue.

"Deliver them, safe from wrath and danger. Preserve their bed and fill their home. Let them see their children's children. Ahem." Sire gets choked up, too. "Unite them into one flesh, and please, dear Lord, we pray, as one family, all of us together."

That's not the vow.

I glance at Sire.

But it seems the spirit has taken him.

"Crown them as king and queen together," he finishes as I cup Ruby's cheeks, pressing my lips to hers, "together, tonight, and in the stars forever."

I kiss Ruby, and it's like every time I do, I'm kissing a wish, a prayer, a feeling so strong that it leaves me tender.

"Only you can touch me, my queen," I whisper over our lips.

"Only you can own me, my king." She gazes into my eyes.

"Damn," Jace sniffles. "Fuck, y'all are beautiful together."

"Someone hand him a tampon," Grant mutters.

"Shut up," Delphine whispers. "That is a word? No?"

"It's two." Zar chuckles. "And yeah, congratulations, you two."

We laugh. We hug. We celebrate.

Everyone mingles as Ruby tries to hide her gag at the caviar we serve, but I laugh, handing her a napkin so she can spit it out.

But she devours the Korovai, the traditional, hand-braided Russian wedding bread that my mother always prepares for the occasion.

"Can we serve this at our wedding?" she asks.

I grab her by the waist, pulling her near. "I'm going to *spoil* you at our wedding. Jesus fuck. Between our families, imagine all the bridesmaids and groomsmen."

"We can just elope."

"We can just get our asses handed to us by The Queen if we do."

That makes her stare turn, sharply aiming it across the room. "So is that *my* queen's throne beside yours?"

I glance at it, and want her to know. "Yes, and it's new."

"Really? When did you buy it?"

"The day after I hired you."

Her sapphire eyes gleam. "Liar."

"No, baby. Never again. I value you, our love, and my dick

head way too much to not tell you the truth, and nothing but the truth, so help me God and every queen who will kick my ass if I don't."

"So, that's my very own throne?"

"Yeah. It becomes yours tonight."

A wicked thought takes me. My darkest fantasies with her are about to come true. They're swelling my cock. Pressing my thumb to her lips, she obeys, sucking it while I ask, "Do you want everyone to watch how you're mine?"

She nods.

"Do you want my brothers to be a part of your initiation?"

She moans, and I lean down, steaming my lips over her ear, "Do you want me to let them touch you while you earn your throne?"

"Please, my king," she pants over my thumb.

Yes, jealousy prowls through my veins. But this possession? This taboo? This claim and pure control I have over her, and who touches her? Yes, Ruby's complete trust in me is far more intoxicating.

"Go put your collar on and get ready."

"Yes, my king." She kisses me, then aims for the door.

"I'm coming with you." Vale jumps up.

"Me, too!" Wren joins them.

"Finally." Delphine follows, clapping.

The women close the door behind them, and Nash laughs. "You know what they're up to, right?"

Sire reclines on his throne. "Butt plugs, I hope."

"Listen," I order. "I want this to be perfect for her. Ruby deserves a real initiation."

"Do you mean...?" Jace raises an eyebrow.

"Ask," I bark. "Ask her before you do anything. I want her ecstatic consent."

"While you ecstatically kill us?" Loch laughs. "Not like

I'm going to touch her anyway, but I'd prefer not to bury my brothers for touching your queen."

When Loch fell in love with Alena, we all agreed it would be different for them. One, because Loch has already fulfilled his duty. He's Delphine's second king. And two, because Nash won't tolerate Loch being with any woman but Alena. Not that Loch wants to be. And three, it feels like Loch and Alena are the next generation. They'll start a new custom.

But not us.

We crave this one.

"Yeah," Jace agrees with Loch. "When it comes to Ruby, you're like Nash and Nick. You won't share."

"And yet, we did share," Nash reminds Jace. "And we liked it."

What the fuck?

Did Jace, the biggest beast of all, just blush?

"Will you share your mystery woman one day?" Nick clocks it, too. Sipping his vodka, he challenges Jace because we're all curious.

"Fuck," Jace shakes his head, "if I ever claim her, I'll give her every goddamn fantasy she wants."

"I'm going to hold you to it," Grant goads him, "... and her."

Of all the brothers, they're the closest in age, in looks. They're like twins giving each other merciless shit ... and love —most of the time.

"I won't kill anyone," I growl, fighting the instinct. "Only tonight and only for Ruby's initiation. Make it mean something to her. Earn her trust. I want her to feel our bond."

Respectfully, Nash nods. After Vale's initiation, he gets it, and the others copy him with knowing grins.

In perfect timing, Vale swings the door open, proclaiming, "All rise for the queen!"

But the moment I see Ruby, stripped out of her elegant

Chanel suit and standing before us in hot-as-fuck, lacey, lilac lingerie and nude heels, I whip my glare to my brothers. "I changed my mind."

Sire rolls his eyes. "No, you didn't."

"My king." Ruby stalks toward me, something primitive rousing my cock when she offers me the black leather handle to her gold chain leash.

I could make this about me. About my sociopathic jealousy and raging possession over her. How I want to reach for knives and salt at the thought of anyone touching Ruby. *Ever.*

I'm still tempted to kill everyone before me.

But, as the queens sit on their thrones, Ruby kneels before me on the velvet purple pillow I bought earlier and left for her before my throne.

Obediently, she bows her head, giving me everything.

Her body.

Her trust.

Her love.

So I make this about Ruby.

What she wants. What she's proven and earned. My God, she is truly our first-chair queen.

I tug on her leash. I make her proudly lift her chin as I step and glance down her luscious backside...

Oh, my Wildfire.

I spy her fluffy purple bunny tail anal plug.

"Good girl," I praise as my cock thickens. "Are you preparing your tight little ass for me to fuck?"

"Yes, my king."

"Do you want me to fuck every hole that belongs to me? In front of the kings and queens tonight?"

I want everyone to hear her. We never claim without consent. We will not repeat the evil that brought us into this world.

No, we're the opposite.

Under her purple lace, Ruby's nipples are hard. Her lungs are heaving. Her eyes are an ocean of lust. Her beg is a command.

"Please, my king."

Something I'll never allow again will happen tonight. Once. And for her.

I don't have to worry about Ruby's innocence. She's mature. She's as experienced as I am.

I don't have to fear she'll betray me. Or leave me. I'll always trust her.

Yes, we've earned this together.

I tug her collar. "Stand."

She obeys, and I reach for her elbow to help her.

"So fucking beautiful." I drink her in. Fire and ice. Curves and lace. Freckles and goosebumps. Alabaster and blushed skin.

"Let me show them," I command, "how beautiful my queen is."

She stands in the center of the semicircle of thrones as I take my place behind her. Unclasping her bra, I sweep it off her shoulders, letting it fall to the floor.

With my glance, I catch Jace licking his lips at the sight of Ruby's exposed breasts. Loch is riveted, too. He adjusts his pants.

Reaching into my jacket pocket, I take out the nipple chain with clamps that Vale suggested earlier today.

Tracing my hand over Ruby's collar, I open the clasp in the center of the gold chain and secure it to the ring on her collar before I tease the thin clamps over her pearled nipples.

"Can I show you off? Can I show them what a good girl you are for me?"

"Please, my king."

"Tickle your clit while I do it. Make the pain pleasurable."

In her lilac ouvert panties, she doesn't have to take them off. Her beautiful ginger pussy is already exposed.

Proudly, Ruby leans against me as she reaches down, moaning while she plays with herself, and I look over her shoulder, carefully pinching and securing her nipples between the golden tweezers.

"Oh fuck," she gasps.

"Look at your kings," I demand. "Look at them and tell them who these pretty little nipples belong to."

I tug the chains, pulling her nipples taut, and she gasps, "Axel. I belong to Axel."

"Fuck, yes, you do."

I bite her neck, then gently kiss the mark I left.

"Kneel," I order her. "Kick off your heels and kneel on the platform and show them how your pussy belongs to me. Show them how wet it gets while you suck my cock."

I yank Ruby's chain, and she moans. When she turns around to follow me, I check her eyes. They're brimming with desire. She's entirely in the moment.

"Is that what my queen wants?" But I make sure. "You want them to watch how you come with my cock in your mouth?"

"Please, my king," she sighs. "I need your cock. I want to feel your cum all over my face."

Fuck, Wildfire. You're my queen.

Gently tugging Ruby's leash, I walk around to the other end of the platform.

I've trained her so well at home.

I've taught her to crawl to me, to bow and serve. To let me play and degrade. To bind and torture her with pleasure. I love leaving her tied up, exposed and naked while I stare forever at her mouthwatering pussy and waiting ass before I fuck them all night.

And I've trained her to let me care for her afterward.

God, sometimes that's my favorite part.

Okay, second favorite part.

So now, obediently, seductively, she crawls across the leather tufted platform, putting her pussy and ass on proud display for the others.

I catch Sire fixated on her bunny tail. It's his kink with Wren. No doubt, Wren gave the new plug to Ruby as a gift. As a way to please Sire, too. Because right now? Wren's reaching over the arm of Sire's throne, and stroking the raging erection under his black pants.

It makes me smile to see Ruby on all fours for me, in front of everyone.

Dragging my zipper down, I order her, "Arch your back, baby, and spread your legs. Let them see how wet you'll get for this cock."

Silently, she submits.

Fuck, I wish they could see how she opens her mouth, too. How she's eager to have my cock in it as I wedge my erection free to jut, thick and dripping before her eager lips.

On initiation nights, the kings don't wear boxers under our pants. We want easy access so we can unzip and expose enough of our bodies to share with our queens, to please them.

"Now be a good girl, and don't tease me. We have a long night." I unclasp her hair from its elegant twist, loving how it tumbles free. "Suck my cock and choke on it. Get me ready to come on you."

She stares up at me, smiling. "Please, my king. Shoot your load all over my tongue."

God, she's going to kill me tonight.

Plunging her lips down my shaft, Ruby moans over my swollen tip, her gag on my length sudden and loud.

It sends tremors like lightning up my thighs, straight to my dick.

"Fuck, baby." I fist her hair. "Fuck, yes, such a good girl. That's it. Show them how you can suck me fast and make me come."

I've waited too long. I've wanted this too much. I will keep every vow I make to Ruby—sacred and profane.

I will love her forever.

Only her.

And I will claim her every hole tonight. I'll have her taking, wet, shaking, sweaty, dripping, squirting, screaming my name and covered in my cum before I offer her to her second king.

So now, I don't hold back, and she doesn't either.

She tilts her head, bobbing her mouth and twisting her lips, her tongue teasing my foreskin, her mouth sucking, her lips drooling over my swollen shaft. The lewd, loving *glucking* sound of my cock fucking her throat fills the room.

I stare at her, aroused, adoring, praising, "Mmm, baby, yes. You know how I like it. You're such a good girl with my cock in your mouth."

Ruby moans. She gets off on praise and degradation.

"Sire," I growl. "Come here and serve our queen."

I see the surprise in Ruby's eyes, weeping at her lustful performance, her moan caught in her gagging throat.

With eyes hooded, almost evil with lust, Sire approaches the edge of the platform closest to Ruby. No one can miss his thick hard-on, too.

"Play with my queen's nipples," I command him. "I know you know how. She's being such a good girl, so give her a nipple orgasm while she chokes on my cock."

He kneels beside Ruby, but he knows to ask. To coax. "Can I touch you, my queen? Do you want to come with your king's cock in your mouth?"

"Please." Spit webs from Ruby's panting lips to my tip.

"Please," she begs, "make me his good girl. Make me come for him."

While she drags her tongue over the swollen vein in my shaft, knowing every contour of my cock and making me groan, Sire reaches under her, fondling her breast.

"Mmm." She moans, her eyelids fluttering with lust and possession fires through me. Rage, too, but I clench my jaw.

I love her more than myself.

This is our bond. I want her to feel it. To trust it.

"Your queen has pretty little nipples," Sire praises. "I bet she's a dirty girl who likes me to pinch them and pull at her clamps. Like this..."

Sire does it, and "Mmm," Ruby moans again, her body shaking while I clasp my hands tighter around her head, my fingers laced in her fiery strands.

"Fuck yes," I growl. "Make her come. She loves it. Torture her nipples until she's streaming down her thighs. Nash," I bark at him. "Can you see my queen's pussy? Is she soaking wet for us?"

Ruby trembles, arching her back more.

"Fuck yes, I can," Nash boasts lustfully. "She has a pretty, wet pussy for you."

I lift my stare toward his throne, spurred on when I see how Nash has his hand tucked into Vale's white cotton panties. He's fingering her and making Vale writhe while he's watching my queen's pussy get so fucking wet for this.

"Oh, Wildfire." I glance down at her. Loving. Admiring. White heat coiling in my spine. "They can see your pussy. How you're so swollen and wet and need to come for us. Don't you?"

She moans. She drools. She almost closes her eyes.

"No, baby. Eyes on me," I command. "That's it. Look at me while you let my brother play with your nipples and you suck my cock."

I shove my length, as much as I can, down her throat, while Sire cajoles, "You're such a good girl for us. So pretty with his cock in your mouth."

He rattles her nipple chains, pulling them. I can't see it, but I can feel Ruby's shaking pursuit. How she's about to come. How I will as soon as she does.

"Fuck, baby," I beg her weeping eyes. "Do it. Let them watch your pussy come. Come for your king."

Ruby lets go, convulsing, her eyes rolling back, her deep groan stifled by my mass in her mouth.

"Fuck, she's coming," Jace murmurs. "She's dripping."

"Oh, fuck yes." I devour the sight of Ruby. I crave her pleasure. I relish how everyone can see it, too.

My breath thins, my thighs shaking. My cock swells even more. I can't hold it back. I'm a fucking animal.

"Open your mouth," I rasp, and Ruby obeys, ripples of her orgasm still shaking her shoulders while she pulls back and obediently opens her mouth, extending her tongue.

"Oh, fuck yes. Good girl," I snarl, jerking my length slick with her spit. In two fast tugs, I grunt, I explode, painting her tongue, and shooting over her chin. I fist her hair, yanking her up fast so I can come on her tits, her pinched nipples, aroused and full of blood.

They drive me insane.

The fire in my veins won't stop.

It goes on and on for her.

This erotic christening gets me off.

"Fuck yes." I spurt again, watching my creamy ropes splatter her beautiful breasts. "I'll cover you in my cum tonight."

Ruby moans, arching her back for more, and I milk my cock, watching my open slit spurt every last drop, my breath huffing until I'm spent as Sire pulls away.

God, what a beautiful sight.

Ruby's lifting her chin. It's dripping with my cum. It's trickling over her collar, my thick creamy drops falling from her nipples.

My Wildfire.

Never during an initiation have I felt such pride, such love.

Yes, it's primal urges, kinky play, and raw sex. It's carnal beyond our wildest dreams, because it conjures the animal in us. The bonds. The attachment. The connections. It's in our nature.

Forever, Ruby will be mine. I'll die trusting it.

But after tonight, nature will nurture her bonds with my brothers, too.

Like me, they'll protect her because I know.

No, I fear ... she'll need it.

Smoothing her hair, I gently order her, "Now turn around and show them how you're my queen."

CHAPTER FORTY-FIVE
RUBY

I'VE NEVER BEEN SO PROUD, KNEELING BEFORE A CROWD. My nipples ache, pinched in clamps hanging from Axel's collar around my neck. My lips, chin, and breasts drip with his masculine claim. My exposed sex weeps, waiting for him. My toying ass is ready to receive him, too.

Axel's dominance is the penultimate drug.

I'm euphoric.

I'm his.

He walks to the side of the platform where Sire knelt.

Where Sire tickled, tugged, and tortured my swollen nipples with his expert fingers, sending luscious shocks through my core, his touch and Axel's filthy praise making me orgasm without a touch to my clit.

God, Sire's just like his brother, a natural Dom, and the fact that I felt it, know it, *trust it*...

That taboo thrills me even more.

"You look incredible like that, my queen." Axel lowers his lips, tugging my leash so I'll lift my chin and eagerly return his kiss.

He laves his tongue over mine, moaning at his taste in my

mouth before he sweeps my lips. He cleans his cum off my chin, too, but he leaves it dripping and drying on my breasts.

Then he nuzzles his forehead to mine.

"Does your pussy want more?"

"Yes, my king."

"Spread yourself open and prove it."

This complete trust. Complete exposure. Complete control and total submission.

And I was born to do this for him.

I sit on the plush platform and lean back on my elbows. Drawing my knees up, I let my legs fall wide open for Axel. His brothers can see me, too. So can the queens.

Desire leaks from my cunt and I clench it for him. I make my ass pulse around my naughty bunny plug, too, and Axel growls, "Fuck yes, that's mine."

"Nash," he calls to him while his stare admires my wanton pride. "Come here and serve my queen's pussy for me to eat."

Oh.

My.

God.

Nash Allen. Our second king. Vale's king and fiancé is almost as menacing and mouthwatering as Axel. Tousled bronze hair. Rich brown eyes. He's tall with ink and muscles galore.

Wearing black suit pants and an unbuttoned starched white shirt—it's what all the kings wear tonight—he rises from his throne.

Axel shrugs off his black jacket, tossing it on the platform while Nash stalks my way.

I'm sure in time, I'll get to know Nash. I've grown so close to his queen already. But the fact that Nash feels like a stranger, but one I want to trust as a king, makes this more erotic.

I guess Axel meant it.

Every king will touch me tonight.

And I want it.

I want to belong. To bond. To be owned and adored.

"Come here, Wildfire."

Tenderly, Axel beckons me to rise, guiding me to wrap my hands around his neck while he lifts me, hooking his arms under my legs and setting me like a doll into Nash's waiting grasp.

With my naked back against Nash's exposed, smooth chest, I can feel his hard heat. I can smell his cologne: vanilla and leather. I can sense how my weight is nothing to his strength.

"You good, my queen?" Nash asks me while I lean against him, my legs dangling over his arms. He holds me, splayed open ... and I love it.

"Yes, thank you."

It doesn't feel right calling Nash or anyone else *my king*. Though I know our roles, that's not my heart. It belongs to one man. One king.

"Bring her to me."

Axel sits on his throne, summoning Nash.

Beside Axel's throne sits mine, waiting for me.

Next to mine is Nash's empty throne. Beside his throne sits Vale with Sire beside her and Wren next to him.

They have a full view of what Axel is about to do, while the others can imagine it. They can hear Axel taunting me, "You were such a good girl, getting so wet for me while you sucked my cock. So, now relax and let Nash hold you while I feast on your cunt."

In two steps, Nash stands between Axel's spread legs, his knees brushing Axel's throne. Nash holds me, hovering my body so close to Axel's mouth that my toes brush the wooden arms of Axel's black throne.

"Pulse that pretty pussy again, baby." Axel sits like a king, regal and relaxed, his breath steaming under my splayed lips. "Pulse it and make it drip on my tongue."

I'm an animal, feral and caught by one man, who's serving my pussy to another.

Yes, please.

Make me do it.

Fucking serve me.

I squeeze and make one little drip leak from my entrance, and Axel groans, the tip of his tongue licking it up before he spears my tender hole. I can't help it. I moan. I fight to keep my eyes open. Held like this in Nash's arms, I can't hide my nature. My pussy is open, weeping, and craving more.

With his eyes glaring up at me, Axel flicks his tongue over my raw clit. It's been hard and aching for over an hour, and I urge, "Please, Axel. Make me come."

He smirks, teasing, "So impatient when you taste so fucking sweet. Watch, my queen. Watch how sweet you taste to me."

Expertly, he circles, sucks, licks, and flicks my clitoris for minutes. Forever, he edges me until I'm shaking in Nash's arms.

"Please, my king," I beg, glancing over at the others watching us. Our lustful audience only makes me need this more. "Please, finger me. Fuck me. Just make me come for you."

"Mmm. Yes, be such a dirty girl for your daddy." Nash's husky voice taunts me. It taunts Axel, too, "Make that pretty pussy squirt all over your daddy's face."

I moan as Axel smirks at Nash's kink. Sinking two thick fingers inside my creamy pulsing cunt, Axel starts playing Nash's game ... *and me*.

"Damn right I'm your daddy," Axel coaxes. "You want to

be a dirty girl for me, Wildfire? You want to squirt on your daddy's face in front of everyone?"

"Oh my god," I sigh, my eyes rolling back, pleasure erupting through my senses when I feel Axel's fingers curl inside me, pressing against that tender spot. Violently, he starts jerking his fingers inside my walls as his mouth starts ruthlessly sucking my clit.

It's the most degrading pain and delicious pleasure I've ever felt. "Oh my god!" And Axel does it to me. Always. He's claiming me so fast. "Oh my god, I'm coming!"

"Come on your daddy's face," Nash taunts. "Come all over your king."

I stare into Axel's icy eyes and burst, shaking and releasing the pressure he built, the pleasure he created. I explode, screaming and squirting it into his open mouth, showering his waiting tongue that won't stop licking and drinking more from me while my thighs quake.

I make myself watch. I make myself witness the woman I am for Axel. The woman I'll always be.

His sub. His queen. His wife. His everything.

Lustful moans spill from me while my cum drips from Axel's beard, his mouth gently slurping on my pulsing cunt until I stop shaking and his deep voice praises, "Such a good girl, making your thirsty daddy get so hard for you."

Nash chuckles, holding my trembling body. That's when I realize that I can feel Nash's swollen tip in his pants, poking at my bottom. Nash is hard, too, and Axel sees it.

His taunt was meant for him, as well, while I hear Vale sigh, "Good god, that was hot."

I agree, but I need to catch my breath, and Axel reads it in my eyes.

"Give her to me," he orders Nash to lay me in his waiting arms.

I soaked his chest and shirt, but I don't care. I nuzzle Axel's neck, curling up in his lap.

"You okay?" he whispers over my hair.

"More than okay," I sigh. "I want more."

"Bring her water," Axel commands the group, and Jace complies. He rises and fills a crystal glass on the antique credenza before crossing the room and offering it to me.

I lick my lips, thirsty and thankful, but also noting the heavy erection hanging in Jace's pants, too.

I thank Jace and sip my water.

And Axel smirks, watching Jace return to his throne before he asks me, "Are you ready for more, my queen? Can I lay you in the lap of another king while I fuck you?"

THE SWEET SHOCKS WON'T STOP TONIGHT, BUT I DON'T overthink Axel's question.

"Yes, fuck me like a queen."

Axel nips at my demanding mouth before his kiss claims it, his tongue sharing our taste: my tang and his salt. I breathe against his lips. "Now, my king."

"Stand up and take off your panties."

"Her *ouvert* panties," Vale interjects cutely, and Axel winks at her.

I love the relationship he has with the other queens. It's respectful. It's affectionate. It's warm and protective, but it's not like the intense love we share.

I'm beginning to feel what Axel has told me all along.

This is building a bond, rare and revered. You can't describe it from the surface. You have to dive in to feel its warmth, its depth.

I already feel connected to the queens, and I've loved Zar and Nick for so long.

But now? With the other kings?

I feel safe with Sire and comfortable with Nash.

As Axel's queen, the first-chair queen, he'll make sure I bond with all of his brothers tonight.

It's like he needs it.

And I do, too.

After my little rest and water, I stand on firm legs, confidently stripping off my panties for the room. Not like they were concealing anything, but now, there's no pretense of hiding.

I'm in my collar and chains, and I'm all Axel's.

He holds out his hand and I place my soaked panties in it.

Then he rises, leaving my panties on his throne before he leads me across the room to the other side of the semicircle.

Now, I'm staring down Grant, Delphine, Jace, and the empty throne beside him.

For a moment, my heart hurts for Jace. He deserves a queen, a love like what Axel and I share.

What woman would stay married to an asshole, as Vale described, and not run into Jace's waiting mammoth arms?

Whoever she is, she'd be lucky.

You can see it in Jace's steel blue eyes. They're warm. They're ready to give so much love.

Beside his empty queen's throne, sit Nick and Zar. Of all the kings, they're closest to me. They're a line I don't cross, and Axel knows.

Next to Zar sits Loch, alone.

And of all the brothers, I know him the least. He doesn't live in Charleston. He lives in the mountains, where he works as a forest ranger with Alena.

I know her throne will remain empty. She'll never be initiated or learn about this room. And I don't imagine her with Axel anymore.

I'm too overwhelmed, feeling how Axel's all mine. I trust it, and I can see that Alena lives in Loch's heart.

It's obvious by the lost look in Loch's stunning eyes. He looks hurt without her. It's an odd aura against his rugged persona and beefy appearance with ink crawling up his thick neck. His pain is almost beautiful, but if I could, I'd make it go away. I want him to have love, too.

Suddenly, I feel close to all the kings. Like I want to take care of them, too.

That's what makes the act of Axel, guiding me to sit on Jace's empty lap, so intimate and erotic.

Jace sighs as I settle over him. He smells like lavender, citrus, and wood. His body is rippled concrete covered by fine wool pants and starched cotton. His hard form greets my soft, naked body, and I relax. I feel that I can trust him, too.

"Hold her open for me," Axel commands Jace.

"Like this, my queen?" Jace's gravelly voice vibrates in his exposed chest pressed against my back. As Nash held me, Jace does the same. Carefully, he hooks his corded, inked forearms under my legs and spreads them open. "Is this comfortable?"

Comfortable?

I'm watching Axel peel off the wet shirt I soaked before he shucks his pants down and kicks them free, along with his shoes. Of course, he leaves his socks on.

Only I can see his feet.

That's what makes this one of the most tender and taboo things I've ever felt. How Axel's cock soars, thick and hungry for me, while his brother holds me open to receive him.

"Yes," I answer Jace. I answer the question in Axel's eyes.

He wants this, and I do, too.

"Play with her nipple chains," Axel orders. "Give her pleasure."

Jace unhooks his wrists, leaving my legs to drape over the padded arms of his throne. Gently, his massive hands pull at the dainty chains attached to the golden tweezers clamped over my nipples, tugging at them...

And, oh fuck.

I groan.

I slip into the pool of lust that Axel's plunged me into twice already. Once, sucking his cock. Twice, when he devoured my pussy.

And now, while Axel tugs my thighs, making me slide down Jace's lap, my back resting against his groin. I can feel Jace's thick erection, urging against me. He's very aroused, watching his brother about to fuck me.

I can feel it in Jace's deepening breath. How he's gazing at my wet open cunt. How he needs a woman, too.

He must be in pain, waiting for his.

"Watch." Axel teases his swollen tip over my clit. "Watch this pretty wet pussy take every inch of this cock."

I set my moan free while Jace stifles his. I start to shake when Axel circles his crown over my clit before he glides his tip to my entrance and brutally thrusts inside me.

Oh my god!

This is going to happen fast. Fast, intense, and explosive again. I feel it. I need it.

"Oh fuck, please," I beg Axel for mercy. For more. For his sweet stretch. His total possession as he gazes down, and all three of us watch his penetration.

How he fills my aching cunt. How I trust him, love him. How he makes me shudder with a wave of emotions. I'm overwhelmed by the sight of Axel's steel piercing for me. How it gleams like his rare wedding ring on my finger, too, my hands bracing against his granite shoulders.

"Axel," is all I can sigh, so damn open to him. Taking him.

"Yes, baby," he growls. "You like this? You like taking my cock while my brother holds you open for it? While he plays with your naughty nipples and watches you get fucked?"

"Yes." I can't think straight. This feels too taboo, too good. The truth escapes my lips. "I've never been fucked like this before. Do it. Make me your dirty girl. Play with me. Fuck me."

"Oh fuck," Jace mutters, his cock twitching against my back.

"You're so beautiful." Axel gazes down at me, at us. "You're so fucking beautiful, loving my cock fucking you like this, Wildfire."

Bracing his hands against the arms of Jace's throne, Axel's inked muscles rip across his shoulders and pecs. His whole body flexes as he planks his form, his washboard abs locked with his effort. He watches his shaft, plunging in and out of my split, creamy pussy.

I can feel every thick inch of him and...

Oh my god, he looks so hot. He feels so good.

"Can you see how her wet pussy is mine?" He thrills Jace. "Can you feel her cum dripping down her sweet ass cheeks and all over your pants?"

"Yes," Jace grunts.

I can, too. I'm moaning, taking, and releasing. It's as if Axel's found my well of lust tonight, and I won't stop leaking, dripping. Little convulsions and deep pulses tease what he's about to do to me. What I *need* him to do to me.

"Please, Axel," I beg. "I need your thick cock. Fuck me so hard with it. Make me squirt for you again like a good girl."

"Fuck, Ruby," Axel groans, his eyelids dropping heavy with lust.

"Fuck, y'all," Jace groans, too. "Fuck, you're going to make me come, too."

"Let him come with us." I gaze up at Axel. "He needs to."

I don't know why I suddenly feel it, but I do. I feel bound to Jace. To everyone. They're watching as Axel permits, "Do it. Come if you need to."

He knows Jace is lonely, that he needs a love like ours.

In a quick movement, I feel Jace's warm hand slide down my back while he rips open his zipper, freeing his cock to rub against my back. It's as if he's desperate for any touch, any warmth, and release.

It's so heartbreaking and hot.

But when Jace growls, "Goddamn, she feels good. She's such a sweet slut. She wants to make us come on her. She wants to come and be so fucking dirty for us."

I'm shocked by Jace's kinky mouth ... and *oh fuck*, thrilled by it, too.

Jace tugs my nipples harder, thrusting his hips, and that unleashes Axel. Like he half-regrets unleashing his brother, too, but he'll show him who's in charge. Who owns me.

They become animals, beasts even. Grunting and thrusting. Fighting and feral.

"Play with your clit," Axel growls, hammering his cock into my cunt. "Strum that sweet clit while I fuck you so hard and make your tight pussy squirt. That's it. Squirt, baby. Show him who you belong to."

I obey. I let go. I'm engulfed in their power and heat. Jace's thick cock drips against my back but it can't match the brutal claim Axel is making of my cunt.

Like a piston, he knocks the breath from my lungs, his mass erasing my mind. His piercing, *my piercing*, strikes my fingers feverishly rubbing my clit for him. And his eyes. *Axel's eyes.* They won't stop watching me do this for him.

"Oh my god," I pant. "I'm gonna come."

"My sweet little slut," Axel praises. "Squirt on my cock. Squirt on my brother."

That takes me. It takes Jace, too. Axel knew it would as I buck so hard in Jace's lap, the friction makes Jace grunt while Axel pulls out, watching me gush, pulsing and moaning.

Then Axel leans down, lapping at my dripping cunt like a thirsty dog and Jace groans, "Oh fuck, yes."

Jace must feel me. He must feel a lot because he dares to grab my hips, thrusting into my backside with pained sounds while he shakes. While his warm cum paints my back. It makes me shudder. The last quivers of my orgasm can't hide the erotic thrill, but then I search Axel's eyes, worried about his wrath.

Oh my God, he's going to kill Jace.

But Axel smiles.

Gently. Knowing. Almost kind to his brother.

Jace couldn't help it.

Yes, Axel will kill for me. But he wants his brother to feel love, even if it's the edges of our love that we share with him. At least until Jace finally has a love of his own.

"Fuck," Jace huffs. "Thank you. Fuck, that felt good. I needed it."

"You're welcome," I sigh, feeling tendrils of the taboo and tender still swirling through me. But it felt right. I feel closer to Jace now, and I try to turn my head to comfort him, but the angle is too awkward.

"It's what I wanted for us, man." Axel still hovers over me in a plank of muscles and ink. His cock remains raging hard. He didn't come, though his beard and cock drip with my plea-sure. "My queen is so fucking beautiful, isn't she?" He gazes warmly at me while assuring Jace, "I promise, you'll love your queen one day like I love mine."

"Thanks," Jace answers softly, and I glance to my right. At Delphine and Grant. How she's in his lap. How he loves her, too. Sire and Wren are the same. So are Nash and Vale.

Then I glance left, and Zar is curled up with Nick.

But Loch?

Why does it hit my heart so hard that he's sitting alone?

"You still with us, Wildfire?"

Axel leans down, softly kissing me. He'll always worry, care, and love me.

And I don't fight it anymore.

I trust it.

"Always."

CHAPTER FORTY-SIX
AXEL

In life, there's the man you're raised to be. Then, there's the man you become.

Violent. Cold. Immoral. In charge. That's who my father wanted me to be.

He half succeeded.

Noble. Loyal. Protective. Loving. That's how my mother made me.

And she won.

It's a duality. A war that used to wage inside me.

But with my new queen, with Ruby, all I feel is peace.

Don't get me wrong. Touch her. Hurt her. Dare to even speak to her with disrespect, and I will disembowel you, alive, and fill your insides with salt.

The beast in me will never die.

But let me witness my breathtaking queen give her body to me, while she wants to comfort my brother, too? While she can feel his pain like I can?

Fuck, yes, that's my Wildfire. My queen. My wife. My goddamn life.

You don't deserve to call yourself a man if you're not as

willing to be changed by a woman as she's been changed by you.

I'm a new man, and Ruby is my woman.

She's already close to Nick, and now she's accepted Sire. Nash. Jace. She's bonded with them as I will only allow.

Hell, it's more than I thought I'd *ever* allow.

But that's what initiations do.

I told you.

It's something in the sandalwood-scented air.

Candles flicker around the room, while I'm tempted to stop. To give Ruby a break. We still have the other part of her initiation, when Grant will become her second king. Fuck, I fear that'll finally summon the beast in me. *I'll kill him.*

But as she cuddles in my lap, sipping water after we refreshed and the others did, too, Ruby lifts her lips to my ear and whispers, "Loch."

"What about him?"

I look across the semicircle. Since I'm the first king, in this arrangement, he's the youngest and sitting directly across from me with his queen's throne glaringly empty beside him.

It matches how Loch looks.

Picking at lint that's not on his pants, he looks defeated. Left out. Like he wants to be somewhere else.

I know where. I know with whom.

We all do.

And I've always protected my baby brother. From letting him hang out with me when he was little to going to his football games when he grew up. Loch never suffered our father, but he needed one, and I tried to be the closest he could get.

But I'm not his father. I'm his brother, and I can't fix this for him, either.

"I want to include him," Ruby whispers. "I want to get to know him and make him feel better."

"Uh, my queen." I pull back, tenderly lifting her chin. "I

know what happens in initiations *stays* in initiations, but we're sticking to our double penetration agreement. Because it will be a double murder if you have Grant *and* Loch."

"I'm not saying that." She smiles. "Jeez, I have my limits."

"You sure? Because I'm fucking loving how you won't stop gushing for me tonight."

"Okay, whose cup wouldn't runneth over with all this virile masculinity and your dirty Dom talk?" She hushes her voice even more, though the others are talking and distracted. "And who knew Jace could be so dirty?"

I smirk. "Me."

"I thought you'd punch him for calling me that."

"I still might."

Her eyes widen, worried.

"But then again. All's fair in kinks and kings. And you didn't seem to mind. You got off on being our sweet slut, and oh, Daddy," my cock stirs, "you liked that kink, too."

"And I feel you getting hard talking about it."

"Mmm, definitely so." I lace my hands in her hair, tugging her neck open to feast on it. "We'll be married for decades, so I promise to spice up our sex life for you."

"Speaking of..." She lets me suck and bite. "Loch: include him somehow."

"Nash will kill him if he touches you, and—"

"We'll respect his boundaries, but still..."

"Still what?" I bite softly then suck hard on her neck. This conversation is making me possessive and *fuck yes*, aroused.

"Still, he's a man. He obviously appreciates watching us."

"What do you want him to watch?"

Her hand glides down my abs, her fist tightly wrapping around my thickening shaft. "Let him watch you fuck my ass."

Jesus fuck.

Just when Ruby thrills me more than anyone, she does it

again. And again. I swear this woman will stand by my side for the rest of my life, but I'll never stop chasing her.

I hunt her lips, nipping them, tempted to make them bleed, but the pain from her new piercing is enough. So I ask between our hungry kisses, "You want me?" Kiss. "To fuck your luscious ass?" Kiss. "And make you come?" Kiss. "In front of my lonely brother?"

Kiss.

And another ravenous kiss.

I'm raging hard.

"Yes," she pants over our lips. "You said you want to, and you know we'll love it."

Call me deviant. Call me devoted. Call me the luckiest goddamn man in the world.

How can my beautiful woman be so cum-driven and compassionate at the same time?

No need to answer.

I'm not waiting for it.

I glance around. Everyone's back in the room and settled into their thrones or sitting on laps. They know what to do. These are epic nights, and who knows when the next initiation will be.

So...

"Stand up and walk across the room." I tug her hair, pulling her nose to mine. "Turn around, and spread your cheeks open for my brother, and don't say a word. Just stand there and let him look at your naughty ass before I fuck it."

Ruby licks her lips before climbing off my lap.

Lifting her chin, she sashays naked across the room, and it falls silent.

I watch her. I watch Loch. I watch the look on his face as she obeys and stares right back at me while she spreads herself open for his gaze.

He licks his lips and rubs his scruffy chin. Tilting his head, he sees my smirk and he shakes his head.

He's not refusing. No.

He's amused. Aroused. He's one of us. He knows what I'm offering.

Loch doesn't want to touch another woman, but he'll always worship the sight of a queen.

I glance at Nash, and he glances back. Reading my mind, he nods his head like, *Yeah, go ahead. The poor man needs something.*

And besides. This is Ruby's initiation. If she wants me to fuck her ass in front of Loch?

All hail my queen.

I rise and, in quick strides, I cross the room. Pulling Ruby's cheek to rest against my chest, I praise, "Good girl. Now, keep spreading open for him."

I reach around and tug on her tail, making her moan while I tempt Loch, "My queen needs me to fuck her ass, and she really wants you to enjoy it, too."

"Please," Ruby sighs against my pec while she pleads to Loch, "we want you to join us somehow. Don't be left out."

"Go for it," Nash calls from across the room. "It's her initiation night. Give her what she wants. Just don't fucking touch her."

My salacious sentiments exactly.

"Alright," Loch agrees, the loneliness evaporating from his aqua eyes. They start glimmering again. "How can I serve you, my queen?"

Ruby rubs her nipples against my abs while she demands, "Watch my king fuck my ass. Get off on how he makes me squirt when he does it, and come with us."

Holy.

Fuck.

My queen.

Dig my grave and roll me in it. I could die as the happiest, horniest man right now.

Scratch that. Let me fuck Ruby first. And then a million times.

Then I can die. After a million more fucks with her.

"Goddamn, Wildfire," I growl into her hair, a primal frenzy charging through my veins. "Baby, I'm about to go beast mode on your ass and make you fucking love it."

"Promise?" she giggles.

"Prepare," I warn.

Pulling on her bunny tail, I make Ruby moan over my chest. Sweetly, I hold her here while I give Loch a lewd show, coaxing her, "Keep spreading your ass for him. That's it, baby. You're doing such a good job. Let me show you off. Let him see how wet I make you when I play with your ass."

I turn and tug at her naughty anal plug and Loch licks his lips, his eyelids getting heavy with desire.

Dragging his hand down his face, he lets it trail over his chest, then his abs, before cupping his hard-on.

While I kiss her, I slowly pull Ruby's plug out, and swallow her moan with my mouth as I push it back in. Over and over, I do it, preparing her ass until she's begging and gaping for me, and I'm feral to do this.

Fuck, here comes the animal again.

I toss the tail aside and spin her to face Loch.

I reach around, unclasping her clamps. She cries out at the rush of blood back to her nipples, so I carefully rub one then the other, helping the pain go away, while I tug the gold chain looped through her collar.

Vale showed me this feature of the jewelry, and it's perfect for right now.

For what I want with Ruby and what she deserves.

With the chain unclasped, it's long enough for one end to reach her clit, while I clip the other end to her collar.

When Ruby feels me teasing her hard nub with the smooth gold tweezers, I press my lips to her ear. "Do you want this, my queen? Do you want to feel so much pain that you're going to squirt with unbelievable pleasure?"

I'll always protect Ruby and take care of her body, just as she does. Her body has its limits, but we've explored them slowly and safely at home.

She loves nipple and clit clamps. We've used them before, and I don't have to worry that it'll be too much for her now.

In fact...

"Please, my king," she begs. "Make me feel amazing. Fuck me like your little pain slut."

"Oh fuck, baby." I nip her ear. "You're driving me insane."

"Shit, yes you are. Like this," Loch murmurs, unzipping his pants, and exposing his swollen cock to Ruby.

It rests thick against his abs, and she moans while I cup her breast. Gently, I knead her nipple, soothing one then the other, before I slowly pinch her clit between the tweezers.

Instantly, her thighs start shaking. "Oh shit. Oh shit," she cries out and I know my baby.

She's going fast.

Holding her back against my chest, I reach down and gently wedge my swollen tip into her ass. She's already slick and open from the plug and its lube. She's ready ... but still, I keep my lips pressed to her ear. "Now be a good girl and tell me the whole time how much you love my cock fucking your ass."

"Oh god. Oh god." Her hands reach for my arm holding her. She scratches it as she begs, "Please, Axel. Do it. Fuck my ass."

Slowly, I breach her while I bite her neck. It makes me find my restraint as I groan, holding her hip until she's pushing against me. Until she wants more and takes every inch of my dick inside her.

Goddamn, she's so tight. And wet. And shaking for this.

She lets me pump into her ass while I hold her neck and play with her hard nipple, my cock relishing her tightest little hole. With each thrust, I feel her ass clenching around my dick and...

God, I love fucking her.

I grit out, "Tell me how badly you want me, baby. Whose ass is this?"

"It's yours," she pants. "I'm yours, Axel, so go harder. Fuck me harder."

"Pull her clit chain," I growl at Loch while I bend Ruby over, palming her fiery hair and making her brace her small hands against the arms of his throne.

She's not touching him, and he's not touching her, but he's doing this with us. He's getting off on this, too. Our heat. Our scent. Our sex. Our sight. He's tugging on the gold chain clamped to Ruby's clit while he hungrily strokes his leaking cock.

"Does this feel good, my queen?" And Loch is such a service Dom. When he was a virgin, Delphine taught him well, and now he gets off on giving pleasure. "Is this what you like? Are you going to come while I play with your clit and your king fucks your ass?"

"Please, yes," Ruby cries out. "Oh god, yes. Harder."

"Fuck." I listen to my queen. I thrust my hips harder. Every inch of my swelling dick is disappearing inside her. "Fuck, Wildfire, your ass exists for me to fuck, doesn't it?"

"Yes, Axel. Take it." Her legs buckle. "Holy shit, I'm coming."

"Good girl. Take my cock in your ass and squirt for me."

I hammer my hips harder, ordering Loch, "Pull harder. She's my little pain slut."

"Yes. Yes." Ruby bucks against me, and her legs give out. Wrapping my arm around her waist, I hold her up while she groans. She convulses. She can't even speak while she showers me, Loch, and the floor.

And I explode.

"Fuck, Ruby. *Fuuuck*, I'm coming," I groan into her shoulder, my thighs, drenched in her cum, violently shaking with my release. I grunt, fighting to stand and hold her up, too, while I pulse, over and over, spilling inside her. "Oh fuck, baby."

Then I hear Loch. He groans, and I catch him closing his eyes and arching his back while he shoots over his tatted abs. The look on his face when he comes is ecstasy and relief twisted with a bit of pain.

But at least he's not feeling it alone.

He's one of us.

Carefully, I pull out of Ruby. Reaching down, I scoop her up, cradling her in my arms. She wraps her hands around my neck, sighing, "I love you," before kissing me.

Then she turns to Loch. She sounds hoarse but happy when she asks him, "Do you feel better now?"

She worries about my brother as I do.

"Yeah." Loch cracks his eyelids open and smiles. "Yes, my queen. Thank you."

I whisper over her strands, "Goddamn, I love you."

After we refresh, I lie with Ruby on the platform. I need to hold her. I need to marvel that I found this woman, and not die in awe that she's mine. All mine.

Of course, the other kings and queens take the opportunity to couple.

At moments, it's erotic.

But always, it's intimate.

"I feel what you mean." Ruby glances around and smiles at what warms me, too—the sight of Jace sitting beside Loch.

They're talking, and as long as their queen's thrones are empty, why should they sit apart? Jace is man enough to sit in the seventh queen's throne so that Loch won't be alone.

"Don't you mean that you *see* what I mean?"

"That, too," she replies with her head on my chest. "But I *feel* what you meant all along. I'm sorry I called it a gangbang, because that's not what it is. Yes, it's the most erotic night of my life, but it feels safe and sacred, too. I finally feel like I belong with everyone. Like I love you the most, but I trust them, too."

I squeeze her tighter and kiss her hair, knowing that's a big step for Ruby, and it's all I wanted tonight. Her belonging. Her trust.

Then I remember...

But can we trust everyone?

I don't get time to go down that rabbit hole.

Sire stands and begins the final part of her initiation.

So, I guide Ruby to kneel with me, facing me on the platform, while everyone else settles into their thrones.

Grant pecks Delphine's cheek while Sire asks, "Which brother here will vouchsafe as a second king, declaring this union between Axel and Ruby as honorable and protected? Who here is pleased to join their bed, mercifully granting that they may live long and bountiful lives but pledging, should her first king perish, he shall guard our queen and their children in his stead?"

I've heard this sacred vow so many times.

But now?

I gaze into Ruby's sapphire eyes, and like a bullet through my heart, I think of Lev. I think of my father, and a shiver whips through me because for the first time, I fear...

My queen may need her second king.

My children with Ruby may need one of my brothers.

I may not make it out alive when I rescue my first son.

It makes me nuzzle my forehead to hers as Grant vows, "I do."

"Will you, Axel, allow Grant to honor your queen?"

I swallow, holding Ruby's hands. "I will."

"Will you, Grant, honor Axel's queen?"

"I will."

"Will you, her kings, be subject to her as she is subject to you? Will you love your queen as you love your own bodies? For he who loves his queen loves himself. For no noble man ever hated his own flesh and..."

This is the part that strangles me.

The one that reminds me of Mom.

It strangles Sire's voice, too. I can hear it.

I turn and see Grant's eyes glistening. It's hitting Jace, too. Nick and Loch were too young to remember our father, but they know what he did to our mother. I look over my shoulder, and they're clenching their jaws.

And Nash? He cared for Alena's mom. He'd never tolerate any woman being hurt, and my mom is like his.

We all know her story.

How this vow saved our lives.

And for the first time, I feel what Maxim must've felt when he made this vow to my mother.

Did he know then, as I do now, that he would give his life for her? For us?

That's all I feel turning back to gaze into Ruby's eyes.

Yes, I will live for her. I will kill for her. I will die for her.

"Every king shall protect his queen," Sire continues, "all queens, for they fill our lives with children, with prosperity, and all good things. This is the love you give to her. State your vow if you agree."

I cup Ruby's face. "I vow to my queen."

A tear slides down her cheek.

"I vow to my queen."

I hear Grant's promise and feel it, too.

It's here when he joins Ruby and me on the platform. It's here when he goes slow with her, and I do, too. It's here when I thought I'd be fighting this, but I don't.

I need this.

I need this brother, this one I trust, to always care for Ruby and our children.

I don't know how I know it, but Grant didn't betray us.

I gaze up at her, lacing my fingers through her flaming hair while I feel her take me inside her body, heart, and soul. I watch her open. I feel her wrap around me. I watch her let Grant inside, too. Yes, it's pleasure for her; we make sure she feels it.

We know how to do this with our queens. When I pull out of Ruby's wet cunt, Grant slowly thrusts into her slick ass. When he pulls out, I drive back inside her tight heat. Like pistons, we fuck my woman senseless. She's drenching my thighs.

I play with Ruby's nipples, tugging on them while Grant taunts her ear, "Let me help you with this tight ass, sweetheart. Let me fuck it with my hard cock while my brother owns your wet cunt. Right? You're a good girl for us? Letting us both fuck you?"

"Yes," Ruby pants, gazing down at me, her hands braced on my pecs, her eyes hooded and locked to mine. "Yes, fuck me, my kings."

"Show us what a queen you are," I demand, pinching her nipples. "Move those hips. Take a cock in your cunt and one in your ass. Come on, fuck us."

We hold still. We did this with Delphine, with Wren, too.

We want our queens to take what they want from us. To have no shame about it. Only pleasure.

Ruby's eyes roll, her beautiful mouth open in awe as she moves down on us, taking both of our cocks inside her at the same time. "Yes," she sighs, shuddering, and I reach for her hips. I don't guide her; I want to feel her shamelessly ride us. Take us. And she does. Back and forth, she rocks her hips and I watch her breathtaking face while she takes all the thick cocks she craves, her pussy glossing my shaft with her lust, her eyes anchored to mine.

"Fuck," Grant sighs, "she's such a queen, taking every inch of us."

I gaze up at Ruby. I lace my fingers in her hair again. "That's it, Wildfire. Take us. Fuck these cocks like a queen."

"Oh god, Axel," she sighs like she can't believe it. Like she's finally mine.

My queen.

I pull her into a deep kiss. As always, it's a hope, a prayer, and a vow when my lips meet hers.

I can see our daughters together, our fiery princesses. I can see our son with my icy eyes. I can see our family together, and I fight like hell to have it.

I don't feel my brother. I only feel her.

Need her.

Love her.

I fight for it and fuck Ruby so hard, thrusting my hips, and Grant matches my rhythm. Thrust for thrust, we fuck her until she's crying out on top of me, scratching at my pecs, her lustful stare committed to mine while she drips over my balls, bucking and shaking.

That ends Grant. He groans. He finishes. He leaves us alone on the platform, but I'm not done.

I'm not done until I'm rising to suck her nipples. Until

she wraps her legs and arms around me. Until she's in my lap and moaning for me again.

I gaze down to where our bodies joined and watch her rub her beautiful pink clit over my steel piercing. *Our piercing.* And she gazes down, moaning at the sight of us, too.

Somewhere between her last orgasm and mine. Between her sweet tears and the ones I fight. Between our kisses, and "love yous," and everyone clapping for us. Between her officially becoming my queen and every goddamn reason I breathe, she sighs...

"Can we name our first daughter Violet?"

And I laugh, loving her, kissing her.

Leave it to my Wildfire to negotiate terms right now. *Like I'll fight my queen on this.*

Then again...

I love our little fights. And I'm still her boss. And hell yes, I'm her Dom.

"Only if we can name our other daughters Hazel, Olive, and Iris."

Yeah, I've dreamt about it, too.

Because I'll always be her king.

CHAPTER FORTY-SEVEN
RUBY

When I open my eyes, I'm greeted by soft golden fur and a sexy nipple circled in black ink.

And …

I smile.

Growing up, my mom used to tell me and my sisters, "A man is not a plan. Prince Charming isn't saving you. So, save yourself."

And I did.

When an ex-Bratva prince stalked me, I stalked him back. I saved my heart until he caught it, and now I plan to love him, covered in ink and kittens, for the rest of my life.

Sounds like a fairytale to me.

Axel stirs, naked beside me. His hand starts lingering up and down my back while his other pets the kitten on his chest, and I wonder aloud, "Just how many pussies do you need to sleep with?"

"At least four." He chuckles, and I glance down, grinning at the two curled on his abs.

I wrap my leg over his, loving his warmth, rubbing against him, too.

"Why, is someone jealous?"

"I'm a queen," I murmur. "Jealousy is beneath me."

His voice husky and teasing, he says, "You keep purring on me like that, Wildfire, and you're about to be beneath *me* while I'm buried deep inside you."

I tease his nipple. "While I appreciate your constant horniness for me, let's schedule the next fuckathon for another month because you broke my pussy last night."

"*And* your ass."

I lift my stare and find his icy eyes sparkling at mine, and his bright smile as proud as a peacock with a giant pierced penis.

"God," I huff, "you owe me."

"If you want to fuck my ass while yours recovers, Wildfire, all you gotta do is let me keep our kittens."

"Uh!" I pop up. "But you said you liked the idea that everyone gets a kitten."

"Yeah, but..." He lifts the one beside him, kissing its pink nose. "Who knew I'd get so pussywhipped?"

"Me, after you saw mine for the first time."

"No, I was whipped for you the first time you flipped me off." He reaches over, circling my nipple, and getting that hungry look in his eyes. "All I could think about was where I wanted you to stick that middle finger."

I arch a brow. "Where?"

"Let me roll over, and you can find out."

I laugh, tempted. "Your mom will be here in an hour."

"And dick deflated."

I glance down. "Liar."

Axel's on his back, nude and breathtaking. I'll never stop worshipping the sight of his hot body covered in ink, but it's how he doesn't wear socks to bed anymore.

He lets me see all of him, love all of him, and it stirs something deep inside me.

It does the same to him.

His dick lies swollen, long, and thick against his abs but when I lick my lips at it, he moans and it twitches, aroused.

"You have until the count of three," he orders, "to put my dick in your mouth and your pussy in my face."

I lean over to happily obey, but it happens before I can stop it...

A kitten swats his dick.

"Jesus fuck!"

He jumps up, and I've never seen a man move so fast. The speed of light would be impressed.

He leaps out of bed, and grabs his penis, pointing at the culprit. "That one's going to Grant!"

The little golden monster with one white-socked paw tilts her head at him.

"No, this is the one we're keeping." I pick her up. "She's the runt of the litter."

"She's the runt who clawed my dick!" He paces, fuming, "She's going to be like a dog that's bitten once. Now, she won't stop. She'll be wild and untamed and scratching my dick all the time."

I laugh, falling onto the bed with her. "Good girl!" I cuddle her to my cheek. "I've trained you so well; I'm naming you *Swiper*."

"Ha, ha, fucking ha, Dora the Explorer." He insists, "We're not keeping that one."

I bat my lashes.

"No!"

I blow him a kiss.

"No."

I spread my legs.

"Goddammit, fine. But she's not sleeping with us."

"We'll see." I shrug.

Like I won't teach her how to break his rules.

And I can't stop giggling during our shower, when he mumbles and checks his penis every five seconds. Not like it was injured or even scratched.

Axel's so cute and worried that I kneel in the shower and kiss it until I make it better, until I make him hard and moan, until he picks me up and I wrap around him, and we make everything better.

By the time we're done and dried off, Sire and Wren are knocking on the door.

Thirty minutes later, all the kings, queens, and The Queen circle our kitchen island, covered in dishes everyone brought for brunch.

"Do we get to pick which one?" Wren gazes into the transparent playpen Axel built for the kittens.

"Angel, baby." Sire pops a grape in his mouth, grinning at Wren. "Pray, you pick the one that sleeps the most."

"I want the one that's house-trained," Jace adds, leaning with Loch against the kitchen counter.

"They're all house-trained." Axel pours coffee for me, then for his mom. "Ruby made sure of it."

"They're litter-trained, weaned, but hell on toilet paper," I share, sitting on a barstool between Vale and Delphine. "Oh, and shoes. They love Axel's shoes, so be careful."

It's sweet, the gentle side hug Nadine gives Axel. His shoes. *His feet.* Of course, she knows, and Axel leans down and kisses her hair.

"I have an idea." Nash rubs Vale's shoulders. "Let them out of the pen and see who they go to."

"Ahh, yes, use natural selection," Vale sighs. "When did you get so smart, my king?"

Nash kisses her neck. "Fourteen years before you were born, my smartass, beautiful queen."

"Let's do it." Zar crouches by the gate to the pen. "Let's set these pussies free."

"Like I don't see that cheese cube in your hand," Nick warns him. "We're not taking two home."

Together, Zar and Wren open the gate, and the clowder of little golden lions scamper toward the kitchen while Sparky rests in my lap.

"One of them we're keeping," I remind the others, but it doesn't matter.

They all scurry to Axel, and two start climbing his grey sweatpants.

"Typical." Loch laughs. "Of course, all the pussies go to Axel first."

I glance up and catch Axel's wince. Then I look over and see something flash across Sire's eyes. *Alena.*

Loch doesn't know. Nash doesn't know. No one else does, and yes, I'll stand by my man when all hell breaks loose over that. Like epic hell it'll be, but I'll never leave Axel's side.

Eventually, I hope that Loch will trust like me. That he'll realize it was one night forever ago, long before Axel fell in love with me and Loch fell for Alena.

You have to trust when someone chooses you over their past.

"Please," Grant scoffs at Loch. "Come to the club and you'll see who the pussy king is."

Delphine laughs, backhanding Grant's arm.

And Nadine rolls her eyes. "Please don't," she demands. "I don't need to see my boys' grown-ass peckers poking around more than I already have to."

"Peckers," Nash snickers.

"*Poking* peckers." Jace winks, chuckling.

"Remember when we used to play with them when we were boys?" Sire laughs.

"Like we've stopped." Axel laughs, too.

"Lord, help me," Nadine mutters.

"Oh, come on, Mom." Nick teases her. "Once I come out

on national television, I'm gonna be damn public and proud of my penis poking pecker."

"As you should be." I toast my coffee cup.

"Thanks to you." Zar toasts me back. "And you." He toasts Vale, too.

"Alright." Axel plucks a kitten off his thigh. "Enough peckers and pussies. Who wants this one?"

"Me!" Wren runs over. "What's its name?"

Axel and I did this last night, after my initiation. He held me in bed while we named our kittens and future kids.

Except Swiper.

She was going to be Britney, like *It's Britney, bitch*, but her new name will torture Axel and amuse the hell out of me.

"That's Onyx," I tell Wren. "For the little black spot on his nose."

"And this one." Axel plucks the next kitten off him. "This one is Moose. For his big ears."

He hands the golden furball to Jace, and I get the warm fuzzies, knowing Jace won't be alone. Well, sort of.

"This one with the white tip on her tail is for you." Axel picks up the one weaving between his ankles and hands it to Nick. "She's Xena, the warrior princess pussy. Watch out. She's fast."

"Like my man." Zar wraps his arms around Nick's waist.

"And this quiet, lazy one is Milo." Axel plucks the sleeping kitten off the floor and hands it to Nash. "You need a quiet pussy in your life because God knows you're not getting that with Vale."

Vale flips off Axel, and I laugh.

"And this last one?" Axel smirks, handing the roundest kitten to Grant. "He's Biscuit. He's like you, big fella. He likes to eat."

Last but not least, Axel picks up Swiper, our tiniest and I

hear him whisper to her, "Me and you are going to have a long talk about claws and cocks and how they don't mix."

It's bittersweet, watching everyone cuddle their kittens as they leave. But I know I'll see them all the time. I know we're bonded for life.

Grant hugs me harder than he ever has. Delphine does, too.

Jace gives me a sweet peck on the cheek.

Nash invites Axel and me on a trip with him and Vale, sans kittens.

While Sire and Wren want to do kitten playdates.

Nick invites us to his next game. Zar has luxury box seats.

The Queen wants to go dress shopping next week for my wedding.

And Loch? He's leaving without a kitten because he has dogs, but...

"Hey, man." Axel gently grabs his shoulder before he leaves last. "Can I ask you something?"

Loch turns around. "Sure."

"Will you be my best man?"

"But," Loch smiles, "shouldn't it be Nash or Grant? They're older."

"No, I want my baby brother to do it," Axel answers. "And so does Ruby."

Axel and I talked about this in bed last night—everything we want for our wedding. I don't know who will be my maid of honor. I'm blessed with so many sisters and queens.

But we don't want Loch to be left out and lonely. It's palpable on him. Jace handles heartbreak better, but Loch? I told Axel I'm worried about him, and that only made Axel hold me tighter.

"You're such a queen," he said. "You're already watching out for everyone."

"So, will you do it?" Axel asks him now.

"I'd be honored, man." Loch hugs Axel, then he hugs me. "Thanks." Loch squeezes me tight. "I needed this."

"I know." I pat Loch's chest. "Has anyone ever told you that you kinda look like Reacher? You know the one—"

"No, he doesn't." Axel laughs. "Not even fucking close."

And after Loch leaves, Axel turns my way, his smirk devilish and delicious.

"Run," he demands with flaring nostrils and a sexy nose ring.

"Halt." My palm flies up. "Before you chase me, I need to know just how jealous I made you."

His icy eyes gleam. He licks his lips. "When I catch you, my queen, your ass will find out."

"So, how possessive will you be when I ask you to come with me to see my doctor tomorrow?"

"Why, baby?" His face falls. He immediately cares. "Are you feeling okay?"

"I'm feeling like I love you, Axel King, and I want to have your babies soon, so—"

Axel's face softens. He pulls me into a hungry kiss, cupping my face with his inked hands. "Fuck, I love you." He breathes over our lips, nuzzling his forehead to mine.

"Now, run, Wildfire." He vows, "Because I'll never stop chasing you."

EPILOGUE
RUBY

Six months later

"So, we have to have *the talk*." Wren sets her fork down.

"Which talk?" I speak with my mouth full of red velvet cake.

We just split a piece, and who needs manners around your in-laws?

"*The* talk." She leans back in her chair, rubbing her baby bump. "You know, what if we want to name our daughters the same thing?"

"Not happening." Axel laughs. "My beautiful wife wants to name our kids after a fucking rainbow. ROY G BIV would be so proud."

"That's what I mean." Wren's cute face twists. She's so worried. "I wanted to name our daughter Bluebell and—"

"Don't worry." I laugh, rubbing my non-existent baby bump. I'm only ten weeks along. "If this is a girl, we're naming her Violet. Little Violet King. She'll have her daddy wrapped around her rebellious finger."

"And if it's a boy?" Sire asks Axel.

And Axel falls quiet, drumming his dark, inked fingers over the white linen tablecloth.

In a week, he leaves for Moscow to get Lev back, and no one knows but me, The Queen, and Roman, who's going with him.

Apart from this nightmare involving Lev and who betrayed Axel, life has been perfect.

Our Mykonos wedding was magical. Everyone was there. Even Alena, who snuck away with Loch after our service. God, I kept my fingers crossed for them.

And Jace?

Of course, I noticed how he kept mysteriously disappearing all week, and when I spied on him, I watched him leave a sex shop carrying a big white paper bag. The man was smiling all week.

When we got home, our new penthouse upstairs in The Mercier was ready for us. My god, it's lavish. But Axel insisted on safety ... and spoiling me.

We usually have lunch here with another king and queen in the Mercier's courtyard with its bubbling pineapple fountain.

The first few months of our marriage have been like a dream. And though I've had two seizures since I changed my meds to get pregnant, Axel rarely leaves my side.

And yeah, we both cried when I found out I was pregnant.

"Maxim," Sire answers Axel's silence. "That's what we should name the first boy in our family."

"Yeah," Axel answers solemnly. "Maxim."

I know he wants to tell Sire about Lev, but he can't.

Once Axel goes to Moscow and confronts Katya about Lev, he'll know who betrayed us. Axel has a way of making people talk, and he won't come home without Lev.

"So, after Maxim, who's having Roy?" Wren laughs, and she lightens the mood.

But when I laugh, my lunch threatens to make another appearance.

"Oh shit." I stand. "Excuse me. I gotta hurl."

"I'll go with you." Axel moves to stand too, but, "Please," I insist. "I don't need an audience for version two point O of my chicken salad. I'll be right back."

I peck his cheek, grab the key card to our penthouse, and race toward the golden elevator.

Scarlett told me morning sickness is a good sign, but I'm giving it the middle finger. A wave will hit me, then nothing will happen. It'll go away. Then, a burp turns into *The Exorcist,* and it's not pretty.

The elevator doors *ding* open as the wave passes. But just in case, I'll go to our penthouse and kneel by the porcelain throne and see what happens.

Lost in queasy thoughts, I don't pay attention when a hand reaches in, blocking the doors from closing at the last moment.

I'm in a nauseous haze when a couple joins me in the elevator.

The doors slide closed, and I hear, "Congratulations, Missus King."

"Do I know you?" I crack my eyelids open.

But the moment I turn to confront the voice, I recognize my husband ... thirty years from now.

Black hair. Heavy brows. Chiseled face. Perfect nose. Lush lips.

But this man is dripping with evil.

Ruslan Kholodov sneers down at me, and then I glance to see the statuesque blonde beside him.

Katya.

The hairs on my neck stand. Not afraid. I'm thrilled. And vengeful.

"What floor?" I ask them. "Because you're definitely not on my level."

Katya scoffs, "Told you she would be low class."

"Hey, Bitchie Barbie," I smile, "just because you sold your cunt and soul, it doesn't mean you have a brain left to fuck with me."

Her eyes widen, but I glare at Ruslan. "And you, PacMan. You have some grey-haired balls to show up here. What do you want? A pacemaker for your dead heart or hers?"

Katya mutters curses in Russian while Ruslan narrows his eyes, and *Oh, that's where Axel gets that look from.*

The one that makes grown men piss their pants.

But I'm immune.

"I could just kill you for fun."

He could. I believe him.

"You know what's really fun?" I answer. "A photo booth. Say cheese, mother fucker. There are cameras in here and everywhere. You won't leave this hotel alive."

The elevator rises, and so does my pulse.

I'm right about the cameras. Scarlett's security is watching us. But right now we look like guests in a chat. Like someone farted in the elevator and I'm mad about it.

But all I have to do is press the SOS charm on my bracelet again, and Axel will kill his father in broad daylight. He wouldn't hesitate.

And there would be a lot of salt involved.

"Let us please speak." Ruslan gestures to the elevator doors as they slide open, revealing the parlor separating my penthouse and Scarlett's.

But she's at her beach house with Luca and his daughter. And his staff aren't here today, either.

It's just me and my gut instinct.

I always trust it.

"Okay. We can speak." I step into the parlor, and they follow. "But Bitchie Barbie better keep her mouth shut, or I'm going to fill it with my fist."

"Uh, so trashy." Katya rolls her eyes.

"Damn right, I'm trashy. And it's gonna hurt real bad when I roll my trash out all over your face. You fucking bitch, you stole Axel's son!"

"He is my son, too!" she shrieks.

"No, you chose to be used by this man over being a mother to your son. And you," I point at Ruslan, "are already paying the price, aren't you? Your own blood hates you. All of them. No ice cold pussy in the world can fuck and breed that karma away."

Katya steps to me and I smile. "Bring it. I don't need a goddamn knife to rip your neck open. I'll use my teeth."

"Enough." Ruslan raises his hand, shooing Katya away.

And I see it. The grey pallor of his skin. The lack of life in his eyes. How he was once a sadistic and seductive man. How everyone feared him, but now he fears death. It's imminent.

"I see that my son has chosen his queen well." Reverently, Ruslan reaches for my arm, but I jerk it away. "Strong. Beautiful. Smart. Fearless and proud. I raised him well."

"No," I lift my chin, "his *mother* raised him well, and I'm just like her. And she sends her Fuck Yous."

"She is a bitch," Katya mutters.

"She is a mother whose sons love her," I say. "Spoiler alert: yours won't."

She lifts her nose. "A son always loves his mother."

"Not when he finds out that she stole him from his loving father."

"Axel is a cold man," she scoffs.

I say bitingly, "You would be too if you were married to

the White Cunt Walker from Hell. They can freeze eggs in your womb."

I catch it.

Ruslan's grin.

"Speaking of..." My stomach flips, and not from this.

I'm pregnant with the baby of the man I love.

And he loves me with the ferocity of a lion. Axel will always chase me and come looking for me soon.

And it will be a bloodbath if he finds his father and Katya here, and I don't want that.

Maybe it's the detective in me.

Maybe it's the lioness mother I'm becoming.

But I can sense it: *they need something.*

Why else would Ruslan and Katya be here? Why would they risk showing up in the lion's den? If they wanted me dead, they've had ample opportunities. If they want a war, they'll get one. If they want to die, they'll lay a hand on me.

"You're right," I say to Ruslan, lifting my chin. "Axel has chosen his true queen wisely. So tell me what you need and I'll tell you the price for it."

AN HOUR LATER, AXEL'S GENTLY RUBBING MY FEET, AND why does it look so sexy when he does it with inked hands and his finger, proudly wearing a thick platinum wedding band?

We're cuddled on our sofa, facing each other, and he knows I'm holding something in.

But? I don't know how to tell him this.

It's not bad news.

It's karma.

"Alright, Wildfire." His smile is so bright. "Come on. Scorch my life as usual. Tell me whatever it is."

Sparky sleeps between us. Swiper is having a field day with Axel's golden tie.

"Well," I sigh, "I met some old friends today. You know them. Ruslan and Katya."

His eyes ice. His brows lower. He knows I'm not kidding.

"They took a ride on the elevator with me today and needed to talk."

Axel's lip curls. "Did he lay a hand on you?"

Because we all know what he would do if his father did.

"No," I answer. "But you'd be proud of me."

"I'm always proud of you." He's way too calm. "So tell me. What happened, Ruby?"

"Well, I made a big deal with your father ... then I threw up on Katya."

NOT THE END

Thank you so much for reading AXEL!
This is their happy ending,
but the dramatic story continues.
Find out what happens next in **SIRE.**

For free hot bonus scenes teasing Jace's story and The Queen's, visit kellyfinley.com/freespice

Enjoy Sire's shocking teaser next.

Please take a moment to leave your honest review, too.
It's such a gift to authors.
Thank you!

TEASER - SIRE

You know the saying, "Give the devil his due."

It's to acknowledge the good qualities of an evil person.

Why, thank you. I appreciate it.

Because I am the Devil looking at this Angel.

"Girls, turn around. Full circle. Come on! Show them the goods!" The seller barks, and the girls cry, shaking and obeying...except...

This one.

"Yeah," I gloat. "This one's mine!"

She's no girl. She's a young woman with pert breasts, rouge nipples, and a dark mound, peeking through her white silk slip.

I can't tell her maturity by her body because some of the underage girls in here have mature-looking bodies, too. But it's their eyes betraying their innocence. They're way too young for the hell they're being sold into.

Okay, being trafficked and sold is hell at any age, but I can tell this one is wiser beyond her years. Her eyes don't shake in terror. Her half-naked body doesn't tremble. Her tawny cheeks are dry.

She's the only one not crying.

No, she looks straight ahead, and if looks could kill, every man in this room would be dead.

These girls and young women are being sold, and I'm buying them.

Settle down.

Don't worry.

I won't lay a hand on them, and neither will my brothers, posing as other buyers in the room. They're making us sit in a circle of chairs around the girls.

This fucker, the seller, a hedge fund manager by day, rented a swanky house in Palm Beach, and he has us sitting like we're getting ready to dine. Like we're about to make an evil meal of these innocent girls.

So, the Lord wants me to use the gun strapped to my ankle and hidden under my jeans to kill the seller.

The sloppy pat-down I got at the door missed my Glock.

Amateurs.

But the Devil in me knows if I kill this fucker now, we won't bust his entire network, and that's what we want.

"What's your name, sweetie?" Some old, sick fuck addicted to self-tanner reaches for the youngest girl.

She sobs, and I growl, "Yeah, she's mine, too."

"You can't have them all," he whines.

"Like you can stop me, mother fucker?"

I'm not dressed like a forty-something pastor; I'm dressed like a twenty-something dealer. Guess I look like one, too. Ink on my face. Neck. Hands. My entire body. Most people can't see past my menacing exterior to my tortured soul inside, and fuck yes, that's how I want it.

"No." My brother Axel glares at me. "I'm taking three of them."

"Fuck you." Grant, my other brother, acts along. "I'm not going home empty-handed. I want two."

"I'm taking the blondes." Nash, who's like our brother, fights his rage. He's a father to a daughter, and this shit is eating him alive, but he plays the part. "All three of them."

That leaves the youngest girl ... and this one.

This iron angel belongs to me.

"You know the price, gentlemen." The seller enters the circle. "The bidding starts at a million each."

"You said a hundred *K* each." The old orange man whines again, "That's not a good deal."

They go back and forth, and it doesn't matter. My brothers and I came to get these girls. To get them the fuck out of here and the help they need.

Our brother Jace and our mom are waiting in a van five miles away. They'll take these girls and get them somewhere safe.

This is what we do, and we don't fuck around. In fifteen minutes, we've bought them all, and they're starting to leave. My brothers won't blow their cover.

But this last one?

The Iron Angel?

"I've grown quite fond of her." The seller caresses her long raven curls. "She's special. Such a rare little bird. Right,

Wren?" He grabs her breast, and I clench my jaw as he sneers, "She'll fight back, and that makes it sweeter."

He throws her down on the marble floor. Crashing on her backside, she muffles her cry, her tattoos revealed.

Stigmata tattoos.

Two blood red marks on the inside of her wrists. Two on the tops of her bare feet. They look like the nail wounds of Jesus Christ on the cross.

Days from now, I'll realize her tattoos are my sign. My greatest temptation and salvation.

Right now?

I get in his face. "Don't fucking touch my property."

"She's not yours yet. Maybe I should have her first. We've been saving them all, ten little virgins. But this one? I think I'll break her before you buy her."

"Two million." My lip curls.

He tilts his head.

Fuck, that was too much. He's suspicious.

"If she's worth so much to you..." He pulls a knife from the pocket of his khaki pants. "How about I take a pound of flesh, too?"

A sob breaks the youngest girl, burying her face in her shaking hands.

Dragging herself up, the Iron Angel reaches for her, protecting her like a big sister.

God, save her. The youngest girl barely looks fourteen. The same age as my mother when she was kidnapped and trafficked to my father.

But my Iron Angel? She acts wiser than her years. *Dear Lord, she's brave.*

"What do you want?" I stare down the seller.

"How about I take a pound of flesh from her," he points his knife at the youngest girl, "and the virgin flower from her."

He grabs the Iron Angel, and something in me snaps.

I did this for my brother. I sacrificed myself.

And I'll do this for her—a complete stranger.

From as young as I can remember, a spirit has moved through me. I can't describe it, and I don't need to. It speaks and I listen.

The problem is.

Is it God?

Or the Devil?

"Take a piece of my flesh." I don't care. My spirit speaks, using my mouth, "Take a piece of me and give me these girls."

"Why?"

Yeah, he's suspicious.

"Because I like blood." I'm not lying. "I like mine. I like theirs. I like cutting and breeding, and let's start the fun now."

Quoting scripture, I hold out my left hand, "I remind you to fan into flame the gift of God, which is in you through the laying of my hands."

"What the fuck?" The seller scoffs.

But the Iron Angel...

Her eyes widen, not knowing what she's seeing, staring at me, but she knows scripture. She must be wondering, *Why is God's word spewing from the Devil's mouth?*

"I'm not fucking cutting your hand off, man." The seller gestures to the opulent house. "I don't need a mess and the heat on me."

It doesn't matter.

Tomorrow, Nash will drain this evil fuck's accounts of the money we paid for the girls, and then Axel and I will kill him, the orange buyer, and the hired guns behind him. It's only six men. It won't be hard.

It'll be fun. I'll make sure of it.

"You want flesh or not?"

"Theirs." He points to the girls.

"Nah, they're my toys and I don't share. So, take my fucking pinky and let's roll."

I slam my hand down on a glass table, strewn with tumblers of whisky. Giving a pinky isn't a Christian custom. It's *Yubitsume*, a Japanese mafia thing. My Russian mafia father admired their discipline and rituals. Growing up, he took a lot from our flesh, too.

But the seller keeps eyeing my Iron Angel.

"Come on, man." I keep my voice flat. "Three million and my pinky, and it's a deal, and I get to take my girls home to play. I have a dungeon waiting for them."

He likes the sound of that way too much. In three steps, he presses the blade, poised over my splayed digits.

"No!" The Iron Angel cries out, "Don't hurt him!"

I wink at her. "It's alright. I won't feel a thing."

But goddamn, I do.

At first, the shock hits me, even though I expect it. Numbly, I stare down at him doing it, my blood pumping as flesh and bone are severed. It spills over the glass table, but he wipes it up with a towel one of the gunmen throws at him.

Then it's a throbbing, nauseating pain from my severed finger to my stomach, to every nerve in my body registering the unnatural trauma—the permanent loss.

But I hide it.

I don't want to scare the girl and the Iron Angel any more than we need to get the fuck out of here.

"Done."

I make myself breathe while the seller lifts half of my pinky, holding it to the light like a goddamn diamond.

"Careful," he warns. "With your appetite for torturing virgin pussy, you'll run out of fingers."

No, dumbass, you're out of time.

In twenty-four hours, I'll cut your head off.

With a blood-soaked towel wrapped around my left hand, I signal to my angel with the right. Shockingly, she follows me without resistance and gets the girl to come, too.

I guess the Iron Angel believes I'm the lesser of the evils in the room.

Maybe she's wrong.

When we get to my rented Hummer parked in the driveway, I clock Axel in his rental, acting like he's on his phone when really, he's waiting for me.

His eyes shock wide at the bloody towel around my hand, but I lift my chin. *I got this.*

Yanking the back door open, I bark, "Get in."

The youngest starts to sob again, so I drop my voice to as true as I can make it sound.

"I won't hurt you. I'm taking both of you to a woman who protects girls in your situation."

"Come on." The Iron Angel urges the youngest one to climb in. "It'll be okay. We're safe now."

I don't know where this angel gets her conviction, but she follows it. Holding the girl in the back seat like a sister, she protects her again, while glaring at me through the rear-view mirror. "Who are you?"

I smirk. It's fitting. Fated. "A fallen angel."

"Don't bullshit me. Who are you, and where are you taking us?"

Fuck it. I don't hide this part of me.

My mom has a safe place for these girls. She'll get them all the resources they need, and I'll go back to my cursed soul.

"I'm a pastor at a church that helps trafficking victims like you. I'm taking you to a woman who spends all her money helping girls and women get safe."

Her glare in the mirror's reflection confronts my soul. *Huh.* Only my brothers are brave enough to look at me that way. "You can trust her."

Her eyes narrow. "Can I trust you?"

"No." I don't lie.

"Why not?"

"You have stigmata tattoos. You know what a fallen angel is."

"An angel who rebelled against God, and was cast out of heaven, and now waits in darkness until judgment day."

I wink. "Nice to meet ya."

She gets the idea, and I take the next interstate exit, my heavy heart already lighter after that confession.

"What did you do?" Damn, she's brave. "What's your sin?"

I glance in the mirror again. The youngest girl looks asleep. Or passed out in shock. *Fuck, I need to get her to my mom.*

"Tell me," the Iron Angel insists. "You gave a pound of flesh for me, and I want to know."

Fine.

I'll never see her again.

And I need to confess my sins.

"I lay with men. I lay with women. I have some very dark needs when I do, and while I help everyone else, I don't help myself. I sold my brother to the Devil, and I'll be paying for it for the rest of my life." I pause. "Amen."

She studies me, her topaz eyes never breaking their glare in the mirror, her breath stealing all the oxygen in the car. It's like we're in the presence of something powerful, but I don't know its name as a heavy minute claims the space between us.

"My name is Wren."

"It's *not* nice to meet me, Wren."

"What's your name?"

"It's best you don't know."

This is me, protecting her. That's half of my DNA. The

other half? It's wired for destruction. I could rip her to shreds.

So why do I sense she's doing the same for me? Like she was brought here to protect me, too? How can a creature so small make the molecules around me feel so ... *so right?*

For another potent minute, she's silent before warning, "Lay a hand on this girl and I'll poison you."

Poison? What a biblical way to go.

"You should."

I spot the passenger van up the road in a hotel parking lot. My brother Jace waits beside it. My mom, as well. My brothers, in their rental cars with their victims, have arrived, too. They'll take the girls from here, and I'll never see the Iron Angel again.

It's best that way.

You should only glimpse the Devil, not take a road trip with him.

I park beside the van.

Of course, the Iron Angel fears what's about to happen, so she vows again, "And if you ever lay a hand on me, Pastor—"

"Yeah, yeah..." I meet her gaze in the mirror. *What the fuck?* She makes me smile. "You'll poison me, too."

"No," she answers sweetly. "We'll fall in love."

GET SIRE TODAY

DEAR READER,
THERE'S MORE TO COME WITH THE BELLES & BRATVA
BEASTS. SIRE. LOCH. JACE. THE QUEEN AND SOME
SURPRISES. THE INTRIGUE CONTINUES. MORE SECRETS WILL
BE REVEALED. MORE SPICE WILL BE SHARED. MORE SNARK
WILL FIRE. OH, AND THE HOT, CRAZY, CONTRACT-KILLER,
COWBOY COUSINS, INCLUDING WILDER, ARE COMING, TOO.

FOR FREE BONUS SCENES AND MORE, VISIT
KELLYFINLEY.COM

ALSO BY KELLY FINLEY
"THE QUEEN OF SPICE"

**-Interconnected Books & Audiobooks
Available in Kindle Unlimited and Audible-**

BELLES & BRATVA BEASTS

NASH

AXEL

SIRE

LOCH

JACE

A NOT-MAFIA-MAFIA, DARK ROMCOM SERIES

SHAMELESS PLAY

SHAMELESS GAME

featuring Blair, Beau & Colton

A FRENEMIES TO LOVERS, WHY CHOOSE, FOOTBALL ROMANCE

MAKE HIM

featuring Luca & Scarlett with Zar and Nick

A BILLIONAIRE DOM, MMF, WHY CHOOSE ROMANCE &
AUDIOBOOK

TEMPT HER

featuring Stacey & her husbands

MMMF, WHY CHOOSE REVENGE ROMANCE & AUDIOBOOK

HOLIDAY FOR SIX

HALLOWEEN FOR SIX

with cameos of MCs from characters above and below!

VERY SPICY, LOTS OF FRIENDS TO LOVERS ROMCOMS &
AUDIOBOOKS

ALL FOR HIM

featuring Silas & Eily Van de May with Cade and Redix

A FORBIDDEN CINDERELLA RETELLING POLY ROMANCE

AFTER HIM

WITH HIM

AN ANGSTY SECOND CHANCE TO AN MMF, WHY CHOOSE DUET

PROTECT HER

PIERCE HER

HUNT HER

CHASE HER

A SPICY, ROMANTIC SUSPENSE, BODYGUARD/CELEBRITY TRILOGY

JOIN MY NEWSLETTER.

I SHARE SNEAK PEEKS, GIVEAWAYS, AND MORE.

KELLYFINLEY.COM

ACKNOWLEDGMENTS

My husband and silver fox: Thank you for being my biggest fan and hottest reader.

My Book Team: Big hugs to my BTS crew: Ashley, Ange, Brit, Kenzie, and more. Sharla, thank you for being my sensitivity reader and for sharing your story with me. Hugs. Deborah and Lizzie, my proofreaders! Thank you so much. Thank you, Lori, for another stunning cover design. All hail, Wander Aguiar and his gorgeous photo of Mario.

My Beta Team: I can't do this without you! Anja, Brittany, Heather, Jay, Katelyn, Kayla, Madison, Marie, Pana, Rachel, and Thorunn. I need y'all to be my neighbors because I love you.

My ARC Team: I love our sweet, smutty group! Your edits, posts, reviews, and support melt my heart, while our DMs and chats kick my feet. I truly can't do it without you. Like. Legit. Thank you!

#Bookstagram, #BookTok, and FB Spicy Book Babes: You keep me going. I love hearing from you! I get all teary at your edits and comments. Thanks for your love.

Romance bookstores! I found you! I love supporting you or just popping by. Here's to filling shelves and hearts with smut.

Author Friends & Mentors: Particularly Eva, Maggie, Rachel, and Trisha! I'm not alone with book besties like you.

Best for last - You, my reader: Thank you for sharing this story with me. I welcome your messages, posts, and emails, and promise to keep giving you more spice.

Please leave your honest review. It's the greatest gift to an author.

Xoxo,
Kelly

ABOUT THE AUTHOR

Kelly Finley lives in the Carolinas with her sexy husband and sweet family.

A rebel with many causes, she fancies black leather, dirty jokes, big hearts, and smart mouths.

She believes in shameless love, so much so that her readers started calling her **"The Queen of Spice,"** and she wears her crown with pride.

Dedicated to writing swoony, spicy books, she's most likely at her keyboard putting the next hot story on the page for you.

Want to connect with Kelly and her readers?

Website: KellyFinley.com

for free bonus scenes, her newsletter, special editions & more

instagram.com/kellyfinleybooks

facebook.com/KellyFinleyBooks

tiktok.com/@kellyfinleybooks

threads.com/@kellyfinleybooks

bookbub.com/authors/kelly-finley

goodreads.com/goodreads_kelly_finley

amazon.com/author/kellyfinley